CASEY'S KINGDOM

Darrell Casey had it all. He had a luxurious mansion with all the pleasures he enjoyed, including a pitful of ravenous alligators in the backyard, and the sexiest beauties money could buy in his bed. He had a crew of killers on call that included a Teutonic murder machine named Gunther Steinhorst and a pair of homicidal mercenaries who loved their work as much as they loved each other. Best of all, he had *ten thousand keys* of coke coming in on a flight so perfectly planned that no one, but no one, could possibly stop it.

No one, except maybe Nick Brown, who knew you had to be crazy to mess with the King of South Florida dopers. But then again, Nick Brown had always been crazy . . . like a fox. . . .

NARCS

When you fight drugs, y . . . **k and take off the**

"Bristles with the . . . . er knew existed but i . . . . this minute; it daz . . . . intricate it could only be real; . . . . s with action from first page to last."
—Stuart Woods, author of *Chiefs* and *White Cargo*

NARCS

ROBERT CORAM

A SIGNET BOOK

NEW AMERICAN LIBRARY

PUBLISHER'S NOTE

This book is a work of fiction. Names, characters, places, and incidents either are the product of the author's imagination or are used fictitiously, and any resemblance to actual persons, living or dead, events, or locales is entirely coincidental.

SIGNET TRADEMARK REG. U.S. PAT. OFF. AND FOREIGN COUNTRIES
REGISTERED TRADEMARK—MARCA REGISTRADA
HECHO EN CHICAGO, U.S.A.

SIGNET, SIGNET CLASSIC, MENTOR, ONYX, PLUME, MERIDIAN and NAL BOOKS are published by NAL PENGUIN INC., 1633 Broadway, New York, New York 10019

First Printing, December, 1988

1 2 3 4 5 6 7 8 9

PRINTED IN THE UNITED STATES OF AMERICA

To Jeannine . . .
and lilac time forever

Acknowledgments

I owe many people for their help. Bill Diehl took time from his work to provide guidance and to introduce me to Mel Berger at the William Morris Agency. Don Smith offered the help that only a longtime and trusted friend can give. Ron and Judy Metcalf, fellow cooks as well as DEA agents, told me many stories of law enforcement. Nick Navarro, Sheriff of Broward County, Florida, and Ralph Cunningham, Chief Investigator for Florida's 20th Judicial Circuit, have lived more than this book, or a dozen books about drug smuggling, could contain. There are numerous other state and federal lawmen who helped, but who have asked not to be identified. They know who they are; they know I'm grateful; and they know any mistakes herein are because I didn't listen. Finally, the idea for this book grew out of covering the drug-smuggling scene for the *Atlanta Constitution*. John Schaffner and DeWitt Rogers, two great newspapermen who moved on to other things, gave me considerable latitude in that assignment, and I owe them.

Prologue

When Lance Cunningham saw the hitchhiker, he grinned, slid the long-barreled chrome-plated Magnum under his left leg, and swung toward the curb. As his battered red Toyota screeched to a stop, he flung open the door, leaned over, and said, "Hey, guy. I'm just going a few miles but I'll be glad to give you a lift that far."

The hitchhiker, a carbon copy of countless drifters going south through Fort Lauderdale toward the torpid languor of the Florida keys, was a thin chalk-faced man of about thirty. He wore a green flowered shirt, faded jeans, and high-topped tennis shoes. In one hand he carried a blue day pack and in the other a cardboard box bound with heavy string.

The hitchhiker was less than ecstatic at the idea of riding in the dingy little Toyota. He wrinkled his lips in distaste as he slid onto the front seat, holding the day pack on his lap and looking for a place to put the box.

"You can put that Puerto Rican Samsonite on the floor," Lance said. "Or throw it in the back seat." He ignored the hitchhiker's sharp look as he shoved the car into gear, quickly released the clutch, and grinned in approval at the tiny squeak. "My name's Larry but my friends call me Lance," he said.

The hitchhiker nodded but said nothing. His casual glance at Lance had taken it all in. The driver was in his late twenties, looked to be close to six feet tall, was wearing boat shoes, brown shorts, and a red T-shirt that said, "I Will Drink Any Wine Before Its Time." Another aging beach bum; a flaky south Florida guy who had spent too much time in the sun.

Lance looked in the rearview mirror, darted into the center lane of Fort Lauderdale's Highway 1, and continued to accelerate. He shook his head, turned to the passenger, and said, "This car's constipated. Won't pass a thing."

The hitchhiker tightened his grip on the day pack and continued to stare straight ahead.

Lance coaxed the battered Toyota until it was twenty miles an hour above the speed limit. He was smiling, nerves tingling, waiting. It was time for the hitchhiker to make his move.

Suddenly Lance tensed. His eyes locked on a blue pickup truck, a sun-bleached weary pickup that sagged and drooped over bald tires. The pickup was parked a block ahead, parked on the curb lane. Four Hispanic men clustered under the hood.

"That's it. That's it. I've found it," Lance said in exultation. He whipped the car toward the curb so unexpectedly that the hitchhiker's head snapped to the side.

Lance's way was blocked by traffic backed up behind the pickup. But he laughed, pounded an open hand on the steering wheel, and repeated, "That's it. Holy shit, I've found it. After two years of looking, I've found it."

The hitchhiker, who was rubbing his neck, leaned forward, stared, then turned and looked at Lance in bewilderment. "Found what?"

Lance pointed. "Hey, guy. See that blue pickemup truck? It's from Central Cuban Dispatch."

"Central Cuban Dispatch?"

"Lemme tell you something. And not many people know this," Lance said in a confidential tone. "But somewhere in Broward County is Central Cuban Dispatch. Their job is to send out old shit cars and trucks every morning and every afternoon during rush hour. A lot of the times the trucks are carrying flattened cardboard boxes that slide off and block traffic. You can identify the cars by the hole in the trunk, the hole where the lock used to be. The drivers go up and down main streets until the cars and trucks break down. Then they get out, stand around, and pretend to be working on the motor." He pointed toward the pickup and shook his head. "What they're really doing under there is keeping score on how many other cars they can delay, how far they can back up traffic before a wrecker comes out and tows them away."

The hitchhiker continued to rub his neck. He wrinkled his pale brow. "You think they deliberately stall their cars so they can cause traffic jams?"

"You got it. I think Castro is behind it. Hell, if it works in Lauderdale they might spread it all over America. The whole country could grind to a halt. We could choke on carbon monoxide. That's why it's so important to find the main office. It's a communist plot."

The hitchhiker was bewildered.

Lance looked around, stretching his neck, peering up and down alleys and side streets. "You see a warehouse or some big building that would hold a bunch of cars and trucks? It may be close. I may have actually found Central Cuban Dispatch. If we can find it, I'm gonna burn it down and stop these traffic jams."

"You don't like Hispanics?" The hitchhiker's voice had an edge to it.

"Hey, guy, I like everybody. But what's Hispanic got to do with it? Just because julios have a monopoly on clunker cars and causing traffic jams doesn't mean anything. If weenie eaters were blocking traffic, I'd be looking for Central Faggot Dispatch. You know what I mean?"

The hitchhiker glanced down at his watch.

Lance instantly was filled with contrition. "Hey, guy, I'm holding you up." He looked over his shoulder, shifted into reverse, and quickly backed up. He turned the wheel hard to the right, drove the small car onto the sidewalk, and motored slowly toward the corner. As he drew level with the blue pickup he stopped, reached out the window and rapped sharply on the fender. The four Hispanics raised their heads and stared.

"You guys from CCD?" he asked. He was smiling and his eyes were dancing.

The four men looked at one another. One said, "*Donde está See See Dee?*"

Lance slapped his open palm on the fender. "Come on. I know you're from CCD."

The four men stared blankly. Lance dismissed them with a wave and continued down the sidewalk. He ignored the angry glare of pedestrians. "They're probably from a substation. I bet they don't even know the dispatcher," he muttered as he drove onto the street. A uniformed police officer glared at him, blew his whistle, and pointed to the curb.

Lance threw his left hand skyward and shouted, "*Hola, hombre. Vámonos.*"

He crossed four lanes of traffic and continued down the main highway.

He drummed his fingers on the steering wheel and whistled a tuneless ditty through his teeth. It was time to force the hitchhiker's hand.

"Where you going, guy? Just tell me and I'll drop you."

"South," the hitchhiker said. "I'll show you where I want out."

"Where you from?"

"Different places."

Lance nodded in approval. "That's the life. Just roaming around seeing the world. Sounds great. But, hey, how do you eat? You got rich parents?"

The hitchhiker didn't answer. He was leaning forward, watching. He pointed to a street paralleling the northern edge of Executive Airport. Then he turned to Lance and said, "I'm going down there. About a block. Can you drop me?" He pulled the day pack closer.

Lance knew there was nothing down the access road but a few palmetto thickets where local people sometimes dumped garbage and where Haitian refugees often camped. The hitchhiker was about to make his move. Lance flexed the muscles in his left leg, feeling the sweaty warmth of the big Magnum.

He was ready.

"Sure, guy. Glad to do it." Lance turned down the side street. No traffic ahead. His dark eyes flicked toward the rearview mirror. No traffic behind.

Then it happened.

The hitchhiker looked over his shoulder and jerked a knife from his day pack, a dull black dagger with a six-inch blade sharpened on both sides. He stuck it under Lance's chin, forcing his head upward. With his right hand, the hitchhiker shoved the day pack atop the cardboard box. Then he grabbed Lance's long hair, shoving his head farther back, and through gritted teeth said, "Move and you're a dead man."

Lance squealed and his eyes rolled white. He held the steering wheel at arm's length slowly applying the brakes, and said, "Holy shit, mister, what is this? I ain't done nothing to you. Take my money. Take the car. But don't hurt me." His voice was high and strained.

The hitchhiker snorted and pushed the knife tighter against Lance's chin. "Pull over. Easy. You fuck with me and I'll hand you your goddamn head. Pull over."

Lance pressed the brakes harder. He stopped near a large palmetto thicket.

"Drive behind those bushes. Get off the road," the hitchhiker said.

Lance eased the car into the thick undergrowth. He stopped. "Please, mister, don't hurt me," he said. He paused. When he spoke again his voice was a tremulous falsetto. "I'm a virgin."

The hitchhiker's brows lowered. He paused. "A what?"

"I'm a virgin. I never had any." Lance's voice raced. "But I'm supposed to get some tonight from this woman I been seeing for two years and I don't want to die the day I'm supposed to get my first piece of tooty, so please don't hurt me."

"Tooty?" The hitchhiker's voice was derisive.

"What the hell is tooty? You mean you been seeing some bitch two years and ain't fucked her?"

Lance moaned. "I wish you wouldn't talk about her that way, sir."

"You lame son of a bitch. I might fuck her myself." He flicked Lance's neck with the black dagger, causing a thin rivulet of blood to run down his neck. "Give me your wallet."

The hitchhiker flicked the knife again and, slowly and distinctly, said, "Move very slowly. Don't try anything or your head will be on the floor."

"In the glove compartment. My wallet's in the glove compartment," Lance whimpered.

"You better have some money, buddy. I almost didn't get in this junk car. Hell, I think *you* might be Central Cuban Dispatch. This thing must break down every day." The hitchhiker giggled and twisted the knife. "You're a weird son of a bitch."

"I got about three hundred dollars and all my credit cards in there. You can have it all. Just don't hurt me." Lance was almost crying.

The hitchhiker, keeping his eyes on Lance's face, reached behind with his right hand and located the glove compartment. He opened it, reached inside, and began to grope around, keeping his eyes on Lance. He felt, then shoved aside a few papers. He touched something hard and closed his hand around it. His brow wrinkled in quick bewilderment. There was a quick movement and a loud snap.

The hitchhiker screamed in pain. Involuntarily he turned to look at his hand and his eyes filled with disbelief. A rat trap, the giant size used in warehouses, had snapped across four fingers. SURPRISE was written in orange fluorescent paint across the top of the rat trap and provided a stark contrast to the bloodless white of his fingers. He knew several fingers were broken.

At that moment something cold and hard slammed against his left ear, snapping his head against the door post, and the knife was twisted from his fingers with such force that he thought his wrist had snapped. He rolled his eyes to the left. All fright had gone from the driver's face. The guy had a pistol, a big silver hog leg of a pistol, stuck in his ear and was twisting it, causing the raised sight at the end of the barrel to cut into his flesh.

Lance smiled, a tight, fiendish smile. He leaned closer. His voice was almost a whisper. "Now, dirtbag. Tell me again how you're gonna take my money." He twisted the pistol.

The hitchhiker moaned.

"Tell me what you're gonna do to my girlfriend." He twisted again.

The moan was louder.

"Tell me how you're gonna cut off my head." Twist.

The hitchhiker squealed.

Lance smiled. "Let's see, now. Is there anything else? Have I overlooked anything? Oh, yeah, you don't like my car. Apologize to my car." He twisted the pistol.

"You son of a bitch."

"That's it. Threaten me. Come on, badass. Threaten me."

"You a fucking cop?"

Lance laughed, a high exultant laugh. "Cop? Cop? You dumb son of a bitch. Yeah, I'm a cop. But, hey, I ain't just any cop. I'm fucking bulletproof. I'm invincible. You just locked assholes with a combination of John Wayne and Superman. I'm the best cop that ever strapped on a badge. And you tried to rob me, you stupid bag of donkey shit." He twisted the pistol, gritted his teeth and ignored the hitchhiker's scream. "In my town. In my jurisdiction."

Lance paused. He wiped the blood from his neck and looked at it. The blood was mixed with the heavy salty perspiration that had suddenly broken out on his head and neck and chest. He was sopping wet. The only sound in the car was the sound of his rapid breathing. It was always that way when he got the upper hand after a bad guy came close to killing him.

He took several deep breaths and pushed them forcibly from his lungs. In a moment he had calmed.

"I'm gonna read you your rights," he said slowly. "Then you're gonna tell me how many Lauderdale motorists you've robbed and you're gonna give me their descriptions. We're gonna clean up a big backlog of robberies here before we're through. Then I'm gonna change your zip code, boy. I'm putting your rancid ass in jail."

Lance grinned. He leaned so close to the hitchhiker that their noses almost touched. "And you know what? I'm not gonna cuff you. Ask me why, badass."

Lance rocked his head and in a simpering falsetto said, "Why, Mr. Policeman?" He backed away. His voice turned hard. "Because I'm hoping you'll try to make a bush bond. I'm begging you to run."

"My fingers are broken. My ear is killing me," the hitchhiker groaned.

Lance laughed. "You assholes are all alike. You were ready to rob me and cut my head off and now you're complaining about a little rat trap. Well, you're wearing it until you talk."

The hitchhiker's left hand reached toward the rat trap. Lance rapped him sharply on the wrist with the Magnum and then, before he jammed the pistol back into the hitchhiker's ear, flicked the rat trap, causing it to pull at the hitchhiker's broken fingers.

The hitchhiker screamed in pain and anger. "You son of a bitch. I should have cut your fucking throat."

Lance laughed. His eyes danced. "You never had a chance, guy. Me and my rat trap had you surrounded. Hey, we caught seven hitchhikers this year. I troll for scumbags like you every morning. It gets my pacemaker going before I go to work."

Lance looked at his watch. In a confidential voice he said, "I've got to take on some certified badasses today. Real double-barreled dope smugglers. Now I know you don't want to slow the majestic process of the law. So let's talk."

He laughed a high-pitched laugh of relief. Then he said, "We got to do this in a hurry. I want to go back and check out those julios on the corner. I still think they were from Central Cuban Dispatch."

1

Nick Brown, commander of the Broward County Narcotics Squad, sometimes was referred to as Fluf, by his colleagues. Fluf was an acronym meaning "fat little ugly fucker" and was a term of approbation and respect. Nick did not smoke or drink and rarely used profanity; he was happily married and made no secret of the fact he took his family to church every Sunday, all of which put him so far beyond the experience of most cops that the only thing they could criticize was his physical appearance. Nick was approaching forty, and while he was not fat, he had the beginning of what, in a few years, would be a cantilevered stomach. His stomach appeared larger than it really was because of two things: first, Nick stood only five feet six inches tall; second, he had broad shoulders and a thick chest. His muscularity, combined with the incipient overhang of his belly, gave him the appearance of someone rapidly approaching butterball status.

Today Nick was in his office on the fourth floor of a boxy glass building perched hard by I-95. The building's glass facade was patched with large unpainted sections of plywood. It looked like a building in a combat zone.

Nick looked over his desk at the smiling young deputy who was in a chair sprawled like a teenager. The deputy had taken off his wide-brimmed hat but still wore a wig—a blond wig.

Brown, unlike most cops, did not like scatological humor. He was not a prude. It was simply that he did not like humor having to do with bodily functions. And the man across his desk, Lance Cunningham, would rather talk about his bowel movements than any subject except how to catch drug smugglers. The guy was a good cop, but he was warped. He would call at 3 A.M. and, with no preamble, say, "Well, I just did one that looked like a dense pack missile system. Think I'll box it and send it to Congress." He would hang up, leaving Brown staring at the telephone and fumbling for some way to tell his wife that the caller was a deputy who only wanted to talk about his latest bowel movement. She wouldn't understand. Nobody would understand.

Brown was determined to keep control of the conversation. He stared at the young deputy, mentally going over his record. Three years earlier, as a uniformed patrolman, he stopped a Florida senator whose car was weaving down A1A in Fort Lauderdale. When the drunken politician threatened Cunningham, the patrolman ate the guy's driver's license. He pushed it into his mouth, stared at the senator, and slowly chewed up the license. While he chewed, he grunted and wheezed in a manner that rattled even a drunken senator.

But eating the license was only a warm-up. "Senator, you're a smart ass," Cunningham said. He looked up and down the highway, waved expansively, and said, "As you can see, this is a no-smart-ass zone."

The senator stuck his head out the window and looked up and down the road.

"Besides, you look mopey," Cunningham added.

So Cunningham wrote the guy a ticket charging him with being a smart ass in a no-smart-ass zone and being mopey with gross intent.

"I should add a GP charge," Cunningham added as he passed over the ticket. "But to show you I'm a nice guy, I'm letting you off. We believe in showing the proper respect to our elected officials."

Cunningham threw the senator a snappy salute and was about to walk away when the senator wrinkled his brow and said, "GP. What the hell is GP?"

"Gross person. Sir," the patrolman said over his shoulder.

"What's your name, boy?" bellowed the senator in drunken indignation.

"Geevasheet."

"What?"

"Geevasheet. Don Geevasheet."

That little episode got him transferred to the vice squad.

He was part of the security detail assigned to Great Britain's Princess Diana during her five-day stay in a Fort Lauderdale hotel. But that ended when he came into her suite, said he was looking for explosives, and ripped the toilet seat from her bathroom.

He had the seat mounted on black velvet and framed. It hung on the wall of his apartment. A silver plate on the frame said, "Temporary Home of the Most Beautiful Ass in the World."

A week later, during a slow night, he rode through

the back alleys of Fort Lauderdale using the loud
hailer on his car to tell drunks that a large flying
monster was circling Fort Lauderdale. He said the
monster ate bicycles and people in a prone position.
The next morning several hundred upright drunks
demonstrated at the courthouse demanding that sheriff's deputies protect them from flying monsters.

Except for several stern lectures, he was not disciplined for these acts of individuality. But Sheriff
Hiram Turnipseed, a man zipped so tight he squeaked
when he walked, began to look at him with a wary
eye. Then one night Cunningham took two bullets
from his chrome-plated Magnum, put one in each
ear of a pimp, held a lighted match to one of the
bullets, and demanded to know about the pimp's
sideline business of drugging twelve- and thirteen-
year-old girls and selling them to wealthy tourists.

The pimp, believing his brains were about to be
blown out, confessed. He complained of police bru-
tality, but even television reporters were not interested in a story about a pimp with a blistered ear.

Cunningham received a commendation.

Lance grew tired of working with what he called
"the dork squad" or "the pussy patrol," and asked
for a transfer. Nick Brown, who was always looking
for young and new faces to use in undercover work,
agreed to put him on the narcotics squad. Nick
sensed that Lance's attitude, if it could be called
that, would be perfect in the fluid, highly charged
area of narcotics undercover work.

The first thing Lance wanted to do was change
the name of the squad. Nick Brown called a meeting of some thirty undercover officers to introduce
Lance. Rather than simply standing up and nodding, Lance made a little speech. He proposed the

name of the group be changed to the Coastal Undercover Narcotics Team.

Lance was excited. The room full of gold-bedecked, bearded undercover cops stared at him impassively. "You go out now," he told them. "You're doing a raid. You pull your weapons and you run up to a bunch of guys and you say, 'You're under arrest. Broward County Sheriff's Office Narcotics Squad.' That's too much. The guy's either asleep or split by the time you're through explaining who the hell you are. Just think," he told them. "If you change the name to Coastal Undercover Narcotics Team, we can kick in a door and say, 'Hands up! CUNT!' "

Lance smiled. "Name's got zip to it. And it does two things. It tells the bad guy who you are and it tells him how you feel about him."

It did not take long for Cunningham to become the best undercover agent Nick Brown had ever known. He was not a serious dedicated cop. It was all a big game to him, a game that allowed him to drive go-fast boats, fly small airplanes, race high-speed cars, and most of all, play the undercover gambit with drug smugglers. His zaniness, wildness, devil-may-care attitude and willingness to take chances not only caused smugglers to trust him; they actually liked him. Lance Cunningham could penetrate a drug ring and get next to the ring leaders while other cops were still trying to make the first contact. He was a natural, a genius at what he did.

His fellow officers thought he was a bubble off plumb because he trolled for hitchhikers. Someday he was going to pick up the wrong guy and he would get his ass waxed. And the business about looking for Central Cuban Dispatch confused the hell out of people. Did he really believe Castro sent out Hispanics in old vehicles to deliberately cause traffic jams?

Whatever his fellow officers thought of Lance Cunningham, they agreed he was the best U/C guy in the business. His undercover exploits had won four awards and two promotions. The details of the U/C assignments that resulted in the awards were so sensitive and contained so much secret information regarding ongoing and future investigations that they were locked in his personnel file.

Brown knew the young agent would need every bit of his nerve and skill to stay alive during the U/C assignment the sheriff had ordered he be sent on.

"The sheriff wants you to go to Bimini," Nick said in his straightforward fashion. "He's got some TV reporter breathing down his neck about all the smugglers using Bimini to launch drug flights that end up here in Broward County."

Nick's tone of voice made it clear what he thought of a sheriff who would be influenced by a television reporter. "He wants you to go over there U/C. Gather intelligence. Get enough evidence for indictments."

"Was he wearing his Duck Head pants?"

Nick sighed. The sheriff had one suit, a tight tan suit he wore three days each week. The other two days he wore khaki pants with the yellow Duck Head logo over the left rear pocket. Lance once had put a memo on the office bulletin board calling attention to the sheriff's Duck Head pants and adding, "This could be a misprint."

"Okay," Lance said. "He wants enough evidence for an indictment." Lance leaned forward, eyes bright. "Against Darrell Casey?"

Brown nodded. His flat impassive eyes stared at Lance. He remembered the first time he had met Casey; it was fifteen years ago in a foreign country. A dope deal had gone bad. Casey had never forgiven him for what he thought had happened.

Nick was disturbed that the sheriff wanted to send an undercover agent into a country where the agent had no authority. The jurisdiction of the Broward County sheriff's office ended at the county line, just as it did with any other sheriff's jurisdiction. Now the sheriff wanted an agent to go on an intelligence gathering trip to Bimini. In a technical sense, the mission was an act of espionage. But beyond that, if the agent were caught, the sheriff would deny sending him. The agent would be left to the not-so-tender mercies of Bahamian officials. He could even be sent to Fox Hill Prison, the jail outside Nassau that would have made Devil's Island look like a Boy Scout camp.

"Casey and his Bahamian accomplices," Nick answered.

Lance sat back, looked at the ceiling a moment, then smiled.

"And he wants you to stay out of trouble," Nick said. He paused. "This is a voluntary assignment. The sheriff wants you to go, but you should understand that I'm not ordering you to go. You know what Bimini is like."

Lance was still looking at the ceiling. He reached up, pulled off the blond wig, and rumpled his brown hair. "Darrell Casey," he mused. "The biggest doper in Florida. One of the biggest in the country. Lives right here in Lauderdale and we've never been able to touch him." He looked at his boss. "Bimini is the key. We can do Casey from Bimini. I know it."

"Casey's got a load coming up tonight. I've alerted Customs. Their air-support people have an operation down in Cuba. Maybe they can intercept the guy. If they can track him, we'll be ready when he gets here."

"How do you know about the load?"

Nick scratched his forehead with a thick finger, pulled at his blond mustache, and sighed. He decided to tackle this head-on. That was his way.

"Casey's planning something big," he muttered. "Really big. That's why I didn't fight the sheriff on this business of sending you to Bimini. Casey's working on a deal involving a large aircraft and several tons, maybe ten tons, of coke. It may be coming through Bimini."

Lance's eyes widened. So many drugs were coming through south Florida in such large amounts that the Drug Enforcement Administration wouldn't even bother with a load of grass under several tons. And it took ten kilos of coke to get their attention. Customs had popped Colombian airliners and found fifteen hundred or two thousand pounds of cocaine. But ten tons of coke was unimaginable. It would be the biggest load in history. He tried to figure the value of such a load and gave up. It would be worth somewhere around a half-billion dollars.

"Where'd you get that?" he asked. "Same place you heard about the inbound load?"

Nick stared at Lance, his silence answering the question. Lance shook his head in anger. He stood up, slammed his right fist into his left palm, then sat down. "She's still playing around with Casey, huh?" He snorted in anger. "You tell me this is voluntary, that I don't have to go to Bimini. And she's up

there in Casey's house. She's with him and that
bunch of slimes."

"I didn't order her up there. She wanted to do
it."

The conversation was interrupted by a more pressing matter when a section of the glass wall behind
Nick suddenly shattered. Lance dived for the floor
when he heard bullets striking the wall behind him.

A few seconds later he lifted his head. Nick had
risen from his chair and was sauntering across the
room to look at the damage. Nick walked with his
arms crooked at the elbows and held out from his
body. He reminded Lance of a wet rooster.

"Get up, Cunningham," Nick said. "If you were
around the office more, you'd know they only fire
one burst."

The narcotics office was located in a building
owned by a Lauderdale man who dabbled in real
estate. In return for a substantial campaign dona-
tion, the sheriff had ordered the narcotics squad
and the vice squad to rent offices there. Except for
the three floors rented by the cops, the building
virtually was empty.

It did not take long for Lauderdale's underworld
to realize that all the undercover cops who could
make their lives miserable were in the same office.
And it was not uncommon for undercover cops to
find themselves being photographed as they entered
and exited the building. That's why Lance always
wore a disguise when he came to the office.

The surveillance was a source of constant anger
to the cops. But even worse, occasionally one of the
bad guys would stick a weapon out of his car while
driving north on I-95 and fire a few rounds into the
building. Half the windows had been shot out at

one time or another. And the real-estate guy never replaced them. Entreaties to the sheriff did no good.

Nick looked at the damage and sighed. He picked up his telephone, called his secretary, and told her to have a piece of plywood put over the holes.

He sat down, rubbed his eyes, then looked up at Lance. "Where were we?"

Lance had returned to his chair. But he sat on the edge, feet under his body, ready to move. He no longer was slouched. "We were talking about your alleged undercover person. Does she know about this Bimini deal? I mean, about me going over there?"

Nick shook his head. "But she could find out."

Lance thought for a moment. Then, in a swift change of mood, he made up his mind. "What the hell," he said. "I think this will be a bit of all right." He was doing his British accent. Ever since he had commandeered Princess Di's toilet seat, he liked to occasionally use a British accent. If someone asked him if he were English, he would say no, but that he was very close to Princess Di.

"For this little caper I rather think I should like to have the code name Houdini," he said. "And we should call the mission Operation Limey."

"I don't care what you call it. Just be careful," Nick growled. "Play by the rules and be careful."

Lance laughed. "Not to worry, *jefe*. The mighty Houdini is invincible. I am, as you colonial blokes would say, meaner than a fart pushed through a keg of nails."

He pronounced fart with a broad *a* and a drawn-out *r*, giving it an onomatopoeic sound.

Nick made a grimace. He had to move on quickly before Lance pursued this line of conversation.

"Those people on Bimini don't care and they don't scare. They will flat kill you if they even suspect you might be a police officer."

"A sunny country for shady people." Lance laughed.

Nick knew he wasn't getting through. So he forgot the safety lecture, and the two men settled down to talk about the details of the U/C trip. They talked for almost three hours. The last thing Nick told Lance was not to get caught on Bimini. "We got no authority over there. No jurisdiction. You get caught, don't flash your creds. In fact, leave all your ID here."

Nick paused. "You got any problem working out of the country, out of your jurisdiction?"

Lance laughed. He picked up the blond wig, put it on, then perched the wide-brimmed hat atop his head. It was this sort of work that made being a cop so much fun. He shrugged. "No problems, coach. Hey, I ain't got no headgear. But send me in. I'm fresh."

Nick did not laugh. "You know what will happen if you get caught or if the DEA or the feebs find out about this? And the State Department?" Nick shook his head at the thought. "The State Department will go crazy."

Nick paused. He was not enthusiastic about sending Lance to Bimini. But he would not criticize the sheriff's idea. He believed in loyalty up and loyalty down. He supported his boss and he took care of his troops. "We are operating here on the principle of tracking an investigation to its source," Nick said. It was as if he were trying to convince himself that the reasons for the Bimini trip were good ones. "We have reliable information that Darrell Casey, a suspected major violator living in Broward County, is operating out of Bimini with the cooperation of Bahamian officials. Much of the cocaine on the streets of Fort Lauderdale is thought to have been brought here by the Casey organization. The taxpayers of this county pay us to stop those drugs. That's what we're trying to do here, track them to the source and put Casey out of business."

Lance's eyes widened. For Nick, that had been a major speech. Lance leaned toward his boss. His voice was solemn but his eyes were dancing when he said, "I understand. I'll keep my head down and I'll go by the rules."

2

U.S. Customs pilot Mike Love took off at 2:17 A.M. from Guantánamo Naval Air Station and, even before the landing gear was up and locked, began a left turn to the south. Cuban territory was only a half-mile from the end of the runway and the assumption was that the Cubans would launch ground-to-air missiles if an American aircraft penetrated their airspace. At the very least, they would register a strong diplomatic protest and go to the media to denounce the latest imperialist aggression. Since the U.S. Customs operation was secret and the agency did not want publicity, pilots were extremely careful not to stray out of the tight corridor that had to be used entering or exiting Guantánamo.

Mike Love pressed smoothly on the rudder of the big King Air and tightened his turn. Ahead of him the sky and the sea merged, and he could see nothing but blackness. The softly lit cockpit instruments told him what he already knew: that he was making a smooth, coordinated climbing turn.

The voice of the navy controller at the Gitmo tower came over his headset. "November four five six, track outbound heading one three zero until you reach point X ray."

"Affirmative." Mike glanced at the compass and then the directional gyro. Both were locked on one three zero. After flying out of Gitmo two or three times a day for the past week, he had the procedures down pat. When his distance-measuring equipment said he had traveled seven miles, he would be at point X ray, an electronically designated dot in the sky that marked the boundary of the air-traffic corridor for Gitmo.

November four five six was not the number of the aircraft Mike was flying. It was a number he was using in case drug smugglers, some of whom knew the tail numbers of Customs aircraft, were monitoring Gitmo tower. Mike was part of a little-known operation to track drug smugglers traveling through the Windward Passage on their routes from Colombia and Jamaica to Florida. This flight had been launched when U.S. Navy radar at Gitmo picked up an unidentified aircraft approaching from the south. Radar indicated the bogey was about one hundred miles out, which meant he was somewhere around ten thousand feet. The smuggler was flying at 150 knots, probably a single-engine job. The intercept would be easy, as the King Air had a top speed exceeding 250 knots.

Mike was to track the smuggler visually while calling ahead to alert U.S. Customs in Florida. If the bandit stopped in the Bahamas, special enforcement groups called BAT teams would arrest him, seize the aircraft, and confiscate the drugs.

Mike grinned and leaned forward in anticipation. This bandit was history. He was going down. His ass was grass and Mike Love was a government-powered lawn mower.

Mike had been a Customs pilot for eleven years but still took it personally when smugglers hauled drugs into the United States.

He looked at a small instrument that indicated his distance from Gitmo. Already he had flown more than six miles. But there was no sensation of speed when flying in total darkness. The only outside stimulus was of sound, of the turbine engines whose muted noise inside the cockpit wrapped the two men in a comfortable blanket.

"Dial in Big Bird's freq," Mike instructed the copilot. As soon as the secret frequency showed in the small illuminated window of the UHF radio, Mike pulled the boom microphone closer to his mouth and pressed the radio transmit button on the left side of the yoke.

He spoke in a flat voice. "Big Bird, five six uniform with you at point X ray."

The voice of the navy guy aboard the E-2, a picket aircraft with a pancakelike disk atop the fuselage to give it 360 degrees of radar coverage, was crisp and professional when he answered from somewhere over the Caribbean, "Five six uniform, radar contact. Your target is tracking three five zero. Speed two hundred fifty knots. Say type aircraft."

Mike's eyes widened and he turned to look at the copilot sitting to his right. The copilot, in preparation for the intercept, was wearing night-vision goggles and looked like an extraterrestrial. "Gitmo said the bandit was at a hundred and fifty knots," Mike said. He paused, thinking rapidly. The smuggler must have been climbing if he was showing a ground speed of only one fifty. Hell, the guy could be up at twenty thousand or so.

He pressed the transmit button. "Super King Air."

"Okay. About the same airspeed." The voice of the navy man turned helpful. "You won't be able to overtake the target from the rear. Continue present course and I'll vector you for a ninety-degree intercept, then swing you alongside the target. It'll be close but I think we can do it."

"Say target altitude."

Navy's voice was apologetic. "Height-finder mode is inoperative." Pause. "Gitmo earlier estimated ten thousand. But the flight profile doesn't fit. Target speed indicates a turbine-powered aircraft. Suggest you climb to twenty-five thousand."

Mike shook his head in frustration. Without knowing the target's altitude, the only chance for an intercept would be to climb high and then convert the altitude to speed as he descended on the same course as the target. He cupped his hand behind the throttles, pushing, making sure they were full forward. He was climbing through ten thousand feet. Eight minutes later, as he reached twenty thousand, the E-2 guy called.

"November four five six, turn left heading zero three zero."

"Left to zero three zero," Mike confirmed. He was thinking rapidly, visualizing the compass heading of the bad guy, his own course, and what was needed for the intercept, translating complex computations of geometry and speed into a practical solution of how to put his aircraft directly above and behind the bad guy. Now the navy was vectoring him for more than a ninety-degree intercept. That meant the target was escaping. The doper had the pedal to the metal. Mike rolled out with the heading locked on zero three zero. Occasionally there was a bump as the King Air sliced through minor turbulence. But there was no outside visual reference. Only a few distant stars twinkled. It was like being inside a dimly lit box surrounded by powerful engines.

Two minutes later Navy called. "November four five six, turn left heading zero two zero."

"Shit!" Mike checked his altitude. Twenty-five thousand. He leveled off and peered into the blackness ahead. "You see him?"' he asked the copilot.

"Negative."

"November four five six, turn left heading zero one zero. You are now one mile from target. Do you have a visual?"

Mike snorted. He and the copilot leaned forward. No smuggler coming up from the south would be dumb enough to show nav lights, especially one as sharp as this guy. Hell, he would be lucky to see the guy at a quarter-mile They didn't even know his altitude. He could be thousands of feet above or below them.

"Negative contact," Mike said.

He twisted a rheostat, darkening the cockpit even more. Now only a faint penumbra surrounded the vital engine gauges and the instruments he must monitor to keep the aircraft level. Without turning his head he spoke to the copilot. "See if you can raise a Bat team."

The copilot dialed in a frequency on the second UHF radio and began calling. A moment later Mike impatiently poked him with a thumb. The copilot, earphones pressed tightly against his ears, shook his head.

"November four five six. Turn left heading three six zero. Correction, turn left heading three five zero."

Mike was impatient. Now he was flying the same course as the target. He poked the copilot again. The copilot shook his head and said, "No answer."

Mike was staring ahead, eyes moving, knowing he would see nothing in the darkness by looking straight at it. He had to catch it from the side.

Nothing. Time to make something happen, to take a chance. His gut instinct told him the bad guy was below. He pushed the nose over to build up airspeed.

The copilot turned. He knew Mike was taking a big risk. Prudence demanded they hold their present course, to slowly close the gap, and then if there was no contact, to either climb and search or descend and search. Mike was short-circuiting the process. He could overshoot the target. He could even ram the bad guy.

"Big Bird, November four five six. Continue the vector," Mike said, eyes searching the blackness ahead.

After a slight pause came the now cautious navy voice. "Roger, four five six. I show you less than one mile behind the target. Directly in trail with a good closure rate."

Still searching the blackness, Mike spoke to the copilot. "See if you can raise Nassau DEA."

The copilot looked at Mike in bewilderment. The Drug Enforcement Administration kept aircraft in Nassau, but they had never responded to a night assistance call from Customs. Never. Those guys worked bankers' hours.

After a few minutes on the radio the copilot turned to Mike and said, "No answer."

"Keep trying."

The copilot leaned forward. He was getting nervous about the possible proximity of the smuggler aircraft.

"There he is," the copilot said in relief. The smuggler was slightly below and about two hundred yards out front, a speeding silhouette identified only by the red exhaust glow of the engines, a glow that appeared in the night-vision goggles as two flaming orbs.

Now Mike could see the exhausts with his naked eye. He grinned. His gamble had paid off. He straightened in the seat, flexed his lean six-feet-four-inches, clenched and unclenched his fingers, wiggled his shoulders, got ready. He reached out with his right hand, cupped his fingers over the tops of the throttles, and after a moment, gently pulled the throttles a quarter-inch to the rear.

As the two aircraft bored northward at high speed, the overcast began to thin, causing a slight increase in visibility. The bad guy was driving a Merlin, a sleek high-speed aircraft normally used as an executive transport by large corporations.

Now Mike was a few feet below the smuggler, nestled tightly under him, eyes locked on the tail of the aircraft as he made minute adjustments to the throttles, rudders, and the yoke. Making an intercept at night was flying of the most demanding and dangerous sort. But Mike Love's normal level of intensity had not increased. He was treating this no differently than he would crossing the street.

The voice of the navy radar operator aboard the

E-2 was tight. "November four five six. I show you merged with the target. Do you have a visual?"

Mike squeezed the transmit button. Without taking his eye off the tail of the Merlin, he said, "We have a visual. Thanks for the assist. Good day, Navy."

Without looking at the copilot, Mike said over the intercom, "Let's do it."

The copilot sighed. He knew what was coming and he didn't like it. But it would do no good to argue. He adjusted the bulky night-vision goggles.

Mike had caught the note in his copilot's voice and chuckled. "You only live once, guy," he said. He slowly eased the King Air to the left out from under the Merlin, constantly making minute, almost undetectable adjustments, jockeying throttles and controls, eyes never leaving the silhouette of the Merlin's tail.

'A little more. Just a little more," the copilot said. Then, with satisfaction, "I got his numbers."

Mike eased a few feet to the left and pulled ten feet higher, eyes locked on the Merlin. The overcast had thinned enough that he could see the expanse of the broad vertical stabilizer. It was painted with a bold design. "Not another one of those guys," he said in disbelief.

The copilot was amazed. "He's got an alligator painted on the tail. A big alligator. Vertical position. Mouth open. Lots of teeth."

"You confirm the number?"

"Got it."

"Any response from the Bat teams or DEA in Nassau?" Mike was leaning forward and to the right, never taking his eyes from the bandit aircraft a few feet away. The slightest mistake and the two aircraft, both traveling at almost three hundred miles an hour, would become fireballs hurtling toward the dark ocean almost five miles below.

"Nothing. I can't raise anyone." The copilot took off the night goggles and turned to Mike. He knew what was about to happen and he was nervous.

Mike ignored the man on his right. He eased out another fifteen feet and added a slight amount of power, confidently and with authority but not abruptly. He was in control of the aircraft. It was doing exactly what he wanted it to do. He looked to the right. His wing was slowly moving forward, about five feet above the Merlin wing, and no more than five feet from the fuselage.

The bad guy had flown at low altitude until about one hundred miles south of Cuba. Then he had initiated a climb, knowing he would be picked up on Gitmo radar. He had figured that his slow climb speed would deceive Customs into not rushing the intercept. And he had almost gotten away with it, almost passed Gitmo before Customs launched an aircraft. He had come from the direction of Colombia, not Jamaica, which meant he had burned a lot of fuel before approaching the Windward Passage between Cuba and Haiti. The low-altitude flying had consumed even more. So he was probably short on fuel. That meant he would have to land in the Bahamas. If he could be spooked into descending to a lower altitude, where his fuel consumption would increase, he might not be able to make the pit stop in the Bahamas. The son of a bitch would crash. And Mike knew how to make that happen.

He nudged closer to the Merlin. Now his wing was almost level with the Merlin's cockpit. For a moment Mike was tempted to do what a doper in a

DC-3 once had tried to do to him. Mike was flying close, giving hand signals for the DC-3 jock to land, when suddenly the guy had crossed his controls, jammed his foot against the rudder, twisted his ailerons in the opposite direction, and sent the giant wing of the DC-3 slicing toward the cockpit of the small Cessna Mike was flying. Had he not been wary and poised to quickly react, the doper would have destroyed his aircraft and killed him. Later, after the smuggler had been arrested, he laughed when Mike, voice tight with anger, said, "I was the guy in the Cessna, the guy whose head you tried to cut off."

Mike's copilot instinctively pulled back from the window as the wings of the two aircraft overlapped. Any second the doper pilot's peripheral vision would detect the shape to his left.

Mike smiled. "Get ready," he said.

The copilot reached forward for the switch that controlled the strobe lights. Under optimum conditions a strobe light can be seen twenty miles. If it suddenly began blinking five feet from the pilot's ear, he might spook and dive for the deck before he stopped to think about his fuel problems.

"Do it."

The copilot flicked the switch. In the sudden burst of light the crew of the Merlin was visible. The pilot had dark hair and appeared to be in his mid-twenties. The person to his right was a woman—blonde. Even in the quick lightning burst of white light it was obvious she was beautiful.

The strobe pulsed again and in the light the startled faces of the two people could be seen staring over their left shoulders into the darkness.

"Head for the deck, asshole," Mike said impatiently.

The third flash of the strobe showed the Merlin crew still staring out the window, trying to see the aircraft between blinding flashes of light. But the Merlin continued straight and level, course unchanging. The pilot, whoever he was, was icy cool.

After several more flashes the Merlin crew no longer looked out the window. They knew the aircraft holding position with them was a Customs aircraft and they knew the government agents could do nothing.

An hour later the Merlin began descending. Mike had pulled away and was slightly above the smuggler. Neither the Bat team nor the DEA in Nassau would answer the radio, but he would continue to track the Merlin as long as he had fuel.

Ten minutes later the copilot said, "He's landing at Bimini."

Mike smoothly pushed the nose over, rolled the trim tab forward, flexed his fingers, and grinned. He had one more chance to put this bastard into the water. Mike wished for a fleeting moment he were flying the old B-26 Customs had seized from a smuggler and used as an intercept aircraft for a couple of years. That old bird scared hell out of smugglers, especially when it was flown aggressively. He had used it three times to force smugglers to crash into the ocean when they fled for sanctuary on Bimini. There were several ways to force a doper into the drink. One way was simply to use the superior speed of the B-26 to climb a few feet above a smuggler and then to settle slowly toward him, pushing him into the ocean. He would try that first.

"Look out your side. Keep a close eye on them and tell me what you see," he ordered the copilot as he slowly inched forward over the Merlin.

The copilot's face was anxious as he looked at Mike. He had heard the whispered stories—he thought they were war stories—of how Mike forced smugglers into the water.

The two Customs pilots could see the long line of runway lights on Bimini. The airport there was closed at sunset and did not allow takeoffs or landings after dark. Any aircraft that arrived after dark was refused permission to land. Any aircraft, that is, except smuggling aircraft. Dopers could make prior arrangements, as this one had done, and have lights turned on.

Slightly to the right of the runway lights and a bit higher were the lights of Alice Town and then, still farther to the right, Bailey Town, both on North Bimini.

"We on top yet?"

"Almost. I see the alligator on the tail. Move right."

Mike slid atop the Merlin. "Tell me when you see the leading edges of his wings. And keep me out of his props. If he pulls up, shout. I don't want the son of a bitch ripping my belly out."

The copilot swallowed hard and leaned as far to the right as he could, face pressed against the plexiglass. "Almost there. Almost there. Now."

Mike pushed forward on the yoke, dropping his two propellers closer to the doper, then switching on his landing lights. From inside the Merlin it appeared the Customs aircraft was about to crash atop the fuselage.

Mike smiled his tight smile. Maybe the doper would panic and stall the heavily loaded Merlin. He had found in these circumstances that smugglers either panicked and forgot their airspeed, then stalled and fell into the ocean, or they tried to outmaneuver the aircraft pressing on them from above and simply flew into the water. Mike didn't care which happened. He was not choosy. Either way it would scratch a loaded doper aircraft.

He pulled another fraction of an inch on the throttles and pushed forward on the yoke.

But the smuggler did not panic. He ignored the Customs aircraft. He was flying the Merlin as if it were on railroad tracks. The guy was a pro.

Mike liked that. But he knew the guy was not as good as he was. "Let's see how big your balls are, fellow," he muttered, pushing forward on the yoke.

"You're too low," the copilot said anxiously, his voice rising. "Pull up. Pull up."

Mike could see from the corner of his eye that the copilot was straining against his seat belt so hard he was almost standing up.

"Have I hit him?" Mike asked.

"Just about. You're about an inch away. It's too close." The copilot's voice was strained. Mike sighed. It's tough when your copilot has no faith.

"I haven't heard metal grinding," Mike said. He pushed forward.

But the doper pilot ignored the big propellers spinning a few feet in front of his face. His approach was smooth, unflinching. He could have been shooting practice landings he was so calm.

"Okay, I'll go to Plan B," Mike muttered.

He had time, but he would have to hurry. He banked the King Air in a hard right turn and added full power. The big aircraft, wingtip pointed toward the water, tightened in a steep circle. Mike leaned forward and looked through the top of the windshield, searching for the runway lights and then for the shape of the Merlin. It was low over the shallow water off the east end of the runway. Mike flicked a forefinger at the throttles, indicating that the copilot should hold them against the stop, maintaining full power. The copilot sighed and cupped the throttles, pushing hard against them.

Mike rolled out of the turn and pushed forward on the yoke. He was not sure he had time to try his second method of forcing a doper into the water. The guy was almost on short final. But what the hell? It was worth a try.

The big Customs aircraft roared down on the Merlin, its speed continuing to increase. Now Mike was flying at more than two hundred miles an hour only several feet above the water. His eyes appeared to be level with the runway lights that were rapidly drawing closer. The doper was also drawing closer.

The copilot turned anxiously toward Mike. "We got room?" he asked.

"We'll make room," Mike said.

Then, just as the doper pulled power and settled toward the end of the runway, Mike roared under him. He was only a few feet above the water and a few feet below the Merlin. The split second the Merlin disappeared from view in the windshield, he pulled the yoke hard toward his stomach, yanking the big aircraft into an almost vertical climb for a few seconds. The idea was to have the King Air's wingtip vortices, miniature tornadoes trailing off the wingtips, catch the Merlin at its most vulnerable time, when it was low and slow, and flip it into the ocean before the pilot could recover.

But as Mike pushed the nose over and then turned in a tight circle to the right, he saw his plan had not worked. The doper pilot was too good. He simply had added power and flown through the vortices. He was on the ground.

As the King Air turned, Mike saw two small white pickup trucks near the terminal building at the edge of the lighted ramp.

"There they are. Bahamian Customs and Immigration. Waiting to refuel the doper," Mike said bitterly. He rolled out of the turn and began climbing.

"And provide security until the doper is ready to go," the copilot added.

"Maybe even drive the boats if the bad guys do an air drop," Mike said. He adjusted the power levers. "Any more dope planes land on that fucking island, it will sink. Nothing there but bad guys. And the only way it can happen is because the Bahamians, Bahamian law enforcement, work for them. Fifty fucking miles from the U.S. is this sanctuary, this total outlaw country, and the most powerful nation on earth can't do anything about it. The goddamn wimps and faggots in the State Department are more concerned with playing golf and drinking tea with Bahamian officials than with grabbing them by the neck and saying, Okay, assholes. Clean up this dope business or you're on our permanent shit list. No more tourists. No more trade. No more nothing. You guys are lepers unless you play ball. But, hell, they'll never do that."

The copilot said nothing. Everyone in Customs' Miami office knew of Mike Love's animosity toward Bahamian law enforcement. He was right, of course. But he took it personally while other Customs pilots accepted it.

Bimini was a refuge, a latter-day hole-in-the-wall, where drug smugglers were idolized more than film stars and where an undercover police officer could find a slow and painful death. It was outlaw country; a combination of the Barbary Coast and the Wild West. Tourists went there for fishing, sun, and the bars. Because the tourists never recognized the signs or never understood the coded conversations or never thought it strange to see so many hard-looking young men wearing gold around their necks and driving go-fast boats, they never saw the smuggling.

Mike wiped his palms on his khaki pants, then reached for the frequency selector on the UHF radio. He dialed in the frequency of the Customs air wing at Homestead Air Force Base, radioed a terse message, waited a moment, then began talking rapidly. The conversation continued for several minutes. Then Mike wiggled his shoulders and settled back in his seat for the return flight to Gitmo.

"Who'd you call?"

"I had home plate give me a land line to the Broward S.O. Their narcotics squad guy, Nick Brown, some people call him Fluf, is a friend. And I know one of his agents. Lance Cunningham." Mike paused a moment, then added, "Hell of a cop but really a weird guy. Do anything."

The copilot raised his eyebrows. If Mike Love said a guy would "do anything," the copilot did not want to meet him or work with him. If a man who had moments earlier pushed himself to the brink of death was impressed with a local narcotics officer, that guy must be fruitcake city.

"I don't know if the Merlin is going that way after it refuels. But I told them to be on the lookout," Mike said.

He was not happy. Four dopers had escaped in

the past two days. Each had a rampant alligator painted on the tail of the aircraft. The dopers were beating him. Badly. Regularly.

But he had a plan. In two weeks the Gitmo operation would wind down and he would go back to his office at Homestead. Once he got back, he knew what he would do. The next time he caught a doper doing an air drop in the shallow waters off Bimini, Mike Love would make it an off-loading the smuggler would remember for a long time. He was going to give the smuggler an early taste of what hell would be like.

And he wasn't going to discuss his plan with anyone. There was a security leak. The Merlin pilot's tactics demonstrated that he knew Customs was flying out of Gitmo. The doper even knew the height-finder mode of the radar aboard the E-2 was inop or he wouldn't have used the slow climb to deceive the Gitmo radar operator. Even Mike, who was flying out of Gitmo every day and in frequent touch with E-2 crews, had not known the height-finding equipment was down. He wondered if he had missed a notice on the bulletin board at flight operations or not heard a briefing officer discuss the inoperative equipment. He shook his head. That was unlikely. He paid close attention at those briefings and he read the bulletin board several times a day.

The smuggler had a source inside Customs. Someone Mike worked with. It could even be his copilot.

3

Gunter Steinhorst slowly and carefully pulled the thick bushes apart and held them with callused muscular hands as he stared at the tent pitched near the edge of the slow-moving tidal creek.

It was almost 4 A.M. and the Coleman lantern hanging from the low limb of a casuarina tree cast a soft, almost tired glow over the campsite and onto the dark waters of the creek.

The long needles of the casuarina tree were motionless. Not a breath of air stirred the hot south Florida night. And the cacophony of animal and insect noises that usually pervaded the primitive reaches where the Everglades blended with the Ten Thousand Islands was absent. It was as if the night creatures were poised and waiting. Listening.

Steinhorst, without turning his head, moved his eyes to take in the boat tied to a cypress stump at the water's edge. It was a twenty-six-foot fishing boat with a fifty-horsepower outboard on the transom. The stern of the boat wiggled and twitched in the current.

Steinhorst's eyebrows lowered when he saw the six-foot CB antenna located amidship on the starboard side. A small VHF antenna was on the port side.

Steinhorst stared at the tent. No matter how much advance planning took place before a load was due, no matter how carefully logistics were thought out, there was always the unexpected. Sometime around dawn he would be supervising the off-loading of five hundred kilos of cocaine at one of the most isolated corners of the North American continent. And he had to contend with campers. Campers, for God's sake, out here on the backside of nowhere.

The load was coming into a clearing, the edge of which was only a hundred yards away. The big twin-engine Merlin would make its approach over the campsite. Even with throttles pulled back, the sound of those screaming turbines would awaken whoever was in the tent.

Radios were on the boat. The campers could do a lot of talking to a lot of people.

"If in doubt, take 'em out" was one of the many little mental notes Gunter Steinhorst kept for himself.

Steinhorst stepped through the bushes, holding his hands out to the side, then let the bushes close silently behind him as he stopped, slightly crouched, eyes on the tent.

He was a big man, standing six feet three inches tall and weighing 240 pounds. Even though he was in his late fifties, there was no flab anywhere on his body. He had a thirty-four-inch waist and, from the back, where one could not see the white close-cropped hair, the cruel arctic blue eyes and the hard set of his face, one would have thought he was a twenty-five-year-old fullback for a professional foot-ball team.

Steinhorst moved quietly across the sand toward the boat.

Long ago he had been in Marine Recon. His skill in killing his fellow man was heightened during the time he spent with the Solus Scouts in Rhodesia. That gig had ended when he killed three fellow mercenaries. One, the knot-tough former legionnaire, had called him a "stupid kraut." The other two had laughed.

Steinhorst bought a small farm near Sunnyland at the edge of the Big Cypress Swamp. Raising vegetables was a cover for his job as chief of security for Darrell Casey, who ran the biggest band of drug smugglers in south Florida.

It was a job for which he was well-suited. He was a model of Teutonic efficiency who killed calmly and coolly. Colombian smugglers, who had reputations as quick-tempered killers, jumped about cursing, uttering detailed convoluted threats, and waving automatic weapons before they killed someone. It was a big production. Hell, you'd think Colombian killers hired choreographers and drama instructors.

Steinhorst never raised his voice. He was soft-spoken, even courteous, up until the second before he killed. It was a style that caused those around him to exist in terror. When he walked through a room of Casey's smugglers, sweat popped out on faces like foam in the wake of a motorboat.

Most of his killings were within the Casey gang. Lawmen had an unofficial policy of expending very little effort investigating murdered drug smugglers. Cops knew of Steinhorst but they didn't care if he killed every doper in south Florida. The awareness that he could kill with virtual impunity had increased Steinhorst's self-confidence, a quality he had always had in abundance, until it went beyond arrogance. He was like an pelagic shark, a creature with no natural enemies, a creature all feared.

Three days earlier Steinhorst had killed two smugglers who had left Casey's gang to go into business for themselves. He had lulled the two men into a false sense of security by telling them Casey had no enmity and, in fact, wanted to show his goodwill by allowing them to use one of his air strips in the Everglades. Steinhorst had driven the men into the swamp, stopped in a clearing, then beat them until they barely were conscious. He had tied a leg of each to a large oak tree. The other leg he had tied to the rear bumper of his jeep with a one-inch-thick elastic rope. The outstanding characteristic of the rope was that it would stretch like a rubber band, then jerk back to its original length. Steinhorst had put the jeep into low gear, taking all the slack out of the rope, then stopped and gone back to smile at the two men. He had gotten back into the jeep, put more pressure on the line, then stopped and again walked back to smile at the two terrified men.

He had raced the motor on the jeep, quickly released the clutch, and simultaneously pressed the accelerator to the floor. A few seconds later, as the rope reached its maximum stretch, he had locked the brakes, the rope snapping to its original length and dismembering the two screaming men.

He had taken pictures and showed them to members of Casey's gang. "I help people who want to branch out," he'd said.

Steinhorst had a physiological quirk, so rare as to be virtually unknown in medical literature, that caused his fingernails to be extremely thick and almost as hard as carbon steel. They were so hard he filed them with an eight-inch rasp. Very carefully and with great deliberation, he filed each nail to a fine point. The edges he meticulously sharpened until they were like short-bladed daggers.

Steinhorst walked lightly toward the boat. At the water's edge, he pulled the boat parallel to the shore and opened the console under the Bimini cover. He found the two radios, reached behind them, and with a thumbnail sliced through the wires. He pushed the radios back into place and closed the cover. He looked at the sky to the east. The morning was darker than ever, the deepening blackness that precedes the dawn. The Merlin, the big thundering aircraft with the alligator on the tail and the cocaine in the cabin, would be landing in a few hours.

The sand was hard underfoot as he turned and walked toward the tent. There would be no tracks of this night's work.

He crouched at the front of the tent, slowly pulled the flap apart a half-inch, and peered inside. The campers, there were two of them, looked to be high-school kids, but Steinhorst did not relax. He had seen too many men die of overconfidence.

He backed up a half-step. "Come out," he barked. His voice was hard and gravelly.

After a pause there was a rustle inside the tent. Then quiet.

"Come out," Steinhorst repeated.

"Who is it?" The voice was young and quavery.

"Police. Come out."

"Just a minute." The voice was relieved.

Wilson Cope stuck his head through the flap of the tent. He was a twenty-year-old senior at the University of Miami who was home for the weekend to see his girlfriend, Beth Tarratoot, a high-school senior in Everglades City.

The young couple had told their parents they were meeting three other couples for an all-night fishing trip.

Beth's first thought was that her mother had discovered she was spending the night with Willie and had sent the police to bring her home.

"Yeah, what is it?" Willie Cope was trying not to show his nervousness when he stepped out of the tent and looked up at the shadowy figure of the giant with the short spike haircut.

Steinhorst said nothing.

"What is it, Willie? What's going on?" Beth asked from inside. She sat up in the sleeping bag and fearfully reached for her clothes.

"It's all right," Willie said. "Go back to sleep."

"Who else is here?" Steinhorst asked.

"Just the two . . ." Willie paused. He could see no badge or uniform, and the big man was not wearing a hat as did most policemen.

"You said you were a policeman?" he asked diffidently.

"Yes. We have an investigation under way. There may be criminals in the area. I want you out of here as quickly as you can pack this tent."

All Willie could think of was having to face Beth's mother if he brought her home in the middle of the night. He hitched up his pants. "What could be going on way out here?"

The cold blue of Steinhorst's eyes seemed to harden. He had hoped the kids would pack up and move. Tonight was too important for him to stand here jawing with a snot-nosed kid. He turned his right hand palm up and stiffened his fingers. Quickly, with terrible force, he jammed them into the vee of Willie's rib cage.

The rock-hard fingers hit with such force that Willie was lifted to his toes. His eyes bulged in a blinding second of pain before his heart burst and he died.

With his left hand Steinhorst seized Willie's jeans at the waist and lowered the boy softly to the ground. Steinhorst sniffed. He had hit the boy too hard and the knife-tipped fingers had sliced through the upper part of the stomach cavity before arching upward into the heart. The acrid odor of stomach fluids, combined with the stench from Willie's loosened bowels, filled the soft night air.

The odors, familiar to Steinhorst, did not bother him. In fact, they excited him. He was reminded of combat and blood and gore. His adrenaline was pumping.

Steinhorst wiped the blood from his right hand on Willie's jeans, then opened the flap of the tent and held it wide so the interior was illuminated by the lantern in the casuarina tree. Beth Tarratoot froze in the act of pulling her shirt over her breasts. For a moment the two stared at each other.

Her eyes lowered and she saw Willie's crumpled body on the sand. She opened her mouth to scream. Before a sound could escape, the big man dropped the tent flap and took two quick steps. He slapped her hard, rocking her head, then jerked her shirt away and tossed it aside.

Her white breasts stood out sharply. Steinhorst leaned over and pulled at the sleeping bag.

She was nude.

Beth wiped the blood on the corner of her mouth where he had slapped her. She stared, almost in bewilderment, at the dark stain on her hand. She wondered why it was black rather than red. It must be the dim light. She looked at the big man looming over her, shook her head slowly from side to side, and began to cry. "No, please," she whimpered. "Please don't."

Steinhorst smiled, unzipped his pants, dropped them, and fell atop her, his knees pushing her legs apart. She threshed her hips to prevent him from entering her.

He shoved his left hand under her waist and pulled her hips off the air mattress as he leaned into her, pushing, grunting. Her clenched fist bounced off his shoulders. He moved his right hand to her left hip and with both hands pulled her hips toward him and thrust violently. He fell atop her.

She screamed.

Afterwards, he dressed. She cried softly as he seized her wrists and pulled her from the tangled sleeping bag, stumbling, dark hair over her face. At the door of the tent, he barely slowed as he grabbed the waistband of Willie's jeans and picked up the limp body easily in his right hand. He carried it high off the sand so there would be no tracks.

He threw the body into the boat, then pushed Beth across the gunwale, causing her to trip and fall atop Willie's limp body. She gasped in fright and tried to pull away.

Steinhorst untied the line from the stump, picked up an oar, and pushed into the dark waters, paddling the boat surely and powerfully.

Five minutes later, at the point where a giant mangrove bush jutted into the deep and narrow channel between two small islands, he tied the bow-line to a bush and waited as the boat swung around in the current.

When he was satisfied the knot would hold, he reached into the small bow locker where he found an anchor and more than fifty feet of half-inch nylon line.

The German worked quickly. He tied the line to the anchor, then flipped the line around Willie's body a half dozen times. He doubled the line back on itself, tied a quick square knot, and jerked on it once to be sure it would hold. He turned to Beth, seized her elbow, and pulled her toward him. The motion caused her large firm breasts to wiggle. Long shadows cast by the moon in the mangrove bushes exaggerated the curve of her wide hips and the length of her legs.

Steinhorst paused. He looked at his watch. He sat on the bow of the boat, wound the thick fingers of his left hand into Beth's long black hair, and jerked her toward him as he unzipped his pants.

Her leg caught for a moment on Willie's body. Steinhorst pulled harder, jerking her forward, then forced her head between his legs.

"No. Please."

He twisted his hand in her hair until she cried out in pain.

"Do it." He spoke so softly she barely heard him.

He closed his eyes for a moment as he felt her mouth around him. He braced his feet on Willie's body and pulled harder on her hair until his entire length was in her mouth. She gagged and tried to pull away. He used both hands, pushing and pulling, forcing her into a quick jerky rhythm and ignoring her retching and muffled protests. He continued after he climaxed, forcing her on and on until his penis was flaccid. Then he angrily shoved her across Willie's body to the bottom of the boat. Her head struck the edge of the wooden seat and she was still.

Steinhorst zipped his pants, stood up, and reached for the anchor line. In long doubled coils he wrapped it around her body, placed her face-to-face with Willie, then wrapped the line around both of them, picking up their feet and then their heads to wind the coils of line until they were pulled together tightly from head to toe.

He wedged the anchor firmly between their bodies, pushing hard, then wiggling the anchor to make sure it was tight.

Beth moaned in pain as the sharp edge of the Danforth anchor bit into her ribs.

Steinhorst pulled on the line near Willie's head. Then near the feet. The line was taut and would hold.

With no apparent effort he hoisted the youngsters to the gunwale.

Beth fought through waves of pain and nausea and gut-twisting fear as she realized what was happening.

"I want my mother," she sobbed.

Steinhorst smiled and struck her swiftly with a closed fist hard under her rib cage. As she gasped, seeking air, he pushed them overboard into the dark waters.

The German's face was intense as he watched the bubbles. They did not last long.

4

Lance was thundering across the Gulf Stream in a Scarab, a go-fast boat, at fifty-five miles an hour. The boat was hardly straining in the calm seas and the snarl of the two high-powered engines resonated across the hot afternoon.

Lance handled the powerful boat easily, standing with knees flexed, both hands on the wheel, eyes sweeping the seas.

"Got to be careful," he said aloud. "Don't want to run over a Haitian. The ACLU will sue me for violating his civil rights."

Lance wore a pair of hundred-and-fifty-dollar Porsche sunglasses, three gold chains around his neck, shorts, and deck shoes. His white T-shirt had a red emblem stating, "Everybody Believes in Something. I Believe I'll Have a Beer."

Inside a hidden compartment in the cabin was a small high-powered radio and the long-barreled Magnum. It was loaded with hydrostatic bullets, a real man-stopper.

Anyone who saw Lance would assume he was a guy on the make, a doper, a scammer, one of dozens of hard men in fast boats who hung out around Bimini. No one would think him a cop. Even the most inexperienced smuggler knew cops traveled in pairs, that an undercover agent always had a backup.

If anyone were suspicious and tried to trace the ownership of his boat from the Florida registration sticker, they would find it registered to a salesman of office equipment, a man who traveled constantly and who was impossible to reach by telephone.

Fifty minutes after clearing the channel mouth at Fort Lauderdale, Lance was close to the long low line of Bimini stretching north and south in a dark-green line above the soft white beaches. He knew the island well. He fished in local waters and drank in local bars.

And he knew the history of the island. He knew that, from the beginning, pirates had favored Bimini. Those brigands, flying the flags of six nations, plied the warm Bahamian waters with a vengeance and found that Bimini was perfect for their trade—a small narrow island with the deep blue waters of the Gulf Stream on one side and clear shallow flats on the other.

It was a sheltered haven from which they could launch swift forays against both merchant vessels and the isolated settlements along the southeastern coast of the New World.

The pirates left a legacy of desolation and death that became genetically ingrained in the psyche of Biminites. When five African families settled Bimini in the early 1800s, they became shipwreckers, luring sailing vessels onto nearby reefs, then murdering the crews and stealing the cargo.

It was a tradition that never abated.

During the Civil War, Bimini was a refuge for

blockade runners, and again the waterways of the island, only fifty-five miles from the U.S. mainland, were filled with blood and intrigue.

During Prohibition, Bimini was the favorite jumping-off point for rumrunners in fast boats hauling illegal whiskey into Florida.

Then, in the late 1960s, a trickle of marijuana smugglers began using Bimini. The trickle grew to a flood until, in the mid-1980s, drug smugglers controlled the small island.

The island added another illegal business to its repertory when it became the last waypoint in the smuggling of illegal aliens from Cuba, Haiti, and Colombia into Florida.

The fishing made famous by Ernest Hemingway and the carousing made famous by New York Congressman Adam Clayton Powell continued. Fishermen and tourists often never knew of the tons of marijuana and cocaine and the hundreds of aliens being smuggled through Bimini. They heard the midnight roar of go-fast boats but thought it part of the allure of Bimini.

More than 80 percent of the inhabitants of Bimini were actively engaged in smuggling by the mid and late 1980s. They often began as humpers who off-loaded drugs from aircraft onto boats or acted as refuelers for aircraft almost empty after the long run up Amber-16, the airway that began off the coast of Colombia and ended at Bimini. Then the Biminites grew to want more of the action and began to pirate loads from smugglers who did not want to pay to use the airport. The island became a favored stash point for marijuana and cocaine. Customs and Immigration officers were given a choice— accept bribes and let the smugglers operate with impunity, or be killed and let smugglers operate with impunity.

The officers who would not accept bribes were taken offshore in some of the most shark-infested waters in the world, slashed with knives, and thrown overboard. Occasionally parts of bodies would wash ashore on Bimini or even around Fort Lauderdale. It was as if even the ocean, which had known uncounted millennia of indifference, was appalled at the violence of Bimini.

Bimini continued to be the only island of the Bahamian archipelago with no representative on any Bahamian law-enforcement agency. The centuries-old tradition of breaking the law was too strong for any Biminite to become part of upholding the law.

Nassau, the seat of government, took the attitude that Bimini was a small, remote, and insignificant part of the country. If people there wanted to bring in marijuana, let them. There was little that could be done except order frequent transfers for the police stationed there.

Bimini, in reality, is two islands—North Bimini and South Bimini. North Bimini is a narrow wishbone-shaped island that runs from north to south and then wraps around a shallow sound on the eastern side. The north-south section of the island is littered with bars, hotels, clubs, and marinas. About sixteen hundred people live there, almost all of them in Alice Town on the southern tip of the island.

South Bimini, separated only by a narrow cut from North Bimini, is a low-lying, swampy, bug-ridden island inhabited by about a half-dozen people. Many Bahamians, even those on North Bimini, are afraid to be alone at night on South Bimini.

Even though the island is only about five miles

long, people have wandered lost there for days. It is said that "spirits of the land" are on South Bimini.

Bahamians often are wary of those born on South Bimini. A man from there, at the sight of a waterspout, will rub two sticks together. Often he is a herbalist or expert in bush medicine.

No telephones are on South Bimini. But each house and each of the half-dozen vehicles has a citizens-band radio. A stranger's every move is broadcast.

Two hotels once thrived on South Bimini, but they have been closed for years. If you roam the grounds of the hotels, one at the south end near the cut into the coral, the other at the northern tip across the channel from Alice Town, you will find aircraft seats and fifty-five-gallon drums of aviation fuel stacked in some of the rooms. Remains of half-eaten meals can be found on tables. And glasses, some containing ice, stand glistening on the tables.

In the small hotel at Buccaneer Point on the north end of the island, a black-and-white television set is tuned to a Miami station. The reception is erratic by the miles, but the set blares at all hours of the day and night.

An air of emptiness and desolation hangs over the grounds of the hotel. Nearby groves of casuarina trees are burned and charred. Doors of the once-busy fishing club are off the hinges and swing idly in the breeze.

A vague ineffable feeling of doom hangs like a soft mist over South Bimini. It is felt when a visitor stumbles into the weather-lashed remains of the tumbled-down yacht club and sees in a nearby canal a shiny sixty-foot yacht, brightwork gleaming in the hot sun, and two deckhands staring in frozen silence.

It is in the hostile faces of two men waiting in a door of an abandoned building. Everyone waits on South Bimini. Usually for a boat or an aircraft.

South Bimini's vital ingredient, the only thing that keeps it from being another isolated Bahamian sandbar, is a paved runway stretching more than five thousand feet.

The airport is remote. It is closed and unattended after sundown. It has two powerful navigational devices that enable pilots to track toward it on the darkest night. Boats can come through a maze of canals to within a few yards of the runway.

The airport on South Bimini has the same sleepy sun-blasted ennui of dozens of Bahamian airports. A small one-room cement building contains offices for Customs and Immigration. A nearby building has a tiny restaurant where the menu is as limited as the waitresses' enthusiasm.

But this airport is different because it is at the end of Amber-16. And it is here that many people in the Business land after the long flight from Colombia.

To the discerning eye, signs of this activity are everywhere. A baggage cart riddled with bullets from automatic weapons, a reminder of one of the gunfights so common at the airport. Crashed aircraft up and down the edges of the runway and in the waters off both ends of the runway. The carcass of the Lockheed Lodestar whose pilot landed because he was low on fuel only to have a Bahamian Customs officer wheel a boarding ladder up to the cockpit and shoot him. The marijuana was off-loaded but the pilot's body stayed in the cockpit for a week. Aircraft sought by every state and federal narcotics officer in Florida are parked on the ramp, but even when U.S. officials fly low over the airport, photograph the aircraft, and then show the pictures to Bahamian officials, the Bahamians deny the aircraft are there.

The men who base their aircraft on Bimini, the men who fly Amber-16, can sleep well in the hotels of Alice Town. No one will harm them and no one will bother their aircraft. Bimini is safe and secure. As it has been from the beginning, Bimini is a sanctuary.

Lance smiled as he thought how he was about to violate that sanctuary. He angled the boat a few degrees south, aiming for the deep cut through the coral near the end of South Bimini. The cut became a canal stretching into the interior of South Bimini and was lined with vacation homes.

As he swung toward the cut, Lance smiled in anticipation. He was alone on an undercover assignment in a foreign country. He was in Bimini in the belly of the beast.

He reached forward with his left hand and slowly pulled the twin throttles. The sharp bow of the Scarab settled and the loud snarl of the engines subsided to a threatening rumble. He kept the boat in the center of the narrow cut.

No one was about the grounds of the deserted motel to his right. Good. If someone saw him coming in, he might have to do some fast talking with Bahamian Customs. They would ask for his papers and then want to know why he had not officially entered the country. But once here, it would be assumed he had cleared Customs.

He stood straight behind the wheel of the go-fast

boat, watching the thick mangrove bushes on either side. He glanced at the houses as he passed. No sign of anyone.

At a small dock on the south side of the canal, he drifted to a stop, quickly snubbed a stern line over a cleat, then walked forward on the dock to secure the bow. He jumped lightly into the cockpit and cut off the ignition switches.

With a soft rumbling bubble, the twin underwater exhausts quieted.

No one was on the narrow sand road. Lance went below, grabbed two heavy canvas bags, and pushed them through the companionway into the cockpit. He locked the companionway, hoisted the heavy bags up onto the dock, then jumped to the dock. He looked around again. No sign of anyone. He picked up the bags and trotted across the road to a two-story house half-hidden in a grove of casuarina trees. All Nick knew about the house was that it was owned by a friend of the sheriff, some wealthy guy who made the house available.

The canvas bags, filled with special equipment, were heavy. Sweat beaded on Lance's forehead. But he was smiling. Tonight he would take the go-fast boat to Alice Town, the small village controlled by drug smugglers. It was a two-minute ride.

Lance thought again what Fluf had said about playing by the rules. There were no rules on Bimini. That's why Darrell Casey was so successful, that's why last night Casey had successfully moved a load of cocaine through even when the cops knew it was coming. Casey made his own rules. For the next few days Lance would follow the same guidelines. His only rule would be to do whatever he had to do to stay alive. This was a dream assignment, the sort of thing every narcotics officer—well, *many* narcotics officers—would long to do. He was going to bust Darrell Casey's ass. He was going to get the evidence needed to indict crooked Bahamian cops, then find a way to lure them to Lauderdale, where they could be arrested. He was going to put the big hurt on the biggest group of smugglers ever to operate in Broward County.

The house was built on stilts near the edge of the shallow waters off South Bimini. Blinding white sand stretched from the steps of the house to a grove of casuarina trees and then on down to the clear green waters. It was a view of unsurpassed beauty. But Lance ignored the view. A soft breeze from off the water stirred his dark hair as he climbed the steps, lugging the two heavy canvas bags. As it was for most of the year, the weather was hot and sultry. Perspiration beaded on his forehead, but Lance hardly noticed. He had to secure the equipment in the bags, then get ready for the night.

In a few hours it would be rock-'n'-roll time.

5

"Stop a minute," Darrell Casey said from the bed. He pushed up on an elbow and looked with unabashed admiration at the nude woman who had just thrown back the white silk sheets and stood up.

Darby DuPree paused, one knee on the bed, and smiled. She was slender, very slender, with lean muscular legs and small breasts. Even in the dim early-morning light her luminescent green eyes seemed to leap out of olive skin tanned to a dark brown by the hot Florida sun. Her straight blue-black hair was cut short and gave her a look of imperious sophistication. She was twenty years younger than Darrell Casey's forty-six and she was the loveliest and most sensual woman he had ever known.

Darrell Casey had been a Fort Lauderdale plumber whose greatest enjoyment was an occasional fishing trip to Bimini until he found he could make a fortune bringing drugs from the Bahamas into Florida. Like most smugglers, he started small; four or five bales of marijuana were easy to hide in a fishing boat and provided more money in one night than he could make during a year of plumbing, even at the inflated prices charged by plumbers.

Then he hauled a few keys of cocaine and thought he had discovered a money machine. His only setback was an abortive trip to Jamaica seeking a new source of supply. That had not worked and he returned to Bimini, where his cunning and toughness soon made him a millionaire many times over.

He virtually had his choice of the beautiful women who flocked to Fort Lauderdale from around the country. And out of the experience of sleeping with more women every month than most men did in a lifetime, he developed what he called his 1-percent theory. He believed that 99 percent of the women a man makes love with rank in the same category of sexual expertise: pleasant but not truly memorable. Six months after making love with most women, one can remember the act, the fact one made love with her, but one cannot remember what it was like. They all blur together in one homogenous lot.

But one-half of 1 percent of the women one goes to bed with are truly lousy. They prove the fallacy of the old saw that even when sex is bad, it is wonderful, that "the worst I ever had was out of this world." Casey privately thought that making love with the one or two women he had known in this category was like fucking a zero. It was impossible to say what made them so forgettable in bed. Part of it was their physiology. Part of it was the way they moved. Part of it was how they talked, how they held a cigarette, the tone of their voice, the quality of their perfume. It was all of these and yet it was none of these. But Casey knew he would rather sit on a wall and masturbate with a sandpaper glove than sleep with one of those women ever again.

Then there is the remaining one-half of 1 percent.

Casey believed that these women were so rare that most men never experienced them; that most men, in fact, neither knew they were roaming the world like some rare exotic species, nor believed it when they heard of such women. If a man ever had the good fortune to make love with someone in this last group, it was impossible to describe the experience to anyone who had not had a similar experience. It was as if one had skipped across the Himalayas from the top of one peak to another, breathing the clean clear rarefied air and looking over most of the world, then trying to describe the experience to one who spent his life trudging across a desert or mucking through a pestilential bog.

After one had made love to a woman in this category, all the remainder of one's days were spent in a fruitless search to replicate the experience. That's why Casey believed that to have known such a woman poisoned a man's life. Everyone else was compared to her, and they all, invariably and inevitably, suffered in the comparison.

Casey wondered if these rare women affected every man in the same fashion. Was she always and with everyone a woman of bliss? Or was there some rare and indefinable synergism that occasionally took place between two people, some arcane alchemy that transmogrified the grinding together of their sweaty bodies into an unearthly experience? Was it some sort of metaphysical prank to let a man and woman know this experience for a while during their earthly sojourn and then to take it from them?

Just as it is impossible to say what makes some women such unutterable sexual mendicants, so it is equally impossible to say what causes others to be such ineffably seraphic creatures of wonder, women who bless and curse the men who know them and cause them to exist in an eternal state of nympholepsy.

Casey, for all his sexual experience, had never known anyone like the young woman standing beside his bed. She was aloof, standoffish, almost haughty, until she came to bed. She did not have the mechanical or gymnastic expertise of many women he had known. In fact, he had taught her a great deal in that area. Rather it was smoky, atavistic, primitive feeling unwrapped from deep within her unconscious. An innocent intensity. A gift she was not even aware she possessed. She did and said and felt things by intuition that women twice her age and with ten times her sexual experience did not know. There were times when Darrell Casey was making love to her that he felt he was in the all-consuming white-hot center of a nuclear furnace.

There was much he did not know or understand about her. Something was burning inside her, something he could dimly sense but not quite isolate or categorize. When he tried to question her, she became like a frightened wild animal. She wrung her hands and rolled her eyes and appeared to be on the verge of running away. "Those things are none of your business," she had told him. "I just need privacy. It has nothing to do with you. You are the only man in my life." Her voice had grown intense and he knew she was deadly serious when she locked her dark eyes on him and said emphatically, "But you have to let me be alone occasionally. Please don't force me to leave you."

So Darrell Casey, a man whose discipline and self-control had made him one of the most successful drug smugglers in America, backed off. He would do anything within reason to keep her in his home and in his bed.

She would stay with him a day, maybe two days, then return to her small apartment near the beach. He had been there only once. He picked the lock when she was not there and entered. The apartment was sparsely furnished and had very few pictures or personal items women like to have around. He had later ordered Steinhorst to run a background check on her, and it all seemed to fit. She had moved to Lauderdale a year earlier—she would not discuss her hometown or family—and she paid her telephone and utility bills regularly. She worked part-time as a waitress in a restaurant about a mile away on the Intracoastal. That was where he had met her.

Darby cupped her breasts, kneaded them for a moment, and then, keeping her eyes locked with Darrell's, slid onto the bed.

He smiled, reached for her, then rolled atop her. She was ready. That was another thing about her: she was always ready, always moist and receptive.

Moments later she slid her arms down his back, squeezed his buttocks, and whispered, "Stop."

He pulled his face from her neck and stared at her in disbelief. "Now?"

She smiled and squeezed again. "Stop," she said softly.

He sighed and did as she asked. She slid her legs together under him so that their bodies touched from toe to neck. Then she moved her head so she could look into his eyes. She stared for a moment, brow slightly wrinkled, and then he felt her muscles seize him.

His eyes widened in amazement.

She smiled. Again he felt her muscles clasp him—clasp him and release, clasp and release.

He groaned and began moving.

"No, you have to be still," she whispered urgently.

"But I want—"

"You will. You will."

He buried his face in her neck. "How do you do that?"

She turned slightly, held his head in her hands, took his ear into her mouth, then pulled back and whispered, "I practice."

"Practice?"

"When I'm watching TV."

He smiled. "You must watch a hell of a lot of TV."

She sighed, locked her arms around his neck, and closed her eyes in concentration. "Don't move," she whispered.

Moments later Darrell Casey cried aloud.

A half-hour later Darrell and Darby lay under the silk sheets and shared the desultory conversation of lovers.

"You working today?" she asked idly.

He pushed back his thick black hair. "Yeah. Got a little problem. Some people are coming over. Won't take long."

He stretched and looked at the heavy gold Rolex on his wrist. "They should be here anytime."

She ran her hand across his chest. "They'll wait for you."

Darrell smiled a smug smile of agreement.

"What do they want?" she asked.

"It's not what they want. It's what I want."

She slid her hand lower. "Okay. What do you want?"

He smiled. "I want things to go smoothly."

She held him and moved her hand. Smoothly.

Darrell placed his forearm over his eyes. "You know about it. The deal on Bimini. Biggest one I've ever done."

"That's pretty big."

"And the goddamn Bahamians are just waiting to rip me off. I've got to send some muscle over there. Steinhorst has got to pay them a visit. That's all they respect. And I'm having problems with my muscle."

"What sort of problems?"

"You know how Steinhorst is. But I got two new guys coming in I think will control him. He's getting too big for his britches."

"He is getting big."

Casey sighed, caught on the tightrope of what Darby was doing and the anticipation of the surprise he had planned for Steinhorst. When he spoke again, his voice was low.

"Fucking Bahamians."

"Why are you having problems with them?"

"I don't know. I shouldn't have problems over there. I own that little birdshit-covered Bimini and half the people on it. The Minister of Tourism, Customs and Immigration people at the airport and the harbor, all work for me. But they are pirates. I can't afford to have anything happen to my stash over there. It's part of the financing for the big load."

"So what are you going to do?"

"I got these three fish-bellied wimps from Harvard working for me, advising me how to move my money around. All of 'em have some kind of business degrees. They're always talking about goals by objective and things I don't understand. This morning I'm going to show them my management style. The only way things work. When you got a problem, you throw everybody down in a hole. You let them fight it out. You let the blood flow. Whoever crawls back over the edge, wins."

She thought of the hole in the back yard out beyond the swimming pool, the deep pit where Casey kept alligators. She hated the pit and rarely ventured beyond the pool, even though she enjoyed sunbathing and the lawn near the deep hole received several hours more sunshine each day than did the pool, which was sheltered in the afternoon by thick oleander bushes. "You're throwing Steinhorst in a hole?"

Darrell laughed. He was finding it more and more difficult to concentrate. "Yeah, him and two other guys."

"The new ones you mentioned?"

"Yeah. Two ex–Green Berets. They were in Vietnam. They'll control that crazy German. And they'll straighten things out on Bimini."

"What did Steinhorst do?" Darby involuntarily shivered. She was frightened of the big German with the spike hair and polar-blue eyes.

For a moment she thought Darrell was not going to answer. He began moving his hips. She slid lower in the bed.

Then, in a loud voice, Casey said, "He killed two people."

Darby paused for a moment. Then she slid lower. "But that's why you have him around, isn't it?"

Casey's voice was loud. "I didn't tell him to do it."

"Do what?"

Casey arched his back. "Kill two kids."

She took him into her mouth.

"Kill two kids," Darrell shouted. His voice fell away. "Kill two kids. Kill two kids."

6

It was 10:30 P.M. when Lance, in his cocky, bouncing fashion, walked across the sandy road and stepped aboard the go-fast boat. The night noises of South Bimini—the frogs, the insects, the omnipresent lapping of the surf—were an unending cacophony. Mosquitoes buzzed about his head like circling, angry airplanes.

He fired up the engines, cast off the lines, and slowly motored down the middle of the canal toward the deep cut through the coral near the end of South Bimini.

The moon was a thin sliver to the west but the stars were bright, and in the clear night air he could easily see the dark thick mangrove bushes along the banks of the canal.

He had no plans for the evening. This was not the sort of operation where one could lay out a course of action. The element of the unknown, his lack of control over events, made him wary and fine-tuned, alert, with every nerve quivering. For the next few days he could make no mistakes. If he did, he would be dead. Lance thrived on living on the edge, on playing the game, on taking the big risk.

He eased through the cut near the abandoned
motel and held his course until he was about fifty
yards offshore. Then he turned ninety degrees to
the right, eyes on the lights of Alice Town a mile
away. He took a deep breath, reached forward, and
slowly pushed the throttles forward. The bow of the
Scarab climbed out of the water and the throaty
guttural snarl of the engines began echoing their
song of power. The warm evening air was salt-tangy
in Lance's face. He laughed aloud, tilted his head to
the sky, and said in exultation, "Hot damn, it's fun
being a policeman."

The go-fast boat, leaving a rooster tail of spray
and a wide trail of foaming white water, hugged the
western edge of South Bimini as Lance raced northward. He aimed the bow a bit to the right of the
lights of Alice Town in order to clear the long
dangerous sandbar off the southern end of North
Bimini. He kept his eye on the white sandy beach a
few yards to the right. Only two houses, one of
them abandoned, were on this stretch of beach, one
of the loveliest in all the Bahamas.

Lance had the boat on the step and the speedom-
eter was indicating forty miles an hour when he
came through the narrow cut between South Bimini
and North Bimini. The sound and appearance of a
go-fast boat preclude a quiet inauspicious entrance.
The audacious thunder of the engines and the long
fine lines of the boat draw the eyes of anyone
within sight or sound.

Lance pulled the throttle. But not too much. He
carried enough speed to rock the numerous go-fast
boats tied up and down the lengthy docks at Brown's
and on the protected harbor of the Big Game Club.
He wanted to let everyone know a heavy breather

was in town. He was trolling for something bigger than hitchhikers.

The Big Game Club is a mecca for fishermen from around the world. And for drug smugglers.

He stayed outside the circle of light cast by the bars and marinas as he motored northward. He slowed enough to leave very little wake. He passed Bailey Town and moved into Porgy Bay. The few people who heard the powerful boat throbbing through the shallows paid little attention. There were dozens of go-fast boats around Bimini. Now the water under the boat was changing color rapidly, going from green to white, indicating very shallow water. Ahead of him the island curved east around the Sound and hooked toward East Wells. The water was becoming too shallow. He pressed two buttons on the throttle quadrant and a soft whine told him the propellers were swinging up and to the rear, enabling him to press on a bit farther. He pulled the twin chrome throttle levers aft until he was barely making headway.

To his left the main road running up the center of the island was coming to an end. A high metal fence topped with barbed wire ran from the ocean side of the island all the way across to the shallow waters of the Sound.

Darrell Casey's white mansion, gleaming under a dozen security lights, was visible on a small knoll in a grove of casuarina trees.

The lights showed a half-dozen beefy dogs walking about the grounds. One stood under a light at the edge of the water, staring toward the boat. A rottweiler, a big male, maybe 140 pounds of muscle and teeth, was staring into the darkness toward Lance.

The dogs moved slowly because of the heat. But Lance knew that, if provoked—and it took very little to provoke a rottweiler—the dogs could explode in savage fury. Those dogs were killing machines. They could eat his boat and use the splinters for toothpicks.

Now the boat was barely clearing the bottom. Lance peered astern and in the moonlight saw clouds of white sand behind each propeller. If it were not for the dogs, he could have anchored and waded ashore.

Lance smiled. He had at least found out the house was impossible to approach from the water. That was something. But even more important was discovering there were no armed guards. That meant the house was not the place where Darrell Casey stored drugs. He probably had a stash house on South Bimini near the airport. This was just a party house, another thing to buy. It was tough being a smuggler. One of the most difficult daily decisions was where to invest money. Smugglers had so much money they didn't bother to count it; they simply divided the bills by denomination, then weighed them.

"Okay, fans. Round one to the bad guys," Lance said in a falsetto.

He lowered the propellers and slowly motored back toward the lights of Alice Town.

He was going ashore, going alone into one of the most violent and corrupt towns in the western world, but he figured the odds were about even: Lance Cunningham against all the smugglers on Bimini.

He laughed aloud. And, still in the falsetto he liked to affect, warned, "Look out, bad guys. The mighty Houdini is on the prowl."

7

Gunter Steinhorst paused, a can of beer at his lips, as he watched Darrell Casey and his little tart leave the house and walk along the edge of the oleander thicket near the pool. He knew from the expression on Darrell's face that something was afoot. His thick protruding white eyebrows lowered over icy blue eyes.

Steinhorst felt grudging respect for Darrell. He was tough. Not afraid to make hard decisions. And the only thing Steinhorst had found that frightened Darrell was alligators. Something to do with an experience in Jamaica years ago when he crashed an airplane. That was why Darrell had the pit of alligators in his yard and why he went out and stood on the edge of the pit almost daily. Steinhorst had seen him there, eyes wide and great beads of perspiration on his face. But Darrell believed in facing up to his fears, in confronting what most frightened him and then pressing through the fear. Darrell had an alligator painted on the tail of every aircraft he owned. It was the trademark, the logo, of his smuggling organization. Steinhorst liked that sort of courage in a man. What he did not like was that Darrell had fears. Steinhorst was afraid of nothing.

Steinhorst's grudging respect for Darrell did not stop him from planning how to get rid of his boss. Steinhorst was living proof of the truth that Germans were always at one's throat or one's feet. He would kill Darrell as easily as he killed the men who worked for Darrell. But he knew that if he seized control of the smuggling ring now, he did not know enough to manage it as profitably as Darrell was doing. So he was biding his time, waiting.

He sat alone at a table under a large umbrella protecting his fair skin from the hot noonday sun. At the far end of the pool were three guys in suits and horn-rimmed glasses. Steinhorst wondered why people who deal with large amounts of money—that is, people who make money their business—always wear suits. Even in South Florida.

He dismissed the three men. Of more concern to him were the two strangers—they looked like twins—who sat at a third table. Occasionally one of the men would glance at him with a mocking look.

Steinhorst recognized professionals, men like himself. He could see it in their eyes. These guys had seen combat. They had looked death in the eye. By their carriage, the way they held their shoulders, they were ex-military. Probably Rangers or Seals, maybe Green Berets. Some elite outfit. One of the men wore a white leather glove on his right hand. Steinhorst glanced casually at his fingernails. He had filed them with the rasp early that morning. He turned up the can of beer and drank half the contents with a long gulp.

It looked as if today was going to be some sort of Come-to-Jesus meeting. Steinhorst had once heard an old Florida shrimper talk of a "Come-to-Jesus meeting." He liked the phrase. Several times, when he had killed overly ambitious smugglers or members of Casey's gang who were suspected of talking to the police, he had begun by smiling and saying, "We're about to have a Come-to-Jesus meeting."

He watched idly as Darrell, a confident smile on his face, shook hands with the two strangers. They were tall, as tall as Steinhorst, but with ropy muscles rather than the great bulk Steinhorst had. He outweighed either of them by fifty pounds.

Darby, wearing a white one-piece bathing suit, stopped at the table where the three Harvard money men sat. They jumped up, stumbling awkwardly, to offer her a chair. When she sat, the sun was in her eyes. But she ignored the three Harvard men who wanted her to move around the table. She pushed her chair under the edge of the oleander thicket. She wanted to watch Darrell.

"Gunter, want you to meet a couple new guys I hired to work with you," Darrell said in his casual voice as he strolled toward Steinhorst, the two muscular strangers in tow. Darrell had a slight limp that caused his dark hair to bob up and down as he walked between the two tall blond men.

Darby watched the two men. They were extraordinarily handsome. Darrell said they had been in Vietnam, so they must be in their forties. But they looked much younger. They were clean-shaven. Tanned. And their casual but expensive clothes were new, stylish and well-fitting. There was something strange about them and she couldn't figure out what it was.

Steinhorst watched also, brows lowered. He stood

up. As Darrell and the two strangers approached, Steinhorst tilted his head and finished the beer.

"Gunter, I want you to meet . . ." He stopped and turned as a shrill scream rang out. The men around the pool turned to look at Darby. She was leaning forward in her chair, pressing against the table, seeking to get as far as possible from the large snake to the left of her chair. It was a six-foot rattlesnake that had crawled from the oleander thicket.

Moving quicker than Darrell Casey had ever seen a man move, one of the blond strangers, the one with the white leather glove on his right hand, ran to her side, crouched, then suddenly reached out and seized the snake by the tail.

The three Harvard money men squealed. Darby stared.

The sun-bronzed man stood, twirled the snake twice around his head, and then, with a harsh martial-arts grunt, reversed his hand and popped the head off the snake. It flew halfway across the yard, rolled over twice, and stopped. The mouth slowly, very slowly, opened and drops of viscous fluid oozed from the white fangs. Then the mouth closed and was still.

For a moment no one moved. The man who held the still-twitching body of the snake turned to Darby and in a kindly voice said, "Don't be afraid. He's dead." He turned and walked toward Steinhorst. As the man walked away, Darby suddenly knew what it was about the two men that had puzzled her. They were homosexuals. She did not know how or why she knew. But she knew.

Darrell Casey had hired a couple of homosexual killers to confront Steinhorst.

The stranger wearing the white glove had a mocking half-smile on his face when he stopped several steps away from Steinhorst, paused, then suddenly tossed the snake toward the big German.

Steinhorst caught the snake in midair with his extended left hand. He paused long enough to fix the younger man with a cold smile. Then his right hand became a blur as his sharpened fingernails slashed up and down the snake's body, turning it into long bloody strips. Before anyone realized what was happening, he flung the bloody carcass around the neck of the man with the white glove. The carcass no longer twitched.

Both strangers took a half-step toward Steinhorst.

With an almost insolent smile, the man with the white glove asked Steinhorst, "Don't you worry about your nail polish?"

Steinhorst did not answer. His cold blues eyes were still locked with those of the stranger. He stepped forward, closing the distance between the two men until they were eyeball to eyeball. He reached out and slowly drew one fingertip down the man's chest. His razored finger nail split the man's expensive white cotton shirt and left a thin crimson line down the bronze skin.

The stranger never flinched or withdrew. He continued smiling and kept his eyes locked with Steinhorst's.

With a soft intense malevolence, in a voice so low that Darrell could not hear him, Steinhorst muttered, "The only thing that hurts my nail polish is when I split open some faggot's chest, reach in, grab whatever I can lock onto, and jerk hard. Sometimes I get a little anxious and hit a man's backbone. That hurts my nail polish."

Steinhorst's mouth moved a fraction. For him it was a big smile. The challenge was there. Out in the open. The next move was up to the two strangers.

Darrell stepped back. He had thought this confrontation would be delayed until the three men were by themselves. But he was glad it was happening. Steinhorst needed to be taught a lesson.

The three fish-bellied Harvard money men were frozen in silence. They could not hear the conversation between Steinhorst and the two men. But they sensed this was a showdown between certified killers. They wanted no part of it. Which proves that, contrary to popular belief, Harvard graduates do have a certain amount of practical knowledge.

Both strangers stared, weighing the German. They were poised, ready to move. The stranger with the white glove looked deep into Steinhorst's eyes. He had killed enough men to know how close he and his partner were to dying. They were not fast enough or strong enough to take on this guy. They didn't mind dying. But they did not want to commit suicide.

"You'll have to teach me that trick," the man said softly, capitulating.

Steinhorst, unblinking, said nothing.

In an effort to save face, the stranger pulled the dripping carcass of the snake from around his neck, held it with his hands about eighteen inches apart, paused, then bit into the snake and chewed slowly.

His partner reached out, seized the body of the snake in two hands, and twisted hard, snapping the spine. He jerked the carcass into two parts and gave his friend one-half. He took the other. He poked the fine lacy rib bones out of the way and bit deeply into the rich red meat, covering the sides of his face with splotches of blood and causing a thin, red watery trail of blood to dribble down his chin and fall onto the grass.

The two men stood before Steinhorst, staring at him, slowly eating the freshly killed rattlesnake. Their hands were upturned, cradling the body of the snake and at the same time making their act an offering to Steinhorst. It was as if they were acolytes standing before a high priest.

One of the Harvard men leaned over his chair and vomited onto the grass.

No one but Darrell Casey ever knew the names of the two men because from that moment they were known only as "the Snake Eaters."

Darrell's plan to tame Steinhorst had backfired. In fact, he now was facing a greater problem. The two new guys would never confront the German. They had been overwhelmed. Darrell could see it in their eyes. They chewed on the snake and looked at Steinhorst as if seeking his approval, as if seeking to demonstrate that they, too, knew certain arcane and esoteric temple ceremonies, as if wanting to prove that they were of the brotherhood.

Darby stood up. She had to tell Darrell good-bye and leave for a few hours. She would tell him she was ill. After seeing those two men eat a snake, he would understand. Her mind was reeling. Darrell had hired two homosexual killers and she knew he would send them to Bimini. Where did Darrell find people like Steinhorst and the two new guys? They were like cartoon characters. But she could not laugh because she knew how dangerous they were.

She had to get dressed and go downtown. Her boss needed to know Steinhorst had killed two kids. Almost certainly the two who were missing from a camping trip in the Ten Thousand Islands. He had talked to her of the big load of coke he was planning on moving through Bimini. And there were the Bimini officials on Darrell's payroll.

She had to report all of this to Nick Brown, head of the Broward County Narcotics Squad. He had to know. Brown was her boss.

Darby DuPree was a narc.

8

Lance tied his go-fast boat at the first slip on the north end of the dock at the Big Game Club. It was an old, unlighted part of the dock, and for a moment he sat in the darkness feeling the warm night air around him. This would be his last night on Bimini. His bags were stashed below. The past eight days had been successful beyond even his eternal optimism. He had catalogued the registration numbers of eighty-seven go-fast boats and forty-three aircraft that he suspected of being involved in drug smuggling. He had located Darrell Casey's stash house on South Bimini. He had met and become friends with boat drivers who worked for Casey. And after coded radio messages had been received from Nick Brown, he had identified the Minister of Tourism and the law-enforcement officials on Bimini who were on Darrell Casey's payroll. He stayed away from the Customs and Immigration officials because he knew he might return to Bimini. But he had met, talked with, and gained the confidence of many of Casey's men. They thought he was a smuggler. Doing them was easy. It was all easy. Bimini was so wide open, the crooks were so much in control, nothing was hidden.

"Operation Limey" was about to wind down as an unqualified success.

Lance stepped onto the dock, secured the lines, and slowly walked toward the bar a hundred yards south. He was wearing what smugglers call "exotics," lizard-skin cowboy boots, sharply creased jeans, a wide leather belt with a large gold buckle, and a Black Sabbath T-shirt that said, "I Want a New Drug."

Suddenly he saw a vessel that made him start. He stopped, leaned over, and pretended to brush off his boot as he eyed the boat to his left. Rocking gently on the outside of the dock, taking up space ordinarily occupied by two boats, was a forty-five-foot black Cigarette boat.

The heavily modified boat had its engines in a special shielded housing. The boat was built like the damn rottweilers he had seen his first night on the island: big, beefy, muscular, looking as if it could rear up out of the water and take on all comers. Lance knew, without looking inside the boat, that its forward cabin had been gutted. His practiced eye told him the boat could haul maybe two tons of contraband through six-foot seas at somewhere around seventy miles an hour. The only thing that could catch this boat was a helicopter. Or a bullet.

The boat's flat black paint reflected no light. But the oiled mahogany trim glinted softly. Black and mahogany. The boat was even colored like the rottweilers.

Whoever drove this monster had to be crazy. It was a raging snarling beast that could pound a man's kidneys to jelly in thirty minutes.

There was only one boat like this in south Florida and Lance knew it belonged to Darrell Casey. The story was that after he paid a builder a quarter of a million to build the boat, he paid him another fifty thousand never to duplicate it. Lance figured he also threatened to kill the builder if the guy even thought of building another one like it.

Lance stood up, kicked his boot as if testing the feel of it, then continued along the dock. He was about ready to break out in song. Cops throughout south Florida had looked for this boat for months. Casey must hide it somewhere, then bring it out only when it was about to be used on a drug run. As soon as he found out who was driving this sucker, he would get on the little high-powered radio, call Nick, and tell him to throw up the barricades. The simple fact this boat was on Bimini meant a big load was inbound, a load belonging to Darrell Casey.

Lance passed the swimming pool, turned right, and walked between the rows of flowering poinciana and bougainvillea, and entered the bar.

I hope I've never arrested any of these slugs, he thought to himself as he walked in. If he had and someone recognized him, he would be in shit city.

"Who the hell are you?" someone asked as he paused inside the door. A heavy hand grabbed his shoulder and Lance's heart began racing the same way it did when a hitchhiker stuck a gun or a knife in his ribs.

But Lance had been undercover enough to know the rules. His reaction was instinct as well as training. He looked disdainfully at the hand. It was covered with a white leather glove. He wrinkled his lips in disgust, picked up the hand as if it were a

piece of garbage, flung it off his shoulder, and angrily turned to face a tall muscular man.

"You look like a DEA agent to me," the man
said, staring malevolently, balancing on his toes,
the thick corded muscles of his arms tensing.

"And you look like a fucking asshole to me,"
Lance said, moving a step closer, eyes dancing with
the light of those who truly do not give a damn.

Deny, deny, deny, is the cardinal rule of narcotics undercover work. Even if caught with a badge, a
copy of police rules and regulations, and a work
schedule with your name on it, deny. Say anything.
Lance knew one uniform officer detached to work
undercover who later had been seen in uniform by a
bad guy. He insisted he was going to a masquerade
party. And he did it with such conviction the bad
guys believed him. An undercover officer should
always deny. Even if the bandits say they have seen
you in court testifying for the government, deny.
Take the offensive. Push harder than you are pushed.

Tradecraft dictates that the undercover officer
always control the situation. Never, never, let a bad
guy put you on the defensive.

"Who the hell are you?" the blond man wearing
the white leather glove repeated. He looked around
the bar for anyone who could be this guy's partner,
anyone who might be looking at them anxiously,
waiting to see if help were needed. The big blond
man was surprised when he saw one of Casey's top
boat drivers step forward.

"He's a friend. The guy's in the business. He's
okay," the boat driver said.

Lance ignored the boat driver. He stepped closer
to the stranger. "What the fuck business is it of

yours, anyway? You the mayor of this place? Or you just nosy?"

Without waiting for an answer, he snorted in disgust, turned, and walked toward the bar.

The big blond man stared after Lance. He was undecided. He looked at the boat driver.

"He's okay," the boat driver repeated. "I know him." The boat driver turned and followed Lance toward the bar.

The bartender, who had watched the confrontation, leaned over the bar toward Lance, raised his eyebrows, whistled softly, and said, "Hey, mon. You know who that is?"

Lance's heart was beating rapidly and a fine bead of perspiration had broken out across his brow and down his back. His shirt felt as if it were plastered to his spine. He took a deep breath. "Who what was?" he said.

"That cool dude what just walked away, mon? That's who. Know who that was?" asked the bartender in his lilting cadence.

Lance stared at the bartender. Bahamians. Always coming on with the third-world independence bit, the to-hell-with-whites party line. But they are Americans in dress, walk, and actions. They try to emulate the speech but their slang is about ten years out of date.

"I have a feeling you are about to tell me, even if I don't want to know," Lance said sarcastically. "Give me a beer." He looked at the boat driver. "You want a beer?"

The boat driver nodded.

"Give us two beers."

Lance's sarcasm slid by the bartender. "Hey, mon, that be one big-time operator. He be in the Business."

"Give us two beers."

"Yeah, we're thirsty," said the boat driver. The stocky, phlegmatic boat driver and Lance had drunk beer together for the past three nights.

As the bartender dug through the melted ice for a couple of beers, he continued talking. "Yeah, mens, you don't want to tangle with that dude. He be heavy-duty. Bad medicine."

"His buddy with him tonight?" the boat driver asked.

The bartender slopped two bottles of beer atop the counter. Both foamed and overflowed. Lance stared but the bartender never noticed. He was looking at the boat driver.

"Yeah, mon," he said. "There be another one just like him back there."

"Who was that asshole?" Lance asked. He took a long pull off the bottle. He wiped perspiration from his face and neck.

"Guy that works for Darrell. New guy. Started a week or so ago. We call him and his buddy the Snake Eaters. They're over here to do some security work for Darrell. Stay away from them. They're mean sons of bitches."

Lance dismissed their meanness with a laugh—a nervous laugh. His heart was beginning to slow down.

The boat driver was gazing at the wall behind the bar. "They hurt people," he said. "They work for Darrell's security guy. Big kraut—but don't ever call him that—named Steinhorst. Somebody else you don't want to meet."

Almost as an afterthought, he added, "They came over yesterday in a big Cigarette. It's that black job down the dock."

Lance's eyes widened for a moment. But the boat driver was still talking and did not notice. "Bastards," he mumbled. "Nobody but me drives that boat. And only on big loads. But Darrell thinks those two are such hot shit he let them drive it over. But I'm the one that's taking it home."

"What makes those guys, the Snake Eaters, so special?" Lance probed.

The boat driver shrugged in dismissal. "They're watchdogs. Came over here to check out security mostly. To take a look at Darrell's stash house and to watch an airdrop about daylight. Think because they were in Vietnam they're hot shit. I don't know."

The boat driver drained his beer and slapped the bottle on the bar. He held up the empty bottle and wiggled it when the bartender looked his way.

The boat driver looked over his shoulder to make sure the Snake Eaters were not within hearing. He leaned closer to Lance and chuckled. In a conspiratorial whisper he asked, "Know where they spent last night and most of today?"

"I give up."

"At the Boca de Mama." The boat driver raised his eyebrows and grabbed his beer.

"That fag bar down near the seaplane ramp? That Boca de Mama?"

The boat driver nodded.

"That's the cesspool of the Bahamas," Lance said.

The boat driver took another long drink of beer. "You believe that? Those guys got papers to prove they are genuine double-barreled fourteen-carat killers. And they got these funny dietary habits."

He shrugged. "I don't know if Darrell knows it or not. But I knew it right after they went to work for him. They were telling me about going to that place in Lauderdale that's owned by the same guy that owns the Boca de Mama. He's got what he advertises as a Hispanic soul-food restaurant on one of the canals. Calls it Nacho Mama. Another gay bar. That's where those two guys hang out."

Lance took a drink of beer. He wanted to talk drugs. "You know, I been in the Business for a while. Moved some big loads. But you people do things on a scale I never attempted."

The boat driver laughed. He turned up his beer and again motioned for the bartender. He looked at Lance's bottle. "You're not drinking much tonight."

"I'll be way ahead of you when the night is over."

The boat driver laughed. He leaned closer to Lance and shrugged in pride. "Darrell is one hell of a businessman. And he looks after his people. I'm taking a load of shit back tomorrow on that big Cigarette. Know how much he's paying me?"

"Depends on what you're hauling and how much?"

"I'm hauling nose candy. And he's paying me a hundred thousand. You figure it out."

"From Bimini to Lauderdale?"

The boat driver paused. "Say Bimini to the mainland."

Lance whistled in appreciation. The boat driver was getting twice the going rate for a Bimini run.

For the next half-hour the two men talked business: boat handling in high seas, techniques for getting extra speed out of a heavily loaded boat, how to avoid interdiction. Lance learned a lot. He shook his head in genuine admiration for a professional.

Then he ordered a bowl of conch chowder, which, to his way of thinking, was about the only thing in the Bahamas worthy of note—that and Bimini bread.

He ate the bread and chowder and drank several more beers. He rubbed his stomach and turned to the boat driver.

"This stuff is good for you," he said, pointing at his empty bowl. "I been over here about a week and I've had the best dumps I've had in years."

The boat driver looked at him in bewilderment.

"Dumps?" he said.

"You know, good regular dumps. Seafood does that for you. I've had some Gulf Stream specials this week. Several. Fantastic."

"Gulf Stream specials, huh?" The boat driver was wavering somewhere between disgust and fascination. He did not know what to say.

Lance did not notice. "Filled with fish," he said. "You know what else? Conch chowder will do the same thing. Good stuff."

The boat driver looked at the remnants of his chowder, nodded, and pushed the bowl away. He was leaning toward disgust and away from fascination.

Lance stood up to leave. He suddenly had an idea. Out of nowhere it came to him how he could take this little Bimini expedition beyond intelligence gathering and into a little street-level law enforcement. He was about to stop a lot of dope that was scheduled to leave Bimini. That was his job: stopping the flow of drugs into his county. Nick Brown wouldn't like it if he discovered the little details. But there was no reason for Nick to know.

Lance took a last drink of beer and sat the bottle down. He knew how to impress upon Darrell Casey the majesty of the law. And the beauty of it was, Casey would not know what was happening. It was a great plan.

The boat driver looked up at Lance and noticed

the grin. "Way you're smiling, that must be either good beer or good chowder," he said.

"All of the above," Lance said, reaching to shake hands with the boat driver. "Got to go. Enjoyed it. I'll see you over here again. Maybe we can do a run together."

The boat driver nodded. "Darrell is like the marines. He's always looking for a few good men."

Lance dug into his jeans, pulled out a twenty, and plopped it on the bar. "Next time, you pay."

"You got it."

The dock was empty when Lance returned to his go-fast boat. He climbed aboard, anxious to proceed. It was at times like this that Lance, who did not consider himself religious, knew some divine power was on the side of cops. Ideas such as the one that had just sprung full-grown out of nowhere made him know he was on the side of the angels, that he was doing good work. It gave him the moral strength, though he would never call it that, to grin in the face of overwhelming odds and to know that no matter what happened, no matter what the bad guys threw at him, he would prevail.

It was past midnight when he pulled away from the dock. "You gotta have balls. Miles and miles and miles of balls," he sang to himself as he edged away from the dock. Then he pushed the throttles to the stop, and as he passed the Big Game Club he was accelerating through forty-five miles an hour. The thunder of the Scarab's engines ratcheted across the night.

Mighty Houdini was on the prowl.

Lance slowed as he entered the cut on South Bimini, turned left, then a quick right, and looked down the long straight canal. No other boats were

on the water. A hundred yards down the canal,
near a road that led to the airport, he nudged the
boat into a clump of mangrove bushes. A quick
burst of the throttle pushed the boat deeper into the
bushes until it was hidden in the thick green growth.

Lance turned off the engines and listened. Then
he unlocked the companionway and went below.
He pulled off his cowboy boots and put on his
scuffed boat shoes. He slipped a black cotton sweater
over his shoulders. Then he rummaged behind a
panel, groping until he found the two wide flat
incendiary devices he had taken from the evidence
room of the narcotics squad in Lauderdale. He
slipped them inside his shirt, jumped atop the gunwale, and walked toward the bow.

Mosquitoes swarmed about him as he forced his
way through the mangrove bushes to the shore. He
looked back. He could not see the boat. Good. He
looked around for visual clues to identify the clump
of mangroves. Then he strode quickly down the
road toward the airport. It was a sandy road that
stood out against the darkness of the night, and he
walked near the edge, in the shadow of the palm
trees.

At the end of the canal he turned right, then left.
The house was ahead, located several hundred yards
from the closest neighbor, and on a point of land
with a dock, only a few feet from the water.

A guard was on the dock. Lance saw him under
the light, smoking, plainly bored, occasionally swat-
ting mosquitoes.

Lance hunkered down, slowly groped about, and
picked up two pieces of coral. He paused for a
moment as he looked about for another guard. Then,
running lightly on his toes and keeping the house

between him and the guard, he scooted around to his right. Once he had passed the house, he paused. Slowly, on tiptoe, moving slowly and carefully and staying within the dark shadow of a row of trees, he moved closer to the guard. When he was about ten meters away, he threw one of the pieces of coral over the guard's head into the water. The sound of the splash caused the guard to wheel toward the water.

Lance tossed the second piece of coral as he ran toward the guard. The splash caused the guard to take the M-16 off his shoulder and crouch, staring offshore, weapon at the ready.

The guard heard Lance as he raced lightly across the small dock. But it was too late. Even as he turned, Lance was upon him, his rigid right hand slicing hard at the back of the guard's neck. The guard dropped like a sack of salt and Lance knew the man would be unconscious for at least an hour.

He checked the two incendiary devices. They were still lodged inside his waistband. He kicked the guard's M-16 into the water, then raced toward the house. He walked quickly across the porch and listened at the door for a moment. Nothing. The other guards must be at the airport waiting for the inbound aircraft.

He turned the doorknob. Locked.

Lance looked around. He listened again for a long moment, then made a decision. He backed up a half-step, raised a muscular leg, and kicked the bottom of his foot against the door, breaking the lock and flinging the door wide. "Good old Georgia search warrant," he mumbled as he walked inside. "One of the wonders of modern law enforcement."

The cloying sweet smell of marijuana caused Lance

to smile in anticipation. He pulled a small penlight from his hip pocket. Marijuana, stacked in burlap-covered bales, reached to the ceiling. Lance walked swiftly down the narrow aisle between the bales into the next room. It, too, was full of marijuana. A third room was full. Even the bathroom had pot stacked in the tub.

Lance pulled the powerful incendiary devices from under his shirt. Nick had confiscated them from Cubans in the Everglades, freedom fighters playing war and plotting to overthrow Castro. The incendiary devices were compact, state-of-the-art equipment. And there was more back in the evidence room—everything from grenades to shoulder-fired anti-aircraft missile launchers.

"Nothing but the best for the friends of the CIA," Lance mumbled to himself as he adjusted the timers on the incendiary devices. Holding the penlight in his teeth, he set the timbers for thirty minutes. That would give him time to be halfway to Lauderdale before the big boom.

One of the devices he jammed deep between bales of marijuana in a back room. The other he placed behind bales in the front room.

He walked to the front door, peeked out, and saw no one. He ran at a steady jog down the road, running lightly on his toes, until he crossed the end of the canal. Then he cut back along the canal toward his boat.

He pushed through the mangroves, climbed aboard the boat, and stood in the cockpit breathing easier, senses alert, turning his head back and forth, listening, looking.

Idly he swatted at mosquitoes. They were horrible, mean and aggressive.

He checked his watch. The sky was going to light up in twenty-four minutes and he would rather watch it from far at sea than from a few hundred yards away.

"I may be wrong, but I think I'm wonderful," he sang softly as he prepared to get the go-fast boat under way.

Civilians, do-gooders, and the ACLU would do backflips over what he was doing. No doubt about it. But what did they know about putting their asses on the line day after day, fighting scumbags, then seeing them walk on a technicality. Sure, the system was supposed to be the American way. But the system wasn't working. And what he was about to do was no different from what almost every cop did at some time or another when dealing with drug smugglers. Smugglers were like bikers. Every cop who ever got a chance would kick a biker's ass from hell to breakfast. And it was rare for either a biker or a smuggler to complain. They knew how the game was played. Besides, they won most of the time. They had all the advantages. So a cop occasionally steps over the line. So what? Keeps the poor son of a bitch's morale up.

Lance reached for the ignition. Then he froze. He looked over his shoulder. He could see nothing through the thick mangrove bushes. But he could hear.

Two go-fast boats were coming down the canal.

9

The fuzz buster on the go-fast boat emitted a shrill whistle, and the driver, the same heavyset man who had been drinking beer with Lance at the Big Game Club a few hours earlier, immediately pulled power and let the long narrow length of the black and mahogany Cigarette boat go dead in the water. He had been rousted out of bed at 3 A.M. by the Snake Eaters and told that the load of cocaine was inbound, that he was to be at the drop zone near the old half-submerged boat south of Bimini within the hour.

"A night drop? What the hell for?" he had protested.

"We did it in 'Nam all the time. You can do it here," the Snake Eater in the white glove said.

The boat driver was impressed with the precision of the air drop. The big Merlin, guided by the Snake Eaters using hand-held radios, came in low from the southeast. One of the Snake Eaters gave a signal and two bright lights suddenly appeared, about a mile apart, in an east-west line over the dark ocean.

"In and out markers," one of the Snake Eaters

said as the Merlin made a wide circle to the west. Their boat was tied to the big Cigarette and both were dead in the water near the jetty off South Bimini. The first of the marker lights was a few hundred yards north of the half-submerged boat and the second was on the flats to the east. "He begins the drop at the first light and finishes before he gets to the second," the Snake Eater continued.

He nodded in approval as the sound of the Merlin indicated it had completed the turn and was inbound. "If he does it right, it can't go wrong," one of the Snake Eaters said. He turned to the boat driver. "Follow his track. Start at the first light and pick up the load. Eight duffel bags," the Snake Eater said.

"How the hell can I see the stuff in the dark?"

He knew the cocaine would be well-wrapped and would be inside flotation collars. He had picked up plenty of loads bobbing around the surface of the ocean. But never at night.

"You ever see those old cartoons, the ones with the bouncing ball?" one of the Snake Eaters asked.

The boat driver looked at him in confusion.

"Well, it's the same thing," the Snake Eater said. "Except here you follow the bouncing light."

The boat driver watched. The Merlin with the modified rear doors that could be opened and closed in flight was approaching the first light. The aircraft was at extremely low altitude, less than one hundred feet. Suddenly he saw a blinking strobe, a bright powerful pulse of white light on the ocean. It was quickly followed by seven more, lined up in a straight line little more than a half-mile in length.

"Son of a bitch," the boat driver breathed. "You put strobe lights on the flotation collars."

"Get out there and do your job," one of the Snake Eaters said. "We got the load in. You get it where it's going."

The crossing from Bimini had been smooth. Now it was first light and the ocean was a flat gray surface under a gray sky.

The boat driver had stopped because his on-board electronics equipment had warned him someone was using radar. He knew the radar warning equipment, his fuzz buster, emitted an audible signal before he was actually painted on someone's radar scope. But the volume of the warning indicated the radar was close. Close and powerful. He had probably been caught in the first sweep as someone turned on their radar after leaving the channel mouth at Fort Lauderdale.

As the Cigarette boat slowed, its broad wake passed under the hull, lifting it several feet higher. The driver stretched and scanned the horizon. He hoped he was being painted by a sport fisherman or yacht. But it could be the coast guard. The war on drugs adopted by the last three or four presidents had resulted in such increased budgets that now everybody wanted to get into narcotics interdiction. More realistically, they wanted the increased budgets that went to those in the interdiction business. And the coast guard was the most rapacious of the lot, expanding from its historic roles of search and rescue, boating safety, and protecting fisheries to wanting the big-budget dollars that went with interdicting drugs. And occasionally they got lucky.

He saw nothing. Not even the usual pleasure craft offshore from Lauderdale. But he was low in the water. He climbed atop the engine housing at the aft end of the boat and looked again. Nothing.

He jumped down, ran forward, put one foot in the skipper's seat, and stood on the small area near the throttle console as he held on to the windshield.

Every second it was growing lighter. He saw thick patches of fog offshore. But the fog would burn off within minutes after the sun climbed a bit higher. Through a hole in the haze he could see that he was dead on course. The two orange-and-white stacks from the power plant in Lauderdale were ahead.

Then, as his fuzz buster emitted another shrill bleep, he saw through a gap in the fog a forty-one-foot coast-guard cutter, a white vessel with an orange slash across the bow. She was steaming down on him at flank speed. He could easily outrun her, but he knew a forty-one-footer carried a crew of three, each armed with pistols and riot shotguns or M-16s. A 50-caliber machine gun was mounted on the bow. Even more important, the coast guard cutters carried powerful radios that could summon helicopters within minutes.

The boat driver cursed, jumped to the deck, went below, opened a panel in a port locker, and pulled out a UHF radio with a scrambler attached.

"Commander, this is Sailor Boy."

Almost immediately came the response. "Sailor Boy. Commander. Go ahead."

"Five miles out. White hats approaching. Request instructions."

"Your cargo?"

"The morning delivery."

After a five-second pause that seemed an eternity came the response. "Activate Plan Copper Pipe."

The boat driver looked at the coast-guard cutter. He cursed again. He would be cutting it close. But when he keyed the mike his voice was calm. "Roger. Understand Copper Pipe."

"Will have a friendly at Pressure Valve. Commander out."

The boat driver was impatient. The Snake Eaters had talked Darrell Casey into using military procedures on the radio but most of his signals and codes revolved around his days as a plumber. Copper Pipe. Pressure Valve. What the hell sort of code was that? Millions of dollars in cocaine involved, and Casey was talking about Copper Pipe and Pressure Valve.

The driver closed the UHF radio panel, dashed back topside, picked up the microphone for the VHF radio, pressed the digital frequency selector to channel 16, and began broadcasting.

"Miami Coast Guard, Miami Coast Guard, Miami Coast Guard, how do you read me?"

The speaker boomed with a laconic voice. "Vessel calling Coast Guard, we read you loud and clear."

"Miami Coast Guard, Miami Coast Guard, Miami Coast Guard. This is a fishing boat needing assistance. Am located, let's see here, about five miles due west of Fort Lauderdale, Florida. Repeat, I am located about five miles due west of Fort Lauderdale, Florida, and I need some help."

The boat driver knew the response would be immediate and that he was going to be very busy for the next few minutes if this plan was going to work. And if it did not work, his capture by the coast guard would be the least of his worries. He was far more concerned with what Steinhorst and the Snake Eaters might do.

He raced to the aft end of the boat, threw open panels atop the engines, and pulled ignition wires from both engines. He hurriedly reached into the engine compartment, pulled out a toolbox, and turned it over, scattering tools across the teak deck. Then he raced inside the cabin, still cursing, sweat pouring from his brow, and pulled two expensive fishing rigs from their felt-edged holders on the starboard side.

He stuck his head out of the cockpit and looked toward the coast-guard boat. A small fog bank had drifted between him and the cutter, but he knew the boat was steaming in his direction.

Quickly he cast the lure from one rod off the starboard side.

"Fishing vessel requesting assistance. This is Coast Guard four one four three five. Identify yourself. State the nature of your problem and repeat your location."

The boat driver cast the lure from the second rod off the port side.

He reached into the still-open engine compartment, pulled out an oily rag, and wiped dark stains across his face and arms. He pulled off his shirt, tossed it below, and wiped the rag across his chest, leaving a dirty streak of oil.

From a cooler he pulled a can of beer, poured it over the side, then tossed the can into the water. In seconds, nine cans were floating near the boat and four more empty cans were on the deck. An open can sat atop the gunwale.

"Fishing vessel requesting assistance. Coast Guard four four three five. I say again, identify yourself. State the nature of your problem and repeat your location."

The boat driver looked around the boat. Any second the coast guard could have a visual on him.

He picked up the radio. His voice was excited. "Miami Coast Guard, Miami Coast Guard, Miami Coast Guard. How do you read?"

"We read you loud and clear. Go ahead."

The radio operator aboard the cutter was bored with the lack of professionalism on the part of whatever idiot was driving the small boat.

"Hello, Coast Guard. Boy am I glad to hear from you guys. I think I've got some kind of electrical problems. Both engines quit on me and I need some mechanical work."

The coast-guard coxswain barely controlled his exasperation. Boaters seem to think the basic function of the coast guard is to provide directions and assistance. Chances are this guy didn't even have life preservers on board. His first broadcast said he was five miles west of Fort Lauderdale. That would put him inland somewhere around I-95. This guy didn't know east from west. Amateur boaters are a pain in the ass.

"Vessel requesting assistance. Coast Guard four three five. Do you have channel one three? If so, switch frequencies and respond with your location."

The boat driver changed to channel 13 and said, "I'm with you now on thirteen. I'm about five miles west of Lauderdale. I need some help. I'm broken down out here."

The boat driver looked up. The coast-guard boat was still steaming toward him. He was almost certain that by now the coxswain had a visual. He turned his back to the coast-guard boat and held the microphone close to his mouth, speaking loud and fast.

"Hey, Coast Guard. I'm a taxpayer. I lost both engines and I need you to provide mechanical help.

I'm five miles from Lauderdale. Hell, I can see the beach."

"Fishing vessel, say your size of boat and the color."

"I'm, ah, let's see, I'm thirty-five feet. Black with mahogany trim. Where are you guys? You going to help me?"

By now the boat driver could hear the throb of the engines from the cutter. But he continued facing out to sea.

"Fishing vessel, Coast Guard four three five. I'm about two hundred yards west your position. Are you taking on water?"

The boat driver turned around, gawked in pretended astonishment, then waved, a big smile on his face. "Hey, Coast Guard, there you are. Boy, what quick results. You guys must have known I would be calling. Can you send a mechanic aboard?"

The coxswain studied the Cigarette boat. It was the most incredible hunk of boat he had ever seen, a customized go-fast boat of the sort used by drug smugglers and by people who had more money than common sense. This could be a smuggler or he could be somebody with money who liked to roar around at high speeds.

The coxswain opened the doors on either side of his command station, slowly circled downwind, and sniffed. A boat carrying marijuana could always be smelled from downwind. The odor could not be disguised. But there no hint of marijuana. The skipper, if he could be called that, referred to the boat as a fishing vessel. And there were two fishing rods stuck in holes on the gunwale. The guy was off his bean to go fishing in a Cigarette boat.

The coxswain continued studying the boat. Beer

cans in the water explained a lot. Most fishermen drank a lot of beer when they were out on the water. But he had never met a scammer who drank on the job. They were too serious about bringing in their loads. Too much was at stake. If they lost a load because they had been drinking they would be dead.

The companionway was open, something a smuggler would never do. And a smuggler would never invite the coast guard aboard. Tools were scattered all about the deck. The guy had grease all over him. The coxswain made up his mind. This guy was a righteous fisherman. A bit flaky and not anyone he would ever get into a boat with, but, nevertheless, a righteous fisherman.

"Fishing vessel. Coast Guard four three five. Are you taking on water?" the coxswain repeated.

The boat driver laughed. "Negatory, Coast Guard. I'm taking on beer but no water. You ten four that?"

"Fishing vessel, four three five. Can you make the necessary repairs to get under way?"

"Negatory, Coast Guard. That's why I called you. I gave up on the engines and started fishing. No luck on fishing either. And I'm about out of beer."

"Fishing vessel, four three five, what was your point of origin and your time of departure?"

"Home port is Lauderdale. Left about five this morning headed out to the Stream, but my boat broke. So I'm fishing here. Can't let the day go to waste. Know what I mean?" He lifted his beer can and waved it toward the coast-guard vessel.

"Fishing vessel, four three five, secure your equipment and stand by to take a towline."

The coast-guard cutter stood off as the boat driver

pulled in the lures and took each rod below. As he came back on deck, he picked up a beer can, put it to his mouth, drank deeply, and tossed the can overboard.

"What a slob," the coxswain said to the engineer.

"I wouldn't mind having one of those beers."

"Okay, Coast Guard, I'm ready. Can you send one of your men aboard to help? I'm a little tired."

The coxswain curled his lip in disgust. "Tired, my ass. He's drunk," he muttered. He picked up the microphone and said, "Negative on that. Stand by to receive the towline."

The boat driver threw up his hands in exasperation. He pulled the microphone close to his mouth and said, "But I'm a taxpayer needing help. And it's your job to help me. That's what the coast guard is for."

The coxswain growled in anger. He was losing patience fast with this guy. He was on a law-enforcement mission looking for drug smugglers and was being held up by a spoiled, half-drunk fisherman.

The towline was attached to the bow of the go-fast boat. The coxswain pulled ahead slowly, paying out about fifty feet of line before signaling the seaman on the stern to snub the line to the cleat.

About an hour later the coast-guard patrol boat entered the breakwater and passed the U.S. Customs station. The boat driver sat in the skipper's seat of the go-fast boat with his feet atop the instrument panel and held aloft a can of beer.

Two Customs officers standing in the big plate-glass window looking over the canal waved indulgently. Nothing but a cutter towing a vessel with a mechanical problem.

The coast-guard vessel turned right, slowed as it

approached the marina, then pulled away from the dock as the boat driver cast a line to a marina employee. The boat driver went forward, cast off the line to the coast-guard boat, and shouted, "Thanks for the tow, Coast Guard. I'll write the president and tell him you did a good job."

The coxswain leaned from the open door of the command station and waved. "Glad to be of help. Have a mechanic look at those engines." He reversed the port propeller and went forward on the starboard prop, spinning the boat almost in its own length, then passed the Customs station, exited from the breakwater, and applied power. He was on patrol.

About the same time the coast-guard boat passed the Customs station, Gunter Steinhorst stepped from a small runabout tied around the corner of the marina from the waterfront refueling positions. He approached the driver of the go-fast boat, who was leaning over the engine compartment, attaching wires.

He paused to look at the boat as several passersby had done, and in his soft voice asked, "Okay?"

The boat driver recognized the gravelly voice and looked up. "Yeah, everything is okay."

"Ready?"

"About a minute."

"I'll follow you."

The boat driver nodded and returned to his work. A few seconds later he had finished attaching the ignition wires. He wiped his hands with a clean towel, turned the ignition switches, and smiled at the satisfying rumble of the two powerful engines. Even marina employees, who had seen every sort of exotic boat imaginable, looked with awe on the black Cigarette. Just sitting there idling, it sounded like Judgment Day.

The boat driver cast off the dock lines, turned the wheel, looked over his shoulder, then pressed the throttles forward and moved into the channel. He leaned to the left and looked inside the companion-way. The duffel bags of cocaine picked up a few hours earlier off the end of South Bimini were stacked in the center of the cabin. A few small folds in the heavy canvas glistened with seawater.

The boat driver sighed. The coast guard had towed in a load of cocaine with a street value of several hundred million dollars. Darrell Casey should send them a thank-you note.

10

Lance Cunningham felt rather than heard the explosion as he roared at full speed through the narrow cut in the coral on the southwestern corner of South Bimini. It was a quick tremulous vibration transmitted through the shiny chrome steering wheel and it was noticeable even above the pounding of the hull in the clear waters.

When Lance cleared the sandbar near the mouth of the cut, he turned south and looked over his left shoulder. A black greasy column of smoke, roiling and billowing, was climbing skyward in the quiet first light of dawn. Lance glanced quickly at his watch. The timers were precise. Good to know. He watched the smoke, knowing it represented the burning of tons of marijuana that had been bound for the United States.

The past twenty-four minutes had been harrowing. As the two go-fast boats idled slowly down the canal, mosquitoes had descended in droves and he was afraid to swat them, frightened that any movement would reveal his position. Already the sky to the east was turning light. If the guys in the go-fast boats were half-alert, they would have seen the crushed branches of the mangrove bushes where he had powered his way into a hiding spot.

But they did not see him as they motored past, bow to stern in the narrow canal, the bubble of the exhausts a muted counterpoint to the powerful rumble of the unmuffled engines.

Lance stared at the men driving the boats. Two julios. They probably worked for Darrell Casey. Julios were known for two things: a propensity for quick mindless violence; and a macho mind set that made them unafraid to confront anyone, be he cop or Satan personified. Both of these guys had those deadly little MAC-10s, the ones with the long ammunition clips, within quick reach on the console. Lance knew they itched for an excuse, any excuse, to use them. Anytime, anywhere, and against anyone, especially a gringo cop. In the sanctuary that was Bimini, they could hose a cop and there would not be a voice raised in indignation.

Lance was terrified. Alone in a foreign country, caught in a mangrove thicket with no avenue of escape, and two trigger-happy julios twenty feet away while mosquitoes damn near as big as flamingos were draining his blood. All of this would be great fun to recount later on when it was war-story time. But right now he was petrified. A sticky salty perspiration, filled with the scent of fear, covered his body.

But now he was free running at high speed on the open ocean, bound for Lauderdale, about fifty minutes away. The stash house was burning. The julios with the MAC-10s had not seen him. Operation Limey had been a resounding success. The mighty Houdini had kicked ass.

11

Mike Love swung the big King Air in a wide descending circle to the left, all the while peering over his shoulder and looking for a tiny speck somewhere ahead. The easternmost spine of the Sierra Madre Mountains blocked the navy radar at Gitmo, but he was getting vectors from a Customs radar operator who was using the equipment aboard a giant balloon tethered at Cudjoe Cay.

Customs used three radar balloons: one at Cudjoe deep in the Florida keys, another at Patrick Air Force Base south of Cape Kennedy, and a third on Grand Bahama Island. Theoretically, the radar balloons, which were tethered to a cable that allowed them to fly at altitudes up to ten thousand feet, gave Customs the capability to detect and intercept inbound drug smugglers, even those flying at wave-top altitudes. But in reality, a breeze of more than ten knots, a frequent occurrence, caused the balloons to be grounded for much of the time. The balloon at Cudjoe was to have been grounded today, but the twenty-knot breeze that had been blowing for three days had unexpectedly died about 6 A.M. Even when the balloon was up, the vagaries of radar were such that fully as many aircraft sneaked through as were detected. And when drug smugglers were detected, there were ways for a savvy pilot to cause enough anomalies on the radar scopes to make the interdiction by Customs pilots extremely difficult.

Now Mike saw the target, a Cessna 210, a high-wing single-engine job that traveled at almost two hundred miles an hour. With additional tanks and a pilot who knew how to conserve fuel, the 210 could remain airborne maybe ten hours.

Mike Love slowed, then swung in tight under the 210. Almost hidden by his beard, his lips were frozen in a tight rictus of a smile. After a moment he edged slowly out to the side, leaning forward and looking up to his right.

"Bastard," he breathed.

The vertical stabilizer of the 210 was painted with the big green rampant alligator, mouth open, eyes slitted in anger.

"I thought Casey just ran aircraft out of Bimini. Now he's got one coming out of Cuba. That son of a bitch must run a scheduled dope airline out of every place in the pipeline," he said.

He swung under and behind the 210, made a minute power adjustment, then settled back. This time he had the scammer. He was on the guy's tail and was going to track him to wherever he was landing, seize his dope, seize his airplane, and put his ass in jail.

Mike's grin widened. It was a tight feral grin with no humor.

"Lima one hundred, Omaha two three, target acquired. Am in position and tracking," he said into the microphone.

"That's a roger," came the voice of the Customs controller. "Confirm position and time when you expect dry feet."

"Over the Cay Sal Bank. Compass heading of three six zero. If target continues present course, estimate feet dry at plus four zero. Alert Air Support units and have them on standby. Also local jurisdictions in south Florida where this guy might land."

Mike paused. The Cessna 210 was initiating a turn to the left, a quick decisive turn. What was the guy doing? Why was he making a big turn out over the ocean? Mike maneuvered to stay hidden under the smuggler's tail. "Lima one hundred, target turning south. Stand by."

"Roger. We're painting him." The Customs controller's voice was disbelieving.

Mike waited a moment until the 210 rolled out of the turn and became locked on a new heading. "He's southbound. Directly toward Cuba," Mike said.

"Do not, repeat, do not, enter Cuban airspace. At your present speed, you can track south for no more than one-eight minutes. Repeat, one-eight minutes."

"Understood. Did you pick up any radio transmissions from this guy?"

"Negative on the scanner."

It was sixteen minutes later, after repeatedly giving Mike Love his distance from the limits of the Cuban air defense zone, that the nervous controller warned the Customs pilot to prepare to break off his pursuit.

"Lima one hundred, I'd like to go right up to the

edge. Maybe I can orbit there and see if this guy lands."

Mike and several other pilots of the Air Support branch believed smugglers were using Cuba as a refueling base when coming up through the Yucatán Channel from Colombia or when flying out of Jamaica. He had seen too many smugglers coming from over Cuba, a country with a good air-defense system. In fact, there had been several times, as he approached the outer limits of the Cuban air-defense zone, that U.S. Air Force controllers at Homestead AFB south of Miami had called Customs to say electronics eavesdropping of Cuban radio transmissions indicated MiGs were being scrambled to intercept their aircraft.

"Omaha two three, that's a negative. We do not want a U.S. government aircraft intercepted by one of Castro's jets. Break off the pursuit. Return to your patrol position off Cay Sal."

Mike's green eyes flashed and he muttered profanity as he turned back to the north. He took up position north of Cay Sal, flying a slow pattern northeast until he reached Dog Rocks, then turned back toward Cay Sal.

It was typical Bahamas weather, bright sunshine, a few scattered clouds, light easterly breeze, and virtually unlimited visibility. The waters around the Cay Sal Bank ranged from white to aqua to pale blue. To the west the waters turned blue-black where they fell off into the depths of the Straits of Florida.

Mike noticed little of this. He was wondering why the doper had turned south. He knew the smuggler had not seen him. There was no reason for the bad guy to break off.

Mike had been flying the patrol pattern for almost an hour and was about ten miles northeast of Cay Sal when suddenly his UHF radio blared.

"Omaha two three, unidentified target approaching from the south. Speed one six zero knots. Magnetic heading three six zero. Radar indicates altitude less than five hundred feet. Negative squawk and negative talk. No flight plan. Speed same as previous target. We believe it to be the same target. We showed an occasional target orbiting about ten miles inland from Corralillo on Cuba's north coast. But the guy was in and out of our coverage, so we're not sure. Turn right to an intercept heading of two zero five. Maintain altitude until you're behind the target, then I'll put you on his tail."

Mike clicked his microphone twice in acknowledgment as he swung around in a tight turn to the east through a southerly heading and then slightly to the southwest. Minutes later he saw a single-engine aircraft below him boring straight toward Florida. It was too far away to identify it as other than a high-wing single-engine aircraft, but he instinctively knew it was the Cessna 210 he had intercepted earlier. He pulled power and gently eased the wheel forward, maneuvering until he was astern the aircraft.

It was a Cessna 210.

The doper was at two hundred feet, far below the altitude at which ground-based radar could detect him. Mike knew that any single-engine pilot that low over the water had to concentrate on his flying and constantly monitor his aircraft systems. As he dropped lower, he pulled out to the side for a few seconds, just long enough to see the alligator painted on the vertical stabilizer.

It was the same Cessna 210.

Mike descended even more until he was again under the tail of the 210, a position where it was impossible for the pilot to see him.

He pressed the radio transmit button on the wheel. "Lima one hundred, Omaha two three is in position. Same target as earlier. Alert appropriate units." A bit of excitement had crept into Mike's voice. The bad guy had gotten away earlier. He probably had orbited over Cuba, just waiting, then turned north again to give it another shot. But how had the guy avoided detection by the Cubans? Maybe they were having radar problems.

It didn't matter. The important thing was that Mike had intercepted him. This guy had to be running out of fuel. He had to land somewhere. And Mike Love was going to be there.

But it still nagged at the Customs pilot that the guy had turned south for no apparent reason. Why did he do a one-eighty that first time? Did he know Customs—it had to be Customs—was on his tail? If so, how did he know?

"Omaha two three, that's a roger." The controller had picked up the thin edge of excitement in Mike's voice. "We're tracking on radar to see if he comes up the east side or swings west to come in from the Gulf. Will alert appropriate units once he's committed."

Mike wiggled his shoulders and tightened the muscles in his legs. He had been flying four hours and fatigue was beginning to set in. Then, in a moment, all thoughts of fatigue disappeared. The Cessna 210 once again broke left in a tight circle. Mike quickly added a bit of power and swung wide to regain his position on the bad guy's tail. What the hell was going on here? Was the guy so hinky that he couldn't get up the courage to punch on into Florida?

"Lima one hundred, target turning south."

"Roger," came the disgusted voice of the controller. "We show he's picked up a course for Cuba again. We're having a little trouble painting you right now. Suggest you return to patrol off Cay Sal. How's your fuel?"

Mike's eyes quickly scanned the fuel gauges as he turned back toward his patrol station. "About an hour if I return to Gitmo. About three hours if I refuel at Home Plate."

"That's negative on refueling here. Gitmo needs that aircraft."

"For what?"

"To fly intercepts."

"That's what I'm doing," Mike said. He was angry. "And I'm on the tail of an aircraft belonging to the biggest doper in Florida. What are they going to do with it? Why is it so important I go back to Gitmo?"

"Am just relaying instructions, Omaha three four. Just relaying instructions."

"Well, just relay to Gitmo that I'll be on station here another hour and then I'll return."

"Roger that. You think the bad guy will return?"

"He's was gone about forty-five minutes before. I don't know where he came from. But he has to be getting low on fuel. I'm betting he'll loiter to the south a few minutes, then try it again. Are you painting him?"

There was a pause before the controller responded. "He was in and out of the ground clutter there for a while, but we seem to have lost him. He's probably orbiting at low altitude."

"Or he's landed, " Mike said bitterly. "I think the bad guy and I are both working out of Cuba."

Mike waited an hour and ten minutes before he notified Customs that he was returning to Gitmo to refuel.

"You got any other aircraft you can put on alert?" Mike asked the radar controller.

"Negative. The crews have gone home."

Two hours later the Cessna 210 appeared over the Cay Sal Bank on a northbound course. It was flying straight and level at about two hundred feet over the water. The 210 was not intercepted. It landed in a large open field in the western part of Broward County, and in less than thirty seconds, a waiting ground crew off-loaded five duffel bags. Each contained one hundred kilos of cocaine.

12

The bright mercury vapor lights of the U.S. Customs hangar at Homestead Air Force Base illuminated the cement ramp and gave the big Blackhawk helicopter the appearance of a droop-winged bird of prey. The flat black paint of the helicopter absorbed the light, causing it to glow from within, almost as if it were alive and waiting. No numbers or symbols were painted on the exterior, further increasing the helicopter's mysterious and malevolent appearance.

Mike Love was anxious to take off. The special Gitmo operation was over. He was back at Homestead and anxious to implement his plan. Unlike the Gitmo operation, his plan was going to get results.

Mike's level of frustration was high. Just yesterday his supervisor had asked him to come to the office and, in a noncommittal voice, told him there had been a call from "a government agency" regarding the Cay Sal episode. It seemed that the nameless government agency had monitored not only the radio transmissions between Mike and Customs, but also between the smuggler and his controller. The smuggler's contact had been monitoring Customs radio transmissions and advising the smuggler on every move to avoid being interdicted. The smuggler, who knew each time he was intercepted by Mike, had simply waited until the Customs pilot was low on gas before coming north. And he did the last bit of waiting on the ground in Cuba.

Cuba was, as Mike suspected, a safe haven for many drug smugglers. Castro encouraged smugglers to use the island. The more drugs that went north, the better Castro liked it.

Mike knew the anonymous government agency was the National Security Agency, a group so secretive that Customs pilots joked the acronym NSA meant "no such agency." This was not the first time that NSA, long after the fact, had told Customs what had taken place during an intercept. It rankled Mike that NSA, which monitored the transmissions in real time, would never advise Customs during an intercept what the bad guys were doing. NSA computers had the capability of picking up every radio transmission in the Caribbean. But they always waited a couple of days before sending down word through circuitous channels. Then Customs pilots would learn what smugglers had been saying on the radio and how they eluded capture.

In addition to the NSA business, he had discovered the day he left Gitmo that Darrell Casey's snitch was not in Customs, but in the navy. A navy aircraft dispatcher, a young enlisted man, had been caught. He was on Casey's payroll and was letting the smugglers know when navy and Customs aircraft were aloft. He knew in advance which aircraft would be dispatched and what equipment they had inoperative. That's how the Merlin snookered Customs when the height-finder mode of the navy radar was inop.

Finding a U.S. sailor on Casey's payroll had disturbed and angered Mike. His father had been a navy career officer. And Mike felt that if U.S. Customs had been betrayed by a navy man, then the agency had no chance at all against drug smugglers.

Mike walked around the Blackhawk, caressing the fuselage. He was eager to take off, but the preflight was important. He walked slowly and eyed the flanks of the five-million-dollar helicopter, checking the hydraulic lines, air-bleed lines, and the rotor system. He nodded in satisfaction when he saw the ball bearing shining through the oil in the tail rotor gearbox. Then he climbed atop the helicopter and looked into the two inlets where he checked the sight gauge for oil quantity.

After a thirty-day course at Fort Rucker training alongside career army pilots, followed by a course teaching him how to fly while wearing night-viewing goggles, he felt more than competent to drive the 'Hawk. He had graduated first in his class at Rucker, beating out hotshot army pilots who had come out of the U.S. Military Academy and who were fifteen years younger than he. But what the hell? Cunning and guile will win out over youth every time. And cunning and guile were needed to fly the Blackhawk, a temperamental high-tech bitch. If she were not handled properly, if the gauges were not monitored closely and the pilot were not ready to react instantly and correctly, she would fly into the ground. More so than most helicopters, the Blackhawk wanted to self-destruct each time it lurched into the air.

Mike paused at the door of the chopper and glanced at his watch. Then he looked to the east, where the still-black sky showed not the faintest trace of dawn. His timing was perfect. He would arrive over Bimini by first light. Dopers had eluded him for weeks, but today, if the Almighty was on the side of the good guys, he was going to win one. It would be risky. If he were caught, it could mean his job. He might even be brought up on charges. But the potential reward made it worthwhile. Today would be a rare victory.

The official stance of Customs was that the agency interdicted and arrested perhaps 10 percent of the marijuana and cocaine coming into south Florida. Mike Love knew that was hogwash. Maybe, just maybe, they stopped 1 percent. Unless the doper pilot had a mechanical problem and was forced down or unless a law-enforcement agency had a snitch involved, the load got through. It was that simple.

Nick Brown, the Broward County narc known as Fluf, had called last night and said he had intelligence that there would be an air drop of cocaine to a go-fast boat south of Bimini about dawn. It would be somewhere near the sunken ship between South Bimini and Cat Cay. The drop would be from a Merlin—another of Darrell Casey's deals.

Mike had asked Nick Brown about the reliability of the information. Nick would only say it was "highly reliable." That meant he had a snitch inside Casey's organization. Either that or an undercover guy. If it was a U/C guy, more than likely it was that crazy Lance Cunningham. He had not heard from Lance in more than a week.

Nick was a righteous narc. The quiet potbellied

little guy was as straight as a stick. He was low-key
and understated. If he said a load was inbound,
then a load was inbound. It was that simple. At
dawn, a Merlin with an alligator on the tail would
be over South Bimini.

Mike grinned his quick tight grin. He knew what
he would do if he found Casey's man scooping up
flotation collars of cocaine from the ocean. He had
planned it for weeks. It had to be done alone.
There would be no copilot to report him.

Regulations said the Blackhawk had to be flown
by two pilots, primarily because a pilot quite literally had his hands full. One hand was on the collective and the other on the cyclic. Many of the
engine-control instruments and levers were on an
overhead panel. A pilot needed help in the event of
an emergency. But Mike was out to create an emergency for someone else, not be involved in one
himself.

Besides, he had a legal out from the two-pilot
requirement. The exception to the rule was if a
pilot had hard evidence that either a major trafficker was moving a load or a big load was coming
in, he could fly the 'Hawk solo.

Mike had engineered this deal, so he met the
criteria. He called two pilots, men known for not
answering their phones when they were off-duty,
and as he hoped, he got no answer. Just five minutes earlier he had telephoned his supervisor, who
cursed and ranted that Mike was calling him from
the airport when he was ready to take off.

"I just got the intelligence," Mike said innocently.
"Either we're in business to stop the dopers or
we're not. Do you want to cancel a one-hundred-
percent-certain deal?"

The supervisor cursed. He had been boxed and knew it. "All right, dammit. Go."

Mike hung up. Now he was legal.

Mike believed that to be a supervisor, a man had the part of his brain removed that prompted creative and aggressive law enforcement. Supervisors were so concerned with writing reports and covering their asses that they forgot what the agency was supposed to be about. Mike wanted to interdict dope. That was his job. He believed in his job. He loved the flying. He would have worked for half his salary just for the chance to fly the wide variety of aircraft used by Customs. The flying made all the government bureaucracy almost bearable. To him, interdicting dopers was a deadly serious business. His buddy, Lance, the best narc in the business, thought it was a game. But Mike had flown south on numerous special enforcement operations and seen the corruption from South America to the Turks and Caicos Islands to the Bahamas to Florida. He hated smugglers and he hated the torture and violence and corruption that were part and parcel of the Business. Most of all he hated how smuggling upset the natural order of things. Mike Love was a neat and meticulous man. Everything had its place. Smugglers upset the smooth and even course of events. Therefore, anything that would stop them and therefore restore the natural order should be used by the government. The ends justified the means.

Mike Love was a one-dimensional man who would have been thought dull at a party of sophisticates. He knew aviation and he knew how to stop airborne drug smugglers. But he could not talk about his job at parties. Most people thought his work was unnecessary as well as futile. That patronizing feeling toward narcs is one of the reasons narcs stick with their own. They work and party and vacation and entertain among a small group of like-minded men and women.

On the rare occasions when Mike and his wife were among civilians, he was quiet and distant. Some thought him shy. But had those people seen him in the cockpit in hot pursuit of a doper, they would have thought him mad, possessed, obsessed.

Mike opened the door of the helicopter, slid on the green military helmet, plugged in the cord from his helmet to the radios, then fastened his seat belt. He jerked the belt tight, then hooked the over-the-shoulder web belts attached to the inertia reel and, using both hands, pulled them down tightly. He flipped the master switch, and the cockpit was dimly lit with the familiar soft red light. Mike knew, though he could not hear them because of the helmet, that the gyros were humming softly as they spooled up.

He reached overhead and flicked the battery switch, then the APU—the auxiliary power unit—primer switch. He turned the APU control switch to "on" and listened as the powerful little turbine mounted behind the transmission began winding up. Now he had the air needed to turn the two jet engines atop the helicopter.

Mike's long fingers cupped the overhead throttles. The throttles were shaped like upside-down lollipops. He pressed the button on the bottom to initiate the starting sequence. The "start" light came on. He checked the NG strip gauge and pulled the throttle down and forward to introduce fuel. His eyes were intent upon the turbine gas temperature gauge. Behind and above him, the first engine was beginning its powerful shriek. Hot shimmering waves of gases were pouring from the maw of the exhaust stack. NG showed 52 percent and the temp was up to 760 degrees—everything was in the green. In seconds the combined songs of the two jet engines atop the Blackhawk echoed across the darkened tarmac. The chopper rocked and trembled as if eager to leap off the pad.

Mike scanned the panel. Everything in the green. He pressed the transmit button on the cyclic. "Homestead tower. Helicopter Omaha five six. West ramp. Takeoff. Eastbound." His voice was deep and calm and slow and gave no evidence of the intensity he felt about what he would be doing in the next few hours.

The Air Force enlisted man in the tower turned and looked south toward the Customs ramp. He saw the giant chopper, hangar lights strobing off the blades. The Blackhawk showed no anticollision or navigation lights, and the tower operator did not request the pilot to turn them on. The Omaha call sign indicated Customs was launching a tactical flight, probably in pursuit of drug smugglers. An Omaha flight had precedence over all traffic except an in-flight emergency.

"Omaha five six, cleared for immediate takeoff. No reported traffic. East departure."

"Omaha five six."

Mike lifted off, swung low across the long north-south runway, then continued eastbound, slowly accelerating. He carefully watched the instruments. At forty knots the huge stabilator at the end of the tail boom, driven by the air-data computer, should be moving up. As he accelerated to one hundred knots, the instruments showed the stabilator was within five degrees of being level. Good. Temperamental stabilators on the Blackhawk had flown a lot of good men into the ground.

Mike crossed the faint gray ribbon of beach, then dropped down over Biscayne Bay until he was sixty feet above the water. Such low-altitude flying demanded a pilot's full attention and all his skill. Ahead the eastern sky was turning a pale pink, the first harbinger of dawn. Mike leaned forward as if willing the chopper to go faster. He was eager for his confrontation with the forces of Darrell Casey.

He had twenty-two hundred pounds of fuel in his main tanks and twenty-six hundred in the auxiliary tanks. He burned about eleven hundred pounds an hour at full throttle, so he had about five hours of fuel. But, at 150 knots, Bimini was less than a half-hour away. He had more than enough fuel for what he had in mind.

The soft nimbus of white coming from the twinkling lights of Alice Town was his signal to swing a bit farther south, about a half mile south of Big Cat Cay, where he slowed and began orbiting. Each circle brought him out from behind the island for a few seconds so he could look to the north. Occasionally he shifted in his seat and quickly scanned the instruments. His big hand was light and steady on the stick, and the big helicopter flew in wide circles.

He did not worry about the sound of the chopper reaching Bimini. He was too far away and too low over the ocean. Nor did he worry about being seen by the crew of the aircraft that would be dropping the cocaine. The sun was not yet up and in the dim half-light of a fresh dawn, the helicopter merged with the dark ocean.

Mike did not have long to wait. He had been on station fourteen minutes when he had a radio message from a Customs air officer working in the Federal Aviation Administration's Miami center for air traffic control. A remote site on the northern tip of Andros Island, where Customs had secretly placed a portable radar, was reporting a fast-moving target bound toward Bimini. The target was not on a flight plan. The aircraft would arrive over Bimini in minutes.

Mike Love straightened, snugged his seat belt another notch, checked the instruments, and with a small tight smile of anticipation dropped the chopper a few feet lower toward the water.

Moments later he saw the Merlin as it roared out of the gathering light and banked north in a wide circle, bleeding off excess airspeed. The Merlin came out of the turn, straightened its wings, slowed, and headed for the cement ship sunk in open water south of Bimini. The go-fast boat waiting for the drop was a half-mile east of the sunken ship. These guys were good. No needless orbiting and looking around. One pass to check it out and then, *boom*, the drop was under way.

Mike pulled on the collective until the TGT gauge showed 850 degrees, maximum temperature. He was pulling 90 percent torque. The 'Hawk was giving her best. He pushed the cyclic forward.

The SAS—stabilization augmentation system—prevented the chopper from drooping into the familiar nose-low mode of most helicopters as they accelerate to top speed. As the four rotor blades bit deeper into the air and as the speed climbed to a 165 knots, the pitch bias actuator tilted the rotor blades until Mike was almost looking through the whirling black streaks as he raced up the western edge of Big Cat Cay, full bore toward the drop zone, a screaming bird of prey.

Mike looked up as the first package fell from the Merlin's open door. He pressed the radio transmit button. "Lima one hundred. Omaha five six. Am three miles south of Bimini. Bad guys are on station. Air drop in progress."

"Roger that, five six. Keep us updated," came the voice of the Customs duty officer. Mike shook his head. It was the same guy he had worked with earlier on the Cay Sal deal. The guy had seen too many war movies. He was called "Roger" because he used the phrase so often on the radio.

Mike leaned forward and watched the Merlin. The doper pilot was good. He held his course as a crewman kicked out bulky containers. As the collars hit the surface, water-actuated strobe lights began blinking, enabling the boat captain, who was already swinging around to begin his pickup, to see each container in the mile-long line atop the dull gray surface of the sea.

The blinking strobes were in a straight line, east to west, starting near the old cement ship. These guys were good, real pros.

"Lima one hundred. Omaha five six. A Merlin has completed his air drop. I count eight markers. The pickup boat is on station."

"Roger that, five six. Be advised a Nassau BAT team is unable to launch. They advise that if a boat is available, they will be under way in about an hour."

"Big whoop," Mike growled.

"Say again."

"You alert the coast guard?" Mike knew it would

take a coast-guard vessel about three hours to steam over from Fort Lauderdale. He would have plenty of time.

"Roger that. Coast-guard cutter *Steadfast* is south of Great Isaac Light. Making flank speed toward your position. ETA one-seven minutes. You roger that?"

Mike cursed. He looked north where the sky and the sea merged in a gray haze. The cutter was too close, steaming toward him at full power and showing no lights. Damn. The coasties were never there when you wanted them, and now they show up right in the middle of a deal.

"Omaha five six. Lima one hundred. You roger that last transmission?"

"Lima one hundred. That's a big roger."

The Merlin, still low, was turning south as it gathered speed. Mike knew the pilot would see him and radio the boat driver. But it was too late for both of them. Hell was coming toward the boat driver at almost two hundred miles an hour.

The wings of the Merlin rocked as the pilot sighted the Blackhawk racing from the south. The pilot banked hard and rolled out of the turn on a collision course with the chopper. He was above the helicopter, had much greater speed, and had the sun at his back—the perfect tactical advantage. Every benefit was his. The bozo in the chopper was dog meat.

The Merlin jock pushed the power levers forward and felt the sound of the engines as their growl deepened. His eyes never left the dark ominous shape of the helicopter. He knew it was a U.S. Customs chopper. He also knew it was not armed. In addition, Customs had no enforcement authority in Bahamian airspace. This guy was little more than a tourist. A eunuch masquerading as a federal cop. It was a big bluff. Well, the Customs guy had stepped out from behind his badge. And now the Merlin pilot had a chance to see what the guy was made of.

The humper, the guy who had been kicking packages out the modified rear door of the Merlin, scrambled forward through the cabin, into the cockpit, and was strapping himself into the right seat. "That went okay," he said, congratulating himself on how quickly he had kicked out the packages. None snagged up. They were very tightly bunched.

The pilot's snort caused the humper to look toward him in surprise. The pilot nodded his head toward the chopper. The humper glanced out the window. A big helicopter was racing toward them. Head-on.

The humper spun in alarm toward the pilot. Dopers, particularly those new to the business, are more paranoid than people in institutions who have been committed for paranoia. To have an unknown element, a helicopter, show up in a drop zone meant either someone was trying to rip off the load or the cops were about to bust them. Either prospect scared hell out of the humper.

"U.S. Customs," the Merlin pilot sneered. He pushed the nose over. "I got this guy cold," he said. "He's as dumb as every other narc. Look at that. He's too low. Right on the water. I'm gonna force him down or make him overstress that thing and break it up in the air. Either way, his ass is mine."

The big twin-engine Merlin and the much smaller Blackhawk were two miles apart, each locked onto its course.

The morning sun was so bright that Mike Love saw the Merlin only as a growing silhouette. He could not read the gauges on the instrument panel. But he knew the only way to go into battle against a doper was at full speed, everything shoved to the wall, a 100 percent commitment. He reached up and pulled his helmet visor down. The dark sun shield clicked into place over his eyes. He leaned forward in anticipation, the vibrating helicopter causing him to bob and weave with the same motion of a medieval knight riding full-tilt down the jousting lane. He twisted the cyclic slightly and the whistling resonating thunder of the Blackhawk increased. He knew by feel, by instinct, by experience, by the blurred wave tops racing a few feet under the fuselage, that the helicopter was giving him all she had, that she was operating at the extreme outer edges of the performance envelope.

Now the two aircraft were less than a mile apart at a closure rate of more than four hundred miles an hour.

13

The Blackhawk was laboring hard, throbbing and vibrating and pulsating as helicopters do when under stress. The deep thunder of its twin jet engines thumped across the clear and clean waters south of Bimini. The blurred blades were tilted forward in a whirring slicing circle as they bit furiously into the warm morning air.

The humper in the right seat of the Merlin anxiously glanced at the pilot to his left. The pilot's expression was growing less gleeful and was rapidly turning into alarm. What sort of chopper pilot would go head-to-head with a Merlin. The guy must be a psycho.

The Blackhawk was tracking straight and true, still only a few feet above the water and making no effort to escape. Why didn't the guy break off?

Then the eyes of the Merlin pilot abruptly widened in horror. The 'Hawk, just seconds away from a collision, suddenly popped up about fifty feet until it was only a few feet below the Merlin and so close the pilot could see the stern bearded face of the chopper pilot, eyes hidden behind a dark sun visor. He suddenly realized the chopper pilot was going to try to slice into his cockpit with those giant blades. The guy was not going to try to escape by diving into the water or darting off to the side. The crazy son of a bitch *wanted* a midair.

As the thick squat shape of the chopper magnified with the speed of an object seen through a rapidly turning zoom lens, the humper covered his eyes and leaned back in his seat as if postponing, if only for a split second, the collision.

The pilot involuntarily yelped as he pulled hard on the wheel, jerking it into his stomach and turning hard to the left.

Mike did not move his head. His eyes almost casually roamed upward as the Merlin sliced overhead, missing the helicopter blades by mere inches. Mike could see the rivets and the blackened exhaust stains on the wings of the Merlin. And as the big aircraft broke hard to his right, he had a glimpse of the rampant alligator painted on the vertical stabilizer.

He looked over his right shoulder. But the Merlin pilot, still flying low over the water, was bound for a landing field in south Florida. Enough was enough.

A small ironic smile tugged at Mike's mouth. Doper pilots thought they were cowboys, real hot-shot throttle jockeys, airborne Robin Hoods whose loads would bring good times to thousands. But the great weakness of a drug smuggler was that he worked for money. Smugglers did not believe in what they did. Deep down in the most remote corner of their souls, they knew they were lawbreakers, scumbags whose loads were bringing misery to children. And every time they heard of an elementary-school principal complaining that children could not be educated in an environment dominated by drugs, or saw a story about a young person killed in a drugs-related traffic accident, or read of a person killed in a drug deal gone wrong, they knew they had contributed, that their work on earth brought only misery and grief and pain and death.

A man like that could have no moral convictions about what he was doing. He had no moral strength. In a life-or-death situation, he always backed down. Mike had learned this early in his airborne duels with drug smugglers. The first guy he forced into the waters off Bimini demonstrated the same lack of courage. Some of the doper pilots were good. But not good enough to put their ass on the line when he forced them into the water, not good enough to go head-to-head with him at full speed on a collision course.

Mike backed off on the collective, rapidly losing speed as he turned slightly north toward the go-fast boat, whose driver had already scooped up three containers of cocaine and was racing in the smooth waters toward the fourth.

Mike was through with his warm-up. He had shown the Merlin pilot his curve ball. Now it was time to show the boat driver his strike-out pitch, time to do what he had come out here to do.

He again glanced over his shoulder, ruddered the 'Hawk hard to port, and caught a final glimpse of the Merlin disappearing to the west.

"Lima one hundred. Omaha five six. Suspect aircraft, a Merlin, has completed air drop and is westbound on approximate course of two eight zero. Unless he changes course, he will break the coast at Lauderdale. Suggest launching intercept."

"That's a roger, five six. State your intentions regarding the pickup boat."

"That's a roger," Mike said to himself in disgust.

He had no patience with a bureaucrat sitting in front of a radio saying "roger" every other word. Mike pressed the transmit button. "Close observation. I want to ID the boat and determine its course."

"Roger that. The coast guard advises they are seven minutes away. Stand by until they arrive."

The coast guard! Mike had forgotten the coasties.

He dropped lower, slowed, and approached the go-fast boat. It was a black-and-mahogany cigarette boat, the most powerful he had ever seen, a real gut-wrenching beauty of a boat.

Like most pilots, Mike had a deep appreciation for certain types of aircraft and boats. This boat was a perfect combination of form and function. It was a boat whose beauty took his breath.

Too bad.

The boat driver, a stocky young guy, was using a boat hook to scoop up the sixth container. He looked casually over his shoulder at the helicopter. He was not afraid. Bahamian cops had no Blackhawks, but no one else had law-enforcement authority in the islands. The BAT teams were a joke. Casey paid to see that they never responded if one of his loads was intercepted. The chopper probably belonged to U.S. Customs, but they had no authority in the islands. The chopper could not land on the water. All it could do was circle and be a minor nuisance. And if the guy hung around awhile, he would simply wait him out before taking the load to Florida. It would be a minor inconvenience if he had to take the load to Bimini and wait until dark before moving it. Darrell Casey virtually *owned* Bimini. No problem.

The boat driver gave the chopper pilot a laconic

wave and slowly motored toward the seventh container of cocaine.

As he reached the container, slowed, circled, and stuck out the boat hook to snare the load, Mike arrived overhead, the powerful wash from his blades hammering the surface of the sea and filling the air with the smell of burning jet fuel. The noise of the chopper's engines and the *whump-whump-whump* of the blades was horrific even over the sound of the go-fast boat's unmuffled engines.

The boat driver looked up, squinted against the powerful down wash, and saw the pilot, a tanned and bearded guy with his helmet visor pulled down over his eyes. For a moment the boat driver considered unleashing his M-16, the one he always carried when he was doing a deal. But if the Customs pilot was fired on, there was no telling what sort of armament he might unleash in retaliation. After all, the asshole represented the U.S. government. No, the boat driver would play it smart and do nothing.

The driver turned, snagged the container of cocaine, pulled it forward, and with a flick of his wrist hoisted it aboard. He pulled the knife at his belt, punched a hole in the inflated rubber ring around the container, squeezed it once to press most of the air out, then tossed the deflated package through the companionway.

Still squinting, he turned the steering wheel, shaded his eyes, and looked across the ocean. The sun was up now and the ocean to the east was a blinding glare. It was going to be a hot day.

Then he saw the last container. He would hoist it aboard, loiter a bit to see what the Customs pilot was going to do, then blast out for the fifty-minute run to Lauderdale. Darrell Casey would be happy.

And when Darrell was happy, he spent money. Casey had given him a fifty-thousand-dollar bonus for his last little trick with the coast guard. Maybe there would be another bonus for eluding a helicopter. He had no doubt he could elude it. One way or another, this load was going to Florida.

He looked up in annoyance. The helicopter was directly overhead, no more than ten feet above the boat. The boat driver glanced toward the container, pushed hard on the throttles, and twisted the wheel in an effort to leap out from under the chopper. But the pilot had seen him reach for the throttles and seen him twist the steering wheel. The chopper remained overhead, blasting him with hot oily-smelling exhaust.

But what the hell? It would last only a few more minutes. Then the last container would be in the boat. If a few minutes annoyance was the only price he had to pay to make a hundred thousand, he could handle it.

Suddenly a slick sticky substance was raining down upon him. He wrinkled his brow in confusion. It was pouring all over him, a cascade of viscous fluid. His tongue involuntarily flicked out as some of the liquid poured down his upturned face. It was jet fuel! A moment of stark panic swept over him. He was being doused in highly flammable jet fuel. He cried out in alarm, jumped toward the rear of the boat, and looked up. The chopper pilot was dumping fuel, hundreds of gallons. It was pouring from a standpipe under the right rear of the chopper. The fuel was being pumped on him at an alarming rate, covering the boat until it sloshed throughout the cockpit and splashed overboard into the sea.

Then the chopper began swinging its rear end in a

slow methodical dance, spraying the full length of the boat and the sea for twenty or thirty feet on either side.

Overhead Mike held his hand on the fuel-abort switch. He was dumping the twenty-six hundred pounds of fuel from his auxiliary tank at the rate of three hundred pounds a minute. He had nine minutes of fuel to spray the doper, the boat loaded with cocaine, and the waters around the boat.

The boat driver, blinded by the torrent of fuel running down his face, reached for the throttles. He had to jump out from under the cascade. A spark from the two engines could turn him into a fireball. But the boat driver was too frightened and too anxious. As he lunged toward the throttles, his feet slipped on the deck and he fell. Mike was directly over him, only six feet above the boat, aiming the fuel with deadly accuracy toward the companionway.

Mike swung the tail of the chopper away from the boat and into the rising sun. He backed off about a hundred feet and flicked a switch that activated a powerful loud-hailer. Then he reached into a metal box, pulled out a large flare pistol, and placed it on the left seat.

"Okay, asshole, here's the deal," he said over the loud-hailer, his calm voice booming and echoing across the water. The boat driver looked up, wiped his eyes, and saw only the malevolent black shape of the helicopter silhouetted by the morning sun, heat waves shimmering from the exhaust. "You got thirty seconds to get off the boat. Then I'm putting a flare up your ass. Wave if you understand."

The boat driver's eyes widened and almost involuntarily he quickly waved his right hand. He looked toward the beaches of Bimini a mile to the north.

He was ankle-deep in jet fuel. The boat was covered in fuel. It was so slippery he could hardly move. The water for twenty yards in every direction was covered with a rapidy spreading film of fuel. The pilot could not miss such a target. A flare would turn the boat into a raging fire storm. Then when the big fuel tanks in the belly of the boat exploded, it would be like a miniature A-bomb.

The boat driver did not hesitate. Sliding and lurching, he reached the gunwale and fell over the side, diving deep and swimming hard. He came up high out of the water, still in the oily patch of fuel, broaching like a big fish; then he gasped, rolled his eyes in fright toward the black shape of the helicopter, took a deep breath, and fell back into the water, clawing to go deeper, kicking, and reaching. When he surfaced again he was beyond the fuel. He swam with all his power toward the welcoming beaches of Bimini.

Mike watched and waited until the boat driver was several hundred yards away. He turned the chopper a few degrees toward the south, flicked the window to his right open, and stuck the flare pistol out into the down wash of the big blades. He rocked the chopper hard to the left until the blades were beyond forty-five degrees above the horizon, fired the flare, then rocked back into level flight and accelerated rapidly. The flare arched high, a bright lazy white ball that faded in the morning sun then brightened again as it approached the water, trailing a stream of gray smoke before landing five feet from the cigarette boat.

For a moment it appeared the fuel had not ignited. Then the small almost-invisible white-hot fire grew and spread and roared upward until the boat was in the center of a half acre of flames. Mike was a half-mile away when the boat exploded.

The ocean was still aflame when the coast-guard cutter rounded the western edge of Bimini. The skipper watched through binoculars as the Customs helicopter disappeared on a southwest heading. The skipper was a big man in starched whites. His round face was rigid with anger as he reached for the microphone of the UHF radio.

14

Nick Brown sat behind his desk, patted his right foot rapidly on the floor, tugged at his blond mustache, and stared at Lance Cunningham.

Lance wore his scuffed boat shoes, sharply creased jeans, and a green T-shirt saying "I May Not Be Perfect. But Parts of Me Are Pretty Good." That morning before coming to work he had picked up a hitchhiker who tried to rob him. But the rat trap got the scumbag's attention long enough for the big Magnum to take charge. So Lance felt great. His eyes danced and a big smile stretched across his face.

A red fright-wig, a hat, and an old-fashioned full-length cotton coat lay on the floor—the disguise he wore when he had to come to the office.

Nick's mouth was drawn in a tight straight line, what Lance privately thought of as his "Baptist smile" and a sure sign of anger. The chief of the narcotics squad never took his eyes off Lance. It was his "hard look," an intimidation tactic not taught in training but, nevertheless, one of the first and most important tactics learned by every cop. However, it was wasted on Lance. Lance never broke eye contact. An observer would have sworn he was about to laugh. The two sat there for long minutes, Nick tugging at his mustache and occasionally flicking a single blond hair to the floor, glaring, while Lance stared and waited.

In addition to the problem he had to discuss with Lance, Nick was deeply concerned about Darby. She had given him the information about the Merlin loaded with coke and, in so doing, placed Nick in the dilemma faced every day by police officers who supervise undercover agents. Should the information provided by the U/C agent be acted on and, if so, when? A cop had to become involved when the law was being broken. Nick could not let an aircraft load of dope enter the United States, not when he knew when and where the deal was going down. But to act, sometimes could endanger the U/C agent. So Nick did what most supervisors do in such a situation, pass the information along to another agency in an effort to distance the U/C agent from the deal. But he was still worried. Besides, she was too involved in this case. He was toying with the idea of pulling her out. But every time he made up his mind to do so, she came up with an incredible bit of information and he decided to let her go awhile longer.

Right now he had an even more pressing problem.

Nick slammed his fist hard on the desk, and said, "I want to know what happened on Bimini."

Lance was bewildered. "But boss, my report—"

Nick made a grimace, held up his hand—a small hand with thick fingers—and shook his head. "Forget the report, Cunningham. I said I want to know what happened on Bimini." He folded his hands, leaned forward, and softly said, "Tell me."

Lance pursed his lips and looked across the room as if confused. He noticed that the window in Nick's office had not been repaired. The shattered section—it was about two feet across and maybe three feet high—was open. A light breeze came through the hole and rustled papers on Nick's desk. "About my undercover work? The stats? Tell you what?"

Lance could hear the toe of one of Nick's cowboy boots drumming on the floor. Not a good sign. Then the little cop stood up, tugged at his blue polyester pants, and eyes on the floor, slowly walked from behind the desk. His arms were bent at the elbows. He held his arms out from his body.

He stopped in the center of the room, back toward Lance, and began talking in a soft voice. "All I've ever been is a cop," he said. "That's all I ever wanted to be. Just a cop." He turned and looked at Lance as if seeing him for the first time. "I'm not all that smart. Lots of people are smarter than me. But I'm a good cop. I think if you're a cop and your job is to put bad people in jail, then you're in the right and it doesn't matter in the long run how smart you are. Things will work out so that you can do your job. You understand that?"

He paused. Lance nodded but said nothing. He had never heard his taciturn boss speak on such a subject.

Nick pointed to a folder on his desk. "You see that file? You know what's in it?"

Lance shook his head.

"It's a classified report from the coast guard. Some admiral came in here yesterday and gave it to me. It says that eighty-six percent of the marine seizures made by coast guard nationwide were made by the Miami district. That's not surprising. But the report also says that this office provided the intelligence for ninety-two percent of those coast-guard seizures. In fact, if it wasn't for this office, for the narcotics squad here in Broward County, the Miami coast guard would be out there telling people to wear their life jackets and chasing off Japanese fishermen from U.S. waters. The coast guard is not going to publicly give us credit for enabling them to make those seizures. They want their people in Washington to think they are some sort of geniuses. You know all this because it was your informants and your U/C work that provided the information leading to most of those seizures. And it's okay if we don't get the credit. It protects you and it protects your sources. Everybody is happy."

Lance nodded in agreement.

"Cunningham, I've told you this before. I think you may be the best narcotics officer I've ever seen. You make more felony cases and get more convictions than any other police officer in Florida. You're better than any federal agent I know. But you know what, Cunningham? You got a big problem. You and I are different."

"How?"

Nick paused. His eyes were locked on the young officer. Then he spoke very slowly and his voice was hard. "I go by the rules. I go by the book. I will not break the law to catch a bad guy. I will not do that. No matter the circumstances. No matter if a bad guy walks. I'll catch him by the book or I won't catch him. Because I believe if we don't do it that way, then we shouldn't be wearing badges. Do you understand that, Cunningham? Do you understand that?"

Lance shrugged. "You want me to kiss the bastards?"

"I want you to treat dopers the same way you treat the IRS. You use every weapon at your disposal to get everything you're legally entitled to get. But you don't step over the line. You don't break the law."

"You're saying I break the law to catch dopers?"

Nick stood in the center of the room, hands in his pockets, rocking on his cowboy boots. "I'll tell you what I'm saying. I'm saying Darrell Casey's stash house on South Bimini burned the other morning. Burned to the ground. Destroyed maybe twenty tons of reefer. I'm saying his security guard was knocked on the head right before it happened. Guy slept through the whole thing. I'm saying two julios were badly burned when the house went up. They said it exploded. And I'm saying all this happened about the time you were leaving the island. But there's nothing about any of this in your report. Why?"

Lance's smile widened until it was a dazzling display of white teeth in the middle of his tanned face. His eyes widened and he rocked his head from side to side.

Nick glared at Lance for a long moment, then slowly walked to his desk. He sat on the edge, left foot on the floor as his right foot slowly swung to and fro. "Let me tell you something that will wipe that silly smile off your face. Your Customs buddy has been grounded. Grounded and suspended indefinitely."

"Mike? What the hell for? He's the best they got."

Now Nick was smiling. A mirthless smile. "One

of his federal colleagues, a coast-guard guy, the skipper of one of their cutters, arrived at South Bimini yesterday morning while a doper's boat was burning. He said it looked as if half the ocean was on fire. A Customs Blackhawk helicopter was leaving the scene. When the coastie picked up the boat driver, the guy told him he had been sprayed with fuel, then a flare had been fired from the chopper."

Lance nodded in approval. "So why was Mike grounded? Sounds as if he should get a medal."

Nick sighed. He was not getting through. "The doper said the Customs pilot hosed him down with fuel and shot a flare at him. Said he was just out there fishing. Of course the computer lit up like a Christmas tree when this guy's name was entered. He's one of Casey's drivers and a suspect in more than a dozen cases. But there was no evidence on this deal to prove anything. No dope. No boat. No nothing. The coasties brought him back to Florida. He stuck with his story about being a fisherman. His lawyer had him on the street about an hour after he got back."

"How much shit was on the boat before it burned?"

Nick paused. "My information is that it contained eight containers of cocaine."

"Sounds like a bad day for Brother Casey. I bet he is one more kind of upset."

Nick looked away for a long moment. "I've got a theory about that," he said softly. "I think something that happened to Casey a long time ago has influenced the way he looks at cops. And with good reason."

Nick turned back to Lance. He paused, as if

trying to decide whether or not to tell Lance a story about Darrell Casey. He decided not to do so.

"Upset? I don't know why. About ninety-nine percent of his loads get through. Maybe he wants to advertise zero defects. I don't know. But I do know he's not nearly as upset as your Customs buddy. They want to prosecute him. I don't think they can because the evidence is circumstantial. The coastie saw him leaving the scene but didn't see him shoot a flare. The doper recanted when he got to shore. But the coastie snitched off your buddy anyway. Know what Mike said? Said his fuel tanks must have been leaking. Said an electrical short must have caused the doper boat to explode."

Lance shrugged. "Makes sense to me."

"It didn't make sense to anyone else. Mike's lucky he was not brought up on charges."

Lance stood up. He was angry. "So Customs had to be satisfied with grounding and suspending a pilot who destroyed several hundred kilos of cocaine? By bringing in that load, the boat driver would have violated about a dozen international, federal, state, and local laws. You and I both know that a big part of that load probably would have ended up in Broward County. I thought stopping dope was his job. It's *my* job. You pay me to stop dope, to catch smugglers, and to change their zip codes. Does Mike have to fight his superiors as well as the dopers? Do I have to fight you as well as the dopers? What the hell's going on?"

Nick exploded. He jumped to the floor and jabbed a finger into Lance's chest. Almost in a shout he said, "They should have prosecuted him. He's my friend and he's a good pilot and a good cop. But they should have prosecuted him. Cops can't go around squirting gasoline on people and trying to set them afire. You know that."

"That's part of being a doper. That guy knew the risk when he decided to smuggle dope. He could have been a farmer. He could have been an insurance broker. But he decided to become a dope smuggler. Just like looking up women's dresses is part of selling shoes, getting your boat burned up is part of being a doper."

Lance paused. Then he leaned down until his nose was several inches from Nick's nose. Very slowly he said, "Mike did his job. He stopped the load."

Nick leaned an inch closer. "That ain't the point. Casey went to the Bahamians and is getting them all worked up. He told them the U.S. government is conducting offensive operations in their airspace and on their territorial waters. He's going to have them so mad they may throw us out. And it's all because he wants to bring in ten tons of coke on a C-130. He's still planning that. And he's planning to bring it through Broward County. He's going to rub our noses in it. And that little episode of burning down a stash house and blowing up his boat will help him. You and your buddy Mike and your cowboy games may have put just enough shackles on law enforcement to enable Casey to do it. You two have helped one of the biggest dopers in the country."

Lance was angry. He wanted to argue about helping Casey. But he knew where the information about the C-130 was coming from. And that angered him even more than being accused of helping a smuggler.

"Goddammit, is she still out there with that scumbag? Passing along his little comments, his pillow talk, and calling it intelligence gathering? I got more intelligence from Bimini in a week than she's given you in months. Why don't you pull her in?"

Nick ignored Lance's outburst. He turned away, stalked behind his desk, and sat down. He leaned forward, clasped his hands atop his desk, and looked up at Lance. "I'm not going to ask you if you burned that stash house. You'd tell me the truth and I'd have to fire you. As much as I respect you as a police officer, I'd let you go."

Lance leaned over the desk. When he spoke, his voice was intense. "You know what dopers are doing. You know the lengths they will go to when they're bringing in a load. You know the results when that stuff gets on the streets. You know what percentage of all criminal activity can be traced to narcotics. And you know that all the rules are like anchors holding us back, keeping us from doing our job. Dopers are not people. They're assholes, the worst people any cop has to deal with. I don't care if some of them are college-educated and dress in five-hundred-dollar suits. You can drape a silk handkerchief over a pile of shit and it's still a pile of shit. Dopers don't deserve any respect or any consideration. We should be able to go after them any way we can."

Nick's lips were squeezed firmly together as he shook his head in disagreement. He looked at Lance for a long moment. Then he said, "You're going back to Bimini."

Nick could not have said anything that would have been a greater surprise. Lance's eyes widened in astonishment.

"And I'm going with you," Nick said with a smile.

"You what?"

"The sheriff was impressed with what you did over there, with the intelligence you gathered on boats and aircraft. He thinks another trip might enable the department to collect the sort of intelligence that could reelect him."

Lance was confused.

"But I think if you were turned loose on Bimini again, you would either get killed or cause an international incident. So I'm going along." Nick folded his arms and paused. "We're partners," he said. He grinned.

Lance sat down, opened his mouth, rolled his eyes, and made a noise of pain. Nick held up an open hand toward Lance and said, "That's it. No arguing. You work out all the details." Nick paused a moment then added, "Partner." He grinned again.

Lance signed. He shrugged. Then his eyes began to sparkle again. "I'll be glad to get back. It's been a while since I had one of those great big Gulf Stream specials."

Nick was puzzled. "A Gulf Stream special? What's that?"

"Ah ha! First you eat conch chowder with lots of Bimini bread. Then a grouper. Pan-fried because of the oil. Lots of beer. Then—"

Nick stood up and pointed toward the door. "Out! Get out!"

Lance reached for his hip pocket and pulled out a small book. "Hey, I can prove it. It's all in here. I keep a record of every dump." He waved the little book. "I've got documentation for the time and type of every dump I've had for the past six months. And I've got other books at my apartment going back—"

"Get out. Now."

Lance laughed, put on his red fright-wig, hat, and coat. He turned up the collar of the coat, then walked toward the door.

"And stop by my secretary's desk. She's got a note for you from the sheriff's office."

Lance stopped and turned around to face Nick. He thunked the heels of his boat shoes together, then snapped into an exaggerated, back-bowed military posture. He popped up a quivering, open-palmed British salute and said, *"Sí, jefe máximo.* I will prepare a battle plan that will bring us glory and honor. A plan that will have generations yet unborn worshiping our memory. A plan that will be taught in criminal justice courses in every university across the land. A plan that will—"

"Out."

Nick spun toward the door. Outside he paused a moment. He looked down at Nick's secretary, motioned with his head toward the door to Nick's office, and said, "Our Fluf is a wee bit upset."

15

"Somebody's fucking with me," Darrell Casey said. He stood on the shaded porch of his Fort Lauderdale home and idly watched a yacht motoring slowly down the Intracoastal Waterway. He slouched, hands in the pockets of his white cotton pants. Casey wore no shirt, and although it was only 9 A.M., his lean shoulders were beaded with a fine sheen of perspiration. He occasionally rubbed his right leg, the one that caused him to walk with a slight limp.

Behind him Gunter Steinhorst and the Snake Eaters waited. Steinhorst turned up a beer and drained half the can. He did not drink, as do many beer drinkers, by occasionally taking a couple of swallows. Instead, he drank half of a beer with one gulp. A moment later he drank the remainder, then opened another can.

Steinhorst and the Snake Eaters stood erect, shoulders back, relaxed but ready to explode into action. They were warriors awaiting orders. Once they were sent forth, violence would result. The Snake Eaters rocked on their toes and flexed their ropy muscles. Neither bothered to hide almost contemptuous smiles. Even though Casey gave the orders, he was smaller;

he had never been in combat, and therefore he was an inferior being. Much of their attitude came from knowing that Steinhorst planned to kill Casey and take over his organization. They would be the top two lieutenants when that happened. The only hangup now was the multiton load of cocaine Casey was planning to bring in. The guy thought big. You had to give him that. And he planned well—a talent Steinhorst knew he lacked. Once all the plans were made and the Bimini operation achieved a life of its own, Steinhorst would move.

Steinhorst knew that the slight man with the long black hair had not built the largest drug-smuggling operation in the Southeast, perhaps the largest in America, by being soft. Casey would do what he had to do. He was hard, methodical. He saw circles within circles and always thought several moves ahead. Steinhorst looked with hooded eyes at Casey and idly touched the four fingers of his left hand to the tip of his thumb, testing the sharpness of his nails. Then he tested the sharpness of the nails on his right hand. He looked at Casey. He waited.

"Somebody's fucking with me," Casey repeated.

He spun around and stared into Steinhorst's arctic blue eyes for a long moment. Then, hands still in his pockets, he looked down the Intracoastal toward the white yacht. He estimated it was about fifty feet in length. Every fall, as soon as the hurricane season was over, the boats came south by the hundreds. There were days when they appeared like a train, a train of yachts several miles long motoring slowly southward, causing motorists on causeways from North Carolina to Georgia to gripe and moan as they were stopped while bridges were raised and the boats majestically motored south.

They wintered in Miami, where they were kept in a state of constant readiness for owners who occasionally flew down for a long weekend. Then, in the spring, the boats were driven back to home ports in the East, back up the Intracoastal.

"Two things bother the hell out of me," Casey said. He rubbed his right leg and continued to watch the yacht as it disappeared to the south. His voice was soft, almost noncommittal. "Two things. Both of them in Bimini." He paused. "Something's going on over there and I can't figure it out."

One of the Snake Eaters, the one who wore the white leather glove, turned to the other and smiled.

"I lost twenty-two tons of weed over there the other night," Casey said. He sounded as if he were talking to himself, replaying the incident as if the repetition would cause a missing fact, the revelatory key to the incident, to surface. "The guard was knocked in the head. He wasn't killed. And the stash house was burned with the weed inside. So it wasn't a rip."

He looked up at Steinhorst as if the big German could explain. Steinhorst's face was implacable.

Casey held out his left hand, palm up. With his right forefinger he began touching the fingers of his left hand, ticking off the items that caused him concern, going over the incident again, still seeking the answer. "If somebody was trying to rip me off they would have killed the guard. They wouldn't just tap him on the head. They would send me a message."

The Snake Eater wearing the white glove looked at his friend and raised his eyebrows as if in approval.

"But the stash house. The stash house." Casey slammed his right fist into his left palm. "Why would somebody burn the stash house? Ripping the

weed I could understand. But just burning it . . ."
Casey's voice dribbled away. His eyes were locked
with those of Steinhorst. "It's like I've been saying
ever since it happened. This is the sort of thing a
cop would do. Just to fuck with me. I can't come up
with any other answer. Some cop is fucking with
me."

He turned and looked down the Intracoastal. The
yacht had rounded a bend in the waterway. "But I
own the cops over there. They're mine. Bought and
paid for. Not a one of those bastards has the balls
to cross me. Besides, a fucking Bahamian would
steal the weed and sell it. He wouldn't burn it."

Casey snorted. "Those scrounging bastards. I've
known them to dive on a wrecked airplane and sell
the weed they bring up. They call it 'square grouper.' They wouldn't burn a stash house."

Casey shook his head in bewilderment.

"And the load of coke I lost. I can't believe a
Customs pilot burned up a load of coke in Bahamian waters. What the hell does he think he is,
some sort of international cowboy? If the son of a
bitch hadn't been suspended, I wouldn't have believed that story. And he got my cigarette boat, the
best-looking fastest cigarette boat in Florida. All
these fish-faced Harvard MBAs I got working for
me say there will be occasional losses. Goddamn,
they got to go to Harvard to tell me I'll lose a load
now and then. I know cops get lucky and stumble
into a deal from time to time. But I want to know
how and why. When I lose a load, I want to know
the reason. Then I can make sure it won't happen
again. Now I've lost a stash house, my boat, and a
load of cocaine. I don't know how it happened. So I
don't know how to keep it from happening again."

Casey paused. Steinhorst and the Snake Eaters waited. The Snake Eaters were impatient. But Steinhorst knew how Casey operated. Now that he had gotten everything off his chest, he would make a move. He was about to issue marching orders.

Casey stared at Steinhorst. But his eyes had a thousand-yard stare. Then Casey nodded. His right forefinger came up and pointed at Steinhorst. "Here's the deal," he said. "Send these two guys back to Bimini." He glanced at the Snake Eaters. "You guys go over there and find out what happened. I want to know if some Bahamian cowboy burned down my stash house. You find out what happened and you come down hard on somebody. Hard. You got that?"

The Snake Eaters nodded.

"And I want to know if Customs or DEA or anybody else has some kind of operation going in the Bahamas. Is the U.S. government operating in Bimini without the knowledge of the Bahamians? Or is it some renegade cop? Whatever the hell is going on, I want to know."

Again, the Snake Eaters nodded. It was as if their heads were tied together. Now their smiles changed from slightly patronizing to smiles of anticipation. They were going to Bimini with a mandate from the man who controlled the place, and that mandate was to rattle the trees and see who fell out.

Casey turned back to Steinhorst. "You get that boat driver and take him for a ride in the glades. He lost a load of coke and he lost my boat. I want to know if he dropped a dime on me. There's no way in hell a helicopter could pop up at the exact moment a deal is going down unless he knew about it in advance."

Steinhorst's close-cropped head moved a millimeter. He turned up the beer can and drained it. Then he clustered the fingers of his right hand until the fingertips formed a phalanx of five steellike points. He slowly pushed his fingernails into the empty beer can and pulled them downward until the side of the can was shredded. His arctic blue eyes stared at Casey.

After a pause, Casey spoke again. "I'm finalizing my plans for the big load. You guys know about it. It's the biggest deal that's ever been done anywhere. It will make all of you millionaires. I don't want any fuckups."

He paused. "You guys get outta here. Go do what you gotta do."

16

Lance Cunningham leaned back in the white leather chair, crossed his legs, and looked with undisguised curiosity at the two old men across the room. They sat with their backs to the huge wall of glass overlooking the ocean. The spacious and luxurious office was on the top floor of the most exclusive office building on Fort Lauderdale's Gold Coast. The early-morning sun shone into the window, backlighting the two men, making them shadowy outlines and almost blinding Lance.

He was enjoying their little ploy. It was a power play, the sort of thing he did when working undercover. Lance pulled his Porsche sunglasses down from his dark sun-streaked hair, used the middle finger of his left hand to adjust them on his nose, then smiled beatifically. He wore boat shoes, neatly pressed blue jeans, and a bright-blue T-shirt upon which was written, "Fight Gravity."

The two men across the room did not speak. Lance did not break the silence. He could play this game longer than they could. It was part of his repertory. He was a pro and these guys were amateurs. Lance continued smiling and staring toward the shadowy figures.

Finally, one of the old men spoke. "Officer Cunningham, we very much appreciate your taking the time to visit with us," said the man on the left. The man's voice was soft and deferential. He paused, slowly opened a mint from a roll on the table, and inserted it between his thin lips. Lance was not deceived by the softness of the man's voice or his courtesy. The old geezer—he was about sixty-five—had anticipated America's physical-fitness craze, built the first portable exercise machine, called it The Poseidon, and became one of the richest men in Florida. He changed wives as often as some people changed shirts. He was now on number six, a twenty-four-year-old honey who was the television model for his exercise machine. In the TV ads she stood there in a wet terry-cloth exercise outfit plastered to her body. Water, carefully applied to her face and legs, made it appear she was perspiring. At the end of the ad, she grasped the stainless-steel legs of the exercise machine, vamped the camera, and said, "The Poseidon is the shape of things to come."

It was said that the ad had caused near heart failure in several thousand men. In fact, the ad was so popular that television stations published in local newspapers the time it would be aired each day.

The old guy was an ardent supporter of police work. He had set up a million-dollar scholarship fund that sent the children of dozens of police officers to college.

"Yes, indeed. We are grateful," said the second man. "We know how very busy you are." The second man also was a millionaire businessman. He had made a fortune importing cheaply made furniture from Central and South America. A year earlier an aviation magazine had written a long story about the man's collection of World War II aircraft. The guy owned more airplanes than did some of the countries where he bought furniture. He also was a major contributor to the first campaign of Broward County Sheriff Hiram Turnipseed. Lance suspected the old man owned the home on Bimini that he had used as a base for his undercover mission.

Both men were wizened, wrinkled, and extraordinarily courteous and soft-spoken. They could afford to be courteous because they were two tough old buzzards whose urine probably would etch glass.

The first man sucked on his mint and peered over his glasses. "Officer Cunningham, we have asked you here this morning so we can discuss an area of activity that, if all works as we believe, could not only result in a small measure of personal satisfaction to us—quiet *unpublished* satisfaction, I might add—but could also bring a measure of relief to our citizens, relief from what we believe to be the most serious, most harmful domestic problem facing our great nation."

"And what is that, sir?"

The second man picked up a folder from the desk and held it aloft. He smiled at Lance the way an uncle smiles at a favorite but sometimes slow nephew.

Lance stood up, pushed his sunglasses atop his head, and walked across the room. His eyes widened when he saw what the man held. It was a thick red folder with a broad green diagonal band across the front. Lance leaned over, knowing what he would see. His name was neatly typed in bold letters on a sticker in the upper right-hand corner. The smiling old man was holding Lance Cunningham's top-secret personnel folder, a folder kept under lock and key because of what it contained. That folder held information that could compromise years of work and put Lance's life and the life of a dozen informants in jeopardy, information that revealed highly secret investigative techniques about several dozen ongoing cases. It was one of the most classified files in the Broward County sheriff's office, and only Nick Brown and Sheriff Turnipseed had access to the triple-locked cabinet where it was kept.

Instinctively, Lance reached for the folder. But the wily old man anticipated him and quickly pulled his hand back.

"Sir, how did you come to have that file?" Lance's voice was hard and cold. It was his cop's voice, the voice he rarely used except with bad guys. "There's stuff in there that . . ." Lance stopped. He was stunned at the enormous power these two old men possessed. They moved in a universe beyond his imagination. Two civilians, even if they were wealthy friends of the sheriff, should not be granted access to his file.

"Do not be concerned, Officer Cunningham," said the first man in his smooth conciliatory voice. His smile never wavered. "We are well aware of the sensitive nature of this document. And you may be assured that were our discretion even the slightest consideration, we would not have this file. It was brought to us by an armed guard and shall be returned in the same fashion. Security will not be violated."

"It already has been violated," Lance snapped. "Where did you get that file?" Like most cops he was uncomfortable being on the defensive. These two characters better come up with some good an-

swers or he was going across the table and take his
folder, even if it meant roughing up two men who
were old enough to have known George Washington.

"That is not the point, Officer Cunningham,"
said the second man. "The issue here is much
greater." He tapped the folder with a bony finger.
"And the contents of this folder, sensitive though
they may be, are only the foundation for a project
that is orders of magnitude greater in significance.
The point is simply this: we know all about you.
And we are asking you to be a part of that much
greater, much larger idea."

"I don't know what the hell you're talking about.
But I do know what's in that folder."

The old man casually motioned Lance toward the
chair. Lance paused for a second. He was between
the old men and the door. They couldn't get out
without coming over him. He returned to the leather
chair but did not sit down. He pulled the chair to
the end of the table where the old men sat. He
wanted to be where he could look into their eyes
without being blinded by the sun. He sat on the
edge of the chair, feet spread, weight on his toes,
ready to move. Still wary, he looked at the first
man. "Okay," he said.

Now Lance could see the eyes of the old men.
Their smiles were benevolent. But their eyes were
harder and colder and more remote than those of a
homicide detective. These guys made him nervous.
He didn't know how to handle them. They weren't
crooks. They were millionaire businessmen who were
personal friends not only of the sheriff, but of the
governor and—so he had heard—even the President
of the United States. And they were so damned
sure of themselves. Lance had a theory about men:

the men who truly held great power always were quiet, spoke slowly, and never raised their voices— just like these old geezers.

The second man crossed his hands and laced his fingers atop the desk, leaned forward slightly, and smiled. "To answer my own question of a moment ago, Officer Cunningham, the greatest domestic problem facing this great nation of ours is drug smuggling. And you are a front-line soldier in that war." He paused again. These guys were masters of the pregnant pause. "Now, I must ask you a question. Do you know anyone qualified to fly a B-26?"

Lance's eyes widened for a moment. Then he waved his arm in a gesture of dismissal. "Sure. They're real popular on my street. Everybody's into flying. Especially B-26s. All the kids have one or two."

Lance had regained his composure.

The two men stared. He matched their smiles, beaming first at one, then the other. He leaned over the desk. "What about you fellows? You have any friends who fly B-26s? What about P-51s, the old Mustang? I know this waitress at a little restaurant over on Federal Highway; has the best chicken wings in town. She flies F-86s. You know any waitresses who fly F-86s?"

The two men smiled patiently and waited for Lance to finish his little game. But Lance wasn't through. He was still angry that the two men held his personnel file.

"And then there's a day-care center I heard about," Lance continued. "It's over on the beach. Not far from here, as a matter of fact. The kids there go up to the Cape every third Tuesday. They fly missiles. Can you believe that? Two of them are going to the moon next Tuesday. You know any four-year-olds who fly missiles?"

Lance paused and beamed. After a moment the second man spoke. "Officer Cunningham, it is our information that you are close friends with one Michael Love, a pilot for the United States Customs Service and a man whom we understand is qualified in the B-26. We also understand that he has been relieved of his flying duties. We further understand that he is a devoted and committed law-enforcement officer who may be interested in a temporary flying position, a position that may appeal to one of his temperament."

Lance tightened his lips and glared at the old man. How in hell did he get this information? Did he have a NADDIS terminal, an NCIC terminal? Was he plugged into EPIC? Lance shook his head, sighed, and said, "Mister, what do you want?"

The first man stood up from behind the desk. He put a mint between his thin lips and smoothed the front of his blue suit, a suit so blue it was almost black, then stepped closer to Lance. He put his hand on the end of the table and looked deep into the eyes of the young police officer. The morning sun sparkled on the toes of his brightly shined black shoes. The shoes looked new. Lance wondered why the shoes of wealthy people always appeared to be new.

"Let me tell you a story, Officer Cunningham," the man said.

Lance wondered how the old man talked around the mint.

The man looked out the window over the ocean.

He was seeing something no one else in the room could see.

"I had a daughter by my first marriage," the man said softly. "She was a child of light and beauty and warmth. I knew at the time—the reasons don't matter—that she would be the only child I would ever have, so I gave her all the love a father is capable of giving his firstborn who is also his only child."

The man turned to look at Lance. "And let me disabuse you of any idea that, because I am a wealthy man, I bestowed upon her many material things. I did not."

Lance believed him. The old geezer was too tough, too disciplined, to ladle out money to anyone, even to an only child. He probably made her rake the lawn for her allowance.

"When my daughter was fourteen, she began using drugs," the old man continued. "I did not know until much later, when it was too late, that she had smoked marijuana. She moved up to cocaine and then through virtually every substance in the pharmacological lexicon. She began selling drugs to support her habit."

The old man paused. "She also began selling her body."

The old man could have been discussing the weather. His voice was calm and measured. But now the old man's eyes had softened and the pain was clearly visible.

"The first time I knew my daughter was using drugs was the day she overdosed." The old man reached for the mints. He slowly put one into his mouth, and then he turned, hands behind his back, and again looked over the ocean. "She was barely alive when I rushed her to the hospital. I think she would have recovered. But while she was in the hospital, she committed suicide. She slashed her wrist with the jagged end of a bedspring. The guilt and the pain over her past life were too much. I had to bury the child, and she was only a child, who would have been the joy of my old age."

In the morning sun the ocean appeared to be a sheet of hammered silver. It glistened and shone and shimmered. The old man was rock-still for a long moment. Only his hands, clasped behind his back, moved. They clenched and unclenched with such strength that the fingers whitened.

Almost as if speaking to himself, the old man continued. "And I know who did it. I know the man responsible."

The old man sighed, then turned away from the window and walked slowly back to his chair and sat down. For a moment he was weary. He rolled the mint around in his mouth and stared at the wall across the office. Then he took a deep breath, regained his strength, and continued, "Officer Cunningham, unlike many parents in similar circumstances, I did not feel then—and I do not feel now—any personal guilt over this matter. I was a good father. I did all that can reasonably be expected of a parent. There was nothing in my actions, or lack of actions, that contributed to my daughter's drug usage. Even so, because of drugs, she committed suicide."

The old man reached out and put his hand on his friend's arm. "My colleague here had a similar experience. A member of his family died because of drugs. The point is, Officer Cunningham, that we have strong feelings about those who smuggle drugs into our country. We know, if you will forgive us for saying so, that we understand the drug business perhaps even better than you. Because we know from firsthand experience what it does to children. To our children. To our families. To our lives."

Lance cleared his throat. There was nothing he could say. He had a sense of where this conversation was going, and the idea both thrilled and frightened him. Kicking ass among drug smugglers was a game to him, the most thrilling and dangerous game on earth. Nevertheless, it was a game. But these guys were like Mike Love. They were serious. Deadly serious.

The first man opened another mint and slid it into his mouth. He nodded to his friend. The second man, who continued to smile while keeping his eyes fixed on Lance, spoke. "Officer Cunningham, before we continue, let me say that if anyone overheard what I am about to say to you, they would brand me as a right-wing lunatic. They would say that the proposal my colleague and I have for you is beyond the pale, that it makes us anarchists, that we may be even worse than drug smugglers."

"Perhaps it is rationalizing, you tell us," the first man interrupted. "But we believe there is a new feeling, a growing, powerful almost subliminal feeling, slowly being made manifest in the breasts of Americans. Officer Cunningham, Americans are angry. They are fed up. They are becoming more and more willing to do whatever it takes to stop drugs. They know that contrary to what the liberals and the newspaper columnists are saying, drug smuggling is not an issue with two sides. Many of those who contend there are two sides to drug smuggling are people who once were and in fact may still be users. There is only one side to this issue. And that is the horrible, the unspeakable, the unacceptable pain and grief. There is nothing, nothing at all, that comes out of drug smuggling that can begin to balance the scale."

The old man had delivered his speech in a flat unemotional tone. But a person's eyes always tell the story. And this old man's eyes did not blaze with the fervor of a zealot. That Lance could have understood. He ran into zealots every day, people who wanted to stand drug smugglers up against a wall and shoot them. These guys had thought about this a long time. They were not emotional.

Lance took a deep breath and wondered if he would be like this in forty or fifty years. Was this what happened when the broad strong shoulders of a young man were weighted down with the burden of the years?

The second man spoke. He had seen the wary expression flit across Lance's face, and his voice was conciliatory. "Officer Cunningham, it is our belief and it is our hope that you will hear us out. We, my friend and I, simply seek a redress of grievances, a right guaranteed us by the United States Constitution. Normal recourses do not work in this situation. So we are proposing a joint venture. A joint venture with you and your friend Michael Love. We believe such a merger has the potential to cause the drug smugglers more problems and more damage than anything you have been able to do in the, shall we say, normal channels of law enforcement."

Lance leaned forward but the old man held up his hand. "I know what you are going to say. But I also know that, at best, you may, and I emphasize the word 'may,' be stopping one percent of the narcotics coming into America. This is no criticism of law enforcement. It is simply that the administration in Washington believes in waging the war on drugs with press releases."

Lance smiled and nodded in agreement.

"You are simply outgunned," the old man continued. "Smugglers have more personnel, more boats, more aircraft, more electronics equipment, and more money. Considering the circumstances, you—and I use you in the generic sense to mean all law enforcement—you are doing an outstanding job."

The old man tapped his bony finger against Lance's personnel folder. "Being more specific, officers such as you are doing a truly magnificent job."

Lance waited. He was unmoved by the praise. He wanted to see if these two men were going where he thought they were going.

The first man picked up the conversation. "Here is our proposal, Officer Cunningham. And forgive us if we ramble. But it is the way of old men." The old man smiled and continued. "It is our idea to meld the resources of you and Mr. Love with what my colleague and I can offer. You have access to certain local, state, and even federal intelligence information about drug smugglers. Their habits, how they conduct business, where they operate from, even, I daresay, information about future drug flights. Right down to the time when someone—how do you say it? goes south?—to pick up drugs." Lance stared unblinking at the old man. He was wary. The conversation had moved into a highly sensitive area. These guys were friends of the sheriff; the personnel folder on the desk proved that. But they were still civilians.

Lance said nothing.

"Do not worry. We are not asking that you share any of that information with us. We have no need to know. What we are asking is that you and Michael Love simply utilize those sources of information and then apply the information through avenues we will make available."

Lance waited.

"And Michael Love, so we are told, is an eminently qualified pilot. A dedicated, determined, and aggressive man."

"You got him right," Lance said.

The old man's smile grew broader. "Very well. My colleague and I have certain resources. Specifically, a B-26. Mechanically, it is in better shape than the day it was manufactured. In addition, it has certain state-of-the-art modifications that a pilot will find most interesting."

Lance leaned forward. "Does the sheriff know we are having this conversation? Does he approve of this?"

The two men stared unblinking at Lance. After a long moment the man who had been speaking continued. It was if Lance had never spoken.

"There are technological advancements found on this airplane that can be found nowhere else, even in the military." The old man rubbed his hands together. "Discuss this with Mr. Love. He will of course have unlimited access to the aircraft. We understand he has a certain amount of flying hours in this aircraft, about nine hundred and forty-three hours to be precise, but it has been a while, two months and seven days, since he last flew a B-26. He may be a bit rusty. He can fly it as frequently as he wishes in order to become fully proficient. Though, for security reasons, he may wish to fly at night or very early in the morning."

"Does the sheriff know what we are talking about?"

Again, the two old men stared at Lance without answering. And Lance knew that if he followed through with these bozos, he would be on his own. If anything went wrong, the sheriff would hang him out to dry. These guys would probably deny ever seeing him. What the hell? It was always that way.

He sighed. "So, after he becomes current in the aircraft, what, then?" Lance was almost afraid to hear the answer he knew was coming.

The two old men glanced at each other. The one with the mint in his mouth slowly nodded. The second man held his arms out, palms turned up, and smiled. "And then, Officer Cunningham, using the information to which you and Mr. Love have access, we propose that he use the B-26 and the, ah, equipment on the aircraft to fly off-shore to intercept a few drug smugglers. We are particularly interested in aircraft belonging to a smuggler by the name of Darrell Casey. Once he has intercepted a drug-laden aircraft, he will know what to do."

Lance, even though he had anticipated what the man was going to say, was astonished. "You mean . . ." He could not finish.

"Precisely, Officer Cunningham. We want Mr. Love to shoot down Darrell Casey's aircraft and—"

The other man interrupted. "And bomb his sanctuary on Bimini."

17

"Boca de Mama," Nick Brown said with disgust. "What kind of name is that for a beer joint?"

Lance tried not to laugh.

The two cops were near the south end of the main street in Alice Town. They stood in the darkened shadows of the canopy jutting out from the ticket office of Chalk Air Service, the small airline that flies amphibians between Miami and the Bahamas. The steep ramp the amphibians used to exit the ocean was to their left as they peered through the darkness to a small bar. Overhanging the bar were full-bodied casuarina trees that swayed and whispered in a strong breeze from the east. Nick was upwind from the bar but he sniffed as if the breeze would bring the odor of the establishment, which could only be unpleasant, wafting toward him. He looked at the garish sign hanging over the door, the gaping lipstick-smeared mouth of an old woman made all the more bold by the small bright light attached to the top of the sign. The carmine mouth appeared part of a disembodied being hanging in the blackness under the trees, moving slowly in the breeze. Nick shook his head.

"Why do we have to go in here?" he asked as he looked at the small cement-block building. It was painted with a flat black paint that caused it to disappear in the shadows. The windows, if there were any, were closed. Nick Brown did not want to go into a darkened cement box at the end of a street on Bimini. There was no escape route. South of the little bar was only a garbage dump and then the ocean. The little inlet separating North Bimini from South Bimini was behind the bar. The ocean was a few hundred yards west. The only way to run was north, right through the middle of Alice Town, a town dominated by Darrell Casey and his gang of smugglers. He didn't fancy the idea of running past Brown's Marina, The Compleat Angler, and all the other tourist-jammed junk-laden stores along the main street. Just yesterday he had seen several tourist laughing over a T-shirt that said, "I Fish for Square Grouper." They thought it was terribly neat, very chic.

"Why do we have to go in here?" he repeated. "What does this place have to do with Casey? I've known Casey for fifteen years. He's a businessman. He doesn't have time for places like this."

He could not see the smile that creased Lance's face. Lance had a theory that the more upset Nick became, the farther his elbows protruded from his body and the more he looked like a wet rooster parading around a barnyard. If that theory were correct, Nick was now in a state of high dudgeon.

"Hey, boss, this is more than a beer joint. This is where all the bad guys hang out. This is the smugglers' roost. We can pick up more intelligence in here tonight than we've done in the last three days."

The past three days had been fruitless. Nick and

Lance had roamed about Alice Town, especially the docks on the east side of town, always staying separated but close enough that each could keep an eye on the other. They had occasionally sighted the Snake Eaters, who appeared to be rushing about in the company of various Biminites. The Snake Eaters were stern-faced and businesslike, and the two Lauderdale cops avoided meeting them.

Lance was surprised and then annoyed when Nick launched into a breakdown on the Snake Eaters. He even told Lance about their military careers; they were two highly decorated Special Forces sergeants who had served in Vietnam. They had been dishonorably discharged after fragging a lieutenant. One of them had burned off most of his right hand while trying to hold a man on the ground and ignite a star-burst flare in his anus. The man had made the mistake of calling him a "butt-fucker." The then-sergeant used his combat knife to slice a hole in the rear of the man's fatigue pants. But the knowledge that he was about to have a star-burst flare, a rocket-propelled bundle of exploding phosphorus, ignited in his lower colon, gave the squirming man on the ground sufficient strength to twist away from the sergeant. The sergeant's hand took most of the initial explosion. He covered the gnarled and burned stump with a white leather glove.

"You didn't get that info off the computer," Lance said.

"Well, once I had the basic info, I went to the army and got their record," Nick said. "Now it's in the computer. I put it there. Those guys are bad news."

"I know where you got the basic info," Lance said.

When Nick did not respond, Lance said, "Boss, you got to pull her out of there. It's too dangerous. I think she's in over her head. She spends too much time there. She's gotten involved. You know what they'll do to her if they even think she might be a cop."

"She's doing a good job. She wants to stay," Nick grunted.

And that had ended that.

Lance knew he would learn nothing new, except by accident, in walking around Bimini either trailing or being trailed by his boss. Lance thought that working Bimini with Nick was like kissing one's sister—not a hell of a lot to it. Nick was of the bulldog school of intelligence: just hanging out and walking around and looking and listening; picking up a scrap here and a scrap there and then laboriously putting it all together, if there was anything to put together. All of the protocols were observed: no entrapment, no working out of sight of one's partner, no time alone with the bad guys. Lance was impatient. He wanted to work alone, to hang loose, to get down to some street-level law enforcement; he wanted to rock-'n'-roll, to walk into a bar full of bad guys, schmooze his way into their confidence, then talk some trash. He'd drop some technical stuff on them such as the fact there was a hole in radar coverage at Jupiter Inlet so big that a doper pilot could come through at twenty-four hundred feet and not be detected, or tell them how to blast through Baker's Haul Over on a go-fast boat with a load of coke disguised by having three or four honeys in Bikinis lolling about topsides. No cop would ever suspect a boat covered with honey was filled with coke.

That was the way to work narcotics intelligence, not this plodding about like Sam Spade. A convention of accountants was more fun than this.

Talking with the two old men the week before the Bimini trip had wired Lance. He had thought of little else. As soon as this trip was over, he and Mike were going out west of Lauderdale to check out the B-26.

It was out of boredom and a mischievous sense of humor that Lance convinced Nick to go to the Boca de Mama. He did not tell his boss that the small seedy bar was the most notorious homosexual nightclub in the Bahamas, a place famous from Great Inagua to Walker's Cay and from San Salvador Island to Cay Sal.

"Here's the way we need to work this, boss," Lance said. "We can't go in there together. I'll go in first, find a seat on the left side, order a beer, and check it out. Give me about ten minutes. Then you come in and sit on the right. We can keep an eye on each other. We'll check out the haps. What'd you think?"

Nick looked at him in the darkness. "I think you're the weirdest person I've ever seen. You're a sick puppy."

Lance leaned closer. "Weird? You think I'm weird? You invented weird."

Nick snorted and tugged at his belt. "You go around looking for Central Cuban Dispatch. You pick up hitchhikers that pull guns on you. And you talk about all your trips to the bathroom. You even keep that book."

"You mean my dump book? I don't have it now. It's in my apartment. Hell, it's important to know how often you go to the bathroom. Do you realize people in Africa go to the bathroom four times as often as Americans? They never have cancer of the colon. We do. We need to take more dumps."

Nick waved his arms in dismissal. "I don't want to hear about that. It's disgusting. And it proves what I just said. You're a weird person."

"What's weird about trying to get to the bottom of the greatest traffic problems in Florida? What's weird about taking criminals off the street? That's my job, boss. That's what you pay me to do. Hell, that's not weird. What you do is weird. You're the weirdest cop I know."

Nick glowered. "I got a wife and two kids and a dog. My family and I go to church on Sunday. I don't chase women, smoke dope, or stay out late unless I'm working. I spend all my time with my family. What's weird about that?"

Lance grinned. That speech, coming from anyone else, would have sounded like sanctimonious tripe. But Nick was sincere. "Well, let's talk about your all-American dog for openers. What's his name? Elmore?"

"Elmer," Nick said defensively.

"Okay. Elmer. Now what the hell kind of name is that for a dog? Elmer. Sounds like a third-grade teacher. And it's got to be the only dog in the Western world that stands on its head to piss. Hell, you got people who work for you, cops that have seen everything from women preachers to dancing bears, who go out to your house to watch your dog piss. Now that's weird."

Nick looked away. "I ran over Elmer. Broke his hip," he said defensively. "When he holds up his leg he falls forward. He can't help standing on his head to pee. He's lucky to be alive." Nick turned and poked Lance in the chest. "What's that got to do with me? Because I like animals, because I didn't have him put down, you think that's weird? It just goes to prove you're weird. So people come to my house to watch Elmer. Well, I've heard about your apartment. People go to your apartment to see your kitchen. When you open the oven door, your radio comes on."

Lance shrugged. "Some wires are crossed somewhere. But if you want to talk weird, okay. What about your church?"

Nick paused. "What about it? I told you I go to church. That's not weird."

"Come on, boss. I know what happened. That preacher started talking about all the criminals and dope fiends on the street, he was looking straight at you. Then he asked you to pray. You stood up and prayed for everything from rain to brotherly love and ended by saying the thing you appreciated most was that you could go to heaven no matter what some idiot in a pulpit said about you. Then you grabbed your wife and walked out."

"So I transferred to another church. Everybody does that."

"How many cops even go to church? That's weird."

"No, it's not. A lot of cops go to church. You just don't know about it." Nick paused. "Why is it that all the things you say are weird, are family things. You're not married. You're almost thirty years old and you're not married. That's weird. Why aren't you married?"

"Let me ask you this. When you go to the bathroom, do you shut the door?"

Nick was bewildered. "Of course I shut the door."

"Well, there you are. If I were married, I would

have to shut the bathroom door and I like to leave it open."

Nick looked around. "What are we doing standing under a tree talking about who's weird? We could ask anybody in the sheriff's department who's the weirdest guy in the world, civilians included, and they would all come up with you. Now stop this. We're here to work. Let's do it. It was your idea to go in and take a look around. I'll follow you in ten minutes. Move."

"I still think you're weird." Lance held up his hand and backed away. "I'm gone. I'm working. Later."

Nick grabbed his elbow. "We better get something in there," he said.

"Don't worry, boss. This is the mother lode," Lance said. He strode from under the canopy, walking as if he were the sole owner of the universe, knowing if he stayed with Nick another minute he would break out laughing. When Nick discovered what the Boca de Mama was, he would be ready to go home. Then Lance could get back into big-time law enforcement.

Lance walked a few yards, paused briefly under the lighted sign so Nick could see him, and reached for the heavy door. The handle was the grab rail from the companionway of a wrecked yacht. The door was made from vertical strips of weathered, sun-bleached planks that looked as if they had washed ashore in a storm a dozen years ago.

Inside, the only light was behind the bar, a stained and darkened cargo container that had been sawed off to hide a beer cooler, and a box containing a half-dozen bottles of liquor. Four stools lined the front of the bar. A big portable radio, the sort teenagers would call a "ghetto blaster," sat atop a nearby shelf. It was tuned to WIOD in Miami, a station given to frequent playing of the Pachabel Canon in D. A wire mesh protected the radio from flying beer bottles.

The bartender was a large Jamaican who wore gold earrings and a white puff-sleeved shirt with the front unbuttoned to his waist. He sat on a high stool behind the bar gazing benevolently over the patrons or examining his cuticles. He was examining his cuticles when Lance walked in.

To the right, along the wall, were four small booths. Short ragged curtains meant to give the occupants a measure of privacy hung limply from a fishing line stretched across the top edge of each booth.

Lance turned to the left, toward one of the half-dozen small tables made from hatch covers nailed to crossed two-by-fours.

The middle of the floor was open. The small space was for dancing and fighting.

The Boca de Mama was packed. Most of the occupants were black. But one group—from their attire they were the crew of the yacht anchored offshore in the mouth of the cut—sat at the table closest to the door. Near them, wide-eyed and quiet, were two tables of tourists. The only other whites in the room were the two big men at the bar. They were sitting facing the customers, elbows on the bar. They were handsome muscular men with short-cropped hair and wary eyes—the Snake Eaters.

The Snake Eater with the white glove glanced at Lance. His eyes narrowed for a moment and then he remembered where they had met. He relaxed.

Lance waved toward the big Jamaican, who slid

down from his stool and minced across the floor. He stopped at Lance's table, put a hand to his hip, and smiled. "Love that shirt," he said.

Lance looked down. He was wearing a red T-shirt upon which was written in bold white letters, "Nuke a Gay Whale for Christ." He laughed. "Bring me a Red Stripe."

"Sure." The Jamaican dragged out the word so that it sounded as if he were saying "shew-uh."

"You're sweet," Lance said.

"Don't you know it," the big Jamaican said, turning back toward the bar. He brought Lance the icy Red Stripe and asked, "Anything else? We have a few munchies, if you're hungry."

Lance held up the Red Stripe. "This is fine."

The Jamaican minced back to his stool and resumed the study of his cuticles.

It was exactly ten minutes later that Nick hesitantly opened the door and looked around. Nick was dressed in cowboy boots, blue jeans, a wide leather belt with a big buckle—his was a curved gold alligator—and a sport shirt. He walked toward the only empty booth, pushed aside the curtain, and sat down.

Lance looked around the bar, watching the faces of the patrons. The Snake Eaters were staring at Nick and whispering intently to each other.

Nick was talking to the big Jamaican bartender and did not know the interest he was generating.

Lance tensed. Did the Snake Eaters know Nick was a cop?

But after a moment it was clear the two men were having a different sort of discussion. The Snake Eater with the white glove won. He was staring across the room at Nick. And he was smiling the sort of smile that telegraphed his intentions. Lance almost laughed aloud. Then he realized he had to warn his boss. God knows what would happen if the Snake Eater hit on Nick. He tried to catch Nick's eye. But the bartender had returned with Nick's beer and was leaning over the table. As the bartender swished back to the bar Nick's eyes followed him, first in surprise, then in disgust. And as he looked around the bar and caught Lance's eye, the look clearly changed to one of anger. He still was not aware of the Snake Eater's interest. The Snake Eater was standing up.

Lance sighed, picked up his beer, and then, with a big smile, sauntered across the bar.

This was going to be interesting.

"Hi, guy," he said to Nick. "Can I buy you a tequila sunrise?" He sat down, forcing Nick to slide toward the corner. He noticed that the Snake Eater had paused, giving him a few seconds to undo the thinking of a lifetime.

Nick rubbed his hand across his mouth and muttered, "Cunningham, this is a faggot joint. I'm gonna kick your—"

"Boss, we got a problem. Let's dance."

Nick jerked back. He thought Lance had taken leave of his senses.

Lance stood up and leaned over the table. His voice was fast and intense. "One of those Snake Eater guys is putting the eye on you. He's about to come over here. If we can't convince them we belong here, we're in deep shit."

Nick lowered his eyebrows in anger.

Lance reached toward Nick just as one of the Snake Eaters stood up. "This is serious, goddammit.

I don't have time to explain. Just go with me or we'll both be shark bait."

He grabbed Nick's hand, pulled him from the booth, and then, while the short lawman was trying to regain his balance, pulled him close. His left hand seized Nick's right hand and he spun quickly to his right, twirling, keeping Nick off balance as he moved across the small dance floor.

Nick pulled his right hand away from Lance, cocked his fist, and drew back.

"Keep dancing," Lance said. "We're not out of this yet." He seized Nick's cocked fist and drew him close, twirling, then tilting his head back and laughing as if Nick had said something terribly funny.

Nick pulled his hand free and angrily jabbed Lance sharply under the ribs.

Lance winced in pain. "What the hell's the matter with you? You want to lead?"

"Cunningham, I'm putting you back in uniform. You're gonna to be on the midnight shift patrolling the garbage dump. You crazy son of a bitch. You're not just weird. You're a pervert."

Again Lance threw back his head and laughed. He pulled Nick close and said, "Those two guys work for Casey. You said so yourself. We have a chance to socialize with two of Casey's top people. We got to take advantage of it. Boss, I'm serious as a heart attack. We got to do this."

Nick grunted and pulled away from Lance. He was torn between his sense of duty and his dislike of homosexuals. He glanced furtively around the darkened bar. "Anybody recognize me, I'm ruined," he growled. "Ruined. I can't say I'm working because we don't work the Bahamas. How did I get in a Bahamian fag bar? Dancing. Ruined." He tried to pull his right hand loose from Lance's grip. "I'm gonna lead," he said.

But Lance tightened his grip and again twirled Nick, causing the smaller cop to seize his shoulder to avoid being thrown off balance. "I'm a better dancer. I'll lead," Lance said. He smiled and pulled Nick closer. "Relax, boss. It's all in the line of duty."

"You son of a bitch."

When the music ended, Lance draped his arm over Nick's shoulder and walked toward the booth. Nick shrugged his arm off and, unsmiling, walked away. As he slid into the booth, Lance sat next to him and moved closer.

Nick glared at him in anger. Enough was enough. "Cunningham . . ."

Lance put his arm on Nick's shoulder and smiled. "Boss, those two guys are still watching us. One of them will be here any minute. You got to make this believable. If we ain't faggots, we may be cops. Why else would we be here?"

"I'm wondering that myself," Nick sighed. He should have known better than to come to Bimini with a wacker like Lance. Then Lance put his hand on Nick's leg.

"He's coming over," Lance said. "Make this look good. If you don't, we're dead."

Lance looked up as the Snake Eater with the white leather glove materialized by the booth and glanced down with a half-smile.

"We met a few days ago," he said, glancing at Lance then staring at Nick. It was clear he was interested in the short cop with the golden mustache.

Lance paused, wrinkled his brow, then nodded. "I remember."

"Who's your friend?"

Nick looked up, grinned weakly, and said, "My name's Nick." He and Lance had agreed they would use their real names, their first names. In the smuggling business no one ever asked for last names. It was considered bad manners.

Nick glanced at Lance then back up to the Snake Eater. "Who're you?"

The Snake Eater shrugged. "I'm like a lot of people on Bimini. I don't have a name. Just call me Friend."

Lance ran his hand up and down Nick's leg, making sure the Snake Eater saw. He ignored the low growling noise Nick made. Nick turned up his beer bottle and drained it. He waved the empty toward the big bartender. Playing the role of a faggot was a dry business. He needed fuel.

"You married?" the Snake Eater asked Nick when he saw the ring on Nick's left hand.

Before Nick could answer, Lance snorted and said, "Naaaah. That's camouflage."

Now the rumbling noise coming from Nick was steady. Only the noise of the radio in the background kept the Snake Eater from hearing.

The Snake Eater smiled at Lance. "Would you mind if I asked your friend to dance?"

Nick shook his head. "I'm tired," he muttered.

The bartender slid a cold Red Stripe across the table. Nick lunged for it.

"He's a good dancer," Lance said, patting Nick's leg. He slid out of the booth and held his hand toward Nick as if giving the Snake Eater permission.

Nick looked longingly at his bottle of beer, then managed a half-smile when the Snake Eater reached to help him from the booth. His eyes glittered dangerously as he looked at Lance.

As the little cop stood up, Lance whispered, "Let him lead." He pulled back when, for a second, it appeared Nick might punch him again.

The Snake Eater put his hand in the small of Nick's back and ushered him toward the dance floor. Lance sat down in the booth, closed the curtain, and shook in soundless laughter.

18

"He hasn't spoken to me since we got back from the Bahamas," Lance said. He laughed and turned to Mike Love. "He had a hell of a lot to say that last night on Bimini. I thought he was gonna explode."

Mike's large hands were in the ten-o'clock and two-o'clock position on the steering wheel of his black BMW. His eyes were on the road, roaming ahead studying the thick undergrowth in the bright beam of his headlights, then checking the rearview mirror.

"I can't understand that," Mike said with a tight grin. "What did Fluf have to get so pissed about? All you did was leave him in a bar full of faggots so he could dance with a sweetie."

"That's right," Lance said in mock seriousness. "I told him I sensed a budding romance and my hanging around might interfere. I had his best interests at heart."

Lance laughed and shook his head. "That guy really had the hots for Fluf. Danced with him half the night. Played gropy gropy under the table. Really put the moves on him. And I don't think Fluf got shit for intelligence out of it. Zip. He got groped for nothing."

"Fluf got groped. Damn. I see why he's upset."

"Nah. What really frosted him was when I called him 'honey' and asked if he were going to write an intelligence report about what happened. He threatened to kill me. Said if word ever got out what happened he would break my neck. I said, 'Hey, you're talking to the mighty Houdini.' And he said if Houdini talked, Houdini would be in one place where he could not escape: death."

Mike made a ratchety reluctant noise that was his version of a chuckle.

"Are we about there? Damn, this guy lives in East Jesus," Lance said as he peered down the remote dirt road. "We've been passing white fence for miles." He pointed to a large white gate. "Slow down. I think that's it. Let's check the sign. It's supposed to say High Gate Farm. He said to go in the gate and drive to the hangar." Lance turned to Mike. "This guy's got a hangar for his airplanes. We ain't dealing with no cheap Charlie here."

"This is it," Mike said, deftly wheeling the BMW off the road and stopping at the gate.

"I'll get it," Lance said. He opened the car door, jumped out, pushed the gate wide, and motioned for Mike to enter. He closed the gate and hurried to rejoin Mike. "Dumb ass leaves his gate unlocked," Lance said as he sat down. "Somebody's going to come in and lift his silverware if he's not careful. By the way, don't mention that Bimini business to Fluf. He's pissed at you already about spraying gas on that doper. And for God's sake don't touch him anywhere. I put my hand on his shoulder yesterday and I thought he was going to punch me."

"Look at this place, will you?" Mike said as he drove down a long paved driveway flanked by palm trees, neatly tended grounds, and a half-dozen outbuildings. "Does this mean I can't pinch Fluf on his little ass anymore?"

"Jesus."

"I think we're here." Mike glanced at the clock on the instrument panel, then looked at a sky that was rapidly growing light. "Dawn. We timed it just right." He stopped the BMW near a large hangar, opened the car door, and slowly unfolded his six feet four inches. He held his right hand atop the open door as he looked around. He was on a large cattle ranch located at the edge of the Everglades in western Broward County. Everywhere he looked, it was obvious someone had spent a lot of money.

"Did you tell those guys I wasn't dropping any bombs?" Mike asked as he looked around.

"Yeah, I told 'em you would use the cannon but you weren't going to do any thirty-seconds-over-Bimini stuff."

"What'd they say?"

"Ummm. Disappointed. But if they can't get *boom-boom*, they'll settle for *bang-bang*. Teaches them humility."

To Lance's left, limned in a soft glow and stretching for an estimated nine thousand feet, was a sodded, neatly mowed runway. Long enough, wide enough, and hard enough to handle jets. Judging by the number of thirty-six-inch drain pipes opening into a deep ditch about one hundred yards on either side of the runway, the surface was hard and dry year round.

Behind the hangar dimly seen through a grove of oaks was a two-story white house. Mike, who had made almost a half-million dollars through real-estate deals, estimated the house was at least eight thousand square feet.

"And this is just one of that old guy's homes. He told me he came out here maybe two or three times a year," Lance said. "I think we are dealing with the big-bucks boys."

At the sound of an engine, both men turned. A new red Ford pickup truck appeared from behind the hangar. "This is your deal from here on," Lance said. "Talk airplane talk to this guy."

Mike put on his military-style sunglasses. His bearded face was impassive.

A wiry sun-bronzed man with a leathery face stepped from the red pickup. He wore jeans and cowboy boots. Mike figured he was the ranch foreman. The cowboy nodded but made no effort to shake hands. He looked at the two men for a moment and then he spoke. His voice was firm and confident. "You're right on time. I was told you would be."

Mike moved his head in an almost imperceptible nod. He waited.

"What you want is down at the end of the runway. Follow me," he said.

"We were told to come to the hangar," Mike said, looking at the huge building to his right.

"That's where the old man keeps his jet when he flies out here. We've built something special for you. Follow me," the cowboy repeated.

He looked over his shoulder. "Park inside when we get there. Just pull off to the side."

Mike and Lance crawled back inside the BMW and followed the pickup down the edge of the runway. The BMW was five years old but was as immaculate as if it had just been driven off the showroom floor. Mike stayed far enough behind the pickup to avoid any sticks or rocks that might be kicked up by the truck's wheels. He realized after a few hundred yards that his fears were foolish. The runway was hard, smooth, and utterly devoid of foreign objects. Mike nodded in professional appreciation. These people knew their business.

About fifty yards off the south end of the runway, sitting at an angle, was a revetment, an arched reinforced-concrete revetment with bushes and trees growing atop it. Inside, bathed in the hot steamy morning air was a B-26. The aircraft was painted solid black. And the paint was covered with so many coats of varnish that the surface appeared a foot deep.

"Son of a bitch," Mike whispered as he stopped near the port wing of the World War II bomber. He knew that from the air, the B-26 was invisible. It was hidden by the revetment which, in turn, was hidden by the trees atop it. The revetment was so broad and the soil atop it so deep that Mike doubted if even the infrared detection equipment aboard Customs aircraft could detect the presence of the B-26.

Mike opened the car door and stared up at the B-26 in awe as he reveled in the beauty and power of the old war bird.

Lance wandered across the revetment to look at a smaller single-engine aircraft. The cowboy, who had parked the pickup truck outside the revetment, watched Mike.

The Customs pilot walked toward the aircraft. He wanted to see if the B-26 was as immaculate at close range as it appeared to be from off the end of the wing. The front of the large radial engines appeared new. No streaks of oil on the nacelles. Mike wiped the flat of his palm under the left nacelle, then looked at his hand. Nothing. Not a drop, not a smear of grease. He looked at the cement hardstand under the aircraft. No stains from oil or hydraulic fluid. The nose landing gear and the two powerful legs of the main landing gear were spotless.

Mike turned toward the cowboy. Before he could speak, the wiry man sauntered toward him, a half-smile on his face, and said, "The old man keeps his equipment in good order."

"Damn sure does," Mike said.

The cowboy pointed at the awesome snout of a gun barrel protruding from under the nose of the B-26. "Except for the gun, there's nothing I can tell you about this aircraft that you don't know."

Mike glanced at the cowboy. He had said "aircraft," a word pilots use. People who don't fly usually say "plane" or "airplane."

The cowboy handed Mike a small card on which was written a series of numbers. "These are freqs for the old man's private radios. They're secure. Built-in scramblers."

Mike studied the cowboy. He had said "freqs" rather than "frequencies," again a term used by pilots. And he used the word "secure" to describe radios, a term that meant conversations could not be monitored. This guy was more than a cowboy.

The wiry man in jeans did not appear to notice Mike's scrutiny. "I understand you brought several radios you want to install. Two bays on the lower center panel are ready. All you have to do is slide your equipment in."

Mike nodded. In the rear of the BMW were two

radios, one preset to the ten secret tactical UHF freqs used by Customs; the other capable of monitoring military freqs. Both radios were in a locked flight bag and he had no intention of letting a civilian see them. All someone had to do to know the secret frequencies was turn the selection dial until the frequencies were visible in the little window. These guys were turning over an aircraft to him for use against drug smugglers, but he looked on that as a one-way street. If they wanted to provide an aircraft, electronics equipment, and weapons, fine. But he would give up nothing in return. They were getting his pilot skills and that was all.

The cowboy paused. He had decided the tall bearded pilot was not much of a talker. The cowboy nodded at the B-26. "I think you'll find everything aboard in good order."

"How long since this aircraft has been flown?" Mike asked.

"Two months since it's been in the air. But the engines are run up once a week. Two months ago a former B-Twenty-six instructor took it up after the old man rebuilt it." The cowboy pointed to the black snout of the gun barrel. "The boss had to make some CG changes because of the weight of that thirty mike mike. The B-26 pilot took this thing up to test the weapon and check the CG envelope."

The cowboy didn't say center of gravity or thirty millimeter. He said "CG" and "thirty mike mike," military terminology. Mike looked at the cowboy a moment, then asked, "The changes call for any special handling techniques?"

"No. The instructor pilot said she flew better than before the mods." He paused. "Of course, this one's got rebuilt R-Twenty-eight-hundred engines that have been tweaked to better than mil specs. It's better than new. The old man's chief mechanic came out yesterday and did a preflight. He said she's ready."

Mike said nothing. He would do his own preflight. He walked to the trunk of the BMW, unlocked it, and gently lifted out the bag containing the radios. "We'll be taking off in about thirty minutes. You ever have any cows get on the runway?"

The cowboy grinned. "Through three sets of electric fences? Not a chance. The old man flies some expensive aircraft in here. He's not going to wreck one on a cow."

"You be here when we get back?"

"That chief mechanic I mentioned and three mechanics have moved into one of the guest houses for the duration. When you get back they'll go over every inch of this bird. Next time you come out, she will be in just as good shape as she is right now."

The cowboy held up his hand, anticipating Mike's response. "Don't worry. They won't come down until after you two have driven away. I'm the only person here who will see you."

Mike nodded. The fewer people who could identify him, the better.

"Security?"

The cowboy stared at Mike. "I believe if you think about it for a moment, you will agree that the old man has a lot more at stake in this deal than you do. It's his aircraft and it's flying off his ranch. So don't worry about security."

Again the cowboy held up his hand, anticipating Mike's response. "We had video cameras on you two miles down the road. That's why the gate was unlocked when you got there. Armed guards were in the palmettos near the gate. There was no way we could prevent their seeing your car. But no one could ID you."

Mike, somewhat chastened, nodded.

"I'll stand by until you're airborne," the cowboy said. "And I'll be here when you return. You know this area pretty well. There are charts in the cockpit if you need them. The most remote part of the ranch is six miles northwest on a compass heading of three two eight. We moved the livestock out of there so you can practice using the cannon. I'll be monitoring the radio if you have a problem. The weather looks good. But if it closes in, we have a low freq NDB on the runway. I'll turn it on at your request. The freq is placarded in the cockpit. Use procedure turns if you make an IFR approach. You know the drill."

Mike nodded, mentally repeating the instructions. He could think of nothing else. He turned. "Lance, let's go."

Lance sauntered across the hardstand. He nodded toward the cowboy, then looked at Mike and with his thumb jabbed over his shoulder toward a Cessna 210 in the corner. "You won't believe the electronics in that thing," he said. "FLIR, HF radio, dual ADFs; he's even got gyro-stabilized binoculars. You could get on a perch at five grand where nobody on the ground could hear you and use those binoculars to watch two gnats humping on a sandbar. I bet you could even see pimples on their asses."

Lance turned and looked over his shoulder. "And I'll bet it's got long-range tanks."

"You're right," the cowboy said. "Wet wings. Ten hours' endurance at low cruise. It also has inertial nav with a data link to those binoculars. You can attach a camera to the binocs, take pictures, and get both lat-long coordinates and real time printed on the picture."

"Uptown, man. Uptown," Lance said.

"You've got a single-engine ticket, twelve hundred and four hours, and you're checked out in the two ten. I believe you have seventy-eight hours in the aircraft." The cowboy grinned. "Maybe you'll get a chance to fly it. I don't think the old man would mind. Assuming, of course, you used it in a professional capacity."

Lance's little-boy face hardened and his eyes grew flat. Even most of his fellow narcs did not know he had a pilot's license. It was a skill he kept in reserve, believing that one day while working undercover it might get him out of a tight spot. This guy knew too much.

Without speaking he wheeled and followed Mike.

The cowboy smiled.

Mike walked under the B-26 and opened the hatch on the belly. He reached up and stowed the two radios. "Go on up and sit in the right seat. I'll do the walk around," he said to Lance.

Lance grunted. "I'll keep an eye on that bozo," he said, nodding toward the cowboy. He climbed up the small ladder.

Mike began a slow methodical preflight that lasted ten minutes. Satisfied, he climbed aboard, locked the hatch, performed the contortions necessary to get his long frame across the landing-gear spars, and then angled his way up into the narrow companionway that led into the cockpit. He sat in the left seat, hooked the seat belt, and pulled it tight.

A half-smile of anticipation creased his face at the odors permeating the cockpit; a combination of leather, gas, oil, and hydraulic fluid that came together in the unique odor of a war bird. It was, like the smell of a freshly bathed baby or a freshly baked apple pie, a smell that instilled warmth, comfort, and deep contentment.

Mike went through the lengthy checklist. During World War II when army air corps pilots were being trained in Tampa on the B-26, the aircraft were crashing with such regularity into the water off the end of the runway that the unofficial motto of the training squadron was, "One a Day in Tampa Bay." But those pilots were green kids of nineteen and twenty with only fifty or sixty flying hours. They were not ready for a high-performance aircraft like the B-26.

Mike Love had seven thousand hours of flying time, including hundreds of hours on big twins and the Citation jet used for long-range interdiction flights. He had more than nine hundred hours in the B-26 that had been flown by Customs until about two months earlier when the regional director ordered that it be sold. Mike could fly this short-winged, headstrong bitch by himself and he could take her to the outer edges of the performance envelope and show her how to do things she had never done before.

As he performed the cockpit check, he paid special attention to the red armament panel to his left. To arm the gatling gun he had to flip two switches. Red lights would indicate when the gun was ready. To fire it, he would use his right thumb to flip the cover off a button atop the right horn of the yoke. Pressing that button would release Armageddon on a target. The big depleted uranium bullets spit from the mouth of the cannon were the size of bananas. They would demolish and set afire whatever they hit.

"You ready?" Mike asked Lance.

"Kick the tire and light the fire. Let's go do it."

Mike pulled the shoulder straps from the inertia reel and hooked them into the seat-belt buckle in his lap.

He looked out the left window. The cowboy was standing there patiently, holding a portable fire extinguisher.

Mike nodded and began ignition sequence. The cowboy twirled a raised forefinger as the giant three-bladed prop began jerking through its early revolutions. The engine sputtered and spit. The blades whirred faster, winding up. Then, in an explosion of white smoke and a seismic rumble that caused Lance's eyes to widen, the engine caught and began a steadily rising thunder. The propeller blades went from jerky revolutions to a whirling blur.

Mike checked the oil pressure. Good. He retarded the throttle slightly and again checked the oil pressure. The engine was as smooth as that of a sewing machine—a hundred times louder and more powerful but just as smooth.

He stretched and looked out the right window. Lance leaned back in the seat to give him a better view. The cowboy had moved into position in front of the right engine.

A moment later the twin Pratt & Whitney radials were emitting a sound of raw unbridled power. They thundered with the sound of more than four thousand horses. Mike scanned the panel. All instruments within tolerances and in the green. He went through the run-up while still under the revetment. He wanted to minimize exposure of the aircraft to prying eyes.

As he ran the engines up, testing the magnetos and the variable pitch propellers, the screaming power of the engines rose and fell, a crescendo that echoed and flattened out and reechoed across the giant cattle farm. A half-mile away, in a guest house, four men in immaculate white coveralls listened intently. There was no popping or skipping that would indicate one of the magnetos was not performing properly. And the surging sound from the propellers, which was heard twice, indicated the pitch controls were working. The oil that controlled the pitch of the blades was flowing smoothly. The older man, obviously the leader, nodded in satisfaction and hoped the pilot, whoever he was, would treat the B-26's engines with respect.

Mike was ready. His eyes roamed across the panel checking and re-checking the instruments. His long lean fingers pressed one button, turned another, adjusted a third, and patted another in confirmation. Everything was as it should be.

He looked out the window, checked for clearance off the short wings, and slowly advanced the throttles. The cowboy waited at the opening of the revetment, earphones clamped over his head. He stood at attention and snapped off a quick Annapolis-correct salute.

The B-26 began inching its way across the hardstand, lurching in its stiff-legged fashion.

As it arrived at the edge of the revetment, Mike braked to a stop. He slowly pushed the throttles forward. The B-26 trembled and shook like a leaf in a hurricane as she tried to overcome the brakes. Mike pressed harder on the brakes, took a quick look at the oil pressure, checked the stability of the rpm's, then looked up, eyes somehow drawn to the lean figure of the cowboy.

The cowboy was twirling a vertical forefinger, indicating the engines were not yet at full power, that Mike should wait. Mike glanced at the tachometer. The guy was right. Then, just as the tach showed the engines had reached maximum rpm's and stabilized, the cowboy dropped to a knee and pointed a straightened arm down the runway.

Mike snorted in amazement. The guy was an ex-navy pilot. He was using the signal given aboard carriers to launch aircraft. Mike was working with top-notch professionals, people who knew as much as he did about aircraft, people who left nothing to chance. He smiled his tight smile. This was better than Customs.

He released the brakes. The B-26 lurched out of the revetment. A light tap on the right brake steered her onto the runway until she was tracking straight and true, gathering speed, anxious to become airborne.

Rudder control came in. Speed continued to build. Then, as a pilot must do with a heavy, short-winged aircraft, Mike yanked hard on the yoke to break contact with the ground. The B-26 leapt into the hazy air.

19

"Describe him again. One more time," Darrell Casey said. He and Darby DuPree were sitting on a teak bench near the edge of the swimming pool behind his house. The Snake Eaters stood a few feet away. They occasionally glanced toward the gator pit. It fascinated them.

The Snake Eater without the white glove spoke. "He was about five foot six. Hundred and sixty. Blond hair. Blond mustache. Tanned. Late thirties. Good body, wide shoulders with a bit of a stomach. Muscular. Quiet."

Casey held up his hand and wiggled his fingers in encouragement, as if trying to pull more information from the Snake Eater. "His manner? How did he carry himself? Tell me what you *thought* about him."

The Snake Eater paused. "He had a lot of presence. In the military, we called it command presence. He is used to having people follow orders. And his eyes told me he is no pushover. He can be tough if he has to be."

Darrell's eyes were blazing in their intensity. He stood up, rubbed his right leg, turned toward Darby, leaned over, and said, "It's him. I know it. The little son of a bitch. How did he snap to me?"

"It's who? What are you talking about?" Darby said in her soft voice. She sat with one longer-than-long sun-tanned leg stretched forward. The other she had pulled up until her heel was jammed into her hip. Her chin rested upon her knee. The sun shone on her blue-black hair. She had never looked more elfin, more remote, more beautiful. But her stomach was tied in a tight knot of anxiety.

"It's a cop. His name is Nick Brown." Darrell's voice was distant, almost detached. "We go back a long time. A long time." He rubbed his leg. His eyes had a thousand-yard stare and he did not notice the quick flash of fear that swept across Darby's green eyes. But the Snake Eater in the white glove noticed. His tanned brow wrinkled and he resolved to keep a close eye on Darrell's little honey.

The second Snake Eater turned to him and with a half-smile said, "A cop. You spent all evening dancing with a cop."

The Snake Eater with the white glove glowered but said nothing.

Darrell turned toward him in disbelief. "You *danced* with Nick Brown?" Darrell laughed in amazement. "You *danced* with him?" Darrell threw up his arms in dismay. "I send you to Bimini to find out who's fucking with me and you wind up *dancing* with the son of a bitch behind it all? I don't believe this."

The Snake Eater closed his lips tightly. His eyes glinted. He was not used to being talked to in such a fashion. And he didn't like it coming from a man he considered a half-wimp, even if the guy did pay his salary.

"Was this at the Boca de Mama?"

The Snake Eater nodded.

Casey slammed his fist into his palm. "He's onto us. He knows something. That's why he was there. Damn. I thought something was sour on Bimini. But I had no idea that a Lauderdale cop was the problem."

Casey looked up at the Snake Eater. "Was he by himself?"

The Snake Eaters looked at each other. The one with the white glove spoke. "He came in by himself. Some guy who came in later danced with him once, but then left. He's in the Business. I've seen him on Bimini."

"Are you sure they weren't together?"

"The other guy left by himself. The little guy, Nick Brown you call him, stayed for hours."

Casey looked across the lawn again, musing. "Another cop wouldn't have left him there alone." He shook his head in disbelief. "A Fort Lauderdale narc working alone on Bimini? Incredible." He paused and then added, almost to himself, "But he's worked in the Caribbean before. That's how I first met the little bastard."

Casey shook his head and uttered a reluctant laugh, a laugh almost of admiration. "Nick Brown. Goddamn. It's just like him." Then his voice turned hard. "He's not doing to me what he once did. I won't give him the chance."

The Snake Eaters looked at each other in bewilderment. For a few moments Casey was quiet. Then he looked up again at the Snake Eaters. "I know Nick Brown. He would not be in the Boca de Mama unless he had some hard information. He is onto you guys. Knew you worked for me. Was hustling you." Casey snorted in derision. "You thought you were hustling him and all the time he was hustling you. What did you tell him? Did he ask you anything about me, about my work, about Bimini?"

The Snake Eater shrugged. "He tried to. It came up a couple of times. But I don't recall that we talked business."

"Doesn't matter. He knows you. Knows who you are. Knows you work for me. Damn. And I'm still trying to set up that load out of Bimini. I can't afford to have that little bastard on my tail."

The Snake Eater with the white glove shrugged in bewilderment. "He's just a local cop, a little guy. One guy. What can he do?"

Casey did not answer. He stared at the Snake Eater without seeing him. Then he spoke. And he was decisive. "This has to be stopped before it gets out of hand. Too much is at stake. And I'm not going to have that little piss-ant narc screwing around with me again. I've tried to do my business and not give him anything to chase me with. Now he's close. And I can't have that. I can't have that."

Darby bit her lip and looked at the ground. She knew what was coming. And she was frightened.

Casey jabbed his forefinger toward the Snake Eater who wore the white glove. "Go get Steinhorst and tell him to come see me. I've got a job for him. One he'll love to do. One that will take a little finesse." Casey paused, then smiled up at the Snake Eater. "I want him to kill a cop."

20

Darrell Casey remembered every second, every horrible, agonizing, fearful second of that night, even though fifteen years had passed.

After making several hundred thousand dollars smuggling marijuana through Bimini, he had come to the same decision made by many smugglers: to make his buy farther down the pipeline, to pay less money for the marijuana on the front end in the hope of making more profit on the back end. He chartered a Cessna 310 and was flying to Jamaica to meet a new source. He was carrying a briefcase containing a hundred thousand dollars in front money.

His pilot broke through a low cloud layer five miles off the Jamaican coast at 1:42 A.M. A long row of flares stretched like a white knife through the blackness of the night.

"There's the field. Put it down," Casey ordered.

What he did not know was that about dusk the previous afternoon a bulldozer driver had ripped out more than six hundred yards of fence along the edge of an alligator farm just north of the Blue Mountains. Torches were placed every five yards along the fence line to contain the alligators until morning.

What Casey saw was not his landing site, but rather the torches. The pilot was puzzled. According to his watch, they should not be landing for another ten minutes, almost at the edge of Ocho Rios. But maybe there was a tail wind.

"It looks short," he said. "I'll buzz the field before we land."

But Casey was edgy after the four-hour flight from Fort Lauderdale. This was his first trip to Jamaica. After he landed and did his business, he had to drive west to Mo Bay, then fly commercial to Miami while the pilot flew the load back to Florida. He wanted to get on with it.

"Never mind the buzzing. Just land," he said.

So the pilot swung left, reduced power, dropped the flaps ten degrees, checked his airspeed, and then lowered the landing gear. "You got a freq we can raise them on?" he asked, eyes never leaving the row of torches. He would land, as Casey told him, just far enough to the right of the torches for his wingtip to clear the flames.

"No radio chatter. It's supposed to be a straight-in approach. And no lights until we're on a short final. We're landing on a farm and the Rasta we're meeting doesn't want the owners to know we're using their land."

The pilot dropped another ten degrees of flaps. He was settling rapidly toward a landing strip he could not see. He reduced power again. He was seconds from touchdown when he turned on the landing lights and received the shock of his life; the horror immobilized him for five dangerous irretrievable seconds.

First he saw eyes—dozens, hundreds of smoldering red embers scattered the length and breadth of the field. In the white glare of the landing lights, he saw the field was covered with what appeared to be giant logs. And then he knew.

He was landing in a field of alligators!

He cursed and pushed the throttles to the fire wall, but it was too late. The aircraft was behind the power curve and continued to settle until the right landing gear sheared off on the back of a twelve-foot alligator. The aircraft slewed violently. The pilot's head slammed through the window to his left, and as the bouncing skidding turn continued, he was almost decapitated by jagged plastic.

The nose gear crumpled on the back of another alligator. Then the right wing folded and aviation fuel spewed from ruptured tanks.

The door by Casey buckled and popped off the hinges as the aircraft skidded to a stop with a screech of twisting metal.

When Darrell Casey regained consciousness a half-hour later, his first awareness was of the pain in his broken knee, a searing pain that sent flames of agony through his leg. He gasped and realized more pain as the sharp intake of breath stirred sharp edges of broken ribs.

Light from the torches flickered in a macabre dance over the broken aircraft.

Then Casey heard sounds in the night, the woofling and grunting of alligators. Their smoldering eyes glowed malevolently.

One of the gators crawled to the edge of the broken wing, lifted its head, and breathed a fetid hiss of anticipation. Casey was nauseated and terrified.

Blood running down the body of the dead pilot filled the cockpit with a sweet odor and caused the bugs and insects drawn by the light of the torches to swarm around the aircraft. Darrell Casey shivered in terror. He could not move. He was in excruciating pain. And a big anxious hissing alligator was trying to crawl over the edge of the broken wing and reach him.

It was dawn when Nick Brown saw the crashed Cessna 310. Brown, then a young narcotics officer for the Broward County Sheriff's Office, was one of a dozen local officers from throughout Florida who were assisting agents of the Drug Enforcement Administration on a special enforcement effort in Jamaica. The special effort was at the invitation of Jamaican officials and designed to show local cops how to interdict American smugglers.

Nick Brown looked at the tail number on the aircraft and shook his head in disgust. All night he had been at a clandestine airport ten miles away waiting on this aircraft. Another fouled-up dope deal.

He looked over his shoulder. Two DEA agents and a senior Jamaican cop were a few miles behind. He grabbed a torch, poked it toward the nearest alligator, and sent it scurrying away. Nick walked toward the aircraft.

The smell of gasoline caused him to stop. He jabbed at several more gators, planted the torch in the soft ground, then leapt quickly atop the broken wing and peered through the gaping hole where the door had been. His nose crinkled in disgust at the odors inside the aircraft.

The pilot, who had been his informant, was dead. But here was the aircraft, two people on board, and a briefcase that was supposed to contain money. Nick looked at the man in the right seat, a man whose face was twisted in pain, and said, "Looks like you up to your ass in alligators."

"Get the fucking gators away." Casey's voice came in short intense sentences. "They've been here all night. God, the pain. I need a doctor."

"Gators won't bother you. They got too much professional respect," Nick said in his slow, calm, unhurried voice. "I'll get you a doctor." He looked in the rear of the aircraft, saw the briefcase, plucked it out, and opened it. He whistled softly.

"You crashed before you got the load," he said. It was a statement, not a question.

"What load? What are you talking about? You a cop?"

"Yeah, I'm a police officer. Nick Brown. Broward SO."

"What the fuck is a Broward County cop doing in Jamaica?"

"Assisting DEA and the locals."

Casey rolled his head and sighed. "Get me a doctor. I'm bad hurt."

"Hold on. Help's coming."

Two DEA agents and the Jamaican cop were at the edge of the field.

"Hey, Brown, how'd you get out there?" one of the agents asked.

"Pick up a torch and walk through."

Sweat was pouring from the faces of the three men as they came near the aircraft. Nick looked up in sudden alarm.

"Don't bring the torches to the aircraft. Can't you smell the gasoline? It's all over the place. You trying to blow us up?"

"What's in the briefcase?" said the embarrassed young agent.

Nick passed him the expensive leather briefcase. The agent took it, looked at Casey, and smiled. "Tough luck, asshole," he said.

Nick squeezed his lips together and looked away. DEA agents learned early.

"This all of it?" the agent asked Nick.

Nick almost slugged the agent. When he spoke, his voice quivered in anger. "I've been here about three minutes. Where do you think I might have put the rest of the money? Up the backside of one of those gators? Of course, that's all of it. And don't you ever ask me that sort of question again unless you plan on arresting me. Because if you do, I'll tear your pointy head off. You got that, sonny?"

The agent waved his hand in dismissal. "Don't get huffy, Brown. What I meant was, is the aircraft clean?"

Nick was not mollified. "Search it. But Casey still has the money. That should tell you he never got to the dope."

"Pilot looks dead."

Nick did not answer. You didn't have to be a federal agent to realize that some guy with his head attached to his body by only a few threads of skin was dead.

"I need a doctor. Get me a doctor," Casey groaned.

The four lawmen looked up as two men in a nearby pickup truck pretended to ignore the crashed aircraft. Neither the driver nor the man in the rear throwing out food to the alligators looked at them. In this part of Jamaica, one did not inquire about crashed aircraft surrounded by hard-looking men;

not even if one of the men were wearing the uniform of a Jamaican police officer.

The sun had already burned away the thin overcast and the heat was beginning to blast across the
land.

One of the DEA agents motioned for Nick to
follow him. The two moved away a few steps, keeping a wary eye on the gators, even though they were
now scurrying toward the pickup truck.

"What can we charge this guy with?" the DEA
agent asked, tilting his head toward Darrell Casey.

"If Customs was here, you could charge him with
violating U.S. currency laws for hauling that much
money out of the country and not declaring it. The
locals can get him on some Mickey Mouse stuff for
illegal entry. But you don't have enough overt acts
to book him on dope or conspiracy charges. And
the snitch is dead."

The agent looked at Casey. He tapped his fingers
angrily on the briefcase. He did not approve of
Nick's answer.

"You don't really have anything on him. You're
going to have to let him go," Nick said.

The agent glared at Nick, then motioned to the
other agent and the Jamaican. "Excuse us a minute," he said to Nick. The three men moved away.

"This guy needs a doctor," Nick said.

The DEA agents did not respond. They clustered
with their backs to Nick and talked quietly. After a
moment they nodded in agreement, then turned
toward Nick.

"We'll take over. You go on back to the hotel,"
one of the agents said.

Nick looked at the Jamaican cop. The Jamaican
averted his eyes. DEA agents could offer him equip-

ment and uniforms, even money for special enforcement efforts. The little cop from Fort Lauderdale could offer him nothing.

Nick shrugged. "It's okay with me."

"Doctor, I hurt," Casey groaned. He reached toward the agents in supplication.

One of the agents reached into his jacket, pulled out a small handgun, and slapped it into Casey's outstretched hand. Casey looked at the weapon in bewilderment. He dropped it. His head lolled against the seat and perspiration rolled down his face. His eyes were dull with pain. "I need a doctor," he said.

"You need shit," the young DEA agent said. "You're under arrest."

"For what?"

"Possession of a firearm. We're all witnesses. The Jamaicans are gonna put your ass under the jailhouse for bringing a weapon into their country. They don't like weapons down here."

The DEA agent reached for Casey's shoulder and tried to pull him from the aircraft. Casey moaned in pain.

"Get out of the aircraft and assume the position," the agent said.

"Can't move. Broken knee. Busted ribs. Get doctor."

Bugs swarmed about Casey's face, but he was too weak to swat them away.

The agent kicked Casey's bloody leg.

Casey gasped and passed out.

"Guess he is hurt. He wasn't joking," the agent said with a grin.

"You guys are assholes," Nick Brown said calmly.

The young agent turned toward Nick, the smile

slowly leaving his face. He put his hands on his hips. "Brown, this is a federal matter. I told you to go back to the hotel. We are in charge."

"I'm staying until this guy is in an ambulance."

Nick was there an hour later when ambulance attendants, wrinkling their faces in distaste, slowly removed Casey and then the pilot from the aircraft.

Casey, even in his pain, was not worried about jail. He knew that once his lawyer arrived, all would be well. But he knew that he would walk with a limp the remainder of his life. And he knew he would be terrified of alligators for as long as he lived. He hated the idea of being a cripple and of being afraid. He looked up from the stretcher into the eyes of Nick Brown. For a moment his eyes burned as red and bright as those of the alligators during the previous night of hell. This was the guy who had found him, who had brought in the other cops, including the one who had put the gun in his hand and then kicked his leg.

"You fat fuck. One day I'm gonna get you," Casey said. And then he passed out.

He never knew that it was Nick Brown, who, by threatening to go public and reveal how the DEA had planted a pistol on Casey, had been responsible for his being released from Jamaican custody. He thought his lawyer had done it. And the lawyer, being a lawyer, never told him otherwise.

Casey never returned to Jamaica. From that point forward, his smuggling efforts were concentrated in Bimini. And he never forgave Nick Brown.

21

The call came at 6 A.M. only minutes after Nick arrived in his office. He stopped at the door and looked at the broken window across the room. It had been weeks since the window was shot out and the building owner still had not placed a sheet of plywood over the hole. He knew it would do no good to complain. The owner would only go to the sheriff, who would tell Nick to be patient. Nick sighed and made a mental note to buy the plywood and install it himself. As he was walking toward his desk, the telephone rang. He had two lines: one came through the secretary, the other was his straight line. It was the straight line that was ringing.

The caller, who had an accent, said he wanted to talk to the head of the narcotics squad, that he had "some very important information about Mr. Darrell Casey."

"What kind of information?" Nick said in his laconic voice. He did not ask who was calling. Asking the name of a caller, who may be a potential informant, can frighten him away. Maybe this was the call he was expecting. But he had to make sure.

"About his . . . import business."

Nick decided to push hard. See what the caller would give up. See if he would stay on the line. "If you're talking about his smuggling, that ain't exactly news. Give me something that tells me you know what you're talking about."

"I can tell you about a big airplane. A C-One-thirty."

This had to be someone close to Darrell Casey. The cocaine-smuggling deal using a C-130 was the biggest and most sensitive operation Casey had ever undertaken.

"I know all about the C-One-thirty. Tell me something I don't know."

During the pause that followed, Nick had the impression the person on the other end was trying hard to curb his impatience, his anger.

"I can tell you about a killing near an airstrip where a load came in not long ago."

"Was it in Broward County?"

"No, but—"

"Why should I care about a homicide that is not in my jurisdiction? You sure you got the right number?"

"It wasn't one killing. It was two. And Casey was involved in it. He lives in your jurisdiction."

"The victims were probably dopers." Nick sounded bored. But he slowly sat down on the edge of his chair.

"Dopers killing dopers is at the bottom of my priority list, right down there with a burglary in a whorehouse. Mister, you're wasting my time. Give me something or get off the phone."

"It was those two kids who disappeared west of here. I can tie Darrell Casey to that deal. I can tell you where their bodies are." The voice paused. "I can tell you where to find what the crabs left." A soft chuckle.

Nick paused. Casey had told Darby that Steinhorst had killed two kids, that he had done it on his own. So chances were that no one else except Steinhorst knew the details. The caller said he knew where the bodies were. The remark about the crabs meant they had been dumped in the water, probably one of the tidal creeks near the campsite.

If the caller knew that much, he had to be the killer.

Then Nick was certain. Steinhorst was on the telephone!

This was the call he had been expecting.

He slowly leaned forward, telephone at his ear, his right hand over his eyes as if to shut out everything but the call: the voice.

"I'm listening."

The voice chuckled, this time in triumph. "I thought that might interest you. I'm reluctant to discuss this on the telephone. We must meet."

"Fine." Nick thought for a few seconds. "You know the Howard Johnson's at Ninety-five and the Alley?"

The motel at the intersection of I-95 and Alligator Alley was used frequently by Nick's agents for undercover deals. The manager had allowed them to install hidden video cameras. Several booths were wired for sound. It would be easy to have undercover officers in the restaurant as backups.

"No. No public places." The voice was adamant. "If I am seen with you, I will be a dead man. People know who you are. We must meet in private. You must come alone."

Now that he knew who was calling, Nick decided

to throw in a little tradecraft, a little smoke and deception. "Look, buddy. I'll meet you wherever you say. But I need a name. Tell me who I'm talking to."

"I cannot do that over the telephone. But when we meet, I will tell you."

"Okay." Nick smiled to himself. "You pick a place."

"We will meet at—"

Nick interrupted. He spoke rapidly. "Somebody just came in my office. I think we got something going on. Look, think about where you want to meet and call me back. Okay?"

Nick hung up before Steinhorst could answer.

Steinhorst slowly hung up the telephone. The glint in his blue eyes was the only indication of anger. They were like ice reflecting sunshine. Cold. A stunning blue. It had been more difficult than he anticipated to get the cop to agree to meet him. The cop was better than he thought. But his planning had worked out well. The cop was satisfied he had something to offer and would meet him. Steinhorst would call again the next morning. The final arrangements would be made.

"You got pretty mouthy with him. You gave away too much," Darrell Casey said.

Steinhorst looked up. Casey stood over him. "I had to. He was about to hang up." Steinhorst stood up from the desk in Casey's study. He looked down at Casey. "It really doesn't matter," he said softly. "He won't be alive long enough to do anything about it."

Casey tilted his head toward the door and made a noise of dismissal. "Finish it as soon as you can," he said.

"I'll call him back tomorrow morning and set up the meet," Steinhorst said. He walked out the door.

As soon as he was gone, Casey opened the lower right-hand drawer of the desk and pulled out a tape recorder. It was attached to the wire leading to the telephone. He placed the recorder atop the desk, and pressed the rewind button.

22

Gunter Steinhorst preferred to use his hands when he killed. But today he would use a pistol. He looked at the Mauser and felt something very close to sentiment. An uncle had carried the weapon in World War II. He shook his head in reluctance and gently placed the heavy blue-black pistol on the shelf near his bed. Too bad it could not be used for this day's work. But he would not use a weapon that could be traced. Steinhorst reached into his coat pocket and pulled out a .22 Beretta, a pistol so small it could be hidden in his big fist.

Steinhorst did not like Jews. But when it came to killing, he admitted that their secret service, the Mossad, was the most effective group of assassins in the world. The Mossad used this same small weapon. Their agents stood close enough to look a man in the eye when they killed him. Steinhorst liked that. He liked close work. It enabled him to smell the victim, to sense his fear, to see the perspiration on his skin and the desperation in his eyes. What Steinhorst had to do today was close work. He wanted to look the little cop in the eye before killing him. The pistol would be perfect, a cheap,

common weapon that afterward would be tossed
into the swamp. And once the cop's body was found,
editorial writers would go into their predictable re-
actions about gun control and Saturday-night specials.

Today's killing was to be clean and neat and
untraceable. Steinhorst was even wearing a tie. No
one who saw him would ever connect him with the
shooting. After the cop was killed, Casey would be
able to relax and get past his paranoia. He would
complete the plans for the big cocaine shipment and
then Steinhorst could get rid of Casey. By using the
Snake Eaters to create terror throughout the Casey
gang, he could take over the most successful group
of smugglers in America.

Steinhorst looked at the heavy watch on his left
wrist. He slipped the little .22 pistol back into his
coat pocket. It was time to go. He wanted to arrive
early at the killing ground.

Lance Cunningham was already there. He arrived
three hours before Nick was to meet the big German. Lance was wearing army fatigue pants, red
leather tennis shoes, a red bandanna around his
head, and a dark-green T-shirt that said, "Peace
Through Superior Firepower." Aviator-style military sunglasses were perched on his nose. He lounged
behind a large oak tree off the dirt road leading
from Alligator Alley to a pumping station south of
Lake Okeechobee. Two steps and he could be in
the clearing that was to be the meeting ground. His
chrome-plated long-barreled .357 Magnum was
strapped to his hip. An M-16 was cradled in his
arms. Not that he would need either. The deck was
stacked against Steinhorst. But he would have them.
Just in case.

It was hot under the trees. Sweat soaked Lance's back, ran down between his buttocks, and caused the army fatigue pants to stick to his legs. He did not know if the perspiration came from the heat or nervous tension. Stacked deck or not, he was nervous about going up against Steinhorst. That guy invented badass.

Lance moved deeper into the shadows as a long black Lincoln pulled slowly into the clearing, circled to the other side, and stopped. Nick Brown didn't drive a Lincoln. It had to be Steinhorst. Lance's eyes widened in approval. The German was using his car in the commission of a felony. That meant it could be seized and pressed into service by the narcotics squad. Lance decided he might want the Lincoln. Not that he liked big cars; it was just that he would enjoy driving the car that had belonged to Steinhorst. There would be a certain sense of poetic justice in that, a daily reminder that the narcs had won a round over the bad guys. Besides, it might help him while looking for Central Cuban Dispatch. Some people were impressed by big cars. You could roll up beside them, crack the window, and ask the location of Central Cuban Dispatch and, who knows, somebody might spill his guts.

Lance watched as Steinhorst slowly unfolded from the Lincoln. The German stood up, looked around, buttoned his coat, and began to pace slowly back and forth along the length of the car, his big feet stirring up clouds of white dust. Lance wondered where the German was carrying his Mauser. It must be in his belt, probably on the front left side, where he could reach inside his coat and grab it.

Lance smiled in self-congratulation as he remembered how he spent three hours Friday night on a B

and E at the German's farm. It had taken two days
of surveillance on Steinhorst before he left the house.
While two narcs followed him to Casey's mansion in
Lauderdale, Lance crawled in a window, found the
German's Mauser, and by the light of a small flash-
light clutched in his teeth, slowly and methodically
pulled the lead projectile from each bullet, dumped
the powder onto a handkerchief, then replaced the
lead and crimped them inside the shells. When the
German pulled the trigger, all he would get was
click, click, click. Then Nick was going to kick him
in the balls and cuff him. Nick said he could do it by
himself. But Lance was backing him up. Just in
case.

Steinhorst was about to be arrested on charges of
attempting to murder a police officer. Neither Nick
nor Lance had any illusions that the German would
finger Casey in return for leniency. At least not as
long as Darrell provided him with high-priced legal
help.

Nick, as usual, had displayed no emotion when
he summoned Lance to his home, asked him to go
for a walk in the woods, and said Casey was going
to try to kill him.

Lance stopped walking and turned to Nick. "Where
did you get that?" he asked in amazement. Then he
knew. "Does she know what she's talking about or
is she just getting dramatic?"

Nick looked up at Lance. "He called me. Twice.
Said he wanted a meeting out on some dirt road off
the Alley."

Nick did not add that, just as Lance suspected,
Darby had called first and said Casey had ordered
the German to kill him.

Lance looked away. Then he changed moods. He slapped his palms together. "Okay, boss, I got a plan." He stared at Nick's crippled dog, Elmer, the one that fell forward on his chest when he tried to lift a leg and urinate. He started to say something, decided against it, then suggested keeping Steinhorst under twenty-four-hour surveillance. When he left his farm, Lance would go in, find his weapon, and neutralize it. Nick did not like the idea of illegally entering a man's home. "We should get a warrant," he said.

Lance was exasperated. "What about security? What about time? It might take three or four days to get a warrant. Word could get out. We don't know that Casey doesn't have people in the courthouse." His voice turned almost imploring. "Boss, I know how you feel. I know you want to go by the rules. And you're right. But a certified killer is looking for you. And you're worried about getting a warrant, about going by the book. For God's sake, boss, the guy wants to kill you."

Nick looked over his shoulder. "Okay, okay, don't talk so loud. I don't want my wife to know about this."

The two men walked in silence for a moment. Elmer foraged ahead, crashing through the undergrowth, not troubling to walk around any bush or shrub that he could walk through.

"You could rent that dog out to clear land," Lance said.

"That's a good dog," Nick said. He still remembered Lance's comments about Elmer.

"Your plan is a good one," Nick said. "We know he will use a pistol. Casey told him to. None of that fingernail stuff."

Lance made a grimace. Nick could have gotten that only from Darby. But he decided to say nothing. "So I'll empty the powder out of the rounds in whatever pistols he has around his house, you wear your vest, and I'll be there as backup."

"I can arrest him by myself."

"I know that. But you know the procedures. You're always talking about going by the rules. Well, you know what the rules are in this situation. You wrote them."

"Okay. But don't interfere. I'll handle it. It's me he wants to kill. So I'll take him down."

"How will he do it?"

Nick stopped and looked up at Lance. "He won't *do* it. If you mean, how will he *try* to do it, listen."

Lance watched Steinhorst walk slowly around the clearing, occasionally waving a big hand in front of his face to chase away mosquitoes. The big German tensed as he heard a car coming down the dirt road. He patted his coat pocket, then leaned over, left hand on the hood of his car, and waited.

Nick drove up, circled halfway around the clearing until his car was pointing the way he came, stopped a few yards before he reached the tree where he knew Lance was hiding, then slowly stepped from the car. He walked forward, swinging his elbows in such an exaggerated version of his wet-rooster walk that Lance knew he was wearing a vest, a bulletproof vest, under his shirt. Good.

After a few steps Nick stopped. He waited for the big German to come to him.

Lance hefted the M-16 and peered through the thick vegetation. Fluf was playing it right. He had stopped just to the left of Lance's position. He was plainly nervous and not doing a good job of hiding it.

Don't worry about it, boss, Lance said to himself. This deal is rigged. Besides, I got you covered.

The big German slowly walked toward Nick, face immobile, cold eyes locked on Nick. He stopped a few feet away and stared down at the cop. Nick came barely to his shoulder.

"Tell me about those kids," Nick said with no preamble.

The German's eyebrows rose a millimeter. The cop was getting right to it. He smiled. "They're dead," he said.

"I figured that. Tell me something new."

"I killed them." The German's voice was so soft Lance barely heard him. The slight smile continued to tug at the German's mouth.

Lance slowly raised the M-16 and pointed it toward the German. He moved his right foot slowly and carefully, testing to make sure he had a firm foundation. He could feel rivulets of sweat in the small of his back and between his buttocks.

Nick's eyebrows rose. If the guy had just admitted to a cop that he was guilty of a multiple homicide, he was about to make his move. He had hoped to have some conversation with the guy first, conversation that would be picked up on the tape recorder in his rear pocket. But none of these deals ever went as they were planned. They took on a life and a movement of their own. Okay, so let it go down. It was going to be funny as hell when the guy pulled his Mauser and heard nothing but *click, click.* Then he would find his big ass flipped over the hood of his car while he was cuffed. Privately Nick was wondering if he could cuff this guy by himself.

"You killed them?"

"Yeah, I killed them. I screwed the girl. She sucked my dick. The last thing she said, just before I punched her in the gut and threw her overboard, was that she wanted her mother. Ever hear anything like that?"

Nick's voice was calm. "How far was it from their campsite?"

"Two hundred meters east. At a sharp bend in the tidal creek. Where mangrove bushes grow out over the water."

"Two hundred meters east," Nick repeated. He wanted to make sure all of this was on the tape recorder. He hoped the thing was working.

"That is correct. But you'll never see the bodies."

Nick ignored the soft malevolent hint. "And you did that on the instruction of Darrell Casey?"

"No, I did it without his knowledge. He was not there." The German stepped closer to Nick.

Lance sighted down the barrel of the M-16. God, it was hot in the undergrowth. He was soaked. He could feel ticks or red bugs or some damn fleet of insects moving around his groin. But he kept his eyes locked on the German. The guy was big as a mountain. Fluf looked like a midget beside him. Lance was uneasy.

"Now it is your turn to talk," the German said. "You will tell me some things I wish to know." He took another step forward. Now he was within arm's reach of Nick.

Nick leaned back and looked up at Steinhorst. "You must think you're a mean son of a bitch," he said. "Or are you just a son of a bitch?"

"I'm mean enough to kill you and hide your body where nothing but alligators will ever find it."

Steinhorst never raised his voice. He could have been talking about the weather were it not for the almost palpable hate in his eyes. "It's come to Jesus time, fat man. And Darrell Casey wants you to know it's coming from him."

"So Casey sent you to kill me?"

Nick hoped again the tape recorder was working. The damn thing was so temperamental.

"Yes, he did. But before you die, we must talk."

The German held up his large hands, turned them around so the backs were facing Nick, then he wiggled his fingers.

"Do you know what these can do to you?"

Nick took a half-step forward. "That's a nice tie." He slowly reached out and ran the tie between his thumb and forefinger. "Feels like silk."

The German was nonplussed. He had told the cop he was going to kill him and the guy wanted to talk about his tie.

"I don't wear silk," he said. He sounded almost defensive.

"Good. I hate blowing my nose on silk." Before Steinhorst could move, Nick blew his nose loudly on the tie. Then he rubbed the mucous discharge on Steinhorst's face.

The German's mouth tightened until it almost disappeared. He stepped back a half-step, dropped into a combat crouch, and reached for his pocket. "You're a dead man," he said, coming up with a pistol so small that nothing but the tip of the barrel was visible. It was rock-steady, pointed straight at Nick's heart.

Even though he was wearing a vest, Nick was not going to take a shot at such close range. "That's no Mauser," he shouted as he fell to the ground, rolling rapidly and reaching for the pistol strapped to his ankle. "That ain't no Mauser."

"Oh, shit," Lance shouted. He jumped forward two steps and pulled the trigger on the M-16, shattering the quiet of the clearing with a staccato blast that almost cut the German in half.

Death came so quickly to Steinhorst that his face still showed anger. But now a film covered his bottomless blue eyes. And the sand around his body was wet with red blood that seeped downward, leaving behind only a dark-brown stain.

For a moment the clearing was silent. Nick raised his head as Lance stepped forward, the smoking barrel of the M-16 held on the body of the German.

"You okay?" Lance asked, eyes still on Steinhorst's body.

Nick slowly stood up. He had been rolling over so fast he could not reach his pistol. He dusted off his pants and shirt, then anxiously reached into his rear pocket, pulled out the tape recorder, and turned it off. He wiped his face, took a deep breath, and in a voice heavy with sarcasm said, "I'm damn glad you took the powder out of his bullets."

Lance leaned over and, with the barrel of the M-16, tried to roll the German's body over. It was too heavy. He prodded the barrel hard in the German's ribs. No reflex. He pushed the barrel hard against the body's skull, just behind the ear, and reached forward with his other hand to remove the tiny .22-caliber pistol from the big fist. He held it by the barrel. Then he stood up. He looked at the pistol in mock amazement. "You're right. This ain't no Mauser."

He put the pistol on the hood of Nick's car. Then, with the M-16 held aloft, he laughed and danced in a circle screaming, "That ain't no Mauser. That ain't no Mauser."

Nick, breathing hard and still shaking, looked at him.

Lance stopped, wiped one arm across his eyes, and still giggling, turned back to Nick. He struck a jaunty pose. *"Jefe,* do not bother thanking me for saving your life. It was nothing. But I will allow you to double my salary."

Nick was flipping buttons on the tape recorder, searching for playback. "Stop screwing around," he said. "Call homicide and tell them to come out here. Bring an ambulance to pick up this hunk of sausage."

As Lance walked toward the door of Nick's car, he looked over his shoulder. He was smiling and his eyes danced. "Hey, *jefe,* for a guy with a big belly, you can move fast when you have to."

"Want to see how fast I can move you back to vice? You can go back to your old habit of sniffing toilet seats."

Lance widened his eyes. His voice was a falsetto of pretended alarm. "Ohhhhhh noooooooooo."

Nick looked up from the tape recorder and shook his head in disgust. "I don't understand these things," he said. He paused. "Lance."

Lance leaned around the open car door, the radio microphone in his hand.

"Thanks."

"Hey. Don't mention it. Besides, he wouldn't have touched you. You were rolling too fast." Lance turned back toward the radio. He was laughing and saying, "That ain't no Mauser. That ain't no Mauser."

23

At 7 A.M. the Snake Eaters slammed open the back door of Darrell Casey's waterfront home. They wore white nylon running shorts and sleeveless shirts of pale blue. After jogging four miles they were perspiring lightly. But neither was breathing hard. When the first Snake Eater, the one with the leather glove, came in the kitchen door, he moved several steps forward, getting out of the door and giving his partner maneuvering room. It was his military training.

Then both men stopped. Darrell and Darby were in the kitchen. Darrell was wearing the bottom of a pair of navy-blue silk pajamas. He was holding a container of orange juice. His hair was tousled and his face was relaxed. Darby was wearing the top of the pajamas. She was standing at the open door of the refrigerator, waving the door back and forth to cool her body.

Darrell looked up, at first in surprise and then in anger as the two men surged into the middle of the kitchen. Darby hid behind the open refrigerator door for a moment, then turned and walked swiftly away.

"I told you to be here about eight A.M. You're early. And I expect you to knock when you do get here. I live here. Don't ever barge in my house again."

Darrell closed the refrigerator door and carried the orange juice to the table. He poured a glass and sat down. He did not invite the Snake Eaters to sit. They stood in the middle of the room looking like young Olympians, supremely self-confident, rocking on their toes and smiling those cocky smiles. Darrell wondered if they smiled in their sleep.

"We wanted to talk with you about Steinhorst," said the Snake Eater wearing the white glove. His voice was very soft. Darrell almost smiled. The efforts of these guys to emulate Steinhorst were sometimes almost humorous. He took a drink of orange juice and looked up.

"He's dead. What is there to talk about."

"We want his job."

Darrell took another drink of orange juice. Now it was his turn to smile. "What makes you think you can handle it? I brought you here to take care of him. You couldn't. You guys became his . . . his understudies. Now he's dead. He was the best and he's dead."

"We can handle it."

Darrell saw the Snake Eaters look over his shoulder. He turned. Darby was there. She was wearing his white terry-cloth bathrobe. He smiled at her and turned back to the Snake Eaters.

"You want more money, too. Doesn't that usually go with a promotion?"

"That's right." There was no subservience in the Snake Eater's voice.

"Two things you have to understand," Darrell

said slowly. "First, there's no freelance work. You don't move on anybody unless I say so. There's too much at stake."

The Snake Eaters nodded. In unison. Darrell wondered if they practiced that maneuver.

"Second—and this is the reason I told you to come over this morning—I've got a job for you. Do it right and then we'll talk about your taking Gunter's job."

The Snake Eaters looked at each other. An unspoken signal passed between them. Again they nodded. In unison.

"You two have flown on C-One-thirtys, right?"

The two men nodded. "We jumped out of a lot of them in 'Nam," said the one with the white glove.

Darrell's voice was casual. "Then this shouldn't be any big deal for you." He drained the glass of orange juice. He turned to Darby. "Would you like some juice?" he asked.

She shook her head and clasped the bathrobe closer around her body.

Darrell turned back to the Snake Eaters. "Go out to Executive. I've chartered a Lear. The pilot will fly you down to South Caicos. Once you get there, you'll see a couple of C-One-thirtys on the ramp. One is parked behind the fuel pumps on the northwest corner of the parking ramp. The other is parked out near the runway. Go to the one near the runway. The pilot is expecting you. I told him I want you to take a familiarization flight. He doesn't know anything about your background."

Darrell paused and waved a forefinger at the Snake Eaters. "Now, I want you to, uh, *impress* the pilot. He needs a little lesson, a reminder that he's a high-paid bus driver. If you can't *impress* him with a little conversation, I'll want you to take other steps."

"Today?" It was the second Snake Eater who spoke. Darrell looked at him in surprise. Sometimes he forgot the guy could talk.

"Not this trip. Not today. He'll be flying the airplane, for God's sake. Just talk to him. Influence him. But if he doesn't get the message, then stay over down there and in a couple of days you can take whatever action you think necessary." He waggled his finger again. "As long as there is no trace."

The lazy smile on the face of the Snake Eater, the one without the white glove, slowly stretched across his face. When he spoke, his voice was almost dreamy. "I think we'll put him in an airplane, fly out maybe fifty miles offshore, and then throw him out. I always liked doing that in 'Nam."

Darrell sensed Darby's shudder of revulsion. In their private conversations, she often ridiculed them, saying they should be in the comic books. But he knew she was afraid of them. He stood up. "Okay. Do what you have to do. Get on down to South Caicos. And call me after the flight. I want to know how it goes."

The Snake Eaters did not move. "If it goes okay, we get the job." It was a statement.

Casey was not to be intimidated. "You do the job. Then we'll talk." He waved them out. They slowly backed out of the room, closed the door, and jogged across the yard toward the apartment they shared. It was four miles away.

Darby moved to the kitchen window and watched them. She pulled the bathrobe tighter around her neck, shivered, and said, "Brrrrrrr. What a strange pair.'

Darby was deeply concerned. She knew she was in over her head. By sleeping with Darrell Casey she was violating every rule in the book. She knew male agents whose careers had been ruined by sleeping with women involved in drug smuggling. She knew others who did it and were never caught. With a lot of male agents it was one of the perks of working undercover. But for a female agent it meant that when the target—in this case, Darrell Casey—was arrested, she could not testify against him. She would have no credibility. She would either have to perjure herself—and she could not do that—or else not testify. All the undercover work would be for naught. She would have lost her first big chance and she was not sure that any other police department would give her a second chance. There was too much involved here, both personally and professionally, for that to happen. She had to make good. She had to bring down Darrell Casey. Somehow.

Darby had wanted to be a police officer ever since she was a child growing up in Edison, a small town deep in southwest Georgia. The Georgia Bureau of Investigation had used several female contract agents to conduct a local sting operation, and Darby thought they had the most romantic job in the world. She was an only child and her parents were not thrilled with the idea of their daughter being a cop. They hoped she would change her mind. But after graduating from Georgia State University in Atlanta she moved to south Florida, to the epicenter of America's drug-smuggling business, because that was where she could get the most experience. Nick Brown, always on the lookout for fresh faces to work undercover, sent her to the academy and then had a DEA friend spend days with her, tutoring her in the arcane world of undercover work. She began working in a small restaurant frequented by Darrell Casey, soon met him, and it all began.

She knew that if Nick Brown had the slightest idea how far things had gone, she would be fired. She pulled the robe closer around her shoulders.

Darrell seemed preoccupied as he returned the orange juice to the refrigerator. He sounded almost amused when he spoke. "They are pretty tough boys. But not nearly as tough as they think."

Darby turned and walked toward Casey. "What do you mean?"

He reached out and stroked her short black hair. His voice softened. "They are too ambitious, too greedy, too easy to see through." He looked over her shoulder, out the window at the vanishing backs of the Snake Eaters. "Nobody fucks with me and gets away with it." He turned back to Darby and added, "Nobody." He waved a hand toward the door where the Snake Eaters had left. "They think they can move on me. It's written all over them. Just as it was written all over good old Gunter."

Darby looked at him in alarm. "Would they try to hurt you?"

Darrell shrugged. "Gunter wanted to hurt me. Look what happened to him."

Darby was puzzled. "But I thought . . ."

Darrell nodded. "So did he. But it doesn't matter. If he had killed the cop, that little pest would be out of the way."

Casey smiled. "And somehow the cops would have discovered the name of the killer. Cops don't like cop killers." He shrugged. "But he didn't kill the cop. He got killed himself. Now he's out of the way and I don't have to worry about my back when he's around. As for the cop, well, there are worse things you can do to a man than kill him. And the fat Mr. Brown will soon find that out."

"What are you going to do?"

Darrell pulled her close and did not answer. As he rubbed his hand up and down her back and over the fullness of her hips, he thought on his plans. He would finish the C-130 deal from Bimini, a little smuggling trip that would bring Nick Brown humiliation and embarrassment. It would send Brown to a painful purgatory, a purgatory that would last for years.

He leaned back and looked at Darby. "Sure you don't want some orange juice?" he asked. He kissed her on the neck, on the warm spot under her ear, behind her ear, and again on her neck. "We don't have much time," he added.

"Why not?" she whispered. "We have all day."

He nuzzled her neck. "No, I have a lot to do."

Darby pulled away, looked deeply into his eyes for a moment, then untied the belt of the bathrobe. She held her arms down and shrugged her shoulders. The bathrobe fell to the floor, a pool of white emphasizing her tanned legs, the longest legs in Lauderdale.

In a languid motion, she coiled her hands around the back of his neck. "I don't need anything to drink." Her lips slumped forward. She kissed Darrell, moving her lips upon his in a way that was infinitely longing.

24

At 11 A.M. the Snake Eaters stepped from the air-conditioned chill of the chartered Learjet onto the ovenlike ramp of the airport on South Caicos. The one without the white glove looked at the restaurant sign on the first floor of the tower and nodded. "Let's go in there and try their conch fritters," he said. "I hear that the best conch fritters in the world are here on South Caicos."

The other Snake Eater looked toward the tower and the half-dozen men standing in the shade around the front door. Up in the top of the tower, two men were standing at the windows watching him. "Let's wait until after the flight," he said. "We can go over to the Admiral's Arms and relax. That's the place with the great conch fritters. We'll hang around, call Casey, and spend the night."

He glanced briefly at the huge C-130 parked behind the fuel pumps on the north side of the ramp, just as Casey had said it would be. He marveled at the size of the alligator on the tail. He knew it was about fifteen feet from the tarmac to the horizontal stabilizer of the C-130. From there, the vertical stabilizer soared upward another twenty-three feet or so, and most of that broad expanse of tail surface was covered with a rampant alligator, mouth agape, eyes blazing, and teeth gleaming.

The Snake Eater turned toward the other C-130 across the ramp. It too had an alligator painted on the vertical stabilizer. A beefy middle-aged guy was standing by the aircraft's open door waving at them.

He touched the other Snake Eater on the arm and nodded toward the second C-130. "That looks like our boy," he said.

The two men sauntered across the ramp. No one moves fast on South Caicos. It is too hot.

The man standing by the open door of the C-130 waved impatiently. As the Snake Eaters drew closer, he waved again. His shirt was half in and half out of his wrinkled khaki trousers. White socks bagged around his ankles and collapsed over the tops of soiled tennis shoes. He had stringy unkempt hair and a face that had been there and back. He made no effort to shake hands. He simply jabbed a thumb over his shoulder and said, "Okay, Jack. I don't know why you're here. But Casey said to take you on a short flight to familiarize you with this aircraft. So we'll fly down to Haiti and back. It's about an hour's flight. Now get on in here and let me shut the door."

He stood aside as the two men climbed up the stairs. Then he climbed down, removed the chocks from under the wheels of the main landing gear, and walked toward the rear of the aircraft. He looked up at the ten-inch pressurization dump valve. There was one here on the starboard aft end of the fuselage and the other under the flight deck. If they did not operate properly today, he was going to be in big-time trouble.

He climbed the steps into the aircraft, closed and locked the door, then climbed the ladder onto the flight deck. At the top of the steps he stopped. One of the Snake Eaters had taken the copilot's seat and the other was standing, waiting for the pilot to move into the left seat, so he could take the flight engineer's seat located between and slightly behind and above the pilot and copilot. Before he could say anything, the guy in the copilot's seat spoke.

"You fly this thing by yourself?"

"You got it, Jack."

The Snake Eater paused. "I read somewhere that the military uses a four-man flight crew plus a load master."

"This ain't the military, Jack."

Both of the Snake Eaters turned their coiled steel bodies in an almost lazy indolent fashion toward the pilot. Ignoring them, he pointed to the ladder he had just climbed. "You guys find a seat back in the cargo compartment and get strapped in. We take off in five minutes."

The Snake Eaters looked at each other. Their eyebrows were lifted almost as if they were amused. They were used to and expected a lot of respect, even a slight amount of fear, from people who worked for Casey. This guy was too independent, even for a pilot. They knew why Darrell asked them to *impress* this guy. He needed a short lesson in humility.

Neither of the Snake Eaters moved. They smiled.

"You can't sit here. I want you back in the cargo compartment for takeoff. When we get airborne you can come up here."

After a pause, the Snake Eater in the right seat, the one wearing the white leather glove, spoke. His voice was very soft. "Just drive the airplane, buddy. Don't worry about the seating arrangement."

The pilot shook his head. "Not with you sitting there, Jack. You guys can sit on the crew bunks behind the seats if you like." He pointed to the double-decker bunk against the rear bulkhead of the flight deck. "But you're not sitting in crew seats."

"Oh. And why not?" The Snake Eater took off his sunglasses and stared at the pilot. His soft voice did not mask the slumbering violence in his eyes. "And by the way, neither of us is named Jack."

The pilot waved his arms. "Because I'm too busy. Especially on takeoff. You said yourself the military has a four-man flight crew. Well, I'm doing the work of those four men by myself."

He pointed to the overhead panel between the two seats. "I have to reach up and back. Getting this thing cranked with only one person is a bitch. I've got four generators to get on line and get them parallel on the bus." He thrust his right arm toward the right seat. "I have to reach across the copilot's seat. I have to handle the radio, the systems, fly the aircraft, do it all. And that makes me too damn busy to have time to ask you to move or to explain things to you or to worry about you banging something with your knee or elbow. It's dangerous for you to be up here and I won't allow it. That's final. Either move to the bunk or we don't fly." He paused and added, "Jack."

The Snake Eater in the right seat looked over his shoulder at his partner. An unspoken signal passed between them and the two men, without a word, moved to the rear of the flight deck, where they sat side by side on the bunk.

The pilot's hands moved swiftly and confidently through the preignition sequence. He mumbled to himself, reading the scrolled checklist, reaching for the overhead panel, darting his eyes about the cockpit. He slipped the headset with the large soft earpieces over his head, adjusted each side, then looked over his right shoulder. He pointed to the two pairs of headsets on the bunk and the box of earplugs. The Snake Eaters smiled and waved indulgently. The pilot looked out the right window, muttered "Three clear," and reached over his head to press a red button. "Three turning," he mumbled as the number-three turboprop, the inboard engine on the right wing, began its banshee scream. The C-130 is the finest cargo aircraft ever built. It also is the loudest. The sustained shriek of its engines has caused hearing problems in many crew members. Quickly the pilot completed ignition sequence for engines four, two, and one.

After a quick conversation with the tower, he released the brakes and slowly lumbered onto the single taxiway. When he came to the single north-south runway, he turned left and taxied down the middle of the runway until he arrived at the north end. All the while he was busy, checking and rechecking instruments, adjusting dials, tuning radios, activating systems, setting controls.

At the end of the runway he swung first to the extreme right edge, then turned the tiny nose wheel steering gear hard to the left. That gave him sufficient room to turn back to the right until he was facing down the length of the runway. He looked over his shoulder. The Snake Eaters were not wearing headsets. The box of earplugs he had offered them were tossed aside on the bunk. The pilot shrugged. One of the Snake Eaters gave him a patronizing smile and a mocking thumbs-up signal.

The C-130 lurched as it came off the brakes, then began a startling burst of acceleration. The aircraft gathered speed rapidly. The pilot's hands were light on the controls. The C-130 climbed out slowly and sedately. Just as Darrell Casey had ordered.

The pilot turned right. It was typical weather for the Turks & Caicos Islands—a low level of widely scattered clouds and unlimited visibility, what pilots call "severe clear." Out the left window the triangular shape of Salt Cay was visible. And ahead and to the right were the low irregular lines of the Ambergris Cays.

The pilot kept the C-130 low, not using the pressurization or air conditioning. The hot sun and the large windows of the cockpit caused temperatures on the flight deck to rise rapidly. The C-130 was crossing the northern edge of the Mouchoir Bank when one of the Snake Eaters tapped the pilot on the shoulder and shouted, "Turn on the air-conditioning."

The pilot tapped his earpiece and pointed to the pair of headsets on the bunk. With a grimace, one of the Snake Eaters picked up a headset and slid it over his closely cropped blond hair. He thumbed the transmit switch on the cord and repeated, "Turn on the air-conditioner. It's hot as hell in here."

"Can't," the pilot said. "Been having trouble with it and the pressurization."

"Try it. Turn it on."

The pilot shook his head. "I'll climb up to where it's cooler."

The C-130 had no cargo and the fuel tanks were less than half-full, ideal conditions to demonstrate its awesome climbing ability. Within minutes the aircraft was at twenty thousand feet. Ahead all of the island of Hispaniola could be seen.

The pilot unhooked the oxygen mask from the sling near his left elbow and put it around his neck. He was not wearing the mask. But it was hanging, like a giant black medallion, close enough that he could have it over his nose in about a second.

Even over the noise of the engines, he could hear the Snake Eaters laughing.

The pilot heard a click in his ear indicating one of the Snake Eaters had pushed the transmit button on his microphone cord. "Why are we wearing our oxygen mask?" came the voice, barely holding back its derision.

The pilot did not look back. "Safety precaution," he said into the boom microphone pressed against his mouth. "In the event of an explosive decompression, I'll have oxygen."

"That's a relief," said the Snake Eater. He laughed.

At twenty-five thousand feet the pilot pushed the mask on his face and cinched it tight. He took his right hand from the wheel and wiggled the mask, making sure it was snug.

Again the click in his ear. Then the voice. "Are all pilots pussies?"

The pilot shrugged and did not answer.

At thirty-one thousand feet the forward and aft pressurization valves failed simultaneously and within two thousand feet of the altitude the pilot had predicted when he had adjusted them. Almost immediately a dense fog filled the cockpit as the cold air at thirty-one thousand feet replaced the warm cockpit air. For about fifteen seconds, visibility was zero

zero on the flight deck. Simultaneously, the air in the lungs of the Snake Eaters suddenly expanded to the ambient air pressure, causing them to think they were exploding.

About twenty seconds passed before the Snake Eaters regained control, and by then they were feeling the first onslaught of hypoxia. The need for oxygen was critical. Both scrambled frantically for the oxygen masks. But C-130 oxygen masks are not the quick-donning type used by airlines. Rather they are awkward bulky masks with two canvas straps to be secured about the head. Even a person proficient in their use requires about ten seconds to put on the masks and turn on the oxygen regulator. By the time the Snake Eaters had their masks on, they were desperate for oxygen. Both began deep gasping inhalation.

The eyes of the Snake Eater sitting on the right, the one who did not wear a white leather glove, glazed over almost instantly and he slumped forward off the edge of the bunk to fall to the deck. The other Snake Eater looked at him in bewilderment. Then the truth came to him and he reached for his mask. But it was too late. He, too, fell to the deck and, after one mild convulsion, did not move.

The pilot glanced over his shoulder at the bodies of the two men. He began descending in wide circles until he was only two thousand feet above the ocean and back on a northbound heading away from Haiti. He opened the air vents, causing warm air to blow through the cockpit. Then he took off his oxygen mask and pulled the throttles until the C-130 was flying at about 150 knots. He turned on the automatic pilot, unhooked his seat belt, stood up, and walked several steps to where the Snake

Eaters lay. In the corner by the navigator's station was a valve—a new valve, judging by its shiny appearance. He turned the valve.

The valve was not connected to the oxygen bottle used by the pilot but was hooked instead to a small metal container of poison gas that had been installed that morning.

The pilot dragged the bodies of the Snake Eaters to the companionway and, one by one, pushed them over the side to the deck of the cargo compartment six feet below. He clambered down the ladder, grabbed the arms of one of the Snake Eaters, pulled him slowly the length of the aircraft, and left him at the edge of the closed cargo ramp. He did the same with the other. Then he attached a safety harness about his waist as he walked to an electrical box on the starboard side of the aircraft. He opened the door and flipped a lever. At the rear of the aircraft, the wide ramp of the C-130 began lowering. When it stopped, the pilot carefully walked aft toward the open ramp. Attached to his safety belt was a rope with a snap-link hook at the end. He attached the hook to a rung in the floor, then leaned over and shoved one of the Snake Eaters to the edge of the ramp. A push from his foot sent the body, arms and legs flailing, off the ramp. A moment later the second body followed. The pilot watched until he saw the distant splashes, then he walked forward, flipped a lever that closed the ramp, and unhooked his safety belt. He shrugged, rubbed his waist where the safety belt had bitten into his flesh, walked forward, climbed the ladder to the flight deck, and sat in the left seat. He let out his breath with a long sigh. He had just gone through more exercise in ten minutes than in the past ten days. He slipped the headset over his ears, dialed in a special frequency on the HF radio, then pressed the transmit button on the wheel. "Dispatch, this is Plunger. Dispatch, Plunger."

Almost immediately he heard, "Go ahead, Plunger. Dispatch."

"Dispatch, Operation Big Flush is completed. Repeat, Operation Big Flush is completed."

He heard two clicks of a microphone, signifying his message had been received and understood. He turned off the HF radio and muttered a low curse. Darrell Casey's new codes were a crock. What was this Big Flush and Plunger and Dispatch? All he did was snuff a couple of would-be badasses and dump their bodies in the ocean.

25

The Cessna 210, a single-engine high-wing aircraft, orbited in a slow crawl six thousand feet over Bimini. It was 6 A.M. and the pilot had been circling the island since 4:30. The throttle of the little Cessna was pulled back until the engine gauges showed it was pulling only eighteen inches of manifold pressure. The engine turned over at a lazy twenty-one hundred revolutions per minute. While the Cessna 210 usually cruised at speeds approaching two hundred miles an hour, today it was cruising at a leisurely 125 miles an hour. In addition to its regular fuel tanks and long-range tanks, the pilot had insisted on even more fuel capacity. Within the past week, tip tanks had been added and now the Cessna could carry 117 gallons. In its slow-speed configuration, the engine burned a miserly eight gallons per hour. It could stay aloft about eighteen hours. The low power setting and the one-mile offset from the island made the sound of the Cessna inaudible to anyone on the ground. Had they looked up and seen the tiny speck, they would have assumed it was one of the hundreds of small aircraft that use Bimini's navigation beacon each day.

The aircraft fairly bristled with antennae of various kinds. In fact, the Cessna was so loaded with state-of-the-art electronics that with full fuel and only one passenger, it was approaching its gross weight, the maximum weight at which it was designed to fly. The sides and the rear of the cockpit were crammed with instruments, thermal imaging equipment hooked to a video readout. Infrared detection equipment, called FLIR, also hooked to a video readout. An inertial navigation system weighed some eighty pounds, a lot of weight but worth it for this mission. The ground track memory on the INS allowed the pilot to return to a precise spot on earth. Accuracy of the INS was backed up with a new Loran C, an updated model not yet on the market. A precise latitude-longitude reference could be dialed into the INS and LORAN as a reference point for the FLIR. Then, even on the darkest night or the most cloudy and hazy day, the aircraft could return to a precise spot. The combination was accurate within a half-mile. Gyro-stabilized binoculars, extremely high-powered binoculars, also not yet on the market, even for the military, rounded out and complemented the equipment aboard the Cessna.

It was an extremely advanced electronic surveillance platform in the disguise of a widely known aircraft.

Mike Love sat at the controls, bone-weary but erect, bearded face impassive. This was the seventh day of surveillance. He arrived over Bimini each morning about 4:30, circled until about 7 P.M., returned to the landing strip at the cattle ranch west of Lauderdale, drove home, had dinner while his wife tried to talk to him about what he was doing, showered, and fell into bed. The alarm awakened him at 2 A.M. and the cycle began again.

Not only was Mike tired, he was bored. The million dollars or so in electronics equipment aboard the Cessna had revealed nothing of major significance. Small aircraft came and went from the airport on South Bimini. Go-fast boats buzzed around the island like berserk water bugs. He had alerted Broward County about several of them. Broward had called Customs. But there had been no intercepts. Every boat got through. The water ferry between South Bimini and North Bimini ran on schedule, or the closest thing in the Bahamas to a schedule; it went back and forth every hour or whenever airplane passengers drove to the dock on South Bimini and waved to get the attention of the ferry driver a hundred yards away. The Bahamian Immigration and Customs officers, both of whom drove distinctive white pickup trucks, had been videotaped several dozen times taking part in refueling of drug-laden aircraft. The airport closed each day at dusk, and an hour or so later the scammers began landing. There were usually one or two on the ground in the early-morning hours when Mike returned. He had videotaped them unloading shipments of cocaine; Mike assumed for transshipment by boat into Florida. Each time he saw an aircraft refueling, he waited until it took off and settled on a heading. Then he called Broward County, which in turn alerted the Customs air wing. One or two had been popped, but most of them had gotten through and gone on to Georgia or the Carolinas or Kentucky. They were small potatoes. There was no activity that would indicate a major multi-ton stash of cocaine was being assimilated in a stash house on Bimini.

And it would take days, perhaps weeks, to put together a load the size Nick had mentioned. Incredible. Mike had never heard of a load that large. Bimini should be like a beehive as humpers moved the cocaine to a stash house. The stash house would be under heavy guard. It would take numerous loads in small trucks to move the cocaine from the airport to a stash house. Mike had watched the trucks of the Customs and Immigration officers closely. But they remained empty.

Because of the size of the load, it would have to be put together somewhere near the airport. Ten tons of cocaine simply couldn't be trucked from anywhere on the island. There was only one place near the airport suitable for hiding ten tons of cocaine: the old virtually abandoned subdivision on the west side of the island. It was laced with a network of canals and had dozens of houses that were occupied only part-time. But there was no activity there.

The only regular activity Mike had seen during the past six days was the half-dozen or so scuba divers in the lagoon.

The lack of activity was odd because Nick Brown's intelligence information usually was right on the money. Either Nick had come a cropper or Darrell Casey was a lot slicker than Mike gave him credit for being. And he refused to believe that a smuggler could be smarter than he was.

Mike was swinging back in a slow orbit to the east and the morning sun was coming up. It was a brilliant shimmering red ball that almost lunged out of the ocean. Today was going to be hot, even at six

thousand feet. He sighed and reached into his shirt
pocket for his sun glasses. He winced as he put
them on. His nose was sore from the weight of the
glasses over the past six days. Ironic to have a sore
nose as an occupational hazard.

He looked to the side, checking the video readouts on the thermal imaging equipment, adjusting
the dials.

Yep, it was going to be hot. Already he could
pick up temperature differences in ground objects.
The air tanks worn by the scuba divers showed up
clearly on his screen. Mike felt a moment of envy
that someone could spend their days scuba diving
when he had to sit on his ass in a cramped airplane,
circling for hour after hour, day after day. And
apparently for zip.

He wondered if Casey were stockpiling his cocaine elsewhere. There was no sign of it on Bimini.
Well, the best indication would be the C-130 that
was to haul the cocaine to Florida. If it came to
Bimini, then the cocaine was there and Casey had
outsmarted them all.

Mike glanced over the engine instruments. Everything within tolerances and in the green. He
didn't need to worry about the mechanical condition of the airplane. Each morning when he arrived
at the airstrip west of Lauderdale, the Cessna was
in immaculate condition: windshield cleaned, tanks
topped off, ready to go. Mike could tell when he
checked the oil that it was changed on a daily basis.
He never saw the mechanics and they never saw
him. But they left brief notes. One day they had
cautioned him about the left brake, saying it was
worn and the new part would not be in until the
next day. He had never noticed. And they apolo-

gized one day for putting milk, rather than cream, into the ice chest to use in the thermos of coffee. Mike never drank coffee. He hated the taste and was afraid of what caffeine would do to his body. He always brought a bottle of mineral water, several apples or oranges, a chunk of cheese, and a piece of hard bread. But each morning the ice chest was half-filled with baked chicken and deserts. And the thermos was always there, filled with hot coffee. What the hell? They were just trying to be nice.

He took a deep breath, let it out slowly, wiggled his shoulders, moved his head around in a circle exercising his neck, performed a few isometric exercises with his leg and stomach muscles, sighed, and settled back in the seat.

He looked at the video screens and carefully examined the area around the airport on South Bimini.

It was as if the island were asleep. The brown lifeless-appearing vegetation was flat. No vehicles moved, not even those of the Customs and Immigration officers who usually were scurrying about attempting to extort money from one person or another. The ferry moved slowly across the hundred yards or so of pale-green water, the heat signature from the small outboard showing up on the video screen with metronomic regularity. It was part of the island's almost undetectable system of vital signs. The airport was devoid of activity. No cars or people moved on the streets of the old subdivision. No boats were in the canals or in the waters near the eastern end of the runway. Even the scuba divers were gone, underneath the waters of the lagoon.

Mike fine-tuned the video equipment and leaned closer to the screen as if seeking to peer inside and find the hidden secrets. Casey's people were on Bimini. The best intelligence available said they were putting together ten tons of cocaine. He had to find them.

He had to locate the cocaine. It was there. But where?

26

It was 4 P.M. when Darby DuPree walked through the gate to Darrell Casey's house. She could not control a shiver of fright when she saw Darrell standing by the alligator pit. She had asked him several times to get rid of the alligators, but he had refused.

Darby jumped as she realized a man had suddenly materialized by her side. She did not see where he came from. He suddenly was just there. Then her training took over and she catalogued his features as she gazed at him with a questioning look. He was about five feet eleven inches tall, weighed about one sixty, hair medium, no mustache or beard, nondescript appearance. The only thing that stood out was that he wore no shoes.

And he was standing too close to her.

"Who are you?" she demanded.

He looked at her and did not answer.

"Darrell," she called. But he did not hear her.

She looked at the black man in fright and hurried toward Darrell.

The black man, without seeming to move, suddenly was in front of her. He held up his hand, motioning for her to stop.

When she continued, he planted his feet and his right hand moved toward his belt. Few other people would have noticed his hand movement. But she knew when a person was reaching for a weapon. And she knew that she had neither the experience nor the poise to handle the situation. She had been taught to always control the situation, to take charge, to seize the initiative. But that was not always possible.

She stopped. "Darrell," she said loudly.

He turned and suddenly was running across the lawn toward her. His limp was particularly noticeable when he ran.

"Darrell, this man—"

"It's okay," Darrell said to the black man. "She lives here. I forgot to tell you." The stranger looked at Darby as if memorizing her features. He nodded, but his blank expression never changed.

Darrell put his arm around Darby and said, "This is Bobo. He works for me. You'll see him around a lot."

Darby nodded. She was still frightened.

Darrell motioned for Bobo to leave them. The black man sauntered toward the shade of the trees near the gate. He merged into the shadows and disappeared. One moment he was there and the next he was gone. Darby knew he was under a tree or behind an oleander, but she could not see him. How could someone simply disappear in broad daylight?

She looked at Casey. "Who *is* that?" she asked in her intense and earnest voice.

"Bobo. From Colombia. He's working for me."

"Doing what? What can he do?"

"Whatever I tell him to." He pulled Darby and said, "Let's go in the house."

Inside the house, Darby looked at Casey, smiled, and raised her eyebrows. "I go out for a day and come back and you've hired someone new." She looked out the window toward the gate. She had the feeling the Colombian was watching even though she could not see him. "He's strange. Bobo? What sort of name is that? He jumped out of nowhere and then disappeared. What's going on?"

Darrell shrugged. He leaned over and unconsciously rubbed his leg. "You know what's going on. I've got a lot to do."

Darby turned away. "I'm so hot. I wanted to go swimming, but the alligators are bad enough. I can't go out there when that scary man is here." She lifted her hair off the back of her neck. "I think I'll take a shower." She turned and reached for Darrell's hand. "Come talk to me while I get undressed."

As they walked through the long hall toward the bedroom, Darby looked over her shoulder. "You said you have a lot to do. Are you talking about the Bimini thing?" she asked. Her voice was casual as if Bimini were of little interest.

"Yes."

Darby stopped by the bed and began to unbutton her blouse. She looked at Darrell and smiled. "You know, you could have been a success in anything you did. Why did you go into smuggling?"

She tossed the blouse on the bed and reached behind to unhook her bra. Casey smiled. She must be the only female in Lauderdale between the ages of fourteen and sixty, who wore a bra with everything but a bathing suit.

"What do you mean?"

She tossed the bra atop the blouse, rubbed her breasts, then pulled the zipper on the back of her slacks, hooked her thumbs into the waistband, and pushed them down her legs. Darrell watched, mesmerized as always by the sight of her legs. My God, what legs.

She turned toward him. "I mean, the same things that make you so good in this business could have made you good in any business. So why get involved in a business where, if you get caught, you can go to jail for years? Is it the money?"

Darrell shrugged. His eyes were locked with hers. "We all do what we all do."

Darby smiled and walked toward him. "Take a shower with me?"

She put her arms around his neck and kissed him. As always, the world disappeared for Darrell Casey. She leaned away from him and looked up with a smile. "And then. . . ."

He shook his head and slowly pulled her arms from his neck. "I have to go back to work."

And suddenly he had turned and was striding down the hall. She stared after him in surprise.

It was the first time he had ever said no.

27

At 1:30 A.M. Mike Love sat up in bed and said, "It's the scuba divers."

His wife, Mary, rolled over, squinted into the darkness, and mumbled, "What?"

Mike was staring straight ahead. "The scuba divers. The goddamned scuba divers." He made an angry noise that sounded almost like a growl. "Why didn't I see it?" Mike looked at the fluorescent face of his watch, turned on the small lamp near his side of the bed, and reached for the telephone.

"What are you talking about?" Mary asked. "Mike, are you okay?" She reached for his arm.

"I've been so stupid. I've seen them every day and didn't realize what they were doing."

"What who was doing?" Mary sat up in bed. "Who are you calling?" she asked.

"Lance. He can call Fluf."

"What time is it?"

"One-thirty-one."

"In the morning?"

Mike chuckled. "No. Just past noon. Mary, go back to sleep. I gotta check this out."

He leaned forward as Lance answered. "Hi, guy," Mike said. "You awake?"

"I am now."

Mike reached back with his right hand and caressed Mary's back as he talked. It was twenty minutes later before he hung up the telephone.

"Mike, I can't believe it," Mary said. "I've never heard of anything like that. Are you sure?"

He stood up. "I'm ninety-nine percent sure. I'll know for certain by noon. Goddamn. I can't get over it. Taking place literally right in front of me. And I didn't realize it."

His voice was filled with reluctant admiration. "It's perfect. The lagoon is just a few hundred yards from the end of the runway. It's deep enough to hide the stuff. And it's landlocked so nobody can come in by boat and pirate it."

Mike walked swiftly toward the shower. Today was going to be a big day.

"He's up now, trying to get confirmation," Lance told Nick Brown. He sat across the desk from Nick. He was slumped in a chair, black wig, big hat, big orange-tinted sunglasses, and a raincoat on the floor. He wore a white T-shirt. Emblazoned across the front in rows of black lettering was: "Only One Thing Tastes Better than an Oyster. And You Don't Eat It on a Cracker." His eyes were sparkling with excitement. At last there was some movement in this case, something solid. There was only one course of action open to Fluf.

"I thought I had heard it all," Nick mused. He was turned facing away from Lance and looking at the wall of his office. He leaned back in his chair, hands behind his head, and thought hard about this new information. It changed a lot of things. It was forcing him to rethink some basic beliefs about law enforcement.

"Hey, boss, when you gonna get that hole in your wall fixed?" Lance asked.

"I keep forgetting," Nick mumbled. He was thinking, remembering that only a few days earlier he had laced into Lance about Mike Love's squirting gasoline on a doper's boat and setting it afire. Now Mike, evidently flying in a private aircraft and working on his own, had discovered Darrell Casey's cache of cocaine. If Mike were correct, it would enable Nick to break this case wide open. He could stop ten tons of cocaine from entering Broward County. But it would mean working with a federal officer who had been suspended from duty. And, to Nick, being suspended was almost as bad as being fired. In addition, he would have to return to the Bahamas. The sheriff liked this business of gathering intelligence in the Bahamas. But it was fraught with peril, not only from the dopers and the crooked Bahamian cops but also from the sheriff. Nick knew that if the operation turned sour, the sheriff would have a public hanging. Whoever was involved in the operation would be sacrificed.

He turned to Lance. His sleepy eyes were deadly serious. "We've got a lot of work to do," he began. "First, we've got to confirm what Mike said. Even if he eyeballs them this morning, we've got to have independent confirmation."

Lance waited. He knew how that confirmation could be obtained. But Nick had to give the word.

"If the stuff is there, we've got to know when it is going to be moved."

Nick tapped his fingers on the top of his desk.

His eyes were worried. "And we've got to find out why Darby didn't know about this. Why she didn't tell us. Is he onto her? Did he withhold the information? Or did it somehow fall between the cracks?"

Nick continued tapping the desk. Lance knew there was something else on his mind; something else he wanted to say.

"Speaking of Darby, Casey has a new man up there."

"Dopers don't have any trouble getting hired help."

"This guy is more than hired help." Nick opened his desk drawer and pulled out a two-page twx. "He's bad news." He glanced at the twx, skimming the contents. "Goes by the name El Bobo. Colombian national from Bogotá. Sometimes passes as a black man. No distinguishing marks. Five feet ten. One sixty. Goes barefoot about half the time."

"Sounds like a houseboy to me. What's so bad about him?" Lance interrupted.

"He's known to have killed fourteen people in Colombia and is suspected of killing another couple of dozen. Does contract work for drug cartels down there. His MO is unusual. He goes into a town, into the black section, hangs out around pool halls and beer joints for a few days, apparently gathering intelligence from yardmen, maids, and blacks who have service jobs that take them into white communities. Then he moves on his target. Never missed." Nick looked up from the teletype. "And he uses a knife."

"He kills people with a knife?"

Nick shook his head. "This twx says he cuts the testicles off men and stuffs them in their mouths when he kills them; it's his trademark." Nick threw the twx on the desk.

"Well, he'll be easy to identify if he comes after me."

"How?"

"He'll be carrying a chain saw."

Lance threw back his head and laughed. "I got my Magnum. And I got an M-Sixteen. Let old El Bobo come on. I'll have his ass for breakfast."

"A lot of other people who are now dead felt the same way. What the hell can a bare footed Colombian with a knife do? Apparently a hell of a lot."

Lance was staring at Nick. "Are you wondering the same thing I am?"

"I've been wondering why it took mister hotshot undercover agent such a long time to figure it out?"

Lance sat up straight. "What happened to the Snake Eaters?" he asked.

"Exactly. They must be gone or Casey wouldn't have brought in this Colombian. But where?" He answered Lance's unasked question, "She doesn't know. Said the last time she saw them, Casey sent them down to the Turks & Caicos to lean on some pilot. She doesn't know what happened. Then this Bobo guy shows up."

Lance looked at the ceiling. "She's losing it. Things up there are out of control. You should pull her in."

Nick stared at the wall and said nothing.

"Hey, boss, lighten up," Lance said. "Don't take all this so seriously. We know what's going down over there now. All we have to do is stop it. Easy." He folded the fingers on his right hand, held his fingernails near his mouth, exhaled, buffed his fingernails on his shirt, and displayed his beatific smile.

Nick looked at Lance as if he were some unusual specimen discovered under a microscope. He leaned across the desk. "Look, this is a joke to you. But I don't see anything funny. We have to stop this load. You said yourself that's what this job is all about, stopping the loads. I know that, in separate individual loads, Casey has probably brought this much and more into the country over the past fifteen years. But our job is to stop it. We do that like a cat eating a grindstone, one lick at a time. Within the next few days we're going to have the chance to take not one little lick, but a big bite. Casey is an arrogant man. He's bringing in a C-One-thirty. He's doing this to rub our noses in it. If that load gets through, you can bet that word will get out. And half the people in this department will be fired. I'll be fired. And since you're involved in the case, you'll be fired. Now that may not bother you. But I've got a wife and kids."

Lance turned serious. "Boss, if some civilian overheard this, they would think you want to get Casey just to keep your job. And I don't believe that. You are too good a cop."

"There's nothing wrong with wanting to keep your job."

Lance expansively threw his arms out and said, "Then not to worry. Your job is safe. Casey is dog meat. Houdini is on his ass. The mighty Houdini. And Houdini can take on even old Bobo Billy Badass."

Nick shook his head and sighed. "You're going back to Bimini," he said.

Lance stood up, clenched his fist, and twirled in a circle. "Look out, badasses." He turned to Nick. "To do what?"

"I should have said 'we' are going to Bimini."
His eyes narrowed and he pointed a forefinger at
Lance. "Two things. You will not carry a weapon.
Over there we have no authority to carry weapons.
We don't even have any authority to be there. But
if we get caught, we can say we're tourists. And
second . . ." Nick paused and blushed. "And sec-
ond, we are not going anywhere near that Boca de
Mama joint. You even mention it, and I'll have you
in a uniform working traffic."

Lance shrugged. "Does this mean I can't call you
sweetie anymore?"

Nick's eyes narrowed.

"Can I bring my dump book? Bimini food really
does something for—"

"No. No. And no more talk of that stuff." Nick
closed his eyes tightly for a moment, then, his voice
calmer, said, "You can fly a single-engine airplane,
can't you?"

Lance nodded. "Hey, I'm part eagle."

"I hope you're part fish. Get your scuba equipment together. You're going down in that lagoon.
According to the map, it's only a hundred yards or
so off the east end of the runway."

Nick looked at his watch. "I'm late for a meeting
with a DEA guy." He stood up and walked around
the desk.

"DEA?" Lance was horrified. "They sleep with a
night-light and eat kitty litter. What the hell are you
doing talking to DEA? They are not your friends."

"This guy is. I've known him for years. He may
be the key, the secret to what I want to do over
there. If he helps, we can put the big hurt on
Casey."

"You got somebody in DEA? Is it Ron? I know him. I met him several times."

Nick poked Lance in the chest with a short stumpy finger. "Go get your scuba tanks charged. Call the air wing and tell them the narcotics squad needs a single-engine job, maybe a little Piper, for a U/C job." Nick paused. "Cancel that. I'll have my secretary do it. I don't want them to know you're flying. She can handle that. Wear your beeper because Mike may call. If he confirms what he told you, work out some frequencies we can get together on tonight. We're going to need him flying air cover while we're on the ground in Bimini. That's crucial."

Lance put on his wig, his hat, and slipped on the raincoat. He held the large sunglasses in his hand.

"Why do you wear a raincoat when you come to my office?" Nick asked. "It's not raining outside."

"It was cloudy. It could rain." Lance pointed to the hole in the glass wall. "And if it's raining outside, it will be raining inside." He put on his big orange-tinted sunglasses, gave Nick his go-to-hell smile, and said, "Houdini is on the move."

Nick turned to leave. Over his shoulder he said, "Don't forget. No weapons. No Boca de Mama. And no . . . no literature."

Lance paused. He smiled. That was the first time his dump book had ever been referred to as literature.

28

Ron Williamson puffed on his pipe, quickly sliced his eyes about the restaurant, and said, "Let me tell you how the thing works." Nick noticed that Ron's mouth did not move when he talked, the mark of a long-time cop and the certain indicator of an experienced undercover agent.

Ron held his big hands about eighteen inches apart. "Each one is about so big, no more than an inch thick. Weighs about two pounds and most of that is battery. The battery life is about three months, but from what you said battery life is not a factor. You expect the load to move within a matter of days?"

Nick nodded.

"Okay, you just attach this to the load. Know what sort of containers the stuff is in?"

Nick shook his head. "It's got to be done underwater."

Ron's eyebrows rose. "Underwater? Hmmmmnmn. I'd guess the stuff is in vacuum-sealed bags that are packed inside canvas or rubberized containers. Probably black. So you slide one of these inside one of the containers, maybe get some black masking tape to make sure it stays there. Are there many packages?"

Nick paused for a second. It was difficult to overcome his reluctance to discuss the case. But Ron was going to provide him with a beeper to track the cocaine, so he had to be told. Nick pulled at his blond mustache, glanced around the restaurant, and behind his hand, said, "About ten tons."

Ron almost bit his pipe stem in half. "What?" He leaned across the table and laughed in amazement. "Oh, shit. If Dumnik finds out I knew the locals were onto ten tons of coke and I didn't report it . . ." He shook his head. "Ten tons." Then the professional took over. "Boat or aircraft?"

"Is this gonna get you in trouble? Will Dumnik find out?" Nick was concerned.

Ron dismissed his concern with a wave of his hand. "I don't worry about Dumnik. That son of a bitch is living proof that the Miccossukee Indians fuck cows. Now, is the stuff coming in by boat or aircraft?"

"Aircraft."

"Then the doper has a problem. If he has too many bags, it will take too long to load and unload it. Security could be a concern. So he'll want to have big containers. But the biggest I've ever seen on an airplane deal is about forty kilos. More than that and the humpers have a hard time. Especially on big loads. But who knows? He might have hundred-kilo bags and intend to use a couple of humpers on each one. That's around a hundred bags. Jesus, he must have a hell of a lot of humpers."

"Half of Bimini."

Ron puffed on his pipe and smiled. After a pause, he said, "So you're about to pop Darrell Casey?"

Nick pulled at his mustache. "I didn't say that."

"He's the only scammer I know who would try to pull off a deal that size." Professional curiosity tugged at Ron. "Tell me how you're going to do this. Maybe I can help."

Nick pulled at his mustache. He had been hoping to hear that. Ron Williamson was the most experienced street agent inside DEA. He was forty-nine years old and counting the days until his fiftieth birthday and he could take an early retirement. Ten years ago, Ron had been in charge of DEA's Special Action Division, a secret group that planned DEA's enforcement programs around the world. Ron had conceived and executed some of the most successful antismuggling programs in DEA history: a marijuana spraying program in Mexico; the first poppy eradication effort in Hungary; and the shutdown of heroin labs in the south of France, part of the so-called French Connection. He was not only bright, he was idealistic. He had written the DEA creed, a short paragraph that hung on the wall of DEA offices all over the world.

But his career took an unexpected turn during a cocaine bust in Atlanta when a young agent named Ray Dumnik was standing beside a car with a shotgun pointed at the head of the man in the driver's seat. The driver was one of a half-dozen people arrested in a parking lot at Lenox Square, a popular shopping center in north Atlanta. Dumnik was holding the gun on the driver as agents worked their way through the other cars, booking and cuffing the occupants. Dumnik had been drinking. And he was nervous. He usually worked the airport detail and had never drawn his weapon. When the driver reached to turn on the radio, Dumnik pulled the trigger and blew away half the instrument panel. He became one of the few men in history to fire a shotgun and miss a target from two feet away. He told other agents the driver had been reaching under the seat for a pistol. But when he looked under the seat there was no pistol. So Dumnik walked up to an Atlanta cop, a uniformd officer, and said, "You got an extra weapon?"

The officer gave Dumnik the pistol from his ankle holster. Dumnik walked off, returned a few minutes later, and said, "Can that weapon be traced?"

"Sure," the Atlanta cop said. "Why?"

"I just dropped it," Dumnik said. He had slid the pistol under the seat in the car. Now he could prove he had fired in self-defense.

"Oh, shit. I'll be fired." The Atlanta cop was astounded that a brother officer would deliberately incriminate him. "You've got to get it back."

But a DEA agent had found the pistol and put it into the evidence bag.

The Atlanta cop was fired, creating a bitter enmity by Atlanta cops toward the DEA. Ron Williamson threatened to go to the newspapers unless Ray Dumnik was disciplined. But Dumnik knew his immediate supervisor was sleeping with a stewardess from Piedmont Airlines. He made it clear that he expected leniency and he got it—a letter of reprimand.

Ron Williamson was so disgusted that he asked for a voluntary demotion and pay cut. He wanted to be a street agent so he would not have people working for him like Dumnik. Williamson was sent to Miami. And then, five years later, Dumnik, who had been made a supervisor, came to Miami as the assistant special agent in charge. Two years ago he had been made special agent in charge.

And about the only thing about Dumnik that had changed over the years was that he drank more. Two weeks earlier he had come to work, got drunk at noon, and could not find his car when he was ready to go home. He had reported it stolen and had half the Dade County police force looking for it. Last week he had gone to Atlanta for a meeting of SAICs from around the country. He drank enough liquor to decide he wanted to depart early for Miami. He packed his suitcases and then passed out. When he awakened, he looked in the closet and thought his clothes had been stolen. He called the Atlanta police and insisted a supervisor come to his room and take charge of the investigation. The first thing the supervisor did was wonder why, if someone had stolen Dumnik's clothes, they had not taken his suitcase. Out of curiosity he opened the suitcase. He stared at the contents for a long moment, turned to Dumnik, and said, "You're still as stupid as you used to be."

Dumnik went out of his way to make life miserable for Williamson, the legendary former Washington big shot who now worked for him. Whenever a new agent applied for a job with DEA, it was Ron who had to do the background investigation. Anytime a suspected smuggler had a car seized and then petitioned to have it returned, Ron had to do all the paperwork justifying why DEA should keep the car. Anytime a DEA agent had an accident in a government vehicle, it was Ron who handled the DEA side of the accident investigation. And he had to stay in the office and pull base duty more than any other agent.

But what hurt Ron the most was that his years of experience were overlooked and ignored. Dumnik ridiculed him as an ineffective old fart who should have been fired years ago.

So Ron counted the days until he could retire.

"You can help," Nick said. "Tell me more about this beeper and how I can know the minute Casey starts loading the coke. That will give me time to get my people in line and alert Customs."

"You think he's bringing it into Broward County?"

"I know he is."

"Why?"

"Because once it's here and distributed, he'll make sure word gets out. Wants to make me look stupid."

Ron puffed on his pipe and blew the smoke toward the ceiling. He was always careful about not letting smoke drift toward nonsmokers. He slid his cigarette lighter around the table for a moment, then said, "Maybe we can do something." He puffed on the pipe and stared at the ceiling. Then he put the pipe into an ash tray and pushed it to the far edge of the table. He leaned forward. "I'll get two beepers. That way if one fails or is discovered, we have the backup. When you put them on the dope, don't put them together. Go to one edge of the packages and install one of the beepers there. Then go around to the other side and put one there. That way, no matter which side they start loading from, you'll know early. It's going to take almost a day to load that stuff."

"Tell me how the beepers work. I know you guys have them, but I don't understand how they work."

"When the beeper is not moving, just sitting there, it emits an electronic signal, a beep, every five seconds. When the load to which it is attached starts moving, any motion, a truck, airplane, just picking it up and moving it, anything, causes it to go into another mode. Then it emits the signal twice per second rather than once every five seconds. Sounds like a typewriter."

"So you could put a beeper on a load then forget it? You know when it's just sitting in a warehouse or a stash house, and you know the minute it starts moving?"

"Right."

"How do you track it once it starts moving?"

Ron's eyes sliced around the restaurant again. Nick had to strain to hear him when he spoke. "Satellite."

"What?"

"Satellite. It's pretty good. We have a much bigger battery, but the basic beeper is the same one used by Fish and Wildlife to track turtles. We use their satellite."

Nick could not believe what he had heard. "You mean the U.S. Fish and Wildlife Service?"

Ron nodded.

Nick looked away and shook his head. "Turtles? I'm trying to keep my eye on ten tons of coke and you give me a thing that tracks turtles?"

"It works. There are no geographic limitations on its operational capabilities. The bird can track it anywhere in the world. The bird comes over every fifty-eight minutes, but it starts picking up the signal about ten minutes before it goes over and holds it for about ten minutes afterward. So there are only about thirty-five, thirty-eight minutes, maybe less, it depends on atmospheric conditions, when we are blind. We get the signal in real time. We've done a lot of good stuff with this system. It's the best technology available."

Nick pulled at his mustache. "Turtles. This is the same beeper that somebody ties to a turtle so they can track it?"

Ron nodded. "That's pretty important to Fish and Wildlife."

"Why do they track turtles?"

"Well, in the case of loggerheads, no one knows where the females go after they lay their eggs along the Florida and Georgia coasts. The beepers are helping track them to their breeding grounds."

"So I got the biggest bust in history depending on the same technology people use when they want to know where turtles go to screw?"

"Well, I never thought of it that way. But . . . yes."

Nick shook his head.

"I'll get the two beepers when I go back to the office. Our tech people have them. I'll make sure they have fresh batteries. And they're easy to operate. All you have to do once they're attached is to flip a switch. Where do you want me to meet you?"

"We'll fly down and meet you at Opa Locka, at the hangar where that guy does all your radio work. We'll be in a Piper. I don't know the number. How about nine or ten o'clock?"

"Fine. That'll give me plenty of time. We'll exchange phone numbers and radio frequencies so we can stay in touch. That way, as soon as the load moves I can let you know. Who's going with you?"

"Cunningham."

Ron rolled his eyes and laughed. "The wacky coprophiliac."

"The what?"

"The guy who keeps a record of—"

Nick stood up. "I gotta go. Lot's to do before tonight." He held out his hand. "Thanks, guy."

And then he was gone.

Ron stayed in the booth in the restaurant, watching through the window as Nick walked across the parking lot toward his car.

"He walks like a wet rooster," Ron said to himself.

29

It was 10 P.M. and the glittering sprawling lights of the south Florida coast had disappeared. The little Piper Arrow had crossed the black line that, at night, is the signal to aviators they have crossed the beach and are over the ocean. Ahead was only blackness.

Lance, who was flying the Piper, wore his scuffed boat shoes, loose cotton pants, and a long-sleeved cotton shirt. He had been on Bimini enough to have considerable respect for mosquitoes, especially at night. Under the pants and shirt, he wore a green bathing suit and a T-shirt featuring an exploding nuclear bomb over a crumbling world and the caption "Whoops."

He hummed a tuneless ditty and acted as if he flew single-engine aircraft over the ocean every day. Actually, he was nervous. Lance was not instrument-qualified; he was not rated to fly an aircraft solely by reference to its instruments. And there are few visual references over the ocean at night. Lance was paying close attention to his instruments, correcting the slightest deviation of the directional gyro, the altimeter, or the artificial horizon. He knew that small corrections were important, that he had to keep the aircraft under control.

Nick sat in the right seat. He wore cowboy boots, jeans, and a sport shirt. He sat there pulling at his mustache, plainly concerned about this night's work. "All we're going to do is put these beepers on the coke," he said. It was the third time he had told Lance this would be a quick in-and-out—no intelligence gathering, no surveillance, no confrontations; just land, do the deed, then get out of Dodge.

He turned and saw Lance's eyes scanning the instruments. "Can you keep this thing in the air?" he asked.

Lance shrugged. "Hey, don't worry, boss. If we crash, so what?" He flicked his thumb toward the rear seat. "I got my masks, fins, and scuba tank. I could last for days with just the mask and fins. I could swim to Key West."

"What about me?"

"Hhmmm." Lance laughed.

"Well, at least tell me how much longer before we're supposed to be there. Can you find Bimini at night?"

"Boss, I can find Bimini day or night, rain or shine. It's got its own little aura."

Lance leaned forward and pointed toward a distant glow to the left of the nose. Then he pointed to a centered needle on one of the aircraft navigation instruments. "Look at that. I'm a regular Magellan."

Nick snorted. "A thirty-minute flight to find a patch of light in the middle of a black ocean. How could you miss?"

"You got to be a combination of Einstein and King Kong to fly an airplane. Don't you know how lucky you are to have me? Hey, don't I make you look good?"

Nick pulled at his mustache. "All right, tell me how you plan to do this. You gonna pull an Einstein and do it the smart way? Or are you gonna pull a King Kong and bull your way through?"

Lance slapped an open hand to his chest and exhaled sharply. "I am wounded in my heart. Have I ever done anything but the right thing?"

"So tell me."

"Just like we discussed." Lance reduced the power two hundred rpm's, adjusted the trim, and kept his eyes on the instruments. "When we are two or three miles out, I'll shut down the engine and make a dead-stick landing. We'll land toward the east; land long, way down the field, and let it roll out. When we get to the end I'll taxi off the north side, into a big cleared area, whip her around so she'll be ready to go, and we'll be in business." He looked at Nick for approval.

Nick interrupted. "Can you land at night with no lights?"

"We're not dopers. They won't turn on the lights for us. So we don't really have a choice."

Nick, lips tight, nodded. "At least we got Mike up there. He can direct you to the airport."

"I don't need directions. I can find it." Lance shook his head in mock dismay. "*Jefe*, you really know how to give a lot of support to your troops. Now, as I was saying, after we land, you stay with the airplane. Monitor the portable radio. Listen out for Mike. I'll grab my scuba gear, boogie on down the lagoon, dive in there, plant these two handy-dandy beepers, get out, come on back, and we'll fly home. Slam, bam, thank you, ma'am. Nothing to it."

A slight bubble of static from the UHF radio caused Lance to hold up his hand for silence. "Victor five one. Lone Ranger," came a low voice.

"There's Mike. Right on time," Lance said. He picked up the microphone. "Hey, Sky King. What's the haps?"

"I'm showing you guys about eight out. On course," Mike said. He looked at the green video screen to his right. It showed a target, a small dot, inbound from the west. As Mike watched, the dot slowly changed shape until he could identify it as a low-wing single-engine aircraft. Mike was at five thousand feet where he had been slowly orbiting since 7 P.M., watching all of South Bimini. A fifteen knot wind was blowing from the east southeast and masked the sound of his engine. Now that Lance and Nick were inbound, he would drop lower, another two thousand feet, to enhance the reception on his infrared equipment.

"Any activity?" Lance asked.

"None at the site," Mike radioed. "But we have two guys, Bahamian Customs and Immigration, in the building at the west end of the field. They're dirty. They're usually not here at night unless a load is coming in. So you need to move fast once you're on the ground."

"Great. Great," Nick said in disgust. "We're landing right before a deal goes down. We'll be surrounded by dopers. We're probably using their parking space."

"No, those guys always use the ramp at the other end. No problem," Lance said. He keyed the microphone again. "Okay, Sky King. I'm pulling power. Let us know if you have any activity on the ramp."

"You got a fifteen-knot wind at one three zero. It should cover your sound on final."

"You a regular eye in the sky."

"You better be glad."

"I am. I am."

"Lone Ranger standing by. Stay tuned this freq."

Lance was three miles from the runway. Even though the runway was dark, he knew it was about one hundred yards right of the lighted ramp. He had been reducing power slowly. Then he pulled the throttle to the rear, changed the pitch on the propeller until it was turning at minimum rpm's, dropped his landing gear, and pulled the fuel control mixture all the way to the rear. The engine stopped. There was no sound except for the slight whistling of the wind around the doors of the aircraft.

Nick cleared his throat and shifted in the seat. Then he cinched his seat belt tighter. "I hope you know what you're doing," he muttered.

"Hey, boss. Have I shown you the latest entries in my dump book? Hey, I've had some really great. . . ."

Nick held up his hands. "I don't want to hear it. Just fly the airplane. Get us on the ground without killing us." A moment later he muttered, almost to himself, "You're a sick puppy."

Lance laughed. Then he and Nick grew silent. Ahead and to the left was the small cement-block building used by Customs and Immigration. Ramp lights revealed two white pickup trucks parked near the door of the building.

Lance looked out the window to his left. He was at three hundred feet when he passed the little building. He could see the men inside. He reached to his right, pressed the button on the end of the flap lever, and with one smooth motion lifted. He pressed forward on the wheel as the sudden lowering of the flaps caused the aircraft to change attitude. He quickly adjusted the trim and glanced at the airspeed indicator. Outside, he could see the faintest shadow of the runway below.

"You're right on target," came Mike's soft voice.

Lance, sweat beading on his face, pulled with finger-tip pressure on the wheel.

"Call Mike," he said, keeping his eyes on the runway. But before Nick could lift the small portable radio in his hand, Mike's voice was heard. "I show you halfway down the strip. No activity down at the other end. Looking good."

Nick, eyes locked on the runway, lifted the portable radio, whispered "We copy," then turned toward Lance.

At that moment the main landing gear touched with a slight squeak. Lance grabbed the flap lever and pushed it back to its normal position between the seats. The aircraft nestled firmly to the runway and began its rollout. Nick sighed in relief. So did Lance. Landing an aircraft on a darkened strip was not his idea of fun. Then he laughed.

"Cheated death again," Lance said. As he looked up, his expression became curious, then worried. The aircraft was rolling to a stop and the end of the runway was more than one hundred yards away. The little Piper stopped.

Nick looked at Lance in bewilderment. "Why are you stopping here?" he asked.

Lance was sheepish. "Uh, boss. We gotta push."

"Push? To the end of the runway?"

"I can't crank it up. The wind is blowing down the runway and the bad guys will hear us. We have to push. Well, it's not actually pushing. You're not supposed to push on the control surfaces. So we'll have to pull."

"Pull."

"It's easy." Lance pointed toward the door handle. "Open the door. Let's get out of here and I'll show you."

A soft squawk from the radio caused the two men to freeze. "Victor five one. Lone Ranger. I show you guys parked in the middle of the runway. Any trouble?"

"Tell him it was the head wind," Lance said.

"I got an idiot for a pilot," Nick whispered into the radio. "He got his flying license through a correspondence course with some outfit that makes kites."

Mike's soft chuckle came over the radio. "I'd get the aircraft off the end of the runway ASAP."

"Open the door. Open the door," Lance said.

Nick, mumbling and grumbling, opened the door, then unbuckled his seat belt and stepped onto the wing. He looked around and cautiously put a booted foot onto the step and then onto the runway. Almost immediately he slapped at a mosquito on his arm. He felt his hand sliding through the bloody remains and said, "I forgot how big the mosquitoes are over here."

Lance leapt from the wing to the ground and said, "I've seen 'em stand flat-footed and fuck a turkey." He took a deep breath, looked around, and said, "Don't you love Bimini? Garden spot of the universe."

"Let's move this thing." Nick pulled a tiny electrical cord from his pocket. The end with the small metal jack he stuck into the portable radio, then jammed the radio into the rear pocket of his jeans. He placed the earpiece on the other end of the cord into his left ear, wiggled it to make sure it was inserted snugly, then said, "What do I do?"

Lance walked to the front of the aircraft and turned the propeller until the two blades were parallel to the ground. "You grab the prop on that side, as close to the hub as you can, and I'll grab it here."

"It's easy, boss," Nick mimicked. "All I have to do is let it roll to the end of the runway, then whip it around." Nick looked toward the tail of the aircraft.

"What are you looking at?" Lance asked. "We have to pull it from here."

"I was looking for the training wheels. I thought I might push on those."

"Come on. Grab it."

The two men seized the propeller, bent forward and began pulling. "I thought you could fly an airplane," Nick whispered.

"I can. I just can't taxi too well."

"This thing must weigh a ton."

"Aren't you amazed at how easy it is to pull it?"

Nick was wheezing. "Why is it that every time I come to Bimini with you I get in trouble? The last time you take me to some faggot joint where I almost got attacked. This time I'm pulling an airplane down the middle of the runway where a dope plane is expected to land. For all I know it may be on final. We could get squashed by a doper. Everybody would think we had gone bad and were smugglers."

"We're almost there, boss. Hold on."

Then the little aircraft was rolling to the left, past the large white "27," then off the runway and onto a grassy area. "Just a little more," Lance said. "Let's turn it around in case we have to get out of here fast."

Then the aircraft stopped. Nick had his hands on his hips. He was breathing heavily as he looked around. To the east was the open sea. Behind the aircraft was a thick mangrove swamp. To the north was a small road that paralleled the runway, an access road that went from the north side of the parking ramp, along the runway all the way to the east end.

"Time to go to work," Lance said. He jumped atop the right wing of the Piper, leaned inside, and hoisted a dark canvas bag. Inside was his scuba gear and the two beepers Ron Williamson had given them an hour earlier at Opa Locka.

"Check with Mike about any security around the lagoon," Lance said.

"Lone Ranger. Victor aircraft."

"I see you guys finally decided to go to work."

"Could you give us another check of the site? Any targets at all?"

"Negative. No sign of anything. If someone was there, the equipment would pick them up."

"Okay. We're proceeding."

"Lone Ranger. Standing by."

30

Mike stiffened and leaned toward the FLIR. The equipment, made by Texas Instruments, performed in a fashion that could only be described as outstanding. The manufacturer said the equipment could distinguish temperature differentials as small as one-tenth of a degree. In actual practice, the difference was closer to a half-degree. But that was enough. A skilled operator could read volumes from the green video screen attached to the FLIR. When Mike arrived over Bimini earlier in the evening, his first pass showed a thermal signature on the ramp, the silhouette of an aircraft that had been parked there earlier. The shadow cast by the aircraft meant that a silhouette on the ramp was several degrees cooler than the surrounding cement. From the shape and size of the silhouette, Mike knew the aircraft had been a Merlin.

Now Mike turned a switch and changed the FLIR from "black hot" to the "white hot" mode—best in the evening when temperature differences had begun to even out. He was north of Bimini, with about a one-mile offset from the airport, when he saw what appeared to be a dot, then two dots, move onto the edge of the screen. Something was moving on the ramp of the airport, but whatever it was was being blocked by the top of the little white building. He turned the Cessna hard to the south so he could give the FLIR a better angle.

"Victor aircraft, stand by. We may have some movement."

Nick pulled the portable radio from his back pocket and whispered, "Standing by."

Within seconds Mike had a confirmation. The green video screen clearly showed two men standing by a pickup truck in front of the small building. They opened the doors and moved inside, and a quick blossom of white on the screen indicated the truck's motor had been turned on. Then the truck crossed the ramp and entered the access road leading to the east end of the runway.

"Victor aircraft, company's coming. The access road behind you. Two men. Customs and Immigration. They're bad guys. My guess is they're just checking out the runway. The load they're expecting must be inbound. Stand by."

Mike quickly moved the FLIR search toward the end of the runway and then toward the south. He made a small sound of approval when he saw a white dot on the screen. Lance was emerging from the lagoon.

"Victor aircraft, your partner has dry feet. His ETA is plus ten. You're going to have company before then. I'm landing."

"Negative, negative," Nick said urgently. "You stay out of this. You got enough troubles. Just keep us under observation. If anything happens, let somebody know what went down. I'm going to try to stall them until Lance returns. How far away are they?"

Mike glanced at the white flower on the screen as it moved along the runway. "Thirty seconds," he said. "Why don't you hide in the mangroves? That should stall them a few minutes."

Nick thought for a second. "They might damage the aircraft. I'll stay here."

"I'll land and extract you."

"That's negative. If a federal officer gets on the ground here, there are too many problems. Just keep an eye on us. Where is Lance?"

"At the edge of the mangroves. He'll be there soon. Put the radio in your pocket. Leave it on and I'll monitor the conversation. You got your earplug in?"

"Affirmative."

"Okay, get it in your pocket. They're right on you."

Nick slipped the radio into his rear pocket. He could see the lights from the pickup truck moving through the undergrowth. He jogged to the edge of the clearing away from the lights. The two guys would be bewildered for a moment or two. That would buy him a couple of minutes.

The pickup truck stopped at the edge of the clearing and the lights washed over the little Piper. After a moment, the doors opened and two men, both wearing uniforms, slowly stepped out.

"They are not armed. Repeat, not armed," came Mike's voice through the earplug. "They haven't seen you yet. They're looking at the aircraft."

The two Bahamians fanned out from the pickup, staying behind the glare of the headlights. One of the men was walking toward Nick. But his eyes were on the aircraft. Nick looked at the man's silhouette against the truck's headlights and instinctively

categorized him: black male, about forty, five feet
nine, one-fifty. His uniform revealed he was with
the Bahamian Customs Service. The hat revealed
he was a senior officer. Then Nick saw the swagger
stick and knew the Bahamian was Inspector Rolle,
a man made wealthy by drug smugglers, a cop on a
permanent retainer from Darrell Casey. That meant
the other Bahamian was Inspector Saunders, the
senior Immigration official on Bimini, also a man in
the employ of Darrell Casey.

These two men controlled the airport and the
waters around Bimini. They had made an early
choice to take the money offered by drug smugglers.

Under normal circumstances, Nick may have identified himself as a fellow law-enforcement officer.
The brotherhood of law enforcement crosses international borders. Many times, even when enmity
exists between two countries, the lawmen of those
countries have unofficial one-on-one relationships.
They share information. They share snitches. They
may even allow the outside officer to go along on a
raid as an "observer." But these guys were dirty;
they were crooks wearing badges, bad guys in uniform. They would put more grief on a cop than they
would on a drug smuggler. Nick looked on them as
dopers who had the authority to arrest him. His
only chance was to let them think he was a smuggler.

Where was Lance? It was time to get out of here.

Inspector Rolle was closer. But his eyes were still
on the aircraft. Why was the little Piper pulled off
onto the grass at the end of the runway? Where was
the crew? Why was the aircraft here? The mind set
of the two Bahamians was such that they instinctively knew the aircraft was involved in a drug deal.
But what sort of drug deal? It could not be mari-

juana, not with that little aircraft. And who would
trust several hundred kilos of cocaine to such a tiny
single-engine aircraft? If it were a drug deal, why
had they not been consulted? Only the rankest amateur would attempt to bring a load through Bimini
without making the proper financial arrangements.

Nick knew he was about to be discovered and
decided to take the initiative. He took two steps
forward out of the shadows and said, "Hello."

The Bahamian made a sudden sound of alarm
and spun toward Nick. A look of relief washed
across his face when he saw that the man who
stepped out of the shadows was not holding an
automatic weapon.

"Inspector Saunders. Come here," the Bahamian
said over his shoulder. "And who might you be?"
he asked Nick.

Nick motioned vaguely toward the Piper and said,
"I came in on that."

"When? Don't you know this airport closes to all
traffic at sundown? It is almost eleven P.M."

Inspector Saunders, eyes wary, walked up. Inspector Rolle turned to him and said, "This man is
flying the Piper. I have just informed him the airport closed at sundown. He was about to explain
why he is here."

Both men turned toward Nick. He stayed in the
edge of the shadows, the side of his face containing
the earplug turned away from the Bahamians.

"Who else is with you?" Saunders asked.

Nick looked from one man to the other. Where
was Lance? This thing had turned to crap.

"I'm having problems with the aircraft," Nick
said.

"How long have you been here? When did you

arrive? What was your point of debarkation?" Rolle
was firing questions in rapid-fire order.

Where was Lance?

"Have I broken any laws?" he asked.

"You have not answered my questions. When did
you arrive? And why did you not clear Customs and
Immigration?" Rolle turned toward his partner. "Inspector Saunders, would you question this man,
please. I wish to look into his aircraft."

"There's nothing in there," Nick said.

"Then, of course, you will not mind if I have a
look," said Inspector Rolle as he walked away. He
was sharply etched in the bright light of the headlights, an imposing figure in his crisp uniform.

Nick looked up at Saunders. "Look, I just flew in
here. I had a problem with the aircraft. And I was
walking around trying to figure out what to do."

From the nose of the Piper came Rolle's voice.
"The cowling is still warm. This aircraft landed
within the last half-hour." He walked around the
wing toward the door.

"Are you an American citizen? May I see your
identification, please?" asked Saunders.

"Of course I'm an American," Nick said. He
reached into his pocket.

"Get ready," came the soft voice of Mike Love
through the earplug. "Lance is over near the aircraft. He must have seen the truck's headlights.
He's stopped. And more bad news. The ferry is
coming over from North Bimini. Eight people
aboard. Probably part of the ground crew for whatever deal is about to go down. You two have to get
out."

Nick was perspiring. A dope deal was going down
soon. But he had a more immediate problem. What

was Lance planning? He knew he would not approve, whatever it was.

Nick's voice was surprised when he spoke. He raised his voice so Lance could hear. "I can't find it. I must have left my billfold in the airplane."

"This aircraft is empty," Rolle said from the wing. He was puzzled. "Inspector Saunders, bring that man over here in the light. We must have some answers."

Saunders, face grim, motioned for Nick to walk ahead of him to the aircraft.

Rolle waited on the wing, looking down at Nick. "Now, you are in rather serious trouble. I suggest you answer our questions. Who are you? Where is your identification? What time did you land? What is your purpose in being here? Why . . ." Rolle stopped and peered at Nick. "What is that wire in your ear?" he asked. He jumped to the ground and walked closer.

"It's a hearing aid," Nick said loudly. He was getting ready to move on these guys. If he moved fast, he could take them down with no problem. But Lance was going to have to fly the Piper. Had he planted the beepers? Was he okay?

Suddenly Rolle pulled the radio from Nick's pocket. "That's not a hearing aid, it's a police radio," he said. He leaned over and stared closely at Nick. "And you're . . . I know your face. You're a police officer in Fort Lauderdale. Why are you on Bimini?"

"Son of a bitch," Lance screamed as he jumped out of the palmettos ten feet away and strode rapidly toward the three men around the right wing of the Piper. Lance was sodden, his hair was matted. He looked over his shoulder toward the bushes.

Nick noticed he was not carrying the bag containing his scuba gear.

"Son of a bitch," Lance repeated. Now he was in the middle of the group. He turned and pointed toward the bushes, then held his hands about eighteen inches apart. "There's a land crab in there that big. The son of a bitch came at me like a bulldozer. He almost got my balls."

Lance turned toward Saunders. "You ever been taking a dump and been attacked by a crab? You people are going to run off all the tourists if you can't do something about the crabs. People have to be able to take a dump without worrying about a crab with a three-foot pincer trying to squeeze his balls off. Son of a bitch. He almost made me a eunuch."

"And who might you be?" asked Saunders. "Why are you wet?"

"Because I sweat when I take a dump, especially if I'm being attacked by killer crabs. And the mosquitoes are as big as the crabs. Two of them are in there now fighting over my clothes."

"Who are you?" Saunders repeated.

Lance paused and looked at Saunders as if seeing him for the first time. He tapped himself in the chest with his forefinger and said, "Who am I?" He turned to Nick and said, "He wants to know who I am." Lance had turned back to Saunders and did not notice that Nick was pointing at his ear. He had just gotten a message from Mike, an alarming message. Two aircraft were inbound.

But Lance was angrily telling Saunders, "I'm the guy that almost got his balls squoze off by a crab the size of Rhode Island. I'm the guy that became anemic from the loss of blood to mosquitoes. I've had enough. I'm leaving. Any country where you can't take a peaceful dump is not a place I want to stay." He looked at Nick and motioned toward the Piper. "Ready?"

The two Bahamians started to speak but their attention was diverted when an aircraft roared past at no more than fifty feet overhead, the deep roar drowning all conversation. The two Bahamians looked up. Saunders began speaking. "A Cessna two-ten. Did you see the num . . ." Then Nick swung, a long looping roundhouse that he brought up from the ground and connected on the point of the Bahamian's upraised chin. It lifted his feet off the ground, knocked him through the air for several feet, then dropped him on the grass where he lay unmoving.

Saunders was still flying through the air when Lance swung. But Rolle saw the blow coming and moved. Lance's fist caught him a glancing blow and knocked him to his knees.

"Let's get the hell out of here," Lance said. He ran for the Piper, bounced from the wing through the open door, then screamed, "Shit. Where are the keys?"

Nick, breathing hard, stopped at the door. "What did you do with them?"

"I left them here."

Neither man spoke for several seconds. "That Bahamian was in the airplane. He must have taken them."

"Which Bahamian." Lance was back on the wing, looking at the two men. Rolle had struggled to his feet.

"That one."

Lance jumped from the wing. Rolle swung and

hit Lance squarely on the nose, causing it to spurt blood. But he was groggy from the blow he had taken a moment earlier and could not muster much power. Lance grunted and swung a short right uppercut that knocked the Bahamian to the ground. Lance grabbed and squeezed his pockets, felt the key, opened the pocket, grabbed the key, and ran toward the aircraft. Behind him, Rolle was struggling to his feet and lurching toward the Piper.

"We got to hurry," Nick said. "Mike says we got two aircraft inbound. They're a few miles out. Big ones. And the ground crew is driving down from the north end. They'll be here in about two minutes."

"Couple of those damn Merlins," Lance muttered, wiping blood from his nose and groping for the keyhole. He pushed the fuel mixture to full rich, adjusted the propeller control, turned on the master switch, then turned the ignition key. The engine quickly caught and washed a blast of warm air over the cockpit. Lance pushed on the throttle.

"Shut the door," he said. "We're making a downwind takeoff. You got a handkerchief? I'm bleeding all over the place."

"I can't."

"What do you mean?" Lance looked at Nick. He was pulling on the door. But on the wing was Inspector Rolle, also pulling on the door.

"I can't close it."

Lance pushed harder on the throttle, breaking the Piper free of the grass and sand. Now it was crossing the number "27" at the end of the runway and quickly gathered speed.

At that moment the runway lights came on. The ground crew had reached the building near the ramp and turned the lights on. That must mean the doper aircraft were on a short final.

"We taking that son of a bitch to Lauderdale?" Lance asked. Rolle was braced on the wing, holding the door with both hands and exerting far more leverage than Nick could manage.

"I know who you are. You illegally entered this country," Rolled shouted grimly through the open door. "You will not take off."

"Watch." Lance laughed.

Suddenly Nick released the door. Rolle pulled it wide against the slipstream and was about to jump inside the cockpit. But Nick had unhooked his seat belt, spun around sideways, then brought his left foot up in a vicious kick. Rolle screamed, released the door, seized his groin, and fell off the wing onto the runway.

The Piper jumped into the air.

Neither man spoke for several minutes. "When you hit somebody, hit them hard enough to make them stay down," Nick said.

"What do you mean?" Lance was watching the instruments, adjusting the throttle and fuel mixture. Blood was streaming from his nose. He leaned forward to turn on the radio.

"I hit mine and he stayed down. You hit the guy, he gets up and slugs you in the nose. You hit him again, he tries to take a county-owned aircraft away from you. I have to save your ass. I don't believe it. Two doper aircraft inbound and you're standing there talking about how a crab attacked you during your . . . your functions."

Nick reached under the seat and pulled out a cloth used to clean the inside of the windshield. "Put this on your nose. You're bleeding all over county property."

Lance held the cloth against his face. "That son

of a bitch almost reversed my polarity," he mumbled through his nose. He looked at Nick. "Why did you hit him?" he asked.

"Because I didn't like what you were talking about. I got tired of hearing you talk about that stuff. It was the only way to get out of there."

Lance paused. "You mean you slugged a cop because I was talking about taking a dump? Hey, that was my Einstein routine. I was playing it smart, distracting them. I could have talked us out of there. You did the King Kong number."

Lance adjusted the radio and suddenly heard Mike's anxious voice. He motioned with his thumb for Nick to pick up the microphone.

"Lone Ranger, Victor aircraft with you."

"You guys okay? Looked like you had a little problem?"

"We're okay. But they eye-deed me."

Mike grunted. He knew the trouble Nick would face from being identified as a Lauderdale cop who had illegally entered the Bahamas and assaulted a Bahamian official. "What about the job?"

Nick turned to his left. Lance held up a circled thumb and forefinger.

"He says he installed them."

"Good timing," Mike said. "You must know something you haven't told me."

Nick looked at Lance. Lance shrugged. "What do you mean?" Nick asked.

"The traffic I alerted you to?"

"Yeah, what about it?"

"It was two C-One-thirtys. They landed about five minutes after you guys took off."

Nick and Lance looked at each other. "Two," they said with one voice. Nick pressed the microphone to his mouth. "Confirming *two* C-One-thirtys?"

"That's affirm."

"Then the load will be moving soon," Nick said. "My guys are going to be busy."

Mike paused. He did not know how much Nick knew about the plan to intercept a C-130 with the B-26. And he said, "My guys," deliberately excluding Mike. Mike would talk with Lance later by telephone.

"Okay, guys, I'm putting it in the barn," he said.

"Good night, Mike. Thanks."

As the little Piper droned toward the long line of white sparkling lights that was the Florida coast, Lance and Nick were silent, each lost in his own thoughts. What was going on with two C-130s? Was Casey going to bring them in together? Was one ten-ton load going to follow another? Was one aircraft a backup? And why hadn't Darby told them about the second aircraft? Did she know?

Then Nick spoke. His voice was sad. "You know the bad thing about my hitting that Bahamian officer? About slugging a cop?"

Lance looked at him, face dim in the glow of the cockpit lights. "What was that?" he mumbled into the cloth he was holding over his nose. His nose was badly swollen and his voice was high and nasal.

For a long moment Nick did not answer. Then he turned to Lance and said, "I enjoyed it."

31

Hiram Turnipseed, Sheriff of Broward County, was living refutation of the adage that fat people are jolly and compassionate. According to this widely held belief, the ridicule experienced by fat people transforms them, through some mysterious alchemy, into warm and loving people. They are said to have hearts as big as all outdoors. But, at his best, Hiram Turnipseed was mean and morose. This morning he was not at his best. He sat behind the big wooden desk in his office in the Broward County Courthouse and glared through beady, heavily lidded eyes, at Nick Brown. Sheriff Turnipseed was dressed in the beige suit he wore three days each week. It was, like most of his clothes, too tight. It was tight in the shoulders, tight in the arms, and, of course, tight around his stomach. His puffy hands protruded from the cuffs of a tight shirt. All in all, he had the appearance of an overstuffed sausage, an appearance heightened by the broken blood vessels in his cheeks, the sign of a long affinity for the bottle.

Turnipseed was something of an anachronism in south Florida politics, a vestigial remnant of a time when sheriffs survived by cronyism, favoritism, nepotism, and despotism. He had been in office eighteen years, and although his margins of victory in the last two elections had grown smaller, he was reelected each time. But he could hear the distant trumpet. He knew, at some deep primordial level, that he was like a great bison running loose in a city park. His days were numbered. But he could still roar. He could make his hooves sound like thunder upon the earth. He could yet instill fear in those who ventured too close. He was, in short, a dangerous man, and more so to the people who worked for him than to criminals.

He leaned over, thumped the newspapers atop his desk, tilted his head to the side, and asked Nick Brown, "Do you know what they are calling me? Calling this department?"

"I read the paper," Nick said. He pulled at his mustache.

Hiram Turnipseed continued as if he had not heard Nick. He picked up the paper on the top of the pile, the *St. Petersburg Times*, and waved it aloft. "The international sheriff's department of Broward County," he said sarcastically. "The local papers are eating my ass. The *Miami Herald* quotes some State Department guy who says I have gone beyond my jurisdiction, that by illegally entering the Bahamas, we are guilty of espionage. Espionage. They're accusing American police officers of espionage."

Sheriff Turnipseed was plainly bewildered at being charged with espionage. That was a charge for spies during wartime, or something the Russians did in the dark of the night.

He waved another paper. "The *Atlanta Constitution*. That guy up there who's written about smug-

gling for years, even he is on my ass. Quotes the
DEA as saying we assaulted a brother officer and
exceeded our authority. They even have an editorial saying we endangered our working relationship
with the Bahamas. Horseshit! They know those guys
are dirty. And what relationship do we have with
the Bahamians?''

Nick remained silent. When Turnipseed was roaming through the ozone, it was best to let him travel
alone. Just sit and wait. He would return to earth.
Nick's thoughts were on the two C-130s that had
landed on Bimini. When he had returned, a call had
been waiting from Ron Williamson at DEA saying
the beepers were working, that he was getting a
loud-and-clear signal. Both men knew the load would
be moving within a day or so. Nick had canceled all
leaves, put his men on twelve-hour shifts, and had
every aircraft in the air wing on standby. He was
going to throw up a screen of aircraft that nothing
could penetrate without being detected. When the
C-130 came in, his men would follow it to wherever
it landed in Broward County.

Turnipseed was still ranting. "Even the *New York
Times* is in the act. They have an editorial saying
my department is guilty of the most''—he looked at
the editorial—''egregious—what the hell is e-greg-
us?—excesses of law enforcement. That we assaulted
a Bahamian official. That we need to be restrained.
That the voters in Broward County may wish to
consider the feasibility of a recall election. Consider
the feasibility of a recall election,'' he mimicked,
tossing the paper on his desk.

"They quote some Bahamian minister as saying
that every member of the BSO is being declared
persona non grata in the Bahamas, that we are not

welcome either officially or as civilians. That means nobody in my department can even go over there to fish."

He waved a beefy hand at the newspapers. "Brown, this department doesn't want that kind of publicity. We don't need it, don't want it, can't have it, won't have it."

Nick was brought back to the present. He looked up, saw the windows of the sheriff's office, and the thought crossed his mind that none of them were broken, none were shot out.

"You're relieved of duty as of this time," Sheriff Turnipseed said. He tapped a pudgy forefinger on the desk. "Badge and weapon right here. Turn them in."

Nick's face was impassive. The sheriff knew he had been operating in the Bahamas—in fact, had encouraged it. And Nick had known that if anything went wrong there would have to be a sacrifice. Well, something had gone wrong. The only good thing was that the Bahamians had not identified Lance. They thought he was a charter pilot.

"I'd like to ask two questions," Nick said.

Turnipseed stared, waiting.

"How long am I suspended for and can I suggest a temporary replacement?"

"I'm announcing that you are suspended without pay for thirty days. And I have picked an acting head of the narcotics squad. I'm putting Larry Cunningham in there. He's a good man."

Nick's eyebrows rose. He had planned to recommend Navarro, a more senior officer. Lance? Running the drug squad? God help the Bahamas.

"He said that because of his undercover work he doesn't want any pictures or any public announcements."

Nick looked at the sheriff. He knew why Lance did not want any pictures. Somebody in the Bahamas might recognize him.

"Do you want a briefing on the Darrell Casey investigation? Do you want to know what's about to go down?"

"The only thing I want is for Cunningham to do his job. I want results, not this kind of publicity. If I get results, fine. If I get publicity, he will be on the street."

Nick stood up, reached into his pocket for his credentials, and reverently placed the worn leather wallet on the sheriff's desk. For a moment he held his hand over the bulge made by his gold shield. Then he pushed it across the desk with his fingers.

He unhooked the brass belt buckle, the one fashioned in the shape of a curved alligator, pulled it through two loops on his blue polyester pants, and removed the holster containing his Browning. He placed the holster on the desk, threaded his belt through the loops, pulled up his pants, and hitched the belt tightly. He turned without a word and walked away. As he walked, his elbows were out from his body.

Lance Cunningham stood in Nick Brown's office. He was wearing a cowboy hat, sunglasses, and a long Australian raincoat that reached to the top of his boat shoes. Under the raincoat was a white cotton windbreaker and then an orange T-shirt that said, "When I Go By, Listen for My Doppler Effect." Under his left arm, in a snap-in holster, was his chrome-plated Magnum. It hung upside down so he could reach under his coat, seize the grip, and quickly pull it out.

"Where's Navarro?" he called through the open door to Nick Brown's secretary.

"Right behind you," she said.

Lance turned. The little Cuban with the theatrical shock of combed-back white hair was standing beside him.

"You know what's happened," Lance said.

Navarro nodded. He combined the rare qualities of being an excellent undercover narc with being a man of unusual administrative skills. His fellow narcs considered him a fellow cop while courthouse bureaucrats considered him a skilled administrator. He was a quiet professional who did his job.

"Fluf played by the rules and they put his ass on the beach," Lance said. His voice was heavy with irony. "They're talking about charging him with aggravated assault. That's bullshit. Fluf might have assaulted the guy, but he didn't aggravate him. Hell, if anyone was aggravated, it was me. That guy was trying to stop a Broward County aircraft. That's the only reason Fluf popped him."

Navarro said nothing. Sometimes it was difficult to know when Lance was serious.

Lance glanced at Navarro and said, "Look, I don't know why the sheriff put me here, but he did. I wouldn't take it, but it enables me to finish a deal I'm working on. You're in charge of the squad. For the next day or so, you're running it. Take care of all the ongoing investigations, keep the paperwork flowing to the courthouse, handle the duty roster, and keep whoever Fluf put on the Darrell Casey investigation working on that."

Navarro nodded.

Lance looked across Nick's office to the broken window. "But the first thing you do, your top priority, is moving this office."

He handed the surprised Navarro a slip of paper containing an address in a small shopping center two miles away. "The sign on the door says Broward Realty, but it's our office as of today. You handle security during the move. I want everybody out of this shit box today. Have the telephones changed. Get everyone over there before the sheriff knows about this. He won't do anything once we're there."

Lance looked at the broken window through which the breeze was blowing, lightly stirring papers on Nick Brown's desk. He shook his head in disgust. "Moving furniture is a risky business. I wouldn't be surprised if a desk or a chair knocked out some of those windows today."

"You never can tell," Navarro said. Then he asked, "Will you be around?"

"I've got some business to attend to," Lance said. "I'll be in touch. Who's off sick?"

"Fullerton," Navarro said, not missing a beat.

"Okay, I'm not going to be on the radio. But if there's a problem and you need me, use Fullerton's call sign. Victor two six, right?"

Navarro nodded.

Lance lowered his voice. "Until this deal goes down, there are only three people other than you I will talk to. If Fluf calls, put him through. Forget his being suspended. You and I both know this is his department. The second person I'll talk to is one of our people, woman U/C type Fluf sent to work the Darrell Casey case. Her name is Darby DuPree. She hasn't checked in lately. If she does, tell her the shit's coming down today and to get out of there. Keep a couple uniform guys on standby in case she needs them. Fluf is concerned about her. Keep him informed of anything regarding her. The other person is a DEA guy, Ron Williamson, a friend of Fluf's. He knows what's going down. We've got our own channels, but if something happens, he may call here. If he does, put him through."

"He called earlier," Navarro said. "He heard about Fluf and wanted to make sure you got the message that he was getting a good strong signal. He said you would know what he meant."

Navarro paused, his thick white eyebrows raised in a question mark.

Lance put his hand on Navarro's shoulder. "Look, I'm not trying to keep you in the dark. But you saw what happened to Fluf. It's best you don't know some things. If they go bad, you'll be out of the way. I can only tell you that a long-standing investigation of Darrell Casey is about to come down. You don't need to know the details. But I'm working with DEA and we're using these military radios that we have when we need tight security."

He handed Navarro the powerful compact radio. "You monitor this one. The others are all locked up. If for any reason, somebody wants to go into the evidence room, especially the section where we store those weapons we confiscated from the julios in the Glades, keep them out. Okay."

Navarro nodded. He had been the undercover officer on the investigation that resulted in the seizure of some very sophisticated weapons from Cubans who were training in the Everglades, training to overthrow Castro. The CIA had provided them with an incredible array of weapons, some of which were so new they had not yet been issued to the U.S. military. If Cunningham were using weapons from that cache, he was after big game indeed.

Navarro looked up at Lance and grinned. "Man,

you are not looking for Central Cuban Dispatch today, not with that sort of firepower."

Lance's eyes brightened. "Did I tell you that I think I've found CCD? I'm almost certain this time is it."

"Where?"

"Yesterday I was out tooling around in my Lincoln U/C car, the one we got from Steinhorst. I was over near ninety-five, down south of the airport. I found it in a shopping center. I'm checking it out. There were julios everywhere. And everyone had either a pickup truck or an old car."

Navarro grinned. "Maybe I should look for CCD. I'm a julio."

Lance snorted. "You ain't a julio. You're a cop."

Navarro laughed aloud. "My friend, don't worry about anything here. I've got it under control." He paused. "Good luck."

Lance squeezed Navarro's shoulder and turned toward the door. "Navarro," he said, "you're a good man. One day you're gonna be sheriff."

Navarro smiled. "I know."

32

Darrell Casey was celebrating.

He sat in the cool opulent living room of his home on the Intracoastal Waterway and hoisted a water glass half-filled with champagne.

When Casey built the house, he hired an Atlanta decorator to furnish it in exquisite and extravagant detail. Price was not a consideration. Casey wanted whatever it was that rich people put in their homes. The decorator had bought two sets of Waterford crystal, one in the bold and graceful Curraghmore and one in the more traditional Lismore, but there were times when Darrell became excited and forgot the crystal. He reverted to the days when he was a plumber and drank out of whatever was available. Today he had ordered six bottles of champagne— "The most expensive you have," he told the proprietor. "Already cold." When the champagne arrived, Darrell popped the cork on the first bottle, reached into a cupboard, pulled out a water glass, and began pouring.

Now the second bottle, already half-empty, sat in an antique sterling-silver serving bucket atop the low table in the living room. The drapes were open and Casey could see down the long sloping lawn to the water. Next to him, sitting on the soft leather sofa with her feet drawn up under her, was Darby DuPree. She hesitantly sipped at the champagne. Darby was not used to drinking and, in fact, did not like the taste of champagne. But Darrell's ebullience swept her along.

"What are we celebrating?" she asked. It was the second—or was it the third?—time she had asked. But he had not answered. The first time, he went to the kitchen for another bottle. The second time, he changed the subject. This time he looked at her, weighing her, appraising her, for a long moment. He made her a bit nervous. It was as if he were trying to decide whether he should tell her.

She had heard a radio story saying Nick had been suspended and she felt very much alone. She had tried to call the office the previous night, but no one answered. Then there was a recording saying the number had been changed. But she did not have time to call again.

She needed to report but did not know who was in charge. Only two or three people in the narc squad knew of her undercover work with Darrell Casey. Lance knew because he was working the same case. But he opposed the assignment. She was alone, cut off from her office, with no one to call on for help except in the most dire circumstances.

She was frightened. But at the same time she knew it was a chance to prove her mettle, to prove she could improvise, that even when alone in the middle of a group of smugglers, she could take care of herself. It would be good for her and good for all the other women in police work. She had to perform. She had to overcome the mistakes she had made on this case.

One of the things that made her so singularly attractive to Darrell Casey was an almost mystical quality. She had what in ancient times was reverently and deferentially called "power." She saw things other people did not see. She knew things they did not know.

Today that mystical power was telling her something was not right. Darrell's aura, his eyes, his body language, something intangible, all told her that he was a man in conflict, a man torn by emotion, a man undecided about what course to take. The tension in his body was palpable. And the ebullience and the champagne did not hide it.

She wondered the same thing that every undercover narc wonders: does he know?

"Let's go outside," Darrell said. "Let's put on our bathing suits and sit in the sunshine."

Darby did not answer. She was afraid of Darrell, afraid of the alligators that so fascinated him. For the past several weeks she had not enjoyed sitting by the pool.

Darrell stood up, grabbed an expensive linen blanket from the end of the sofa, and repeated, "Let's go sit in the sun. You like the sunshine. Come on. Bring the champagne."

She pursed her lips, reluctantly said, "Okay," and uncoiled her achingly long legs from the sofa. She stood with her feet apart and stretched. And for a moment there was an expression of great longing in Darrell's eyes, a longing for the way things had been between them long ago. Then he turned and motioned for her to follow. "And bring another bottle," he said.

She walked into the kitchen and picked up another bottle. Then she picked up the sterling champagne bucket, cradled it to her waist, and with the bottle under her arm, followed Darrell.

She stopped when she saw he had walked past the swimming pool and spread the white linen blanket at the very edge of the alligator pit. He took off his shoes, pulled his cotton shirt over his head, and tossed it aside, then sat on the blanket. The alligators saw the movement and became restless. Several raised their heads and emitted long slow warning hisses.

"Come on," Darrell said.

"Darrell, I'm afraid. Let's move the blanket near the pool."

"This is a good place. Come on."

"Darrell, please don't make me do this. I'm really afraid of the alligators."

Darrell looked over his shoulder and stared into the pit. He looked at her and after a long moment said, "So am I. Come on."

Darby came to the edge of the blanket, sank to her knees, placed the champagne bucket on the grass, then turned and slowly lowered herself to the blanket. She lay on her side, supported by an elbow, and looked at Darrell. His eyes were closed as he soaked up the warm afternoon sunshine. After a moment she took a long drink of champagne. Maybe the champagne would help her forget the alligators. She took another long drink. She giggled.

"Pour the rest of that bottle in our glasses, then put the other bottle in the ice," Darrell said.

Darby looked at her glass, turned it up, and drank the remainder, then reached for Darrell's glass. She poured from the bottle until it was empty, then nestled the other bottle in the ice.

She turned her face up to the sun, shut her eyes,

and sighed. She looked around. The fenced yard
was empty. There was no sign of Bobo, the creepy
Colombian. She crossed her arms and pulled the
cotton sweater over her head. Then, with an imp-
ish smile, she stuck her thumbs in the waistband of
her shorts, lifted her hips, and pushed the shorts
down her legs. She kicked the shorts aside and was
nude.

She looked at Darrell. His eyes were still closed.
She leaned over, maneuvering, trying to place her
right breast on his lips. But her elbow slipped and
she fell atop Darrell and began laughing.

He grunted, "What the. . . ."

"My breasts are not big enough." She giggled.
She looked down. "I've always had such small
breasts." Her voice was wistful. "Don't men want
women with larger breasts?"

He looked up at her looming over him, a light
sheen of perspiration glowing on her tanned body.
"Some men do," he said.

"What about you?"

For a moment he did not answer. Then he said,
"I don't think I would change a thing about you."
His voice was sad. He turned up the glass of champagne, drained it, then reached across Darby and
pulled the new bottle from the ice. Cold water
dripped on her stomach, causing her to gasp.

Darrell twisted the wire from atop the cork and
opened the bottle. He poured champagne into his
water glass, then leaned over and replaced the bottle in the ice bucket. He looked at Darby's stomach
where a few drops of ice water had pooled. He
slumped and began licking the water from her stomach. She sighed, placed her hands in his hair, and
gently pushed him lower.

After a moment he raised his head and said, "You always taste so sweet."

"Let me," she said, rolling Casey over on his back and pulling at his belt. He picked up his hips and she pulled his white pants off, tossed them aside, then stretched one of her long legs across Darrell's body. She reached behind her, groping, maneuvering, then shoved her hips downward causing Darrell to groan and toss his arms wide. He did not know he had flung his glass of champagne over the edge of the pit.

The hissing of the alligators grew louder.

Darrell seized Darby's wide hips and pulled her closer. For a moment he almost forgot what he had to do. He looked up. Her eyes were closed and her face contorted in intensity.

"Hey," he whispered.

She did not hear him.

He pushed lightly on her hips. "Hey," he repeated.

She opened her eyes. "What is it?"

"Not that way."

She smiled. And in one fluid endless motion she lifted her leg, moved from atop his body, and lowered her head. Darrell looked down. He thrust his hips. He placed his right hand behind her head, held her close, and thrust harder. He wanted to use her. It would make what he had to do easier.

Then he groaned loudly and fell back. Darby moved up higher on the blanket, threw her leg across him, and snuggled her face into his neck. "Hmmmmmmm," she said. "That was nice."

He did not answer.

A moment later he pushed her aside and sat up. He looked around, then reached for her cotton sweater and wiped himself off.

She stared at him in astonishment. "What are you doing?" she asked.

He looked at her. His face was fixed and his eyes were hard and mean. For a second, his eyes reminded her of Steinhorst. "You mean, what have I *done*?" he said.

He stood up and slid on his pants, all the while keeping his unblinking eyes on her. She reached for her shorts but he pulled them from her hand. "Stay just like that. I like that."

"Darrell! What are you doing?"

He backed away. He was holding her shorts. "Stay right there. I'll be back in one second."

He turned and walked swiftly toward the house. Suddenly the hissing of the alligators was strong in her consciousness and she unwillingly looked over her shoulder and down into the pit. With a small cry of alarm she moved away. She looked around. Her crumpled sweater was on the ground. She stood, picked up the linen blanket, and wrapped it around her body. The noise of the door caused her to look toward the house. Darrell was returning. With him was Bobo, the barefoot Colombian. Darrell was smiling. He stopped a few feet away and waited, saying nothing. Then he nodded his head. "Well, my little *undercover* agent. Your time is up. It's over."

Her dark eyes flared in fright and she pulled the blanket tighter under her arms. "What do you mean? What are you doing?"

Darby was terrified. Darrell knew! And the tone in his voice told her he was not guessing. He knew! He stared at her and his face was almost as impassive as that of the Colombian standing to his side.

"You're wondering how I knew," he said. He

went on, pleased that he had discovered her, that he had outwitted the cops, anxious to tell her where she had failed. "Well, I began to suspect you when the Customs helicopter burned my boat. There was no way he could have been there at that moment unless he knew in advance I was doing a deal. You were the only person who could have leaked that information. Then your fat little boss slipped up. I made a recording of Steinhorst's conversation with him. He said he knew about the C-130 load. And that information had to have come from here. Only two or three people in Lauderdale knew." He shrugged. "You were the logical source. Once I figured that out, a lot of other things, things I had not understood, fell into place." He nodded. "You were good. But not good enough."

Darby felt vulnerable. Not only was she dealing with two crooks, she was having to face them while clad only in a linen blanket. She had only one way to go. She tried to push back her fear as she said firmly, "You're making a big mistake. My office knows where I am. I'm not out here on a limb by myself. The best thing you can do is give yourself up."

Darrell laughed. He walked to the edge of the alligator pit and looked down. Then he turned back to her and laughed again.

"You came close to doing me some real damage," he said. "Now I'm going to show you what real damage is."

He looked at Bobo and flicked his right hand toward Darby. "You know what to do," he said.

He walked away.

33

"They're moving the load," Ron Williamson said.

Lance's mouth twitched. This was one of those times when he realized that being a narc was not a game. Not when somebody was shuffling ten tons of cocaine around, ten tons that were being readied to come into Broward County. And it was his responsibility to stop the load.

He looked at his watch. Friday. One P.M. His brow wrinkled. "What do you think they are doing? How will they handle this?" He had met the big DEA agent twice but did not know him well. He did not like DEA, but if Fluf thought he was a good guy, then he was. Lance would listen.

Ron puffed on his pipe. The Friday-afternoon party, a regular occurrence at the Miami DEA office, was in full swing and the noise level was growing. He placed his pipe in an ashtray, pressed his left finger into his ear to muffle the party noise, and leaned forward. "Well, let's see. We got the first indication on the beeper about seven minutes ago. I'm assuming they're working it from the front. Was the beeper placed in a container right in front or was it several rows back?"

"Front row," Lance said immediately. He had no trouble remembering where he had placed the beepers that night in the lagoon.

"Okay, we're indicating one beeper is moving and the other is remaining stationary. So they're still working the load. And my guess is that even with a half-dozen divers working it, they're going to be there for hours, well into the night, probably up into the morning. Was the underwater configuration of the stash such that they would work straight through it?"

"Yes. If they went to the back side, they would have to tow those big bags around the front part. So they will work in from the front in order to have clear access."

"Okay, then, when the second beeper is activated, we'll know they are near the end."

"How long will it take to load that much on the aircraft?"

Ron picked up his pipe and puffed on it for a moment while he thought. "Let's assume the divers are doing nothing but retrieving the stuff and putting it on the banks of the lagoon. It doesn't make sense for them to have to come out of the water, load it on a truck, then drive to the aircraft. You agree?"

Lance knew the answer to much of what he and Ron were discussing. But he wanted the benefit of the DEA agent's thinking. He could not afford to take chances. "Yes. And once it gets out of the lagoon, the only way to move it is by those little pickup trucks. Only one at a time can go down the path to the lagoon."

"But can they load it as fast as it comes out of the water?"

Lance paused. "I don't think so. Not with a half-dozen divers in there. They will be all spread out. It will get damn tiring pulling those bags out of the water. The weights have to be taken off. Then, once they are onshore, the flotation collars have to be removed. The humpers throw the bags on the trucks. I'm guessing they won't put more than four, five max, bags on a truck at any one time. The trucks are small, the road is extremely rough."

Ron knew Lance had been with Nick the night of the big flap on Bimini. And it appeared the young agent had a good eye for detail.

"Where will they take it? Is the aircraft on the ramp?"

Lance paused. "Can you stand by one?"

"Sure." While Ron was waiting, he took his finger from his ear. The party noise was louder. Suddenly a wheelchair whizzed by his open door. One of the blind file clerks was driving. She was wearing a set of earphones with a small, built-in radio and eighteen-inch-long antennae, and she was laughing uproariously. DEA had recently gone on a binge of hiring the handicapped. Two blind file clerks were the latest hires. They were not actually blind, not 100 percent; vision impaired, it was called. And Dumnik had ordered that the file clerks were to retrieve all case files. Agents could no longer do this. So agents had to wait while the blind file clerks searched through the drawers, pulled files one by one, held them up to their eyes, squinted, mumbled, and looked for the large identifying numbers. Both were seemingly oblivious of their handicap and were vibrant smiling women who laughed about bumping into walls. And during the Friday-afternoon parties they would have a few drinks, then ride in the wheelchair belonging to Dumnik's secretary. One of the agents would pick her up—she had been injured in a car wreck—and place her atop a desk. Then the blind file clerks would take turns careening around the office. Occasionally they had run into people, pinning them against the wall, their blindness making them oblivious and the radios making them unable to hear the entreaties of their victims. Friday was truly a happy day at the Miami DEA office. It was good enough that the agents no longer spent Fridays around the corner at Ma Grundy's, their long-time favorite bar.

"You there?" Lance was back on the telephone.

"Yeah, guy, go ahead," Ron said. He took another puff from his pipe, placed it back in the ashtray, then put his finger in his ear and leaned over the desk.

"One aircraft is on the ramp. The other is pulled off onto the grass at the east end of the field. The ramp is down so that's probably the one they're going to be loading. I'll know in a few minutes."

"You have an eyeball over there?" Ron was astounded. After all that had happened, these local guys still had on-site intelligence.

"They're loading the aircraft at the east end of the strip," Lance repeated. He did not feel comfortable telling a DEA agent that a suspended Customs pilot in a civilian aircraft, surrounded by about a million dollars' worth of electronics, had watched the scuba divers enter the lagoon to retrieve the cocaine a half-hour before the satellite reported the beeper was on the move. Mike had reported that one of the little white pickup trucks—it belonged either to Customs or Immigration—was parked at the edge of the lagoon. The other was waiting near the aircraft. And everyone was being videotaped.

Ron paused and thought rapidly. "Is there any activity around the other aircraft? The one on the ramp?"

"Stand by one."

A few seconds later Lance was back on the telephone. "Negative. It's parked on the north side of the ramp just sitting there. No sign of activity."

"That bothers me. Why would they bring it in, then not use it?" Ron was confused. He had asked Lance about one aircraft and then the other in order to determine the extent of the surveillance Broward County had on Bimini. They obviously had an eyeball on the lagoon and one on the C-130 at the west end of the field. But Lance's quick radio conversation indicated they had someone near the airport building also.

He would try something else.

"How many humpers do they have?" he asked.

"Stand by one."

Thirty seconds later Lance was back. "They have six divers working the load in the lagoon. Four humpers loading one of the pickups. Eight humpers at the aircraft." Lance paused. "They have more at the aircraft because they have to off-load the truck and put the stuff in the back of the airplane, then move it forward to distribute the weight properly."

"Well, I never would have known," Ron said sarcastically. He had worked airplane cases when the coprophiliac was still wearing short pants. He was astounded at how quickly and how detailed Lance's response had been. Broward County must have at least a half-dozen guys hiding in the bushes on Bimini. My God, they were all *persona non* grata. If they were caught, they would go to Fox Hill. At the same time he admired their audacity. And how did they get on Bimini? DEA could take lessons in undercover techniques from these locals.

Unless, unless, they had an aircraft up. No, it couldn't be that. No local law enforcement had the money to buy the electronics it would take to conduct that sort of surveillance. It had to be guys on the ground.

Lance interrupted Ron's wondering. "Hey, I forgot, guy. This thing has me—"

"Forget it," Ron interrupted. "I figure they'll finish loading the aircraft sometime early tomorrow morning. The big question then is when will the load move. Will they move it as soon as it's loaded or will they give the crew some down time? Will they come in while it's dark or in daylight?"

Lance thought quickly. He remembered what Fluf had told him about Casey's desire to humiliate Broward County cops.

"Daylight. They'll move it during the daytime," he said.

Ron picked up his pipe, puffed on it, and blew the smoke toward the ceiling. "Why do you need the beeper?" he asked. "You got an eyeball over there. You're watching them in real time. You know every step they're taking. So why do you need the beeper?"

Lance was alarmed. The beepers were crucial, but he could not tell the DEA agent the role they would play. The beepers had to stay in place. "The way Fluf explained it to me, the beepers give you one signal when they're just sitting there and another when they're moving. Is that right?"

"Right."

"So you will know when the second beeper is being moved from the lagoon and then on the truck?"

"Right again."

"When the stuff is on the aircraft, just waiting until takeoff, you'll know that?"

"I went over all this with Nick. But, yes, you're right. And if your next question is, will we know when the aircraft moves, the answer is yes."

"Okay," Lance said. "I've got to know the second the aircraft starts moving. Our plan to stop it hangs on knowing the very second it begins to move. We have to get things lined up. It only takes about twelve minutes for that aircraft to reach Florida. We have to know when it moves. Can you do that?"

"Your eyeball over there can do that. Why do you need me to stay on top of the beepers?"

"I can't explain," Lance said. "But you trusted Fluf enough to do this. He's out of the picture. He gave it to me. So I'm asking you to trust me when I tell you it is absolutely crucial that we know the exact second the aircraft starts moving."

Ron reached for his pipe. He couldn't figure out what Cunningham had in mind. "Okay, guy. You'll know."

Lance sighed in relief. "You have one of the radios and you have Navarro's phone number. You can reach me anytime until this is over."

"I'll call when it starts moving again. And let us know if you need us. Nick had a plan to intercept the load, I don't know what it was. But you guys appear to have it under control. If you need us, give us a call."

"Hey, thanks."

"Talk to you." Ron hung up just as the wheelchair driven by the blind woman careened past his open door. She was being pushed by the other blind woman. He could hear Dumnik laughing in the background. He sighed and looked at his watch. One hundred and four days until retirement.

Lance looked at the telephone and sighed in relief. That had been close. His plan could not avoid having a lull in the surveillance on Bimini. Mike was keeping track of the number of containers being pulled out of the lagoon. When the loading was almost completed, he would take the Cessna 210 back to the farm west of Lauderdale and trade it for the B-26. Then the timing got sticky. The moment Ron notified them that the second beeper had sounded, Mike would take off in the B-26. The nose cannon on the B-26 was loaded. Mike was going to intercept the C-130 over the open ocean and blow it out of the sky.

Lance grinned. He couldn't tell a DEA agent that Broward County planned to shoot down a doper. Feds don't understand that kind of law enforcement.

34

Darby was unconscious.

She was sprawled on the seat of an old pickup truck, her hands lashed to a cross brace in the rotted-out interior of the door. Her matted shirt was tied around her mouth as a gag. The linen blanket she had worn to cover herself was rucked up about her waist.

The dark Colombian known as Bobo fondled her as he drove slowly and carefully through the back streets of Fort Lauderdale, through the poor section where many blacks and Hispanics lived, toward the large open garbage dump.

He was about to enjoy a very pleasant benefit of his job. Back in Colombia the wealthy *padrones* for whom he worked occasionally decided they were tired of their women. Because the women had overheard numerous business conversations, the drug dealers could not afford to simply turn them out.

They had to be silenced.

Then there were the women—girls really, young girls—whom several *padrones* liked to kidnap and bring to their homes for a week or a month. When the *padrones* wearied of the young girls, Bobo was called upon to remove them.

They, too, had to be silenced.

But before the women were silenced, Bobo enjoyed them. Sometimes it was at the suggestion of the women. They thought that granting their favors to Bobo would save their lives. Bobo derived his own peculiar method of satisfaction from these women who had graced the homes of the most powerful men in Colombia. Many of them were the incredibly beautiful young blondes so highly desired by Colombians. But in the end they all died. They had to. Bobo knew that if one lived, he would die.

Bobo had been surprised when the gringo Darrell Casey said this woman should not be killed. Bobo stared, thinking he had misunderstood.

"Do not kill her," Casey insisted. "Use your knife. Hurt her. Make her remember you every day of her life. But don't kill her."

"She will talk," Bobo said. He had been influenced by the men for whom he had worked in Colombia, men whose solution to virtually every problem was to kill the problem.

"Not if you hurt her badly enough. If you hurt her so badly that every day is torture, every day she prays for death . . . if you cause her enough pain to fuck up her mind, she will be too afraid to talk. Even to her cop friends. Every time they ask who did it, she'll remember what happened all over again. She's too young to deal with that."

"She will talk," Bobo repeated.

"Look, just do what I tell you. Hurt her so badly that anytime she thinks of you, her next thought is that you might come back. You do that and I'll worry about her talking. Now do it."

Bobo slowly turned a corner and smiled as he remembered. The woman had thought she was going to be thrown to the alligators. She was almost relieved when he took her across the yard to the old pickup truck. He had knocked her unconscious with a sharp blow to the back of her neck and then had tied her hands to the door of the truck. He glanced down at her long legs and lovely hips. He groped for a moment, causing her to moan in pain. She was dark enough to appear almost Colombian. Too bad. He liked blondes.

Now she was awakening. And when she did, when she realized what he had planned for her, when she saw what he was doing to her body with his knife, then she would wish she had been tossed to the alligators. He would keep her conscious as long as possible. He wanted her to know the horror.

Bobo turned through the gate at the garbage dump and casually glanced around. No other vehicles were in sight. But he continued driving around the edges of the huge open area until he came to the rear side.

No one would disturb him here.

No one would hear the woman's screams.

35

The landing gear of the B-26 was still cycling into the wheel wells when Mike Love racked the speeding aircraft in a steep turn toward the coast. The aircraft was low and the throttles remained at full takeoff power as the speed continued to climb.

A half-mile away, in a guest house at a sprawling ranch west of Lauderdale, four men in white coveralls heard the screaming engines. They had worked all night on the B-26. Their conversation had stopped when they loaded the big rounds of ammunition into the gatling gun in the nose of the aircraft. The B-26 carried the same cannon, albeit a far more sophisticated model, than the A-10, the famous close Air Support aircraft used by the U.S. Air Force. Once the firing button was pressed, the cannon became an urban-renewal project; it chewed up real estate, houses, even tanks, at an awesome rate. It was one of the least known but one of the most effective weapons in the Air Force inventory.

"Power reduction. Power reduction," whispered the older man, the one to whom the others deferred.

He stood up, walked quickly to the window, and pulled the curtain. To the east, low on the horizon, he saw a brief flash of early-morning sunlight glance off the canopy of the B-26. He cocked his head, listening to the fast-fading thunder of the powerful engines. The other three men looked up at him as he turned away from the window. "This is it," he said, rubbing his hands together. "We've done our job. Now he has to do his."

The B-26 was racing flat out, belly low over the water, as it hurried into the morning sun. At 235 knots, Bimini was about ten minutes from the Florida coast. Mike was going up against drug smugglers as he always did, everything to the wall, full commitment, nothing held back. At high cruise, 85 percent power, each of the B-26's two engines was burning about seventy-five gallons per hour. But the old World War II bomber could carry almost fourteen hundred gallons. Even at high cruise, he could stay aloft more than nine hours. But he expected action within the next hour or so. Casey would want to move the load as quickly as possible. No one, not even Darrell Casey, could safely leave ten tons of cocaine in an aircraft on Bimini.

Mike began orbiting five miles west of the island. The C-130 he was waiting to intercept could walk off from him at speeds in excess of three hundred knots. He had to stay between Bimini and Florida. He would get only one pass at the C-130. He kept his speed up, ready to roll toward Bimini the moment he heard over the radio the load was moving. And, as backup, he kept one radio tuned to 122.8, the Unicom frequency at Bimini. The dopers almost certainly would radio a traffic advisory that they were departing, just for protection. Bimini was a busy runway. Why risk a midair with a private aircraft when carrying ten tons of coke?

Finally, Mike utilized a special piece of equipment he had asked the lanky cowboy at the farm to order for him. The cowboy had smiled in approval when Mike asked if he could obtain one of the TOW missile telescopic sight units used aboard the navy's Cobra helicopters. With the TSU adjusted to thirteen power, Mike could cut through the slight haze and, from five miles away, easily see the Bimini runway.

He raced back and forth in a tight orbit, engines snarling, like a dog growling as it waited for a penned-up cat to break through a gate.

Mike knew the rules of engagement for F-4 Phantom pilots operating out of Homestead Air Force Base, and he knew there was only a slim chance the C-130 would be pounced by interceptors. The rules said that *any* aircraft, no matter the speed, that was detected approaching American air space from south of the twenty-fifth parallel, a line running through the Florida keys a few miles north of Islamorado, would be intercepted. Any aircraft approaching from north of the twenty-fifth parallel at speeds greater than 180 knots would be intercepted.

One would think the C-130 could not sneak into America undetected. Its speed was around three hundred knots, well over the 180 knots that dictated an intercept. In addition, the C-130's sheer size made a large primary return on radar. But Mike knew there were several easy ways for the C-130 to avoid detection. First, it could simply slow to a speed under 180. Second, it could get down about fifty feet over the water and come in *under* the radar. Third, the pilot could squawk any number of discrete law-enforcement frequencies that would deceive NORAD and FAA radar operators.

That's what Mike had done. His transponder was tuned to the secret "Spirit" code used to designate Customs aircraft. Any FAA or NORAD radars painting him on the screens would show a Customs aircraft orbiting west of Bimini.

Mike planned to radio FAA once the C-130 was airborne. They would alert the Customs Air Wing that a known trafficker was coming out of Bimini in a C-130 suspected of carrying a multi-ton load of cocaine. If all went well, everything would be over before Customs could launch aircraft for an intercept. But he wanted to give Customs a shot at the coke.

The B-26 raced north and south in a tight racetrack pattern, never going more than three miles north of the island or three miles south. Mike wanted to keep the western end of the runway in sight.

After three hours, Mike grew impatient. The sun was well up in the sky and the cockpit was like an oven, a humid oven. The C-130 should have been airborne. He wanted to call Lance. But they had agreed not to break radio silence until the load was moving.

Two hours later, the C-130 still had not moved. Mike tightened his orbit and moved a mile closer to Bimini. The dopers had to move soon. It was almost high noon.

Then his radio crackled and he heard Lance's voice. "Sky King, Victor aircraft. Target is moving. Target is moving. Do you copy?"

Mike pushed his sunglasses atop his head, leaned forward, and looked through the TSU toward South Bimini. He saw an aircraft rolling onto the east end of the runway. Then a second aircraft pulled in tight behind the first.

The Bimini airport suddenly was becoming very busy.

Lance had used "Victor aircraft" as his call sign. Was he in an aircraft?

"Victor. Sky King. I have a visual. Rolling in."

As Mike turned steeply toward Bimini he heard another voice on his radio. It was the C-130 pilot calling on Bimini's Unicom frequency, advising any inbound aircraft that a "large transport" was departing to the west.

Mike flicked the red arming switch on the cannon, rolled his shoulders, wiped his hands on his pants, wiped his eyes, then put his sunglasses back on, sat up straight, and snugged up his seat belt and shoulder harness.

He pushed the throttles of the B-26 until the snarling war bird was delivering 100 percent power. He was going into battle.

He pushed his glasses up and looked through the TSU a final time. In seconds he could eyeball the C-130. His brow wrinkled. He saw the dark shape of the C-130. And tightly snuggled up under it in a formation takeoff was a second C-130. Immediately after the two aircraft broke ground, they pulled apart, one veering to the north, the other to the south.

Which was carrying the cocaine?

Mike pulled his sunglasses back over his eyes. "Victor aircraft. We have a problem. Two, repeat, two target aircraft."

"Are they together?"

Now Mike could see the black dots of the C-130s. Both were low, no more than fifty feet above the water, and already they had spread far enough that each was about fifteen degrees off his nose, one north of him, the other south.

"Negative. Line abreast. About five miles apart. Course of each appears to be about two seven zero."

Within seconds Mike was going to have to make a decision. He did not have the speed to catch the C-130 once it passed him. He could make one firing pass. That was it.

"Sky King. Victor. Take the aircraft to the north," Lance's voice was intense. "The other is a decoy. Repeat, take the aircraft to the north."

Mike did not have time to question Lance about how he knew. He only had time to roll left and begin the intercept. As he turned steeply, he called Miami FAA and told them to alert "Lima one hundred"—Customs Air Support—on a land line. He switched frequencies before the surprised FAA controller could ask him to identify himself.

The bulbous shape of the C-130 was growing larger in the windshield. He had hoped for a head-on attack but the C-130's speed was too great. It would be about a forty-degree intercept at a combined speed approaching six hundred miles an hour. The firing pass would last no more than three to five seconds. It had to be right the first time.

He checked the arming switch. Hot.

A final glance at engine instruments. All in the green.

The heat and humidity were oppressive down low over the water. He quickly lifted his glasses and wiped perspiration from his face.

Now all of his attention was devoted to infinitely complex calculations of relative speed and vectors and energy management and muzzle velocity.

The humiliation of his suspension, the long nights orbiting over Bimini, the frustration of being beaten by dozens, perhaps hundreds of dopers—it all was about to culminate in one brief firing pass. And in some cosmic way those three, four, or five seconds would balance the scales.

Mike's hands were light as a caress on the wheel. His thumb rested atop the red firing button.

The C-130 was growing in size at an alarming rate. The pressure of his thumb on the red firing button increased by a fraction of an ounce.

Then the C-130 crew saw the B-26 and, in a maneuver that would be astounding to one unfamiliar with the C-130's performance, broke hard to the right. As the big vulnerable belly of the C-130 became visible, Mike knew that in a few brief seconds the target would have eluded him. He noticed, almost subliminally, the bright-green alligator with the gaping red mouth on the tail of the aircraft.

He pressed the red button and held it down. The blow-back of the cannon in the nose was such that the B-26 shook and shuddered and decreased in speed. It was covered with smoke from the cannon and anyone below would have heard frightening staccato blasts.

Then the B-26 passed the C-130. But not before Mike knew the cannon shells had ripped open the belly of the giant aircraft from just behind the wings all the way aft to the loading ramp. It looked as if the rear of the C-130 was covered in dust; then the aircraft shook from the impact and the lower aft portion of the aircraft disappeared. The surface of the ocean was suddenly covered with debris. Had the big aircraft not been so low over the water, it would have broken apart and crashed. As it was, the pilot simply pulled power on all four engines and let it settle into the water.

Mike pulled up to about one hundred feet, then turned on a wingtip. He saw the C-130 when it hit the water, bounced once, then broke apart on the second impact.

"Now we'll see if its true that alligators like saltwater," Mike muttered. He pressed the transmit button on his radio and notified FAA that a transport aircraft had crashed approximately halfway between Bimini and Fort Lauderdale. He saw two men in life jackets and knew the crew had escaped.

And he knew that the C-130 contained no cargo.

The cocaine was in the other aircraft.

36

Darby struggled through a deep vale of pain, reached upward for consciousness, then, fighting waves of nausea and the relentless pull of merciful sleep, slowly opened her eyes. She closed them immediately. The noonday sun was too bright. But it was the warmth of the sun, the soothing healing warmth, that had pulled her from the depths of unconsciousness. She slowly turned her head to the side and again opened her eyes. The first thing she saw was the blurred image of a wadded-up cellophane container. Beside it was a crumpled can with a tattered red label. And there was a puddle of thick green liquid in the bottom of a broken bottle. And filtering through her pain was a horrible repulsive odor, an odor of rot and slime.

Where was she?

The birds were singing. She could hear the birds, hundreds of them, somewhere in the background. She moved her head a few inches, tried to focus her eyes on the distance, and saw that she was in a deep valley. The mountains were high around her. But there were no mountains in Lauderdale. If only the pain, the awful pain of her breasts, her loins, of her body, would lessen, then she could think more clearly. There was something she had to do, something very important. But she could not remember. All she wanted to do was let the warmth of the sun pull her back toward unconsciousness. No. She could not sleep. She must move. There was something about her job, something that must be done now, something that could not wait.

She tried to lift her head but could not. She was too weak. As pain washed over her like waves falling on the beach, she drifted back into unconsciousness.

An hour later, pulled by the sheer force of will, her eyes opened. She slowly pulled her right knee upward and used her leg to push her body to the left. As her right arm flopped over her body, she put her palm down. It slipped off a can but gained purchase on a piece of wood. She pushed and raised her torso enough to brace her left elbow under her body and push herself almost to a sitting position. She heard the birds. There must be hundreds of them. And now the odor was more biting.

Where was she?

Slowly and painfully she raised her head, opened her eyes, and looked about. Her mouth trembled. She had been tossed to the bottom of a mountainous stack of rancid, fetid, and necrotic garbage. The brightness of the sun again forced her head down. After a moment she opened her eyes and gazed upon what was left of her body. Her left breast had been sliced almost from her body. Long shallow cuts had been made across her stomach and legs.

Then she remembered the impassive face of Bobo as he held her and used his knife and told her how much she would bleed there in the garbage dump.

A trembling hand went to her face and recoiled in horror. What did her face look like? She could feel the blood. She remembered the knife. Her loins screamed out in a visceral pain, the intensity of which she had never before experienced, and she knew that somehow he had damaged her internally. What in God's name had he done to her body?

She fell back upon the garbage, tears streaking the blood on her face. And the last thing she heard was the sound of the birds.

It was an hour before she awakened. This time, powered by that bottomless mystical strength that had so drawn Darrell Casey, she managed to sit, then slowly and weakly, with bent knees trembling, rise to her feet. As she stood, a giant flock of small garbage-eating birds ceased their chattering and took wing. Darby almost fainted as she felt fresh blood gush from her body and run down the inside of her legs.

What had Bobo done to her?

She lurched across the garbage, impervious to the crumpled cans and broken bottles, bent only upon doing what she had to do. It took two hours for her to reach the top of the pile of garbage. Once there she fell forward and tumbled down the other side, her body limp, legs and arms flailing, until she stopped, unconscious at the bottom.

When she awakened, she reached out to brace her arm, and her hand closed upon a round wooden object. It was a broken crutch. She pulled herself upward and ever so slowly began to place one foot in front of the other as she inched toward the road.

A half-hour later a Fort Lauderdale police car pulled up beside Darby, and two young officers stared at her with undisguised horror. They had been summoned by a phone call from a garbage truck driver who said a naked woman covered with blood was walking out of the garbage dump.

"Good God, lady, you need medical attention. What happened to you?" asked the driver.

Tears of relief ran down Darby's bloody face. She had thought she would not be able to do what she had to do. Now the cops were here. They would help her. She could finish the job.

She leaned on the door and sobbed. Then she straightened up and, with little other than willpower, forced her voice to be calm. "Darby DuPree. BSO narcotics," she said. "Patch me through on your radio."

The two young Lauderdale cops looked at each other in amazement. Broward narcs were wackers. They operated in a different universe. Nothing they did surprised anyone. There was one guy up there who trolled for hitchhikers. The head of the department had just been relieved of duty for illegally entering the Bahamas and kicking a Bahamian Customs officer in the balls. Kicked him off the wing of an airplane, so the story went. Nobody knew all the details. So if a naked woman, who looked as if she had lost a battle with a chain saw walked out of a garbage dump and said she was a Broward narc, the uniform guys had no doubt she was telling the truth.

"Call sign?" one asked, picking up the radio microphone.

"Victor three six."

A few seconds later, Darby was listening to the calm reassuring voice of Navarro. He was coming to pick her up. All would be well. Then Navarro broke radio security to tell the two cops, "That officer is one of my people. You protect her." He hoped the sheriff had not been monitoring the radio.

The two cops turned to Darby. That was another thing about narcs. Their loyalty to each other went far beyond the loyalty one cop has for another. They were closer than brothers and sisters or husbands and wives. They went crazy when something happened to one of their U/C people.

The cop on the passenger side stepped from the car, hand on his weapon, eyes searching all directions. The other opened his door, looked around, then told Darby, "Lady, uh, ma'am, uh, officer. You need medical attention. And you need some clothes." He pulled a yellow rain slicker from the rear seat and offered it to her. But the heavy slicker was so painful on her slashed and battered body that she shrugged it aside. She would never have believed that she could experience pain great enough to cause her to have no concern for modesty.

It was less than ten minutes when an unmarked car with a small blue light flashing over the driver's side arrived and a rear door opened. Nick Brown, face set in anger and elbows pumping furiously, was out of the car and running toward her before the car stopped. He was followed by Navarro and two uniformed deputies. "Give her your shirt," Nick snapped to one of the uniform guys. She slipped on the light cotton shirt as Nick led her toward the car.

Darby tried to smile. "Thanks for coming, Nick," she whispered.

"I'm taking you to the hospital," he said as he ushered her into the back seat. Navarro sat on the other side and the two uniform guys were up front. Nick leaned out the window and waved at the two Lauderdale cops who had found Darby. "Thanks, guys," he said.

Very quickly Nick and Darby brought each other up to date. "I have to arrest him," Darby said. She refused to go to the hospital until she finished her assignment. She leaned forward and gave the driver instructions to reach Darrell Casey's house.

The driver looked in the mirror, his raised eyebrows a question to Nick. Darby took a deep breath. The pain was coming back. Her slashed breast was bleeding. And she could feel blood pooling in the seat under her hips. "I've got to do this," she said. "You're not going to take this away from me."

"Go to the hospital. Navarro and I will take care of Casey," Nick said.

Darby shook her head and a small painful smile pulled at the corner of her battered mouth. "You're always talking about going by the rules," she said. "One of the rules is that the U/C officer gets the collar. You know that."

Nick looked up. The driver wanted to know should he go to the hospital or toward Casey's house. Nick nodded, telling him to go to Casey's. He turned toward Darby and said, "At least let me give you some medication." He reached for the emergency first-aid kit that the shirtless deputy on the passenger side was holding.

"No. I want to have a clear head. I want to feel the pain until this is over." She coughed and slumped, then sat up. "That's all that's keeping me going."

Nick sighed and tapped the shirtless deputy on the shoulder. "Give me the shotgun," he said. "Give Officer DuPree your pistol and you take the M-Sixteen."

Bobo saw the car as it arrived at Casey's house

and the doors flew open. A big man in a uniform, a man with a drawn weapon, stepped from the driver's side. Another man, this one with no shirt, stepped from the other side. He was carrying a rifle. Then the back door opened and a short plump guy stepped out holding a shotgun at the ready. From the other side came a Hispanic holding a .45-caliber pistol. These guys were not here to check the gas meter.

Bobo turned to alert Darrell Casey. Casey was out by the alligator pit sitting at a table loaded with electronics equipment. Earphones were clamped over his head. He was talking to the C-130 crews. They had just taken off from Bimini.

Then Bobo's eye was caught by movement from the car. Climbing slowly from the rear seat was a woman. Her dark hair was matted and dirty. Perspiration covered her forehead and streaked the blood on her face. She wore a blue police shirt that was sodden with blood. The badge shone in the sun. Blood ran down her bare legs. She was holding a pistol.

Bobo's eyes widened. As Darby DuPree, flanked by four men approached the gate, he turned and faded into the oleander bushes.

Bobo disappeared.

37

"Sky King. Victor aircraft. Say last heading of target."

Mike pushed the throttles of the B-26. But they were against the stops. The B-26 was at full takeoff power in a fruitless effort to catch the C-130 loaded with cocaine. He pressed the transmit button and in a weary and disgusted voice responded, "Victor aircraft. He disappeared on about a two six zero. I lost him. The one I splashed was empty. The crew got out."

"Not to worry. The mighty Houdini is on patrol." Lance was wearing green fatigue pants and a green T-shirt that featured a dagger piercing a skull surrounded by the legend, "Kill Them All. Let God Sort Them Out." He had a red bandanna tied around his forehead. His scuffed boat shoes were on the rudders of the electronics-laden Cessna 210.

Mike grinned. "Are you airborne?"

"That's affirm. And, hey, I'm Sierra Hotel."

Mike laughed aloud. "Good luck, guy. He's all yours. Don't let him beat us."

"Where you figure he'll hit the coast?"

Mike had flown around Bimini for years. He did

not have to look at a map to answer "Lima one hundred."

"Homestead?"

"That's the way he was headed. Unless he changes course, he'll go right over Homestead."

Lance thought for a moment. It made sense. Darrell Casey was a clever and audacious smuggler as well as an arrogant man. What could be more like him than to fly directly over the airforce base where F-4 interceptors were stationed and where the U.S. Customs Air Support Branch was headquartered? From there he could simply punch north into Broward County.

"What do you think he'll do then? If he gets by there, and I believe he will, which way will he go?"

"You said he would land in Broward. Are you certain?"

"More certain than when I sent you after the wrong C-One-thirty."

Mike thought. "Okay, he could continue due west and then swing north, but that would put him over the restricted area west of Tamiami. That's an air-defense area. They've got missiles. I don't think he'll risk that. If it were me, I'd turn northwest as soon as I cleared Homestead. I'd stay east of the Perrine NDB. That'd put me between Tamiami and the restricted area. Once I cleared Tamiami I'd swing back to the northwest to avoid the traffic at Miami. After that, it's anybody's ball game. He could go anywhere."

"So the best place for an intercept would be between Tamiami and the restricted area?"

"You got it."

After a moment, Lance's voice returned. "I can't do it. I'm too slow and it's too far away. I'm going to have to try a bit farther north. Is there any way you can find out from Homestead when he passes over?"

"Sure. I can call the tower."

"Do that. Let me know the time he passes over and his course when he leaves. Then I'll switch on this gee-whiz stuff and see if I can understand it enough to pick him up."

"You're in the two-ten. I can talk you through using the FLIR well enough to pick him up. But what good will it do?"

Lance looked at the short tubular object on the seat beside him. It had come from the locked evidence room of the Broward sheriff's office and was covered with military markings. He patted the object, laughed, and said, "Hey! this is the Houdini war wagon. Track in on the same course you think he will follow. Keep me advised once he crosses Homestead."

"And?"

"Look for the fireball."

The C-130 approached Biscayne Bay at more than three hundred miles an hour and only fifty feet above the water. The pilot, the same middle-aged rumpled pilot who had taken the Snake Eaters for their last airplane ride, was at the controls. He was more abrasive than usual. First, he was hauling ten thousand kilos of cocaine; twenty-two thousand pounds of 98-percent purity cocaine. The value of the load boggled his mind. Behind him were two of the weirdest guys he knew: two electronics wizards called Batman and Robin who hunkered over a panel of instruments installed where the crew bunks had been. Their eyes were glazed as they twirled dials, listened through giant earphones, watched digital and tape-display readouts, analyzed hundreds of bits of incoming data, and constantly fed new information into the equipment. Those guys had the C-130 equipped better than Air Force One. And then there was Darrell and his stupid radio codes. As soon as the pilot broke ground on Bimini, he broke to the south and called Darrell as he had been instructed: "Dump Truck to Commander. Inbound from the Sand Box. Say entry point."

Darrell was so secretive that he and the other C-130 pilot knew neither their route into south Florida nor their landing site. They had coded instructions for four entry points and three landing strips. Plus they had numbers for a half-dozen transponder codes.

Darrell came back and said, "Squawk code one. Entry point is the Cess Pool." The pilot cursed. Code one was the secret "Spirit" code used by Customs when flying drug-interdiction flights. It was a good choice because there were lots of Customs aircraft using this air space on a regular basis. And their "Spirit" code had remained unchanged for years while DEA changed its secret transponder code every year or so. What rankled the pilot was entering over the Cess Pool—Homestead Air Force Base. It was stupid to tweak the nose of the U.S. Air Force and that of U.S. Customs needlessly. But Casey was the boss.

Moments later, Batman and Robin had picked up a brief radio transmission from the other C-130,

code named Pipe Wrench, that indicated he was
crashing into the sea. No explanation.

Now, about four minutes from Homestead, Casey
was on the radio again.

"Commander to Dump Truck, activate Plumber's
Friend. Upon reaching Cess Pool, pick up heading
of three three five and stand by for final instructions."

Batman and Robin did not have to go through
their code sheets. Those two digit heads could mem-
orize a phone book with one reading. They loved
working with coded instructions and they knew that
Plumber's Friend meant they should turn on every
radar-warning device, thermal-sensing equipment,
signal-blocking electronics countermeasures, and
radar-jamming equipment on board. The panel in
front of Batman and Robin lit up like a Christmas
tree.

Off to the right, Fowey Rocks could be seen. The
long low green coastline beyond the bay was etched
sharply in the noonday sun. The tall striped stacks
of Turkey Point were to the left. Then, there it was,
the long straight single runway of Homestead Air
Force Base stretching white and clean, except for
the black tire marks at either end.

Batman and Robin were all atwitter. The pilot
looked over his shoulder, pressed his intercom switch,
and said, "Okay, Jack. Update me. What are you
getting?"

The digit head known as Batman looked up, rolled
his eyes behind glasses thick as Coca-Cola bottles,
and said, "Thermal imaging is picking a twin-engine
turbine aircraft taxiing toward end of active runway. Radio traffic indicates it is a Super King Air
using the 'Omaha' call sign. That means it is a

Customs aircraft being scrambled for a tactical intercept. Against us."

Robin said his computations indicated they would be over Homestead by the time the King Air reached the end of the runway. Their superior speed meant the King Air would never get close.

Batman and Robin were terribly pleased with themselves. The pilot wondered if the gnomish techies would die from the terminal grins.

The C-130 roared directly over the tower. They were so low the pilot could see the tower operators. Then they were gone, turning sharply on the new heading while Batman and Robin listened to the furor of radio traffic behind them. "The air force thinks we are a Customs flight. They're raising hell." Then his face grew puzzled. "They just gave our new heading to an aircraft."

"So what, Jack?" growled the pilot. "It was to that King Air. And you just said they can't catch us." He called Casey. "Commander, this is Dump Truck. Outbound from the Cess Pool."

"Dump Truck, this is Commander. Proceed to Release Valve and go to hot mikes."

"Acknowledge Release Valve." The pilot turned a small switch that made all conversation automatically broadcast without pressing a transmit button. The pilot's scowl lessened. He liked the choice of Release Valve as the landing site. Release Valve was a four-thousand-foot dirt strip carved out of the Everglades. A camo tarp big enough to cover the C-130 and the fleet of swamp buggies, trucks, and campers that would haul away the cocaine was waiting.

The C-130 flew under the inbound traffic pattern

at Miami International, causing near heart failure in two Delta pilots flying parallel approaches to the east. Both complained bitterly to tower operators who said they were painting only a fast-moving aircraft whose transponder signal indicated it was a Customs airplane. One of the tower operators was picking up a telephone to complain to Customs when the other controller said, "Wait a minute. Here comes another one."

At that moment the radio crackled and Mike Love said he was approaching from the south but would swing wide to avoid the airport traffic. He asked if the controllers would track the fast-mover that had just gone through.

Ninety seconds later Lance picked up a rapidly growing blossom of white light on the thermal imaging equipment. Five seconds later he identified the target as a high-wing four-engine aircraft at extremely low altitude—he had the C-130. But that part of south Florida is one of the busiest corners of the nation for air traffic. At the rear of the scope, Lance saw the white traces left by jets inbound to Miami. Multiple dots were in the vicinity of Opa Locka. He had to wait until the C-130 was almost on top of him before he could proceed with his plan. To miss could be catastrophic.

Batman and Robin painted the Cessna 210 and cautioned the pilot that a small private aircraft was four miles ahead. Their present course would take them above and slightly west of the aircraft. Then their equipment showed the small aircraft had slowed and was beginning a lazy turn to the west. It would cross directly in front, although several hundred feet above them. The two men turned from the bank of electronics equipment to look over the pilot's right shoulder. They could see the aircraft less than a mile away. It was a small Cessna.

"What's that private aircraft doing?" Robin asked.

Suddenly the left wing of the Cessna lifted high in the air and they could see something—it looked like a stovepipe—protruding from the window. They stared.

At that moment the Red Eye missile that Lance had taken from the evidence room began to emit a low growl that indicated it was locked on target. The C-130 was so close that target acquisition by the missile was almost immediate once Lance turned it on. The thermal signature of the C-130 was so bright, there was no doubt that the missile was locked onto the giant transport.

He pulled the trigger.

Batman and Robin were looking out the cockpit and saw a puff of smoke come from the window of the Cessna. The smoke moved toward them in a straight line and at an incredible speed.

Robin had time to say only "Missile . . ." before the impact and resulting explosion blew the C-130 out of the air and scattered more than ten tons of cocaine and flaming wreckage across a remote corner of the Everglades.

Lance turned in a wide circle toward the south and then flew over the wreckage on a northerly heading. A white glaze over several hundred square yards where the cocaine had struck the surface was slowly darkening and disappearing as it was absorbed by the water of the Everglades. He knew no one had survived the crash. "You bastards can snort coke in hell," he muttered.

He called Navarro and told him to report the crash to the FAA and then dispatch a helicopter to the crash site and have officers make sure the cocaine had been destroyed. "The alligators in that part of the Glades are going to get weird tonight," Lance said.

Navarro interrupted and Lance's smile disappeared. He shoved the throttle to takeoff power and turned toward the farm. He had to get to Darrell Casey's mansion.

38

Darrell Casey leaned forward over the table and pressed the earphones tighter over his head. He sat at a table in his back yard, a table covered with radio equipment. It was at the edge of the alligator pit. The proximity of the alligators and the nature of the conversations he was having on the radio had made the past few minutes the most intense of his life. Ever since Dump Truck radioed that he had departed the Sand Box, events had swirled past at blurring speeds. Pipe Wrench, the aircraft on the northern track, had crashed. It happened so quickly that the pilot said only that he was going into the water. Moments later Dump Truck was approaching Homestead, the most daring and innovative part of a flight carrying almost a half-billion dollars' worth of cocaine. Casey's career, perhaps his life, was riding on this load. Much of the money Casey had made over the years was invested in this flight. The C-130s cost twelve million dollars each. And one had just disappeared without a trace. It was as if all those stories about the Bermuda Triangle were true. The front money necessary to buy ten thousand kilos of cocaine exceeded the national budget of most Central American countries. And even then, he still owed the Colombian suppliers a small fortune. Those people accepted no excuses—only money. If they weren't paid on time, he would be dead meat. It was that simple. Steinhorst and the Snake Eaters and Darby DuPree did not understand that, did not realize the lengths to which he had to go to preserve and protect that load. Three lives were nothing when balanced against almost a half-billion dollars.

But now it appeared the big gamble had paid off. Dump Truck had passed Homestead so fast that both the Air Force and Customs were left spinning in the prop wash. Neither could launch an intercept. Batman and Robin had radioed that they were approaching the Blender—Miami International Airport—and their electronics equipment showed no threat of any kind. Once they passed under the jet traffic at Miami, they would be home free. From there it was only minutes to the dirt strip west of Lauderdale. When the cocaine was off-loaded, he would see that word got out about the biggest load of cocaine in history coming through Broward County to be distributed all over America. And that would be the end of Nick Brown and Hiram Turnipseed.

Background conversation over the radio caused Casey to lean forward. Robin had mumbled something about a private aircraft. There had been a brief silence. Robin's surprised voice said "Missile . . ." And the radio was dead. He could not raise them. What the hell was going on?

"Dump Truck. Commander. Come in."

Pause.

"Dump Truck. Commander. Come in."

Casey felt something prod him in the back. He

ignored it, thinking Bobo was trying to get his attention. Bobo could wait. He leaned forward. "Dump Truck. Commander. Come in."

He felt the light prod again.

Again he ignored it.

"Dump Truck. Commander. Come in."

He was prodded a third time. Angrily he spun around in the chair and, for a moment, was transfixed with horror.

Darby Dupree stood there. She was weaving back and forth and could hardly hold her head up. She had been prodding him with a pistol. Now she was holding the pistol in both hands. And it was pointed at his nose.

Behind her, fanned out on both sides, were four men, all in a combat crouch. And pointed at him was what looked like enough firepower to take over a small country. Nick Brown, the fat little narc, was holding a shotgun and looking as if he wanted half an excuse to pull the trigger.

Darby wore a bloodstained police shirt with Broward sheriff's office patches. Her hair was plastered to her head. Perspiration beaded on her forehead and streaked the blood on her face. Fresh blood, dark flowing blood, was running down her legs and glistening in the noonday sun.

"Darrell Casey," she said in a soft quavery voice. "You are under arrest. You have the right to remain—"

With a scream of anguish, Casey jumped up, knocking over the table covered with radios. He backed up as if afraid the bloody apparition before him would attack. A keening whining noise of fear came from his throat. He held his hands up as if to push Darby away, as if to protect himself from Nick

Brown. He took another step backward and fell into the alligator pit. And the last sight he was cognizant of before he landed atop a twelve-foot alligator was of Darby's legs, those achingly long blood-covered legs.

Casey screamed once. And then, except for woofling and snarfling and an occasional loud snap, there was no more noise from the bottom of the pit.

Nick motioned for the deputy, the one wearing the uniform shirt, to take a look, to make sure. He slowly ventured to the edge of the pit, took a brief look, and jumped back, swallowing rapidly, trying not to vomit. He looked at Nick and shook his head.

But Nick did not see. Darby had slumped to the ground unconscious.

"Call an ambulance," he said.

Epilogue

It was late Saturday night and Lance, his Magnum by his side, had been riding the streets of Fort Lauderdale since noon. He wore a T-shirt that said, "I Love Toxic Waste," jeans, and his scuffed boat shoes. Lance was searching for Bobo, the Colombian who had so brutally injured Darby. But he apparently had escaped. Broward's airports, the Intracoastal, Port Everglades, all were covered with every deputy the sheriff's department could muster. It was the sort of massive security effort rarely seen except during presidential visits or when a police officer has been seriously injured. Leaves and off-duty days had been canceled. The BSO, much to the displeasure of south-bound tourists, was even conducting driver's license checks on I-95. But more than twenty-four hours had elapsed since Bobo had been seen by a neighbor leaving Casey's house. The APB on him would be lifted Sunday morning.

Lance was morose and angry as he drove the big black Lincoln around Fort Lauderdale. Except for the missing Bobo, the Darrell Casey investigation had been wrapped up.

Lance turned to the left, down a narrow side

street. He reached out to seize the Magnum and prevent it from sliding across the seat.

The sheriff knew virtually none of the details of what had happened. He did not know that Nick had been there when Darby attempted to arrest Casey. All he knew, or cared about, was that he had never experienced such a public outpouring of support. The switchboard at the courthouse had been jammed since dawn. People stopped him on the streets. He felt like a rock star. Everyone wanted to clasp his hand and pat him on the back.

The crash of the cocaine-laden C-130 had been front-page news on almost every paper in America this morning. It was the lead story on network news. They all told how the aircraft had been loaded with cocaine on Bimini. The media types were confused about many aspects of the Casey story. There were all sorts of rumors flying about the role of the Broward County Narcotics Squad. How did Darrell Casey, the most-wanted drug smuggler in America, come to be killed in a pit of alligators? Three Broward officers said he fell. How had the C-130 crashed? There was some evidence of an explosion. And the rescued crew of another C-130 reported they had been shot down by a B-26, an ancient World War II bomber. The story would have had no credence except there were eyewitness reports of a mysterious black B-26 seen flying at high speed in the Miami area. No one had gotten a tail number and no one knew who owned the aircraft. The sheriff told the media it was ludicrous to think his air detachment could afford a B-26. "We have only a few surveillance aircraft," he said.

Lance turned onto Highway 1 and increased his speed. The big Lincoln was a powerful car. Lance smiled at the irony of how only the media were raising questions about the investigation. The people in Broward County did not seem to care about anything except that an aircraft carrying an estimated ten tons of cocaine had crashed and the cocaine was destroyed. Newspaper and television reporters were reporting, with extreme reluctance, the unprecedented outpouring of support both for the sheriff, who was being given credit for stopping the load of cocaine, and for the young female undercover officer in the intensive-care ward of the local hospital. Dozens of people brought her flowers and did not seem dismayed when they were turned away by grim-faced protective deputies. The people gave their flowers to the deputies and said, "We wanted to do something for her."

Through all of this the sheriff nodded and blinked and talked about not revealing investigative techniques. His lack of knowledge came across on television as being protective of his deputies. He was becoming a folk hero. He had gotten so much public support that he realized what the newspaper and television people thought did not matter. This morning he had even publicly criticized Bimini and blamed the Bahamian government for allowing wide open cocaine trafficking. The Bahamian prime minister announced that he was moving a Bat team to Bimini and stationing a full unit of the Bahamian Defense Force on the island.

The State Department stayed silent. But the regional director of DEA was publicly congratulating the sheriff for stopping the load of cocaine and for his "innovative" techniques. "Innovative" meant they did not know how the hell he had done it.

The sheriff called Lance Saturday afternoon and,

after preening himself about the public reaction to the end of the Casey investigation, magnanimously said, "You can keep that new office." Knowing how loyal Lance was to Nick, the sheriff said he would have reduced the time of Nick's suspension, but to do so would set a bad precedent, that he had to stick with his word.

It was the telephone conversation with the sheriff that caused Lance to grab his Magnum and jump into the Lincoln. He wanted to look for Bobo and get rid of the anger he felt toward the sheriff.

A half-billion dollars' worth of cocaine had been destroyed. But the price had been high, both for the bad guys and for the good guys. On the bad guys' side of the ledger, Steinhorst was dead, the Snake Eaters were missing, and Casey was dead. They all deserved whatever had befallen them.

On the good guys' side, it seemed as if those who cared the most were paying the greatest price.

Darby paid the most. And she would continue to pay for years. All she wanted was to be a good cop. She had been so young and so ambitious. But her judgment had been seriously flawed. She had been chewed up by the Casey investigation with the same impassive relentless violence that the sea shows against those who do not respect its power. In retrospect, she had been allowed too much freedom. She had tried too much too soon. She was recovering from extensive surgery and would be in the hospital for weeks, maybe months. When she came out, no one would ever again think of her as a beautiful woman. What Bobo had done to her with his knife resulted in a doctor having to remove her reproductive organs and perform a colostomy. The effect of all this on her mental and emotional health, no one knew.

Nick Brown, the straightest cop Lance had ever known, was on the beach, suspended from duty. Nick accepted the suspension in a fatalistic fashion. He was not angry. He said he had stepped over the line and deserved the suspension.

He should have gotten a medal.

Mike Love, who was the most passionately anti-smuggling pilot in the U.S. Customs service, also had been suspended. He had not harmed anyone. He could have hurt the boat driver. But he gave him time to escape before he burned up a boat and several hundred kilos of cocaine. He did what he got paid to do and then was relieved of duty.

He, too, should have been given a medal.

Ron Williamson, who had a reputation of being a brilliant and innovative federal agent, was being daily subjected to humiliation and embarrassment from a petty and small-minded man. But Dumnik was destined for higher office in DEA and Ron was counting the days until retirement.

The sheriff, who couldn't find his ass with a search warrant, had become a minor deity and would almost certainly be re-elected, probably with the greatest majority he had known in years. The sheriff had given Lance's personnel folder to those two old rich guys. Lance wondered if they had told him about the B-26. Probably not.

Those two guys must be ecstatic—that is, if they could generate enough emotion about anything to climb as high as ecstasy. They had called Lance and Mike, asking them to come out to the farm and pick up a "bonus," but neither man had any intention of going. They wanted no money for what they had done.

However, there may come a time when the use of

the B-26 would again be necessary. Bimini would be shut down for a while. It was too hot right now. But some other place, probably the Turks & Caicos Islands, would fill the vacuum.

Lance made a mental note to himself as he turned left off Federal Highway. It may be necessary for the mighty Houdini to go down there and practice a little street-level law enforcement, impress upon that bunch of brigands the majesty of the law.

That reminded Lance of the greatest irony in the case. All the cops who cared so much about stopping smuggling had, in one way or another, been trampled by events. He didn't really care. Sure, he wanted to stop smugglers from bringing in drugs. But it was a game of wits, not a morality play. And he was the only cop involved who had paid no price.

None of it made any sense.

Lance sighed and looked at his watch. Midnight. He would swing by the hospital to check on Darby, then go to his apartment.

The streets were almost empty.

Then Lance saw him walking down the street. At the sound of the Lincoln, the man turned around and held out his thumb. He was a black man, slender, wearing nondescript clothes. And he was barefoot.

It was Bobo.

Lance grinned and shoved the Magnum under his left leg. The rat trap was in the glove compartment. He wheeled toward the curb and used the electric switch to lower the window. The Colombian leaned over, looked into Lance's sparkling eyes, then opened the door and sat down.

Robert Coram has been writing on drug smuggling for more than a decade for *The Atlantic Constitution* and other publications, and has twice been nominated for the Pulitzer Prize in Journalism. For the past seven years he has also been a part-time journalism instructor at Emory University and currently lives in Georgia.